The Kandahar Talisman

The Kandahar Talisman

intrigue, suspense and romance during World War II

a novel by

J. D. Smithyes

Copyright © 2007 by J. D. Smithyes

All rights reserved. No part of this publication may be reproduced, stored in a retrieval system, or transmitted in any form or by any means without written permission from the publisher, except by a reviewer who wishes to quote brief passages in connection with a review written for inclusion in a broadcast, magazine, newspaper, or other media.

Published by Onslow Publishing, LLC
onslow2007@comcast.net

Interior design and layout by Lee Lewis Walsh, Words Plus Design, www.wordsplusdesign.com

Printed in the United States of America

Acknowledgments

My gratitude and heartfelt thanks to all the special friends listed here:

Carol Gray for the loan of books from France pertaining to WW II (*Femmes sous l'Occupation* by Célia Bertin and *La Vie des Français sous l'Occupation* by Henri Amouroux) as well as German Michelin Guides and maps.

Dr. Edith Kovach, Latin scholar and linguist extraordinaire for proofing my manuscript for punctuation and for making some excellent suggestions and comments on the plot.

Richard Sullivan for research in German.

Jack and Ruth Darin, Rose Rasch and Shirley Wood for their proofing contribution and encouragement.

Missy Chabot for the many helpful and creative discussions; for reading the manuscript, but most of all for her artistic contributions: the cover art and the map.

Bill Heisel for a good literary suggestion.

Cynthia and Richard Cummings for sharing their experience in the publishing process.

Lee Lewis Walsh for her time, patience and expertise.

Lastly, the encouragement and support from my family, especially my husband.

THE JOURNEY

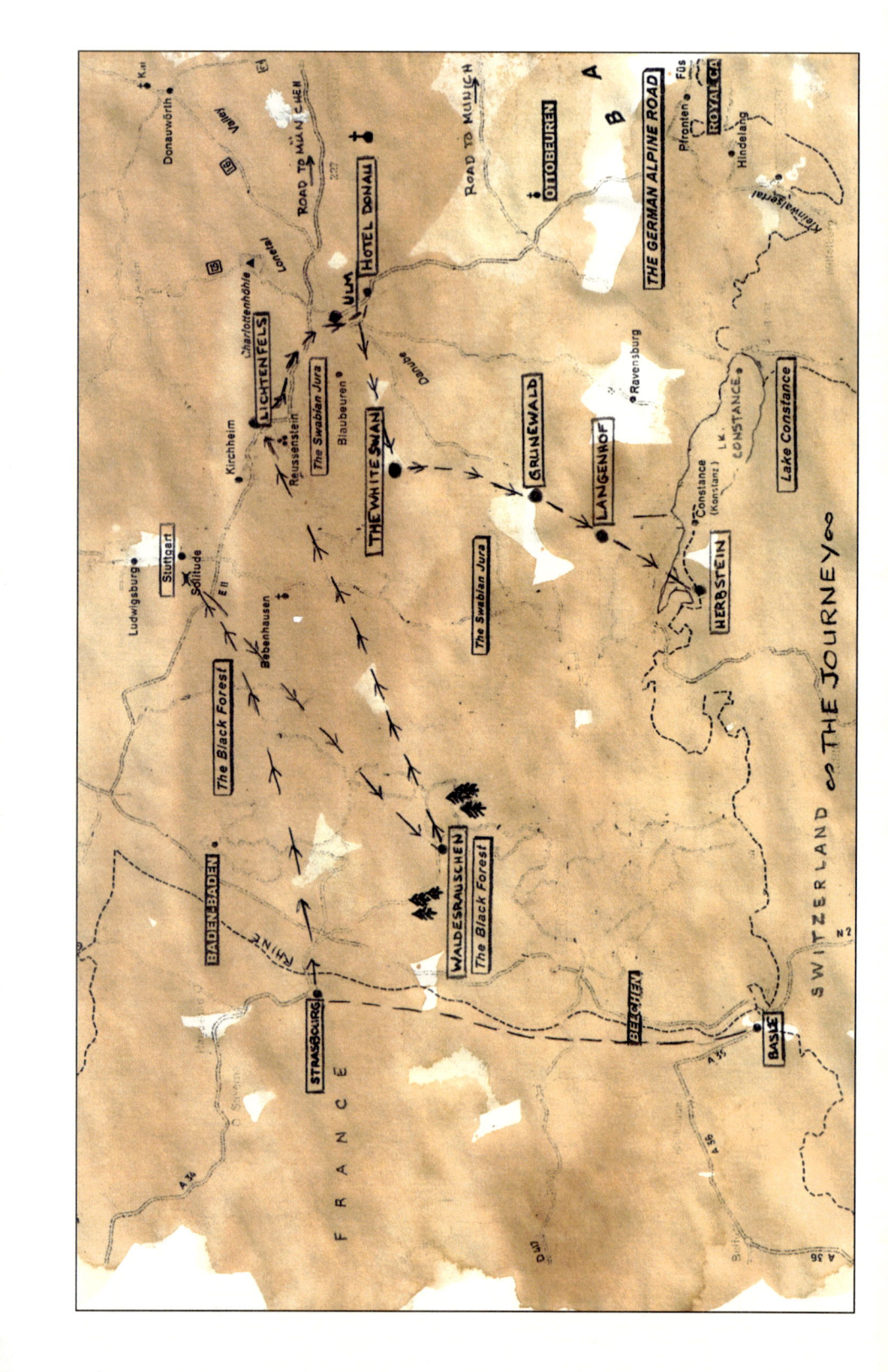

In loving memory of my parents
and
to my beloved family
who challenged me to write this novel

— *1* —

Madeleine awoke suddenly. Her neck hurt and she winced as she massaged it tentatively. She had fallen asleep with her head leaning at an angle against the window. There was neither sound nor movement. The train had stopped. When she opened her eyes, she found it was still dark, the compartment empty. The couple who had been sitting across from her were no longer there.

She peered out the window and in the first grey light of dawn saw only the outline of trees, no buildings. Unexpectedly, the train lurched gently, as if nudged by a giant hand. That was what had awoken her. They were adding extra coaches to the train.

She got to her feet and pulled open the compartment door and looked out into the corridor. There was no one. Through the window she saw a rail network and the outline of a building in the distance. Had she missed her stop? She looked at her watch and felt reassured. She was still an hour from her destination. She went back into the compartment, sat down and closed her eyes again. The coach next to hers had been a dining car. She wondered if it was still there. She had not noticed. She would welcome some coffee and something to eat.

She dozed off again, and was awoken this time by the sound of many feet and loud, boisterous voices. The compartment door was abruptly pulled open and she was staring into the young, raw face of a German sailor. His eyes bulged in surprise as he yelled over his shoulder to his companions. They gazed in at her. "Sehr schoen," murmured one of them as he shouldered his way into the compartment and sat down opposite her. In seconds, the compartment was filled with sailors and their equipment. She was acutely uncomfortable and uncertain how to act. She knew that she must not provoke them. "Guten Morgen," she said. The response was mixed. A couple of titters and some muttered responses. She closed her eyes in the hope that she could somehow pull a curtain around herself and become invisible.

The train jolted again and kept moving, slowly gathering speed. The noise in the compartment increased in volume as the men, having settled in their places, began conversing with one another. However, their focus was still on her. It was obvious that something had gone wrong. As she listened to their conversation, she realized that she was on a troop train, in which case what had become of the rest of the passengers she had embarked with earlier? The first stirrings of fear flitted across her mind.

The man next to her edged closer to her. He smelled of sweat, his breath of stale beer. His face was very close to hers. She kept her eyes shut. A hand was laid on her knee. She turned and swept it off. The compartment exploded into roars of laughter. She looked out the window. It was now daylight and she could see the fields flow by as the train gathered momentum. What was she to do? She had to keep them at bay. The hand was replaced, a little higher this time. She turned and picked it up and placed it firmly on the owner's leg.

"Let us not play games," she said in German. Hoots and titters followed this remark. Had she now mistakenly laid down a challenge? The man opposite her leant forward, his knees touching hers.

"I will protect you," he said. The compartment rocked at this new approach. She stared at him, unable to respond. She sat upright so her knees disengaged from his. At that moment, the compartment door slid open and a seaman with a file of papers and pen stood staring in at them. His eyes alighted on Madeleine and his face reflected both shocked surprise and astonishment.

"I will be back." It sounded like a threat. But in some ways, she was relieved. The compartment buzzed with conversation. Remarks flowed back and forth about her, but now she did not care. No more physical advances were made towards her. It was a long time, but in due course the seaman was back. He beckoned towards her and told her to follow him.

They wove their way along what seemed miles of corridors filled with men and their possessions. Some received her presence in silence, others made loud and crude remarks. Occasionally the seaman would reprimand the men, but for the most part he was too busy working his way through the train to bother. It was hard work. They came at last to a coach that was obviously set apart for administration and other purposes. She was told to sit and wait.

Nothing happened for a considerable interval. However, she was aware of voices coming from the next compartment. At times, they seemed to be raised in anger. The seaman returned with a large pile of papers in his hands. He knocked on the door and was told to enter. As he moved across the threshold he pushed the door behind him, but it did not close. She edged forward to gain a view of the room beyond. She saw a small man standing in profile to her, thin-lipped with wire-rimmed glasses. He was speaking to someone beyond her range of vision. He was obviously angry. His whole demeanor she found very menacing. More words were exchanged; he appeared taken aback by the fury of the response he received. The seaman cleared his throat and the little man swung around on him. At this point, Madeleine moved quickly back to the corner seat, out of range of anyone looking through the door. She felt a red-hot poker of fear run through her. What if he were Gestapo? She had not been able to see enough of his uniform to judge his rank or service.

The seaman came out and closed the door behind him, obviously relieved to return to his other duties. But it was only seconds later when the door opened again and the small, thin man stood on the threshold, his back to her. She tried to shrink further back into the corner. It was evident that he was furious. As he swung away, he said with a steely edge to his voice, "You have not heard the last of this." And then he was gone. She could not believe it. He had not seen her. Whoever was in the next room, she somehow feared less than the man whom she had just seen.

The seaman was back. He knocked quietly on the door. No response. He knocked again. He opened the door and to her surprise waved her in towards a chair beside a table littered with piles of paper. She did not even hear the door close behind her. She wondered later if the seaman had decided that there was no way to prepare his superior for the shock that was awaiting him.

The man standing behind the table facing a map on the wall and speaking into a telephone was tall, over six feet tall, and lean, but with strength in his muscular shoulders. He had very dark hair. She could hardly see anything of his face, just the tip of a long, straight nose. She settled more comfortably in her chair. She began to realize how tired she was. The short, deep sleep that she had enjoyed now no longer sustained her. She turned her head to look around her.

It was at this precise moment that Kapitän Erich von Brandenburg turned away from his map to pick up a pen from the table. He was remonstrating loudly with the idiot supply officer at the other end of the telephone. How could he possibly do his job, or his men theirs for that matter, if he were not equipped in a manner due his rank and the assignment given him? He picked up his pen and saw Madeleine. The shock was so unexpected that it left him speechless. The voice on the other end of the telephone took the opportunity to defend his position and droned on unheard. The Kapitän passed a hand across his eyes and then let it rest there. He was exhausted. He had not slept in 36 hours and during that time he had to field every imaginable difficulty, mishap and miscalculation that it was possible to encounter in a military operation of this nature. He had to be hallucinating, there was no other possible explanation for the vision that he had just seen. He turned back towards the map on the wall and opened his eyes. He could read it clearly. That was comforting.

The voice once more caught his attention. "Another two weeks," it was saying. His mind leapt back into gear. "You will get the supplies to me within the week, or I will personally see that you are shot." There was just time to hear the gasp as he slammed down the receiver.

Madeleine's attention was caught by the conversation which had just ended so abruptly. She turned her head just as the Kapitän turned slowly away from the wall and looked across the table at her. She was not prepared for what she saw. He was very handsome, but she could tell from his extreme paleness and the dark shadows under his deep blue eyes and the lines in his face that he was exhausted. She felt no fear anymore, which was not logical considering her situation.

The Kapitän sat down slowly in his chair and contemplated her. What in God's name was such a beautiful woman doing on this train he asked himself? Was she a spy? But that made no sense! Spies needed to be inconspicuous and there was nothing inconspicuous about this woman. She had short curly hair and a beautiful complexion and long, shapely legs. But the most striking feature of her face was her eyes. A clear, luminous blue. A pretty mouth, soft and very appealing. He took a deep breath.

"What are doing here?" he asked her. She looked surprised but did not respond.

He rephrased the question. "What are you doing on this train?"

"I don't know. There has been some mistake."

"Please explain what you mean."

"I was on a train traveling from Strasbourg to Basel yesterday morning, but when I awoke this morning, I found myself surrounded by sailors. No one told me to expect that." She had struggled a little with this sentence and felt obliged to explain. "My German is not very good."

He contemplated her for a long time. His weary brain was struggling to digest what she had told him. She was obviously French, or French Swiss. What on earth was he going to do with her?

"What is your name?"

"Madeleine Devaux."

"What was the purpose of your journey to Basel?"

"I am a writer. My present assignment was to write an article on travel in Switzerland and other possible destinations in Europe, especially taking into consideration the unsettled situation in . . ." her voice trailed off in confusion.

Von Brandenburg looked at her thoughtfully. Such an assignment could certainly disguise information gathering. He was annoyed, as much because he was exhausted as for any other reason. He needed desperately to feel clear-headed. He did not need one more decision to be made, one more problem to be solved and certainly the presence of this woman on this train was going to present him with huge difficulties, unless he could come to some solution quickly and decisively.

"I cannot understand how you came to be on this train. This train was requisitioned in Strasbourg by the Reich. You should not be on it. I have urgent matters to accomplish. You will have to wait. When I have time, we will discuss your presence here further."

He pressed the bell on his desk. The same seaman entered the compartment and she was conducted back to the place where she had been sitting some twenty minutes earlier.

It was uncomfortable sitting where she was, but during the time she was there, no one else appeared, except the seaman who brought her a jug of water and a glass.

Four hours had gone by and she was feeling exhausted, not only from discomfort but by the tension that was slowly building up in her. She was afraid.

At last, she was asked to go back into the office. She sat down in the same chair.

She thought he looked less haggard. In fact, von Brandenburg had slept deeply for two hours, but it was not nearly enough. However, he felt less light-headed.

"Your papers, please."

She handed him her passport. Her heart beat a little faster. She was fearful of his reaction. She sensed that his fatigue had clouded his hearing earlier and that he was unaware of her nationality. In this she was correct.

The Kapitän looked down at the passport in front of him in disbelief. He had thought she might be French or Swiss, but he had never contemplated that she could be British. His fatigue was going to jeopardize the whole operation if he did not get more sleep soon. He turned the pages slowly. He needed time to think. She was 24 years of age. He might have guessed that at least. He could see that she was now getting anxious, whereas earlier she had not been, which in itself was very surprising. He made up his mind.

"I think that I had better take you into protective custody, while I decide what is to be done with you."

Her response was instantaneous. "No."

His eyebrows went up and he looked a little sterner. "You mean to tell me that you would prefer to take your chances with those animals out there?"

She blushed and looked at her feet.

She shook her head. "You misunderstand me. I just want to get to Basel."

"Impossible. If such a train still exists, which I doubt, I would have no way of getting you there. We have traveled too far. Besides which, I am engaged in a war, and civilians, especially foreign nationals," he added with stern emphasis, "are to be considered a threat to our security."

He was angry that those swine might have in some way violated her. He had let his anger at them and the other burdens upon him be directed at her. She looked vulnerable and very young.

He said in a kinder voice, "Are you hungry?"

She looked up and nodded. "Very."

He pressed a bell and shuffled some papers. He pressed it several times.

Fifteen minutes later, a gentle tap on the door announced the presence of the seaman. "Enter."

"Herr Kapitän?"

"Where the devil have you been?" was the enraged response. "I rang 15 minutes ago. Never mind. We are hungry. Do you think that you could provide us with something edible, Schultz? I do mean edible . . ." He relented a little, for he knew that the seaman, like he was overworked and very tired. "The dinner two nights ago was excellent. Last night . . ." he left the sentence unfinished. The seaman melted away. His office was adjacent to the kitchen. At least he did not have to trek to the other end of the train this time.

"Now I must get on with my work. You can use the compartment next door and the adjoining bedroom through the door on the right." He pointed to the door, opposite to the one she had entered by. She was dismissed.

It was wonderful to be able to wash. It seemed as though she had felt gritty and dirty forever. She was surprised that there was hot running water in the compact little bathroom adjoining the bedroom assigned her. In due course, the seaman arrived, much out of breath, and delivered her suitcase. It was not a large case, but she knew the effort it must have taken to carry it through all those long corridors filled to overflowing with men and their possessions. She thanked him warmly. He smiled weakly and she knew that he held her no special ill-will. She would have liked to ask him when she might expect to have something to eat, but she could not bring herself to do so. He was looking as haggard as his superior and seemed far less fit. He was somewhat overweight, the result no doubt of a loving wife. In this assumption she was correct. Seaman Schultz missed his home and his wife's cooking more than he would ever admit. But he was devoted to von Brandenburg and was prepared to work until he dropped if required. Such was his loyalty.

Dinner finally arrived about four o'clock in the afternoon. She felt dizzy and light-headed with hunger. It was served in the room between the Kapitän's office and her compartment. It was a room used for conferences. A long narrow table sat between two long benches. She caught a glimpse of the passing countryside. It was getting dark already. The Kapitän joined her the moment the dinner was served. He looked even more fatigued than when she had first seen him. He sat down opposite her.

A bottle of red wine accompanied the dinner. He filled her glass and then his own. They were served a bean soup and then roast chicken, with potatoes and vegetables. Von Brandenburg nodded to Schultz and he melted away.

He lifted his glass. "To peace, health and friendship amongst men" he said in perfect English. "I studied at Oxford," he added as though it were the most natural thing in the world.

She almost dropped her glass as she stared at him in astonishment. She drank and felt the warm, mellow wine course quickly through her bloodstream. One glass on her empty stomach and she would be under the table. But it was so good. She was very hungry. They ate their soup in silence. Both were very hungry. A little color returned to the Kapitän's face.

"Your English is perfect," she said feeling obliged to acknowledge his extraordinary accomplishment.

He smiled and her heart seemed to skip a beat. It totally altered him when he smiled. He was very handsome. She had met handsome men before. His smile, however, melted something inside her. She grasped her wineglass as though for support.

"I think that if we talk English at dinner it will help me disassociate myself from my present distasteful job. I am a man of peace, caught up in a war in which I see no future."

"You are not in the army?" she said surprised that she had not really noticed his uniform or that she had accepted it as something else.

"I am a naval officer. A family tradition of seafaring adventurers."

She felt dizzy. It must be the wine, but in her heart she knew that it was also relief. He was hopefully not a hardened professional. She felt less threatened.

They talked about England and his experiences at Oxford. He asked her about her home and her interests. It was very relaxed. Schultz appeared as if by magic when they had finished their main course. Fruit and cheese were served.

"My compliments on the chicken, Schultz. Excellent." The seaman positively glowed with pleasure. When he had gone, von Brandenburg smiled and said, "He did not prepare it himself, but you can be sure that he was in and out of the kitchen supervising its preparation. It would not have been worth the cook's life to have served us something inedible." He smiled.

What a difference it made when he smiled. It washed away the lines of fatigue and stress. He appeared very boyish. She smiled back. He looked at her long and appraisingly as he picked up his wineglass.

Schultz returned and cleared away their dishes. "Be sure to awaken me at 6.15, Schultz. As you know, timing tomorrow is a matter of life and death. Thank you very much, Schultz."

She was aware of a special bond between these two men. Words were not necessary. She could not guess at the origins of their friendship.

"Schultz will prepare your bed next door. You must excuse me. I have to sleep. Tomorrow we have to outwit those who would try to destroy us. They make a habit of bombing this particular line. We have to reach a certain destination in the hope of avoiding detection. A tunnel, to be precise."

She closed her eyes against this unwelcome piece of news.

"Forgive me, I did not mean to alarm you, but I might be very busy tomorrow. I feel you should know this. But please do not lose sleep over it. We Germans are very precise. We shall make it." Please God that we do, he said to himself. His confidence in this train, its engineers and others in charge was not of the highest. He opened the door into the next compartment, and was gone.

— 2 —

She felt very alone. A stranger amongst strangers and to make it worse, the opposition. What a mess. How would she ever extricate herself from this situation? She was going to be in the center of the battlefield soon, being bombed by her own countrymen or those sympathetic to their cause. Schultz reappeared and proceeded to make up her bed. He was quick and efficient. She thanked him. He went out and she was aware of his locking the door behind him. There was a certain comfort in knowing that she was locked in because it also meant that the rest of the world was locked out. The Kapitän's bedroom paralleled hers. His compartment, like hers, had a separate entrance into the conference room too. She was very tired she realized, not so much physically, as emotionally. The dinner had been very good, or perhaps she had just been terribly hungry. In any event, despite the bad news of possible dangers that lay in store, she felt she could sleep for a week. The wine probably helped her feel so sleepy. She prepared herself for the night, lay down partly dressed and fell instantly asleep.

It seemed that she had hardly shut her eyes before there was a knock on the door. It was Schultz. He told her that he had put a tray with coffee and rolls in the adjoining conference room. He left, leaving on a light. She opened one eye and squinted at her watch. It was exactly six o'clock. She had slept 12 hours. She wondered what had become of the Kapitän. Was he already on his rounds? She felt very refreshed. But she suddenly remembered what the events of the day promised to bring and she felt a cold shiver of fear run through her. She got up. Before she picked up her clothes to dress in the bathroom, she looked out into the conference room and noticed that there were two cups and saucers on a tray and some rolls. She found that very surprising. Schultz was not someone to make mistakes. She returned, fully dressed, and sat down and poured herself a cup of coffee. She looked at her watch. It was almost 6.15. She was pouring herself a second cup of coffee, when the Kapitän entered the conference room from the exterior door. He sat down opposite her.

"Good morning. How did you sleep?"

"Without moving. And you?"

"Never better."

"Even knowing what today could bring?" She voiced her amazement.

"I do not recall ever going to bed knowing that a most beautiful woman was sleeping in the next room to me and that she would still be there in the morning."

He was quite serious and she felt there was sadness in his voice.

She stared at him in amazement, unable to reply.

"May I pour you a cup of coffee? Schultz left two cups, so I presume you have not had anything to drink this morning."

He nodded. "Actually, I have already had two cups, but today I need to be as alert as is possible." He took the cup from her and helped himself to a roll. He got up and walked to the window. It was almost light. He stood there motionless for what seemed a long interval. Suddenly, he turned towards her.

"I do not know what to assume from your presence on this train, how you got here, whether by design or unintentionally, but in any event, your being here gives me grave concern. I have to decide what to do about you. However, such a decision will have to be made later. We shall probably not see each other for the rest of the day. If all goes well, I hope that we can dine together tonight. I shall have Schultz keep you informed of anything important."

He means that he will have Schultz tell me if he is killed, she thought despairingly. As brief as their contact had been, she felt instinctively that he would do his best for her, even if she was handed over to other authorities. Without him, she would be totally alone and at the mercy of men such as the small, sinister little man with whom the Kapitän had quarreled yesterday.

He was gone. She turned and went to sit by the window in the conference room, looking out but not seeing.

She thought of her home in England and her parents. Eventually, when there was no word from her they would begin to worry. In time, it would be evident that something had gone terribly wrong. The company that she represented would begin trying to trace her, but the trail would be lost and they would have no way of knowing what had become of her. She was totally cut off from all that was safe and from all those who she knew and trusted. She had no way of contacting anyone. She would be just another statistic of war, another unexplained disappearance, even though she was supposedly traveling in safe, unoccupied territory. But hardest of all was the thought of possibly never seeing her family again.

She was not aware of how long she had sat there, but she could hear that the train was picking up speed. It continued to do so, straining like some great animal with a very heavy burden. The countryside flashed by, the trees close to the track, passing in a blur. Schultz had come and gone. He had left fruit, cheese and more rolls and coffee. It would be impossible to cook in these conditions had it been necessary. The train rocked precariously at times. She had given up looking at her watch. It only increased the tension she felt. She had no idea of their deadline - when they might expect to reach the tunnel or be attacked. It might all come down to a matter of luck.

Schultz came back to announce that a meeting was to be held in the conference room and she would have to move back into her compartment. He left her with the remaining fruit and cheese and a fresh pot of coffee and took with him the remains of her meal. She was locked in her room again. Schultz told her that it would be in her best interests to be very quiet. There were certain parties who might not take kindly to her presence. He need not have warned her of that. There was no way she wished to cross paths with the officer she had glimpsed in the Kapitän's office upon her arrival in these quarters.

There was a murmur of voices. At one point, a voice held the attention of all those present. The discussion went on and on and became more animated. She could distinguish the Kapitän's voice from time to time. On the whole, he said very little. The original voice took over again for about five minutes when there was an explosion of protests. More discussion and then abruptly they concluded their meeting. She wondered what the conflict was all about. She imagined it was probably political. Who was in charge and who would finally gain the upper hand?

She was glad they had gone. It made her uneasy having them so close. Supposing someone had wanted to use a bathroom. It did not bear thinking about.

She lay on her bed trying to keep calm, listening to the throbbing sound of the train, each moment feeling like an eternity. She felt that she had been locked in her compartment a very long time. But slowly the rhythmic motion lulled her nerves and she dozed.

It seemed only a short time later when there was a knock on her door. It was unlocked and the Kapitän was standing looking down at her. His exhaustion saddened her heart. She wanted to reach up and comfort him. It hurt her to look at him. Her saw the compassion in her face and was touched by it.

"We are fifteen minutes from the tunnel and five minutes ahead of schedule. On the other hand, the enemy air force could also be ahead of schedule and we might just as well be a thousand miles from the tunnel."

Fear caught at her, and a tightness gripped her throat and her heart thumped painfully, but she inhaled deeply and tried to focus only on him.

"Against my better judgment, I plan to leave the door unlocked between your bedroom and the conference room. If the train is badly damaged, I cannot contemplate your being trapped in here. I comfort myself that the train can hardly be more conspicuous than it already is, so I do not see how you could sabotage our present plans, even if you were of a mind to do so." He did not add that her luggage had been searched, also her room, and nothing the least bit incriminating had been found. He had found that comforting, which was perhaps foolish since a professional would not necessarily be found with anything compromising. "I hope for both our sakes, the army does not find you. Your presence here would be considered very suspect." They both knew this was an understatement. He felt a sense of relief telling her this. Time was of the essence, but he felt duty-bound to be straightforward.

"Where will you be until we reach the tunnel?"

It was not an unreasonable question. "With the engineer."

She gasped. "They will try to destroy the engine before anything else?"

He nodded.

"How did you come by this assignment?"

"The navy outnumbers the army in this particular instance. Their engine broke down. Since it was an emergency and they were relatively few in number, it was decided to join the two contingents together. Something not normally done. However, I consider that since my men were assigned to this train, I am in charge. The army disagrees. Ground forces normally have priority over other fighting units. However, I can be persuasive, when desperate."

She could not help laughing. He smiled back. She was utterly captivating. He cursed his luck, this situation and the war for bringing them together in such dangerous circumstances.

He turned to go. "Keep away from the window," he said over his shoulder, "should there be any shooting." Then he was gone.

She got up immediately and went to the window and scanned the far horizon. Nothing but mountains and a clear sky. Towards those mountains lay the tunnel and possibly the total destruction of the train. Another ten minutes to the tunnel.

When he left her, he hurried to the locomotive's cabin. It was just beyond the kitchen and a storage car. Not too far. He mostly kept in touch with the engineer by telephone. A hulking brute of a man, but honest. He was quite straightforward as to the train's capacity for speed, its age and ability to survive stress. The train was longer than the tunnel by a couple of cars or so. At the speed they were traveling they would overshoot the tunnel and have to back up in order to be partially hidden from above. The various alternatives were discussed calmly and methodically. The army had its equipment in the rear cars, also an anti-aircraft gun. It really was this that resolved which service took which end of the train, although the army had done its best to eliminate the naval officer from any decisive role.

The Kapitän looked out of the locomotive's left side and peered skyward. His long distance vision was not bad, but his binoculars would be helpful. He discovered with irritation that he had left them in his office. He gave some last minute instructions to the engineer and worked his way back again.

Back in his office he scanned the sky, but could find nothing. He poked his head in the conference room and saw her standing at the window, rigid.

"Did you see something" he asked.

"A flash of light, briefly. Nothing I could identify." He strode towards her. "Where?" he asked.

"Between those two mountains."

A matter of minutes, he thought to himself, and we shall know if it is them. He looked at his watch. He said aloud, "About four more minutes to the tunnel."

The strain showed in her face, but she said nothing.

By being helpful, could she be considered a traitor? She swept the thought aside.

He went back into his office and called the engineer. They discussed distance and speed. It was not unlike steering a ship. One had to make allowances and calculations.

An earsplitting roar suddenly enveloped them. Two planes, flying very low appeared from behind the nearest mountain and swung away from the train. Are they going to attack from the rear? Are others awaiting us at the other end, he wondered? This was an unscheduled train, but then most of the trains nowadays were unscheduled. The French could not have known that this train was coming. For this reason they had traveled through the night to make as much distance as possible before daylight.

He watched the planes circle, before they were lost to view. The tunnel was only minutes away. He held his breath. The planes would aim for the front of the train. He looked quickly into the conference room. She was still looking out of the window. "Into your bedroom, at once." he shouted and ran back into his office. The telephone was ringing: the army in charge of the rear of the train announcing a low level attack.

There came a spine-chilling whine, followed by an earsplitting, thunderous explosion which seemed to lift the train off its tracks and hold it suspended. Von Brandenburg had thrown himself on the floor. He could hear nothing, but he was aware that he lay in darkness, that the train must be in the tunnel. The vibrations told him that it was still moving forward. He slowly picked himself up and was aware of being covered by a blanket of glass. He had a torch in the drawer of his desk. He felt his way carefully around his desk. He opened the drawer and found the torch. He switched it on. The window had been blown out and he saw that his papers were scattered everywhere. Luckily the larger piles he had put away, but he stood as though in a snowstorm of white paper. He crunched his way to the door of the conference room and opened it. It was empty, he noted with relief. The window had been pulled down and therefore seemed intact. He walked into the bedroom and found Madeleine, lying face down on her bed. He touched her on the shoulder and she rolled over. Her eyes were wide with shock, but she seemed unharmed. She grabbed his wrist and he dimly saw blood on his hand. She turned the torch in his hand and shone it on his face. He had a small, but deep cut on his cheek which was bleeding profusely. "You have a cut. Wait a moment, I will get a towel." He was aware she was talking to him but could not hear what she was saying. She got to her feet and felt her way into the bathroom. She touched the switch but the light did not work. She found the towel rack and felt for a small towel. She found him standing where she had left him, holding onto the door jamb. She placed the towel against his cheek and told him to hold it there. "Do you have any dressings." He did not reply. She repeated the question. She took the torch and directed it on her face and pointed to her ear. "Can you hear me?" She touched his ear.

He shook his head. She hoped his deafness was temporary. He touched her on the arm and pointed to her bunk. She sat on it and he took the torch from her. "I have to go," he said and left her.

He looked at the towel in his hand and found it soaked with his blood. He must find a dressing; he could not have one hand out of commission this way. He went into Schultz's office, shone the torch until he found the first-aid kit, selected a dressing and applied it to his face. He took several others and stuffed them into the pocket of his uniform. This done, he worked his way to the front of the train, which was still thundering along, even though he could hear nothing.

He reached the locomotive and found the engineer peering at his dials by the light of a hurricane lamp. "Are we slowing down?" he asked. He could hear himself as if at a great distance. On the way to the locomotive he had been aware of the noise of the train. It was a good sign. The engineer responded but he could not hear him. He indicated that he had been deafened by the explosion. The engineer responded with a wave that said he had things under control.

Suddenly they were out of the tunnel, traveling fast but gradually slowing down. There was a series of other tunnels ahead. They had discussed stopping between two of them and backing up into the longer tunnel, if needed. With the terrain mountainous at that point, an air attack would take more precise calculations. It would all depend on whether an aircraft was waiting for them as they exited the next tunnel. It was a matter of a couple of minutes away. They looked out both sides of the train up into the air and saw nothing. They reached the first short tunnel and were through it. Then another. The train was slowing down. It came to a stop.

Von Brandenburg climbed onto the top of the locomotive, still looking into the air. He saw a plane in the distance swinging away from them. What would the pilot's next move be? He glanced back along the length of the train. It looked as though two of the sections had been badly damaged, but it was difficult to tell from this distance. He climbed back into the locomotive and told the engineer what he had seen. He could now hear the engineer better, although it was obvious that he was shouting at him. They agreed on what the next move should be, depending on the reappearance of the aircraft. In the meantime, von Brandenburg would go back and inspect the damage.

There was no sign of Schultz. Von Brandenburg hoped fervently that Schultz was uninjured. Von Brandenburg was not sure how he could function without him. They had served in the same ship together now for several years and understood and respected one another. He came finally to the damaged end-section of the train. It had not been a direct hit obviously, but the roof was severely damaged and all the windows were out. There were numerous injured men who were not in serious condition and who were binding themselves up. The more seriously injured were being attended to by part of the medical team which had been in the front half of the train. His eye fell finally on Schultz who was organizing a clean-up crew to sweep up the glass and remove as much of the debris as possible. Before he could open his mouth, Schultz had seen him and was hurrying towards him, a look of concern on his face. "Let me put another dressing on your face, sir." Von Brandenburg did not demur. He knew that he needed one because he could feel the warm blood trickling down his neck. The old dressing was deftly removed and a new one applied. "You need stitches, sir," was all that Schultz said.

He was surprised to see von Brandenburg respond with a smile. "Remind me to do it soon." He could not afford to loose too much blood. It would make him weak and faint. He was relieved that his hearing had returned. He had heard every word.

The train had stopped between two tunnels; the front end of the train was thus out of sight and only the middle section of the train and the last carriage were exposed. The men working on the damaged section therefore were able to work in good light. Stationary and with good light, the engineers had a chance to repair the telephone and lighting systems.

Madeleine, aware that the train had come to a stop, got up and went into the conference room. It was in darkness. She went to the window and looked out. She knew they were in a fairly short tunnel because she could see light at both ends. She wondered what she should do, but realized that it was useless to wander far in the dark. The door between the conference room and the Kapitän's office was unlocked. She looked in but could see nothing so closed it again. She went back to the bunk in her compartment and lay down.

Although they were nestled against the mountain wall, it would not take more than a few reconnaissance flights for the planes to find them. The biggest problem for the enemy aircraft was to work out how they could make a successful bombing run without running into the mountain. In the meantime, the train's engineer had to work out how long it would take him to work up enough speed to get back to the long tunnel where they could hide until dark.

They must have been there half-an-hour and had seen nothing. "If only the telephone were working" von Brandenburg thought to himself. "I wish I knew what was going on at the end of the train, not that I care whether that insufferable Colonel Krupp has been blown to bits. But I would like to know where those planes are and what they are doing."

He was a man of action. He selected one of his men and instructed him to go to the end of the train and report to him as to what was going on there. He told him to get off the train and go back along the line. It would be quicker. In the meantime, he busied himself checking on his men.

In due course the young officer returned to report. The end of the train had sustained some damage as had the track. The second plane had dropped its bombs and both seemed to have left. But could they be certain? The men had been kept very busy. Meanwhile, the telephone line had been repaired and communication between both ends of the train had been reestablished.

The damaged line could be repaired quickly by taking replacements from the southbound line. Measures would be taken to give good warning to trains traveling southwards and the appropriate authorities informed of the needed repairs. Then came the question of the damaged tail section of the train. It was in bad shape and had been rendered pretty useless. Would it be better to disconnect and abandon it? This was now a matter of the army versus the navy all over again. There was very little worth salvaging, except the anti-aircraft gun. It would take considerable time to dismantle it. The discussion was heated. Von

Brandenburg was angry, but knew that losing his temper with the Colonel was not only useless, but also dangerous. Focus was finally brought to bear on the need for speedy action. A compromise was reached. The damaged section would be disconnected from the end of the train and left behind in one of the tunnels. A crew would be left with it and the anti-aircraft gun dismantled. The main part of the undamaged train would pick up the gun and the crew when it began its night run northwards.

Schultz was at the Kapitän's shoulder. "Sir, it is time that you had your face stitched. A doctor is available to do the work."

"Very good. Where does he propose to do it?"

"Wherever there is good light and you can be comfortable. The electricity has been restored. It could be done in your private compartment."

"Good. Arrange it and see to it that the Fräulein is out of sight."

He gritted his teeth as he walked through his office towards his bedroom. Papers everywhere. In his opinion, very few of them were that important, but each piece had to be kept as proof of this or that purchase order, or this or that particular battle report. He was nothing but a paper factory. All he had ever wanted to do was to sail the seven seas, in peace. The repair to his cheek was made neatly and quickly. He was admonished for having let it go so long and told to eat a good meal and have a good rest. He thanked the doctor, enquired about his men and the other casualties, and promised to do as he was told. Alone once again, he stepped out of his sleeping quarters and walked to the door of Madeleine's compartment and knocked. A few seconds later, it was opened and she stood there looking fresh and relaxed.

"How are you feeling?" she enquired.

"Tired," he responded. "But at least my face is repaired and perhaps later I can get some sleep, which should make me feel better. If all goes well, we can dine together."

The warmth of her smile made him feel briefly light-hearted.

Schultz had worked miracles in his brief absence. The papers were in piles, albeit untidy ones, the glass swept from his desk and the floor, and some semblance of order restored. He sat down at his desk and pondered his next move. A tap at the door announced Schultz who, in typical fashion, had anticipated his need for coffee and something to eat. "Schultz, if it were in my power to do so, I would see that your wages were doubled immediately." Schultz beamed with pleasure. They discussed briefly the schedule for the next few hours and he was gone. Von Brandenburg spoke to the locomotive's engineer and told him the plan concerning the gun removal. In view of the absence of further enemy aircraft, it was decided to move to the longer tunnel as soon as possible. He had no sooner replaced the receiver, than his words were put into action. A gentle jolt and the train moved briefly and came to a stop. His telephone rang and he was told that the engineers were now working on the removal of the last section of the train from the line. They would inform him as soon as the work had been accomplished. He took a long drink of coffee, took several large bites out of his bratwurst and set about finding his most important papers. He was happy to forget all about the army.

Time had flown. He looked at his watch. Why are the repairs taking so long? Could it have been so difficult to remove the damaged section of the train? He called the locomotive's engineer. The army had been working diligently, he was told, and they had just informed the engineer to be ready to get up steam in another 15 minutes. There had been no signs of aircraft at the front end of the train. This information disturbed von Brandenburg. Had the French given up? Could it be that the French had a second destination and target on this mission and needed to conserve fuel?

The telephone call came and within seconds the train was in motion. It took very little time to reach the long tunnel. They accomplished this without incident. The Kapitän ordered that a good meal be prepared for his men. At least this could be accomplished in ideal conditions. No rocking and swaying to overcome. The conference room was prepared for dinner. The window closed. How fortunate that it had been open and therefore left intact. It made the compartment much more comfortable with it closed.

In due course Schultz served dinner. Madeleine had removed the jacket of her black suit and put on a soft, fresh white blouse. It became her very well and accentuated her lithe body. They talked of the day's activities and the prospects of making the rest of the journey without incident. "We shall wait until it is dark to make the last three to four hours of our journey. Unfortunately, there is a moon tonight, but depending on the weather we may not have to wait for it to go down. The sooner we can reach Stuttgart the better." Her heart sank. Then she would see him no more and what was to become of her in the heart of Germany? As if reading her thoughts, he said. "I have a plan for you." Her eyes expressed her surprise. "I will see that you get a pass, since you have no papers. But your chances of getting out of Germany are very poor. I have a country house some distance outside of Stuttgart. You could stay there with my housekeeper until I can make some other arrangements. It would be a very confined existence, but better than a different type of prison. I can trust Maria. She has been with the family for many years. She probably will not approve. Even if I tell her that you are a distant relative, you will be very suspect, since she will never have heard you mentioned before. However, even if you were German, she would still find the situation very unorthodox She is of the old school, but she will do what I tell her."

Tears of relief filled her eyes. She was enormously grateful and relieved beyond words. Ever since discovering her predicament she had been in a wordless torment of despair.

All too soon dinner came to an end. It was cleared away. He took her by the hand and led her to her bedroom door. He sighed deeply and stood for a long moment, silent, contemplating her. He hoped that this decision to save her from almost certain death would not cause him serious doubts as to his wisdom, to his loyalty.

Her heart beat a little faster, fearful of her fluctuating emotions for this attractive, enigmatic man, but aware instinctively that he had no great enthusiasm for his role as her custodian and that he intended her no harm.

"I have to sleep. I think that I need to replenish my strength again. I suppose it is always going to be like this until it is over." He sighed deeply.

"I think that you have lost more blood than you know. Rest well." She wanted to say more, but how do you thank someone who is prepared to save your life even though you might be the enemy? Was she the enemy?

She lay down, but tossed and turned in her anxiety. Finally she fell asleep. She was aware of the train being in motion, but turned over and slept again.

The Kapitän slept deeply. He had told Schultz to wake him only in an emergency. Schultz had no intention of disturbing him except in the direst of circumstances. The night passed without incident. The train had to wait for the moon to go down, but clouds came up and they were able to set out earlier than expected. They would reach Stuttgart as dawn was breaking, or possibly earlier.

Von Brandenburg tapped Madeleine on the shoulder. She was awake immediately. "Here are your papers. They should give you free passage within the Stuttgart area without too many questions asked. Try to answer briefly." He was right. She could disguise her lack of complete fluency by avoiding long sentences.

"I will provide you with an escort to the station entrance. From there you are on your own. For the benefit of those watching, you will seem as though under arrest." He smiled his apologies. "It might be some time before we meet again." If we ever do, he said to himself. He felt a constriction in his chest. She looked so lovely. It was this memory of her he hoped to hold onto. She stood up. He handed her the papers. He kissed her hand and was gone. She felt bereft. She wanted to cry like a baby. She had never felt so alone or more afraid.

— 3 —

It was dark when the train finally reached its destination. The empty platform became a scene of confused and frantic activity. Men poured out of the train, equipment and personal belongings were handed and thrown out of windows and doors. The noise awoke Madeleine. She realized that they had arrived. There was no longer any motion. She found that she was locked in her bedroom. Understandable. Her presence could be very compromising.

Another heated discussion had been held with Colonel Krupp over the telephone. The Kapitän stated his urgent need to get his men to their destination without further delays. The Colonel insisted that his need for speed was even more imperative. Von Brandenburg wanted the Colonel to be the first to leave. It would make it much easier to get Madeleine out of the station safely. He fenced a little longer and finally capitulated with bad grace. He could see the Colonel smiling at the other end. The army and the anti-aircraft gun would be the first to exit the station. And good riddance thought von Brandenburg.

So it was that the army, in immaculate formation, marched down the length of the platform and out of sight.

The navy gathered itself and lined up in small groups. They were inspected by the Kapitän. He spoke a few words to each group. At a certain moment, he turned and saw Schultz, who had been following at a discreet distance. He beckoned to him. Schultz nodded and walked quickly back to his office. He had already arranged which men were to escort Madeleine from the train. It was now time to put the plan into action. When the knock came on her compartment door, Madeleine was dressed and packed. She was very tense. This could be very difficult. She half hoped that she would not see him again. She was afraid that her face might give something away. Schultz stood outside her door. His face was expressionless. He asked her to follow him to his office. Once there he made a telephone call. The escort was to collect her there. They arrived almost immediately. Four strong looking youths. One picked up her suitcase. Two preceded her and the other two followed. As she stepped off the train, her suitcase was handed to her. This gesture somehow designated her a prisoner, better than anything else could have done. They marched down the platform towards the entrance behind the rows of men. In this fashion, very few witnessed her departure.

They had just exited from the platform and were starting to cross the main hall of the station when the noise of drilling and sledgehammers began blasting their eardrums. She looked briefly in the direction of this overwhelming crescendo of sound. She had noticed a big trench at the exit of their platform. It ran half the length of the station. It was filled with disintegrating pipes of different sizes. Some were cracked, exposing old wires. Workmen had returned to this area to continue removing concrete.

They continued to walk at an angle across the hall. They were not much more than a hundred feet from the exit of the station when the world seemed to explode. A series of explosions were intermingled with the high-pitched whine of erratic projectiles, some flying closer than others. Without hesitation, Madeleine dived under a heavy wooden luggage cart standing a few feet from her. She fell with a hard thud on the cement and covered her head with her arms. She nestled against her suitcase as though in some way it had the power to protect her. The noise was deafening. There was such a confusion of sounds - shattering glass and the wrenching protest of twisted metal. It was all over in a matter of minutes, but it had seemed an eternity. At first, it was as though there was a great silence, after such ear-shattering noise, but in fact there was a lot of noise. Men screaming in agony, others in fear. There had not been a lot of civilians at such an early hour, but a small stream had begun to trickle into the hall and were crouching at gates and ticket counters.

She crawled from under the cart and stood up. She was surprised to find herself uninjured. She looked around her. Her four escorts lay nearby, apparently lifeless. She could not tell whether they were dead or alive. There was glass everywhere. Her first thought was for von Brandenburg. Her fear for him was overwhelming. She had to go back and see if he was unharmed. Without a backward look she started to make her way towards the train she had just left. She could not run. There was too much glass underfoot. It seemed to take a long time to cross the hall and reach the entrance to the platform. The sight that greeted her made her feel nauseous. There were men lying all over the platform, some lifeless, others writhing in pain. Yet others were just sitting, as if in shock. As she picked her way through them, her eyes averted where possible, some of them reached out to her to grab her skirt. They saw her as an angel of mercy, someone who would comfort and help them. Some cried out to her.

It seemed as though half the train was a mass of mangled wreckage, including her compartment. What could have happened? A gas leak; an electrical fire; ammunition which had been ignited?

She stopped. She took a deep breath. Now she had to start looking if she was to find him. What she saw brought tears to her eyes, tears which coursed down her cheeks. She was sobbing. Please let him be alive she prayed to herself. Please, please.

She saw the familiar shape of Schultz's back. He was obviously in charge, giving orders. His arms were like windmills. Every other moment, he would bend down as if to comfort someone and then continue giving directions. She sighed with relief. But as she approached him, her relief turned to fear. There could only be one person lying on the ground who would have Schultz's undivided attention. She was standing twenty feet away, her way blocked by a barrier of injured men. Medics and volunteers were working feverishly to bandage and comfort them. She could not see who was lying at Schultz's feet. He was blocking her view. Fear seemed to have frozen her to the ground. She was unable to move. She called Schultz by name. He did not hear her. She called again. He turned and saw her. She saw a look of genuine surprise cross his face, which was immediately followed by another expression which she could not define. Relief? Surely not. He waved her towards him. She stepped gingerly closer. There at his feet lay von Brandenburg. There seemed to be a gaping wound in his side. She thought she could see his thigh bone but she turned her head away and took a long, quivering breath.

"We must transport him to the nearest hospital immediately." Schultz said to her. "Stay here and let no one take him away. I am going to find a stretcher." With that he was gone.

She bent down and took von Brandenburg's hand. It felt cold. She leant closer to his face and spoke his name. His eyes fluttered. He had heard her. She told him that she was beside him, that she was staying with him until Schultz returned, that they would be getting him to a hospital as soon as possible. Briefly his eyes opened and seemed to focus on her. His lips moved, but no words came out.

She concentrated on his face. She could not bring herself to look at his poor, torn body. That one look at his waxen face was indelibly imprinted in her mind. Torn flesh and gushing blood. How can he possibly survive such an injury? He is going to be bleed to death, before we even move him. She kept talking softly to him, her head close to his, her mouth almost touching his ear.

At last, Schultz was back. He had brought two men with him. One was a medic, the other was possibly a doctor; at least he took immediate action and applied dressings and what might have been a tourniquet. She did not look closely. They had moved him onto a stretcher and were walking away with him towards the end of the platform. She followed.

They got to the entrance of the station itself. There were all sorts of trucks parked there, in anticipation no doubt of their

The Kandahar Talisman

arrival. Schultz walked up to one of the drivers and spoke briefly. He got immediate action. The doors of the truck were flung open and von Brandenburg deposited inside. She touched Schultz on the arm and asked if she could go with them. He hesitated briefly and then beckoned her in. Her relief was overwhelming. She was surprised by his decision. It was probably contrary to all regulations. But the existing chaos was sufficient to exempt him from following the normal rules. In any event, she was sure that he intended to use her for some special purpose. In this she was correct.

The journey to the hospital was made in record time, at least if one judged the speed at which the driver negotiated the intersections and turns. Once arrived, Schultz got immediate action from the hospital staff. They were the first of the casualties to arrive. The Kapitän's rank gave him priority over any civilian. He was whisked away. A nurse in crisp uniform conferred with Schultz pointing in the direction in which the Kapitän had disappeared. Schultz nodded and pointed to Madeleine, continuing to speak. Finally the conversation came to an end and Schultz beckoned to Madeleine. "Follow me." he ordered. They walked some distance down corridors, asking the way from time to time, going from one floor to the next. Finally satisfied, Schultz turned to her and said, "You will wait here for me. Someone will inform you when they have finished operating. I will return when I can. You are to write down where they put him, if he survives his injuries." She felt sick, but nodded. "I have to get back and organize the removal of the other injured." With that he was gone. She was grateful to Schultz. It gave her time to collect her thoughts and to know the outcome, before she set off into the unknown, if indeed that was now possible. She sat and closed her eyes.

The hours ticked slowly by. She alternated sitting with pacing the corridor. Occasionally she stopped and enquired for news, in case they had forgotten her presence. The reply was always the same. They had nothing to report. There were times when she must have dozed. She was exhausted from the strain.

She was standing staring out a window on an empty inner courtyard, when a voice behind said, "Fräulein." She swung around and saw standing before her an elderly, distinguished gentleman with slightly greying hair. "You are a distant relative of Kapitän von Brandenburg, I understand. I am Professor Schmieding."

Her surprise was total, but she responded immediately, if hesitantly. "How is...how did...?" she could go no further. She was terribly afraid.

"We managed to save the Kapitän's leg. It was a very bad wound. A very complicated surgery. He may have difficulty walking for some considerable time."

"He is going to live?" she almost whispered it.

"Provided there is no serious infection, certainly. He was very lucky to get such good medical care before reaching the hospital. He could have bled to death. It will be a long convalescence. I understand he has a country home?"

"Yes." she responded, "at Mitteldorf." Thank goodness she knew that much.

"I will count on you to inform his family, then."

She nodded her assent.

"Good. Now I must go. It is going to be a long day and night." He looked tired. She felt sure that von Brandenburg's injury had tested him to the limit of his skills.

She thanked him warmly and he walked away down the corridor.

She sat down and took a deep breath of relief. Now she would wait for Schultz

She was surprised that Schultz had not turned up before this. What she did not know was that Schultz had every ambulance check at the hospital on the progress of the operation. He got no more information than did Madeleine, but he also knew that he did not need to come to the hospital. He had his hands full with the dead and wounded. He also wanted to get the men out of the station and on their way to the naval base.

She must have dozed off again. Schultz was standing in front of her calling her by name. "The Kapitän. Did he survive"? She was surprised that he did not know. She saw that the nurse's desk was empty.

"Yes, they managed to save his leg."

Schultz heaved a great sigh and turned away.

She sat waiting for him to compose himself. Finally he turned back to her. "Thank you, Fräulein, for your help. Now I do not know how you are going to reach Mitteldorf in such circumstances, but I will try and find you transport at least part of the way."

"Will you inform his family about this?"

"The navy is very thorough about such matters. Now if you will follow me, please." He was all efficiency again. "Did they tell you where he was going to be put?"

She shook her head.

"Then we must wait for the nurse to return. The front desk is far too busy for us to bother them about such matters at the present time." In fact, when they left the hospital, trucks full of the wounded were lined up trying to gain entrance. The traffic jam that had resulted was chaotic. Schultz sat Madeleine on a bench inside the entrance to the grounds and told her to wait. He then stepped out into the road and began to direct the traffic. What an amazing man, she thought. He managed to make an opening for the trucks and the long column turned slowly into the hospital entrance. He continued to direct the traffic for a time, until it was moving slowly but smoothly. At a certain moment, he stopped an old truck and spoke to the driver. He waved him to the side of the road and told him to wait. He came and fetched Madeleine and told her that he had found her a ride out of the city. It would not take her where she was going, but it would get her within 20 kilometers. It was a farmer who had just delivered a load of vegetables to the hospital.

— 4 —

Almost before she knew it, Madeleine had been settled in the back of the truck on a pile of sacks and the door closed. Schultz told her that it would be a three to four hour journey, since her destination was about 120 kilometers outside the city. It might take longer, depending on how badly blocked or damaged the streets were leading out of the city. As an afterthought, Schultz informed her that the driver did not expect payment. With that he was gone. The truck had started up and they began their bumpy ride out of the city.

Madeleine arranged the sacks as best she could and lay down on them. They smelled of onions and cabbage and earth. There was something very soothing about it all. The truck stopped and started very often, but as time went on it stopped less frequently. Eventually, she had the feeling they were on the open road because the old truck kept up a lumbering speed. It finally rocked her to sleep.

She awakened when the back of the truck was opened by the farmer. "I have come to the end of my journey." he told her. You will now have to find your way to Mitteldorf without me."

She climbed stiffly out of the truck and pulled her suitcase after her. "Can you please tell me in which direction is Mitteldorf?"

He went to the front of his truck and came back with a wrinkled piece of paper and pencil. He sketched a rough map, with the names of two or three other villages, and then pointed in the general direction she should go. She thanked him warmly and walked across the cobblestoned yard and out of his gate into the country lane beyond.

She was very hungry and thirsty, but she had not dared asked more of the farmer. He had asked no questions, but she felt that he was not very sympathetic towards her. She did not wish to arouse his suspicions any more than necessary. She had noticed a spigot in the wall of his barn, but it was not necessarily good drinking water. She would have to find another source.

She could probably walk the 20 kilometers were it not for her suitcase, which although not large was rather cumbersome and would soon become quite heavy. She set out at a moderate pace and hoped she would not attract too much attention. If only she could come upon a signpost. But she presumed that most of them might have been removed. At the first crossroad she came to there was no signpost. She saw a church spire in the distance and decided to walk towards it. It turned out to be an inspired idea.

She turned through a gate into a field half-way up a steep hill. She thought that by walking across as many fields as possible, she would be much less conspicuous. The fewer people who saw her, the better. If she was lucky, such a route might be more direct. She had deliberately asked for directions to Mitteldorf, which was the train station closest to von Brandenburg's country home in Riquewihr. She hoped that this might avoid probing questions. The map that von Brandenburg had drawn for her had shown that Riquewihr and his country home would be a closer destination than Mitteldorf. For this she was exceedingly grateful, for her body was very weary and her feet aching painfully.

She had no sooner closed the gate behind her than she heard a truck laboring up the hill in low gear. She crouched by the gate and as it passed her she stood up. What luck. Another farmer going to market? In any event, she walked behind it and looked at the array of produce inside. She hopped up on the open end. There were fruit and vegetables, dried beans and lentils. Household wares, brushes and pails. She must hurry before he came to the top of the hill and gathered speed. There was no way he could see her, so she worked her way quickly through the bundles. She selected a few items and slid off the back of the truck. She turned and walked back down the hill. He had no rearview mirror on her side, so she hoped she had escaped detection.

She picked up her suitcase and walked briskly across the field and into the next one. At last she found a sheltered corner against a hedge and amongst some bushes and sat down, out of breath. She surveyed her spoils with relish. A small, whole cheese and some plums and pears. She still lacked something to drink, but she hoped that she could manage to solve that problem later. She ate slowly. It all tasted wonderful. She had not eaten properly in about eight hours. The nurse at the hospital had taken pity on her and provided her with cups of tea, but there had been nothing to eat. This revived her almost instantly.

In due course she got to her feet and started walking again. She was surprised how far away the church was. She had been walking across the fields for over an hour and the church was still a long way off. Finally, she saw a gate which opened onto a road. She decided to risk taking this route because it looked as though it would lead more directly to her destination. Ahead of her was a high wall. She paralleled it for a considerable distance. Finally, it made a right-angled turn. At this corner, she was surprised and delighted to find a traveler's fountain. It was a green arbor of vines and trailing ivy. A cup hung from a chain that was attached to the wall next to the elaborately sculptured spout from which a steady trickle of water splashed into the basin below. She drank long and deeply.

She had been walking for another half-an-hour, since leaving the last gate, when she came to the crest of a hill. There before her, in a slight hollow surrounded by a wooded area on three sides, stood a wonderful, gothic church with an ornate bell tower. There was a village beyond it, but the church stood alone, at a bend in the road. The village was nearly hidden from view.

She walked up to the main door of the church and set down her suitcase just inside the porch. There seemed to be no one about. She pushed open the door and stepped inside. She was surprised by the intricately decorated ribbed vaulting of the roof which disappeared into the shadows above her. The windows sent shafts of jeweled light from the setting sun. From outward appearances one would have no idea of the majesty that awaited the unsuspecting visitor. It was a most tranquil scene and she took great comfort from it. Candles filled low-hanging wrought-iron chandeliers, but were not lit. She imagined with pleasure how beautiful the interior would be in the flickering candle-light.

If nothing else, perhaps she could sleep here for the night. She realized now how late it was.

She was turning to leave, when a voice spoke to her from the shadows. "Is there something I can do for you, my child?" was the enquiry.

She turned towards the voice and saw a very elderly priest standing a short distance from her.

Without hesitation she responded, "I was wondering if I could sleep here for the night.

There was a long silence as he shuffled towards her and stood searching her face. "Are you lost?"

"No, but I have come a long distance and am very tired. I do not think that I can reach my destination tonight."

"Follow me." was his response. Then he turned back and with an apologetic smile said, "I am Father Hildebrandt,"

He led her half-way towards the altar with its elaborately carved nativity scene in mellowed wood, before turning towards a side door. This brought them into another part of the church. He shuffled on slowly until at last they reached what must be his living quarters. A small refectory table stood in the center of a stone-floored room. There was a fireplace, but no fire, and two old armchairs.

"My housekeeper has been away nearly a week, caring for a sick relative. I am hoping she will return soon. I am a very poor cook. You could have her room for the night. In return, I wonder if you would have the goodness to cook my supper?"

She smiled warmly at him and said, "I would be very happy to do so."

She followed him to a small, neat room which had a bed covered with a white counterpane, a pine chest of drawers and a wardrobe. Through the window she could see the woods. She set her suitcase on the floor and followed the old man to the kitchen. It seemed to be a jumble of pots, pans and dishes. He showed her the pantry which was well stocked with food. There were sacks of potatoes, beans, onions, but no sugar. There was plenty of butter, milk, cheese and eggs. The benefits of living in the country, surrounded by caring parishioners. He seemed to have eaten all the bread, for there were a lot of ends of loaves. She asked him what he had been eating. He said that Helga, his housekeeper, had left him several meat pies, but they were now gone.

"When did you last eat?" she asked him.

"It seems like a long time ago," he smiled at her.

"Then I shall prepare you something that will not take long to cook. Do you often light the fire?"

He shook his head. "I am afraid that my arthritis does not permit such a luxury and Helga has bad knees. It is a great pity. I would love a fire. That can be a cold room."

"If you have some wood, I could start a fire for you."

A smile illuminated his face. He beckoned to her as he shuffled towards an outside door. There was a small shed leaning against the outside wall and inside was a good supply of aged and dry logs. She took as many of the smaller pieces as she could carry and went indoors with them. She got the fire started and returned for some larger logs. The old priest sat in front of it, his frail, old hands outstretched. She left him to return to the kitchen.

She decided to leave the mess of dishes and concentrate on the food preparation. She was very hungry herself and also very tired. But it was a pleasant fatigue, because she was no longer concerned about finding a bed for the night and that knowledge had taken much of the stress out of her. She made a fruit pudding. She found some apples and berries and with the addition of milk and honey, she thought it would provide a substantial dessert. For the main course, she made a cheese and ham omelette. It was soon ready. She walked into the refectory and found the old priest nodding in front of the fire. She laid the table and went back into the kitchen.

When she came back he was awake. She told him that supper was ready and he got slowly to his feet. She brought in the omelette. He said grace.

The omelette was good. She was tremendously hungry. She suspected that Father Hildebrandt was too. In any event, it disappeared from his plate. The fruit pudding was browned and ready when she returned to the kitchen. It was sweet and crispy. Father Hildebrandt ate in silence. She presumed that he was accustomed to eating alone and therefore was not used to conversation at mealtimes. He asked her if she would make him an herbal tea. The meal came to an end and he said grace and blessed her.

She removed the dishes. Father Hildebrandt sat himself in front of the fire with a second cup of tea. She brought him a small footstool. She added more logs to the fire and left him. She wondered if he might not choose to spend the night there. It would surely be much warmer than his room. There seemed to be no heating system in this part of the building.

She decided to leave the kitchen clean-up until morning. She needed to sleep.

She slept for twelve hours, seemingly without moving. She awoke refreshed. She began the day by cleaning up the kitchen. It took her a good hour. But in the process, she cleaned and peeled a quantity of vegetables and began a large pot of soup. The pantry was an ideal storage place. The walls were about two feet thick, a small, narrow slit providing air from the outside; food would keep fresh for weeks in such a place, even months in winter. It was obvious that the parishioners were generous with their gifts of food for the old man, for the larder held a mixed variety of ingredients which helped her in her meal preparations. She began a meat stew, adding more vegetables. She would leave him well provided.

The kitchen was at last neat and tidy. She walked into the refectory and laid the table. The fire was now in ashes, but a faint glow showed that it could be stirred into life with gentle persuasion. She got some more logs and the room was once more alive with firelight.

She had just made more herbal tea and brought it in, when Father Hildebrandt shuffled into sight. He greeted her warmly and enquired how she had slept. As suspected, he had chosen to spend most of the night in front of the fire. He looked better today and she felt glad. He had looked very frail last night. But his frailty did not extend to his mind. They sat down for their breakfast, which was eaten in silence. At the end of the meal, he leant towards her and said, "I wonder if I might ask a very special favor of you?" She nodded and he went on. "Would it be possible for you to remain a little longer with me? I believe that my housekeeper will be returning soon, although I have heard nothing yet. Today, I have a very busy day in the parish and it would be such a help to me not to have to worry about caring for myself."

She smiled. How could she deny such a gracious request? His need was great. She did not know what a busy day in the parish would involve, but he was certainly not physically capable of enduring anything too demanding.

"I will be happy to remain." In any event it would give her more time to find the best route to Riquewihr.

He smiled his thanks and got painfully to his feet. "Then I will leave everything in your capable hands."

She got up too and walked up to him. She suspected that his hearing was very poor and that he spent most of his time lip-reading. It was for this reason that their meals had been eaten in silence. He was too far away from her to read her lips. Also, he was accustomed to eating alone.

"I think that I will spend part of the day exploring your church." He smiled his approval. "I will tell you some of its history at dinner tonight."

It had been a pleasant day. She had wandered through the great shadowy church drinking in its peace and serenity, its history and the names of those who were buried there. It had an intricately carved pulpit above which hung a crimson fringed canopy. She knew that Father Hildebrandt was busy hearing confessions for there were several women gathered at that side of the church.

After lunch she walked into the woods behind the church, careful to do so while no one was in sight. She wandered under the canopy of soft green, enjoying the damp, rich smell of earth and vegetation. It was a peaceful place. She followed the slope of the terrain and found that it led her down to a broad and quiet stream. She followed its course and it finally brought her out into the open. It led her eventually to a simple bridge and a path across it. She wondered where it went and decided to try and find out.

At dinner that night Father Hildebrandt looked tired. He complimented her on the stew and thanked her again for her kindness in staying with him. He asked few personal questions and she wondered if it was because he sensed that her life had been disrupted by hostilities, like so many others, or because he truly lacked a sense of curiosity. After all, he probably knew so much about the personal lives of his parishioners, what could be of special interest about her?

She had built another fire and he was seated beside it. She handed him a cup of tea and sat herself opposite him. She had asked him if there were many other churches the size of his church in the vicinity. For such a relatively small community, she thought it was rather large. He smiled. He explained to her that at a certain time in history, it had been quite common to build a church in every community and that in some cases communities competed with each other in this respect. Many of the landed gentry were the main benefactors of such projects, seeking out famous architects and renowned artisans. The most beautiful church in the area was the small church at Riquewihr, St. Annenkapelle. A church built of natural stone with a slender and elegant steeple. Inside it was very plain, he told her, which accentuated a gloriously painted beamed and paneled ceiling. Only the most celebrated craftsman had been employed in its construction hundreds of years ago. It was considered the personal and private chapel of a large estate just outside the village. Generations of the family were buried inside the crypt. In earlier days, it had been a place of pilgrimage because of its relics.

Her heart had taken a leap at this. She had asked him if it would be close enough to visit on foot. His response had been in the affirmative. He told her of a path across the fields which followed more or less a small stream. She could pick it up behind the church.

The following day dawned very wet and Madeleine was confined to the church and the living quarters. She spent most of the time in the kitchen preparing various simple dishes. She also added some more fresh vegetables to the soup which seemed to get better each time she served it.

They had just finished lunch when there came a knock on the kitchen door. Without waiting for a response, someone opened it and walked into the refectory. Madeleine was in the kitchen and remained there, hoping not to be seen. She heard a woman conversing with Father Hildebrandt. The visitor had just received word on the telephone at the post office from Helga. Father Hildebrandt was to expect Helga to return after lunch the next day. Soon after this announcement, the woman asked if she could be of help in any way. Then she excused herself saying she had to return to work, as there was only one other person left in charge at the post-office. She left as quickly as she had come. Madeleine was relieved not to be seen and felt sure that Father Hildebrandt had not mentioned her presence.

She sat briefly with him after dinner in front of the fire. He was obviously very tired. He had visited two parishioners in the village. That had been very draining for him. She asked him if he did not have someone who could take on some of the more demanding tasks. He smiled and replied that he had once had more help than he had now, but his assistants had been moved to other parishes with a greater need. He said that he felt that he should retire to a smaller parish, but that there was no one to replace him. She told him that she would leave after lunch the next day. He nodded and closed his eyes. She could not tell whether he had gone to sleep or was meditating. She added some more logs to the fire and since he remained with his eyes closed, she left the room quietly.

— 5 —

The day of her departure dawned dry and she set out briskly, following the path across the little stream that eventually turned and meandered side by side with it through the woods. She took deep breaths of the clean, fresh air and felt invigorated. Her stay at St. Nicolas had given her a chance to rest and review her situation which, at best, was one of great uncertainty. Lunch had been eaten in silence, as usual. As she handed him tea in his chair by the fire after the meal, Father Hildebrandt thanked her warmly for her great kindness in staying and expressed the hope that her friends would not be worried about her delayed arrival. She had not mentioned her destination or any details about it. She assumed that Father Hildebrandt was aware that her life had suffered a disruption. These were stressful times. He obviously could not hear that her spoken German was not that of a native, but he could perhaps sense it from reading her lips? She decided it was of no consequence any longer. He had accepted her and would not deliberately endanger her.

The path eventually led to open fields and the sun came out and warmed her. She had a sense of her direction from some of the things that Father Hildebrandt had said. She would come out on the rise of a hill and would look down at the little hamlet of Riquewihr. There she should see the beautiful St. Annenkapelle nestled in one corner of the small hollow, a few houses encircling it. There would be a narrow road winding away in a wide curve to her left leading passed two large stone pillars which were the entrance to the von Brandenburg's estate. The details of the village, von Brandenburg himself had given her. It was good to have some confirmation from a local source.

She had been walking for about an hour. She felt there was no guarantee that Maria, von Brandenburg's housekeeper on the estate, would necessarily be in residence. Supposing she had decided to visit family or relatives? She pushed that thought aside. At last she came to the point where the path started downhill towards Riquewihr. She sat down and surveyed the scene. She did not want to walk through the village in daylight.

The light seemed to be fading. She decided to refresh herself with a quick snack. On her feet again, she kept working her way in the general direction she hoped would bring her to the front gates. She had just rounded a large bush and saw ahead of her the beige-colored stone wall surrounding the estate. It was a relief. She began now to parallel the wall.

She had been working her way through thick undergrowth and around small bushes when she heard the sound of a truck engine quite close to her. When it seemed to be receding, she stood up and caught sight of it as it disappeared.

It was important for her to get inside the gates without being seen. She was about 20 yards from the gates. The ground had been kept clear and she would be in the open while approaching the entrance. She could hear motorized vehicles, even though they were hidden by the high wall. She would have no warning of bicycles. It was an eerie feeling, listening for some sound that might indicate an approaching traveler. She had decided that she could not rush through the gates. She might run straight into the arms of a groundskeeper or local tradesman. She could wait until dark, but then it was possible that Maria would not open the door to her.

It was time to move. It would soon be dark. She looked at her watch. She pushed her suitcase into the undergrowth and walked quickly to the entrance and was just looking inside when she noticed a bicycle. She held her breath and froze. The old man passed without noticing her. Very cautiously, she looked through the gates. She saw a long driveway lined by a low hedge of yews, about waist high. There seemed to be no one in sight. She paused and stood listening. She walked quickly back to her suitcase. Then to her consternation someone on foot. She lay flat. She could hear nothing. Had he passed? There was no way to tell. The grass and growth were not very deep here. Could she be seen she wondered? Very gingerly, she raised her head a little and was shocked to find the man standing in the middle of the entrance half turned towards her. What could he be doing? She felt sick. It would be so easy for him to discover her. In this posture she would be very suspect, much worse than on her feet with suitcase in hand. There was a crunch and then another. She held her breath. The steps seemed to be receding. She waited another eternity and then raised her head. There was no one there. Had he gone inside the gates or away down the road? She lay listening. More vehicles and then silence. She stood up with her suitcase and walked as calmly as she could through the gates. No one in sight in front or behind. She darted quickly behind the hedge just as a car approached.

It had been a stressful experience and she sat a few moments to calm her nerves. She decided that she had better find the letter that von Brandenburg had written to Maria. It would be wise to have it in her hand in case Maria did open the door and immediately try to turn her away. There was a moment of panic when she could not find it. Keep calm, she told herself, and search for it methodically. She came upon it where she remembered putting it. I must teach myself to do things more slowly, it might make the difference in a moment of grave danger.

She could not see the house as she walked up the driveway behind the yew hedge. But as she approached the crest of the gentle rise she saw it nestled in a slight hollow. It was a handsome stone and timber dwelling, with one long wing and a smaller one joining the main facade at right angles. A large gable framed the front door. Smaller ones were situated above the upper windows along the length of the building. Several elaborate chimneys rose from the lichen-covered soft red tiled roof. A beautiful cedar of Lebanon stood dividing the circular driveway. She stepped onto the driveway. She had no idea what she would do if Maria were not in, but she pushed the thought aside and walked slowly towards the massive carved oak front door. She pulled the bell which hung on the right-hand side. She could hear it ringing as if at a great distance. There was an almost immediate response in the deep-throated baying of a dog. She had forgotten Max. Max was a wolfhound. Von Brandenburg had told her that Max would like and accept her, even though he was not generally friendly towards strangers. Supposing von Brandenburg were wrong? And how could he possibly assume such a preposterous thing? Her heart beat a little faster. She had heard no sound from within, but suddenly the door was pulled open and in front of her stood a short, thin woman. She was attired completely in black except for a white cotton apron around her waist. Her dark, greying hair was drawn tightly into a bun at the nape of her neck. Her face was wrinkled, but her skin soft and pale, typical of someone who did not spend much time outdoors. Her dark and unfriendly eyes appraised Madeleine. It was disconcerting and Madeleine was about to open her mouth to speak when she suddenly noticed another pair of inquiring eyes looking at her over Maria's shoulder. Max. He was huge. His grey brown flecked eyes were unblinking.

"I have a letter for you from Kapitän von Brandenburg." she said as she held out the letter very slowly and deliberately. No sudden moves, she thought, so as not to stimulate any aggressive behavior in Max.

Maria was obviously totally surprised. Few people came to the house any more, especially with the family not in residence. Deliveries were generally made at a rear door. She took the letter from Madeleine and looked at it as if it might bite her. She stood looking at it and Madeleine wondered what she would do next.

"You are to read it right away." And don't shut the door in my face, she said to herself.

Maria looked up, noticed the suitcase for the first time and invited Madeleine in with some reluctance. She closed the door behind her. "Please wait here."

She turned and hurried away.

Madeleine had decided that she would tell Maria of the Kapitän's injury later.

Madeleine was left standing face to face with Max. His gaze had not wavered.

Max," she said softly, "Are you Max?"

He cocked his head on one side, a look of surprise in his eyes. Nobody called him by his name, or at least not very often, only his master. Maria did not like Max and Max did not like Maria. But he was dependent on her because she fed him, generally complaining loudly at how much he ate and how long it took to prepare his meals. There was no love lost between Max and Otto, the gardener, either. Max dug trenches in Otto's flower and vegetable beds.

Max took a tentative step forward. He was within touching distance. She looked about her, trying to find a way to calm herself. She was standing in a two-storied paneled hall. In front of her was a beautiful oak staircase that divided half-way up, branching right and left to a balcony that ran above her head on three sides. On each side of the staircase at ground level were doors leading to another part of the house. It was through one of these that Maria had disappeared. Portraits hung on the walls, a large one over the fireplace to her left. There were also heads of various deer and wild boar. The floor was of oak too, a few rugs scattered here and there. A large and very old table sat across from the fireplace, a big empty urn in the middle, with two large tapestry arm chairs on either end.

As she stood there, taking in all the details of her surroundings, a cold, wet nose touched her hand. She slowly stretched out an arm and gently stroked Max on the chest. He took half a step closer, leaning against her hand as if to indicate that he did not wish her to stop. She curled the hair of his coat around her finger gently several times and then let her hand travel up his neck and behind his ears.

Maria could not see to read the letter from her beloved young master without her spectacles. She hoped that she had left them in the kitchen. She only used them to read and there was not much time during the day to do that. It took her several minutes to find them. She opened the letter slowly, a quiver of apprehension running through her. She read the contents with surprise. "A distant relative... to stay at the house... needs new papers to travel... best not to mention this to anyone.... I will be in touch soon." She read it three times. She was perplexed at this unexpected turn of events. Now she had to decide which bedroom to prepare for this so-called relative and get it aired. She felt resentment at the extra work involved in caring for a family member she did not recall hearing about in all her years of service with the family.

Walking back into the hall, Maria was very surprised to find Max leaning up against Madeleine, his eyes half closed, and Madeleine with her arm resting on his great shoulders. Maria's dislike of Max was based on her fear of him. His unblinking eyes followed her every movement throughout the day and she found it unnerving. It would have surprised Maria if she had been told that Max was starved for attention and affection and had immediately sensed in Madeleine a friend on whom he could count for all these.

Maria did not waste words. "Let me show you to a room, I am sure you must be tired."

"Thank you," said Madeleine. "I wonder if it would be possible to give me something to eat." Silence greeted this request. It was obviously an imposition. She followed Maria to the staircase and followed her up it. Max remained at the bottom. He let out a loud bark which took both of them by surprise.

"Is he not allowed up?" Madeleine asked sensing Max's frustration.

"Only when the Kapitän is home." was the curt response.

"I suppose you like to have Max near you. It looks like a very large house." This tactic provided the response that Madeleine sought.

"You may have him sleep in your room, if you wish." Maria was relieved that Max's unexpected attachment to this stranger could provide her some freedom of movement. She found Max's baleful gaze an unwelcome part of her everyday life. But the Kapitän loved his dog very much and she had to accept the situation.

Madeleine turned and called to Max. He was up the long staircase in what seemed like a couple of huge bounds. He disappeared down the corridor as if he knew where they planned to go.

Maria had decided to put Madeleine in the corner guestroom, where the two wings came together. The view over garden and the paddocks to the woods was one of great tranquility. Madeleine could not wait for the sun to come up so that she could see it better. Maria said, as she left, that she would bring some thick soup as well as some hot water bottles to air the bed. Then she was gone.

Madeleine sat on the edge of the bed, relieved to get off her sore and weary feet. Max came up to her and put his cold nose in her face. She stroked his head and whispered in his ear, "Willst du mein Freund sein?" He wagged his tail as though understood. He sniffed her shoes and the arm of her jacket. Was there some telltale scent of his beloved master, she wondered. Or was he just a lonely dog who had found a friend? Yes, he would be her friend, she felt sure.

She drew a hot bath in the adjoining bathroom and lay luxuriating in the warmth that engulfed her, the steam penetrating every pore in her body and gently relaxing her. She could not remember when she had enjoyed a bath so much. In due course she got out, pink and steaming, wrapped in an enormous towel, to find a large bowl of soup on a tray with some fresh bread and some fruit. She sat eating wrapped in her towel. She could feel the energy returning to her body. Max, in the meantime, had settled himself in the middle of a thick rug, his head on his front paws. She unpacked a few things from her case. The rest of her clothes she would hang up in the morning. She was truly exhausted.

Maria had also placed three stone water bottles, quite hot to the touch, in her bed. She moved them several times. She could hardly wait to lie down and go to sleep. She stroked Max on the head, turned out the light and was instantly asleep.

She awoke to a day of sunshine. She lay and stretched. She felt that she had slept without moving. She rolled over, remembering Max. His eyes were on her. He wagged his tail and got to his feet and gave her a cold nuzzle with his nose. She sat up and he pranced in front of her. He had been so patient, she thought. It must be long after his breakfast, if that is when he ate. She walked to the door and opened it and he bounced out and down the corridor.

She opened the curtains and looked out on a breathtaking scene. There was a curved brick path winding its way around the house. It was bordered on one side by a profusion of flowers. From there the lawn stretched away down a slope to a walled garden on her left. Beyond that were trees and large bushes and a glimpse of a lake. To the right, the lawn swept in a large circle with clumps of bushes surrounded by flower beds. A sundial, near a small pond stood centrally in this area. There was a backdrop of huge trees. It was a misty, sunny morning and the scene had the look of an impressionist painting. She drank it in and wished that she were home again. As lovely as it was, it made her terribly homesick for her parent's familiar garden.

After she had dressed in a fresh sweater and skirt, she unpacked the rest of her suitcase. The Kandahar medal she hung around her neck under her sweater. It gave her comfort. A precious gift from her father. It was an unique piece which her father had asked a jeweler to design into a locket for his beloved daughter. It was a Persian gold coin of ancient origins, one facade covered in intricate script. The other gold side, which had been worn smooth by time, was hidden by a beautifully carved circle of green and lavender jade. The two pieces were bonded together by sculptured and worked gold which blended the two elements to perfection. She liked to think it brought her good luck. She looked for a place to hide her passport and finally taped it to the bottom of a drawer. It was not a very original scheme, but for the time being she felt it was sufficient. She had completed this when she heard a sound behind her and turned to see Max. He looked expectant. She smiled. He was ready to play.

They went down the staircase together and out into the kitchen. Maria was nowhere to be seen, but a place was set at a table. There was hot coffee in a pot, rolls and jam and some sausage. There was no butter. She was very hungry.

She had finished her breakfast and was removing her plate from the table when Maria came in from the outside.

"Thank you for the breakfast. Can I help you by taking Max outside for some exercise?"

"He is accustomed to exercising himself." she responded. "I do not have time for such things. However, you may take him out. I have told Otto that the Kapitän has a relative staying here. Otto lives in the small cottage near the barns. He rarely leaves the property and has probably already forgotten what I have told him. He will not mention your presence here, which is what the Kapitän wishes. As long as you keep Max out of the vegetable garden, Otto will not bother you. Lunch will be ready at one." With that she was gone.

Madeleine felt dismissed. She decided that she would try as much as possible to keep out of Maria's way. It was obvious that she had very much added to her workload. Maria was prepared to do her duty, but that did not extend to being conversational.

Once outside, Madeleine forgot Maria. It was the most glorious day. Max was excited as a puppy at the prospect of having a companion and a playmate. He bounced in circles around her.

She had to find some suitable toy for Max. She wondered if there would be anything in one of the barns. She glanced through a wrought-iron gate which protected the enclosed kitchen garden where Otto obviously spent much of his time rearing fresh, healthy vegetables. She walked on under a stone archway covered with roses onto the lawn sloping down to a walled rose garden. A brick path wound between the rose beds. There were climbing roses on three walls. The fourth wall contained espaliered trees that looked like peach trees. She could tell it was a wonderfully warm and sheltered spot.

She came to the barns at last. There were three of them. This is where the horses must have been kept. The first barn was empty. The second held a collection of tools and equipment. The last was a surprise. It contained a magnificent Daimler convertible. Other than a little dust, it looked as though it were in perfect condition. She walked all around it and peered in the windows. It was very impressive. She was tempted to open the door and sit in it, but was afraid that someone would discover her doing so. Anyway, Max was getting impatient. She looked around in the hope of finding something like a ball, but there was nothing. She went into the second barn, not hopeful of doing better, and was delighted to find an old and worn leather glove resting on a pile of rope. She picked it up and went outside.

Beyond the barns was the paddock. The grass was long and overgrown and it was obvious that the paddock had not been used in a long time. She turned back the way she had come and climbed the slope up to the house. She made her way to the large open lawn which lay behind the house. It was a perfect place in which to exercise Max. She threw the glove to him, but he seemed surprised and let the glove fall at his feet. She went and picked it up, touched his nose with it and threw it again. He bounded after it, grasped in his mouth and raced in ever widening circles around her. She laughed. She felt sure that no one had played with him for a long time. It was wonderful to see his carefree abandon.

They played in this fashion until Max was tired. They walked back to the barn and returned the glove and then wandered down to the small lake that lay in a sheltered hollow surrounded by reeds and a variety of trees. It was a very tranquil spot and she sat down on an old bench and watched waterfowl who were busily foraging amongst the reeds and water-lilies. Max waded into the lake and had a long drink.

In the weeks and months that followed, her routine did not change much from day to day. She and Max spent most of the time together. The dog became her faithful shadow. It was difficult to fill the day, alone as she was. She instinctively knew that it was a waste of time to try and befriend Maria. Maria was always polite, but very distant. At one point, she had the courage to enquire about the Kapitän and whether he was recovering from his injuries. Maria's response was that the authorities would keep the Kapitän's parents informed of his progress. Surely, they in turn would keep Maria informed, if only in the process of enquiring about conditions at the country estate. She wondered, with a sinking feeling, what von Brandenburg's parents knew of her presence at Waldesrauschen. Worse still, when would the authorities be alerted of her presence. She tried to suppress her great anxiety at this ever-present thought. She was afraid for herself, but also very concerned at what might happen to von Brandenburg for the risk he was taking on her behalf. Their fate was linked. Madeleine realized Maria would only impart information to her that she felt obliged to tell her and nothing more.

It was many weeks before she found the courage to visit St. Annenkapelle, which sat at one corner of the property. From all her observations, it did not seem as though anyone from the village ever came there. She found that the door was locked. In some ways, she was relieved. To be discovered inside could give rise to unwanted questions. But she longed to see it. From Father Hildebrandt's description, it sounded unique.

She had been down at the lake all afternoon sketching. Max had sat beside her. It had been a peaceful interlude and she had been pleased with her efforts. If she could find pen and ink she would like to transpose her sketches into something more solid and permanent. She would have to broach the subject with Maria. It was annoying to have to do this, because it would be another irritation to Maria. She had worked very hard at trying to keep out of the way, but as large as the house was, there were days when wet weather forced her to remain indoors. She had discovered the library, and had taken comfort in some good books, including a few in English. But she had to be careful not to have Maria find her reading these. This meant that a lot of the time she was reading in German which was not as relaxing.

Madeleine often sat in the library before going to bed. She did that most evenings. It was a comfortable and cozy place and she enjoyed curling up in one of the big armchairs with a book. She sat this particular night in the library and found it difficult to concentrate on reading. She was very worried about her future.

She could not remain here indefinitely. What if von Brandenburg were not to return? She had an equally frightening thought. What if he returned home and had no recollection of her at all? Such a possibility would not be surprising after such a serious injury. His mind might have sustained as serious an injury as his leg. She shuddered in dismay. She was sure Maria would not continue to give her shelter in either of those circumstances, but would notify the authorities and she would be arrested. That night she slept fitfully and was later than usual for breakfast.

Since her arrival at Waldesrauschen, there had been very few visitors. Those who did come were mostly tradespeople. Madeleine was careful not to walk near the front of the house or the driveway, so that she should not bump into some unexpected stranger. It was difficult to remember as the days went by that she was in enemy territory. She even avoided Otto as much as possible, although when she did see him, he took very little notice of her other than giving her a brief greeting. He always seemed very preoccupied, whether working in the garden or around his cottage. She felt he might be older than some suspected.

On this particular day, she entered the house through the kitchen garden door. Maria was not around and she cut herself a slice of course bread and covered it with jam. She was sitting eating this when she heard the clatter of loud footsteps coming down the staircase. There was the sound of men's voices. The front door closed and she heard the sound of a truck engine as it moved away down the drive. Her heart began to race. This was something new and unexpected. She wondered if it had anything to do with her presence? What if she had been observed by someone during the days she was outside with Max? What if Maria had chosen to mention her presence in the house and the explanation had been unsatisfactory? Would they be back soon to arrest her? Had they been upstairs to search her bedroom? She had moved her passport to a better hiding place, but it gave her little comfort. She decided to sit where she was until Maria returned to the kitchen.

But she sat there almost half an hour and Maria still did not return. The house was silent, so she got to her feet and quietly walked out into the hall. She stood at the bottom of the staircase, listening. She could hear nothing. Quickly and quietly she climbed the stairs and went to her room. Max followed her, hesitating briefly at the top. Her room seemed untouched. She checked her passport in its hiding place and found it as she had left it. She sighed with relief.

Later, Maria knocked on her door and announced that her dinner would be a little earlier that evening. She gave no reason for this change and Madeleine did not feel she should question it. She had supper alone, as usual, in the sun-room adjacent to the large dining room. Maria only stayed long enough to serve the meal. Madeleine felt that Maria's resentment of her was growing, so she continued to avoid her as much as possible.

— 6 —

Von Brandenburg returned home to his country estate in an army truck. The journey had been a long and painful one for him. He could not remember much of his hospital stay. He had been told that there had been a violent explosion at the station, as a result of workmen igniting some ammunition shortly after the arrival of their train. One of his last memories was of talking to his men. The surgeon who had operated on him had been an eminent professor. He had received the best possible care and attention. They had managed to save his leg. It had been a terrible injury and he would need many months of rest and recuperation. How well he would be able to walk was unknown. He was young. He might be lucky.

It was wonderful to enter his own home. Many times he had thought that he might never see it again. They carried him swiftly and expertly up the steep staircase into his bedroom. Maria had been at the door to greet him. He could see the joy and the pain in her face. He knew what an effort it was for her not to weep. It would not have been seemly in front of the medical staff and driver, all of whom had entered the house to see him safely delivered. She hurried after his stretcher and turned back the covers of his bed even further to permit the orderlies to lay him down with the least disturbance possible. Maria placed water beside his bed and some fruit and asked if he would like something to eat. He shook his head. He needed to sleep. He would eat later.

They had left him then and he had settled more comfortably on his pillows. He looked up at the familiar ceiling with its old beams, at the solid and friendly furniture and the photograph of his parents looking gently at him and he sighed deeply and closed his eyes. His poor battered body was throbbing with pain, but he was home and safe and he was very grateful. He closed his eyes and slept.

When he finally awoke, the sun was shining softly into his room. He felt refreshed, despite moments of restless discomfort. What a luxury not to have someone poking and prodding him awake every hour or so. There had been a few extraordinarily handsome nurses, but even they had been heartless to a fault. He had grown sullen under their continual intrusions. They had seemed undeterred and when he complained loudly and angrily, they had smiled and said that one day he would thank them. Perhaps he would thank them if he ever managed to walk again, but all he had ever wanted was to be able to sleep, as much as the pain would permit.

It was time to focus on getting up. He had done it several times in hospital with a whole group of nurses hovering over him; an excruciating experience. He hated making a spectacle of himself. He had tried it just once alone and had come close to falling. He noticed that they had left his crutches within reach beside his bed. There was also a bell-pull draped over his headboard, but he certainly did not want Maria to witness his helplessness.

He despised his crutches. They were treacherous things. It was very difficult to get to his feet with them, especially feeling as weak as he did. Finally he managed to stand. He waited for the pulsating pain in his body to subside. He walked himself to the dressing-table mirror and was shocked to see a stranger looking back at him. He had not seen himself all the time he had been in hospital. He was hollow-cheeked and haggard. His skin looked almost grey which was accentuated by the deep blue of his beard which had not been shaved for two days. His brow was moist from the physical effort. It was disconcerting to see himself like this. He looked like some wraith from another world. He propelled himself to the window and drank in the beautiful scene below him. It was enough to give him courage. He loved this place, which brought back so many happy childhood memories.

He was back in bed by the time Maria arrived, knocking on his door with his breakfast. The smell of coffee filled his nostrils and he welcomed Maria with a warm smile. She had always spoilt him, ever since he could remember. He had no idea how she could have found such a rare commodity as coffee, but he was grateful at the thought of the pampering he would enjoy at her hands. She fussed over getting him settled with enough pillows for support. He realized how hungry he was. He really had not eaten a proper meal in 24 hours.

They chatted briefly about family matters and the property. She filled him in on all of importance that had happened since he had last been home. He asked about Max and a slight shadow crossed her face. He knew that she had only tolerated the dog because of him.

"He does not like me," she said with a shrug.

Von Brandenburg laughed and said, "You do not like him and he knows it."

"He has grown very big," she said trying to deflect the direction of the conversation.

"I cannot wait to see him," he answered, "but I am not strong enough yet to tolerate an enthusiastic welcome from him."

After a few more words, Maria left him to eat his breakfast.

He savored everything she had put before him and felt the energy flow into him as he ate. He knew that with rest and good food his strength would soon return. As to the ability of his leg to regain its mobility, that was something that only time would reveal.

His breakfast finished, he lay looking out the window and wondered about his parents. He had not been able to reach them by telephone before leaving the hospital. He had better write and tell them he was back home. The family estate was some considerable distance from this country residence and to come here would be a journey that they would not undertake in such uncertain times. Besides which, he knew his father was not enjoying the best of health. But he would like to have seen them. He had felt very alone in the last few weeks.

His mind flitted back unbidden to the face of that beautiful girl who somehow had found her way onto their troop train. He had forced himself not to think of her. She had surely been killed in the explosion in the train station. At best, she could not have got far without capture. He must not waste time dwelling on the possible horrific ending of her life.

He slept again and awoke in time for his lunch. His appetite seemed to be better and better and Maria was gratified to see that he could eat all that she served him.

It was time for a little exercise. He carefully got on his feet and, and with the support of his crutches, limped over to the window. It was such a lovely sight, the soft contours of the trees at a distance, the symmetrical shapes of flowerbeds, paths and lawns. The variety of greens and the vivid contrasts of blooming flowers. He wished that he could be sitting out there. He hoped that would be possible soon.

He was turning away from the window when a movement caught his eye and he turned his head. It was Max. His heart swelled with pleasure. Max was carrying something in his mouth and was tossing it into the air and pouncing on it when it landed. He was the picture of carefree abandon. He was out of sight again, but he reappeared almost instantly running gracefully in great easy strides. He was up on the main lawn and circling it like a racehorse. He was surely not out there alone putting on such an exhibition? There must be an audience somewhere. It could not be Maria and he was sure that old Otto would have nothing to do with his beloved Max. He had disapproved of the dog from the first meeting. Curious, he stood looking. Max was now seated in the middle of the lawn, his ears up, looking expectant. Someone had called him and he raced away out of sight. How big he had grown in all these months. He looked wonderful. He was glad that Max had found a playmate. He had feared that he would be very lonely in his absence.

He slept some more. When Maria brought his supper, he had planned to ask her who Max's playmate was, but she said she was late for a meeting in the village and hurried away.

Von Brandenburg was looking out the window the following morning when Max appeared once more. He was walking sedately, not in the playful mood of the previous day. He seemed interested in some scent in the air for he kept raising his great head high to sniff the wind. He eventually disappeared into the woods and was lost to view.

Von Brandenburg was upset at his disappearance for he knew that Otto set traps in the woods. He half suspected that Otto would be equally as glad to trap one of Max's great paws as to catch a rabbit or a pheasant. He was about to turn away and ring for Maria, when he saw Madeleine appear walking towards the woods where Max had roamed. He was flooded with an excitement that took him by surprise. He could not believe his eyes. There she was, even lovelier than he remembered. She was unharmed. She had made it safely to his home. She had not quite reached the woods when Max reappeared. She must have called him for he bounced up to her and pranced around her. She held out her hand and he came to her and she leant down and hugged him.

Von Brandenburg's first impulse was to ring for Maria immediately, but he changed his mind. Why had Maria not mentioned the guest in his house? There had been much to talk about, but he would have expected her to say something soon after his arrival. He was puzzled. But concluded, rightly, that Maria was jealous of her charge and did not wish to share him with a stranger.

That night Madeleine was sitting in the library as usual, when she became aware of a slightly irregular tap-tap-tap above her head. At times it would stop, but then it would start up again. She went on listening, but it had stopped and she did not hear it again. She was mystified. She could not place the sound.

She had not been upstairs in that wing of the house. She presumed that it was the main family living quarters, since her wing of the house seemed to be guest rooms. The more she thought about it, the more she was convinced that it was possible that the Kapitän had come home. That would explain the men in the house. It would explain why no one had come to arrest her. Her spirits rose at this possibility. She would no longer be alone if he were here. He would find some way to help, she felt sure. She prayed that he would remember her.

The next day was like all the rest. The weather was good and Madeleine spent a considerable time outside with Max. It was the most carefree time of the day. Maria, as usual, kept to herself and spoke only when necessary. Madeleine was always polite, but had given up trying to make conversation. Madeleine had seen less and less of Maria in the last few days. Maria seemed to spend more time in her kitchen

Madeleine had taken the opportunity, when she knew that Maria was outside talking with Otto, to walk through the other wing of the house. She had heard no sounds as she had listened at all the closed doors. She did not dare open any of them. After supper the room above her was silent. She was disappointed.

Van Brandenburg felt some of the weakness leaving his body as he alternately slept and ate. He had been so exhausted. Each short exercising period, which he had not tried to extend, left him grateful to be back in bed and able to sleep for several hours. He was uncertain how to address the problem of Madeleine's presence in the house. He had hoped that Maria, seeing that he was more alert, would bring up the subject. She was not going to do so. He hoped that Madeleine herself would ask to see him. It was a ridiculous situation.

Madeleine was again sitting in the library after dinner. She was waiting to hear the tap-tap-tap above her. She was not disappointed. The irregular tapping began. To and fro, it came and went over her head, stopping periodically. She envisaged him as she had last seen him and quickly pushed away that ghastly image of torn flesh. She understood the sound she now heard. He was walking with crutches. It did not last too long. He could not be very strong. She felt sure that he was forcing himself back to strength. She was eager to see him. She wondered why he had not sent some sort of message to her, even if he did not feel like seeing her. Maria would have told him of her arrival. She tried to push away the possibility that he might indeed be shell-shocked. She could not believe that this thought had never occurred to her much sooner. Perhaps that was why Maria had said nothing of his home-coming. She went to bed feeling helpless and depressed.

The next day dawned wet and dreary and did nothing to lift her mood. She took Max out for a walk, but it was not a day to linger outside and even Max, who did not mind cold weather, was eager to get indoors as soon as possible.

Maria was nowhere to be seen. Madeleine was hesitant to ask Maria about the Kapitän. If she got some sort of negative reply from her it would take the initiative away from her. It would be better to act on her own. At some point, she was going to have to get up her courage and go to his room.

Von Brandenburg awoke feeling the sharpness of the pain in his left side was not as severe. He had slept better, always waking to turn over, but less frequently. He felt encouraged, until he saw the darkness of the day. These were the days that were the hardest to bear. There was nothing to lift the spirits. If only the girl would come and see him. What was keeping her? How dare she live in his house and ignore him in this way? After all he had done for her. And after all he had suffered, he thought, as he gritted his teeth and got himself to his feet.

Maria brought him another substantial breakfast, but he treated her sullenly and she left without lingering too long to chat. He ate heartily and felt better. He must begin to find some way to entertain himself. He could not lie in bed all day long looking at the ceiling. He did not have the concentration to read. He must devise an exercise plan for himself, but he was not really strong enough yet to do much.

Lunch came and went and he slept a little. He walked up and down a few times. He now awaited his supper. It seemed as though his meals were the highlight of his day. He had to admit that he felt a little stronger, the more he ate. He must thank Maria for her efforts. Without her, where would he be?

Maria was surprised to find her charge in a good frame of mind when she brought in the dinner tray. He thanked her warmly for her culinary efforts and they chatted about this and that. He asked her if there was anything of special interest going on in the village. She had replied that a group had been formed by the principal of the school to report anti-Nazi activities in the area. She had attended the meeting, but did not feel sympathetic towards their intention of spying on each other. Surely the enemy was not fellow Germans, but the English who were bombing their cities. Von Brandenburg was taken aback by this information. He wondered what Maria's true feelings were. He would never question her loyalty to his family, but could she be trusted not to report their guest? He must take action soon in some way. Finally, Maria left him saying she was going to another meeting.

There was a knock at his door. He did not turn. Maria, no doubt, to collect his tray. He was looking out the window although it was dark and he could see nothing, except the black outline of the trees against the sky. He had the glimmer of an idea in his head, the beginning of a plan that might work, although it would require every detail to be fail-proof. It was probably madness to attempt it at all, but sometimes daring paid off. In a way, he was trapped by his own impetuosity. If he had not chosen to extend a hand in compassion to a beautiful girl about whom he knew nothing at all, he could just lie in bed and wait for his body to heal. Whereas now, he would have a lot of explaining to do if he handed her over to the authorities. He could not bring himself to do that for he could see in his mind's eye what they would do to her. So what if she were a spy, she was surely neutralized by the mere fact that she had no means by which to get in touch with any of her contacts. If he could get her out of the country, he would be doing everyone a service, he hoped. In the meantime, he had at least something to occupy and challenge his mind.

His mind clicked back to the present and he was aware that whoever had entered his room had not left. He turned then and what he saw made him catch his breath. Madeleine was standing there looking uncertain. She wore a dark brown tweed skirt and the softest light blue sweater that complemented the blue of her eyes and the pinky-white complexion of her skin.

"Forgive me for entering without an invitation," she began. She could have sworn that there had been a glimmer of a smile on his lips when he first saw her, but now he seemed furious and she took a step backwards.

"How dare you take refuge in my home and then have the effrontery to ignore me," he roared at her. "How dare you accept my hospitality and leave me to look at the ceiling while you romp around in the garden with Max. Who do you think you are to eat at my table and leave me to dine alone? You are here at my misplaced generosity and I expect you...."

She smiled. She was no longer afraid of him, and her smile transfixed him in mid- sentence...."to be very grateful, which I am," she said, finishing the sentence for him. She recognized his outburst as one of frustration and impotence, the anger of a normally healthy man trapped in a situation over which he had no control. A man who was accustomed to directing others, who was used to being in control of his destiny. A man who was possibly a little interested and intrigued by her. She hoped that he was not regretting his decision to help her.

"Forgive me for seeming to ignore you, but I had no idea that you had returned home. Maria did not choose to tell me. I think that she is perhaps very possessive of you."

He gave her a long look. He was surprised by her astuteness.

"I hope that Maria is not going to be a problem for you. She also did not tell me you were here. I will have to give that some thought. In the meantime, I would like you to entertain me. I am very bored. Tell me how you found your way here. Tell me how you have filled your time, other than make Max your friend for life?"

"Without you, I think Max was the loneliest dog in all of Germany. Does he know that you are home yet?"

"We have not been reunited yet because I do not think that my battered body could withstand the onslaught of his welcome."

She nodded. "I think it may be difficult to keep the secret much longer. I think that he has sensed that you are home. Perhaps we can protect you with a wall of cushions."

He laughed then and her heart did a somersault. It was the first time that she had seen him so carefree. As pale and gaunt as he was, he was still exceedingly attractive. "I am very grateful that you have been kind enough to exercise him. He has never liked Maria, perhaps sensing that she does not wish to share me. In any event, I think she is afraid of him. Of course, Otto and Max are often at war. I am sure Max digs in Otto's garden out of sheer boredom."

"So fill me in on the events between the present and when we last met."

She carefully retraced her footsteps. He did not remember that she had returned to him as he lay injured on the platform. He also did not know that she had been to the hospital. He thought she had been fortunate in finding her way to Riquewihr and Waldesrauschen as she had and hoped that the farmer who had driven her out of the city did not choose to make enquires about her.

"You shall have lunch and dinner with me from now on. I shall inform Maria."

"She will not be pleased. I am afraid that Maria disapproves of me, or more precisely is suspicious of me," she said.

He nodded and frowned.

"Maria's loyalty to my family is beyond question. However, the fact that she is only seeming to tolerate you makes me uneasy. She would do nothing to compromise me, but if she had any suspicion of your true identity I have to wonder whether she would not devise a scheme to betray you in some way." A shadow had crossed his face as he remembered the disturbing news Maria had mentioned of village meetings. He looked at Madeleine long and thoughtfully.

"What kind of prognosis did the doctors give you?" she asked, eager to change the subject.

"They did not choose to make any specific predictions. They said that I was young and healthy, that provided I did not abuse myself and rested until I felt fully healed, I might be lucky and regain a lot of mobility - they were rather vague. Typical. I think that I was rather lucky to survive." He looked at her quizzically.

"I think you were extraordinarily lucky. Between Schultz and Professor Schmieding..." she left the sentence unfinished. "I think that I had better go." She did not want to have Maria find her here. Better to let the Kapitän prepare the way.

"Then I shall look forward to seeing you here at lunchtime. And from now on, please call me Erich. Remember, we are distant relatives." He gave her a long look.

She turned and went out. It was ridiculous, the thrill of excitement she felt in his presence. She hardly knew him. Perhaps it was just relief that he remembered her and that she no longer felt so terribly isolated and alone. She knew it was more than that.

She had just reached the door of her room when she heard Maria come into the hall below. She was relieved the timing had worked out as it had.

The next few weeks seemed to be a time of special enchantment. They dined twice a day together. It began casually enough. But inevitably they got to know more and more about each other. They laughed often.

It was finally decided that they could no longer keep Max from his master. The wall of cushions proved to be an adequate protective barrier. Max was beside himself with joy, but seemed to sense that his master was in some way incapacitated and limited his excitement to licking Erich's hands and face with whimpers of delight, his tail wagging continuously. Max did not leave Erich after that, except for the walks he took with Madeleine which he enjoyed with the same enthusiasm as before. Erich had asked Maria why she had not informed him of Madeleine's presence. Her answer had been simple. He was not well and needed his rest. He did not choose to argue with her. He needed to have Maria as an ally and did not wish to antagonize her in any way. She was disgruntled enough at first at having to bring two meals to his room. However, in other ways it meant not having to serve two separate meals in two different places. He was relieved to see that Maria seemed resigned to the inevitable.

Erich's strength began to return. The more he exercised the more mobility he seemed to gain. Madeleine cautioned him often at not over-extending himself. For the most part he did not. One day she was surprised to find him in the dining room for lunch when she came in from the garden with Max. He was pleased with himself at surprising her. Maria was cluck-clucking like a mother hen over him and rebuking him for pushing his recovery. However, it was evident that she was relieved and happy at his progress.

Soon, he was outside taking short walks, much to Max's delight, as he bounded in graceful circles. Color came back to Erich's face which had seemed so deathly pale for too long. He discarded the crutches and used a heavy, gnarled stick.

They were sitting at dinner one night when Erich brought up the subject of how much longer it would be possible to keep Madeleine's presence a secret now that he had returned home. She suddenly felt helpless and very vulnerable. With Erich home, she had been able to push away the thoughts of having to face an uncertain future.

Only yesterday there had been a visit from one of the town's representatives enquiring after the Kapitän's health. It was known that he was home convalescing. The visitor had been admitted to the house. Madeleine had just come indoors with Max and was walking into the hall when she heard voices in the library and was about to run up the stairs, when the door opened. The visitor had his back to her, his hand on the door knob. She quickly stepped into the dining-room and stood behind the door.

"It is so good to see the Kapitän is on his feet after such a serious injury. If there is anything we can do to provide assistance, the Kapitän has only to let us know. And as I have already mentioned, when you are fully recovered we should be most honored if you would address our local unit. We need to be prepared to deal with all eventualities and even the possibility of enemy agents..."

"Admirable, admirable," Erich cut in, anxious to be rid of his visitor. "Thank you for coming. I will get in touch with you in due course."

The visitor left after several more offers of help and promises to visit again soon.

Madeleine heard Erich return to the library and shut the door. She stood listening a little longer and then ran up the staircase. How long could she avoid being seen by one of the local townsfolk? For some considerable time now, she had taken Max to the lower meadow to exercise. Now that it was known that the Kapitän was home, she would have to be much more circumspect when outdoors, even though strangers were not apt to wander around the house.

They were in the library after dinner later that day. She was sitting with her hand caressing Max's head.

"I think that I am envious of my dog. He gets so much attention," he said with great seriousness, looking at her over his glass of port.

She found herself blushing. He had not made such a personal remark before. She did not know how to respond.

"How is it that you are not married?"

She was taken aback and shook her head. "I suppose the right person has not come along. I could ask you the same question or do you have a wife?" She desperately wanted to change the subject.

His long, appraising look disconcerted her and she wished she could escape his penetrating gaze.

"It would make my mother very happy if I were to marry." he smiled reflectively and she realized that he was somewhere else.

"This is not the place where you grew up?" she asked, knowing that she now had a lead she could follow.

He shook his head. "No, my parents' home is near Passau which is some distance from here."

"They must have been very worried about you. Did you manage to speak to them often?"

He shook his head.

"Will they come and visit you here?"

"No, it is a difficult journey for them, especially in these uncertain times. Also, my father is not well. I would not encourage them to do so in any event."

Her eyes widened.

"It would complicate my life. I am very content to have Maria look after me and have you entertain me."

She was surprised. She smiled softly.

"More importantly, it is imperative that I get well as soon as possible. I must find a way to get you out of the country. It will not be easy, but it would be far safer if you could travel with me. There are so many times you could be stopped and even if I am able to provide you with authentic papers that might not always be enough. You have to leave here soon. I am very concerned that your presence will be discovered and questioned."

She knew he was right. She was flooded with gratitude that he was still willing to attempt this for her.

"I have the beginnings of a plan," he continued. "We will have to make the journey in several stages. I have various friends who own small planes, but it would be very difficult to use one without detection, but not insurmountable." He smiled at her, for her forehead was creased in worry.

"I am not without resources," he said as he took her hand and kissed it. Her heart constricted and left her breathless. "All I ask of you is to be very careful from now on when you go outside. The villagers are apt to be more attentive now that they know I am in residence and well enough to receive visitors."

Several more weeks passed and Erich's mobility was much improved. They were in the library after dinner one evening when Erich put down his coffee and said "I think that I am almost fit enough to travel. I think that I have devised a basic plan. There are many blanks but I am hopeful that they can be filled."

The implications of this sent a small shiver through her. She would have to leave behind all that had become familiar and launch herself into the unknown.

"When would we leave?"

"In another three nights. There will be no moon. Maria plans to attend a village meeting and I have received word from some friends that they would welcome my visit."

"How would we travel?"

"In my Daimler."

Her eyebrows raised in query. He responded to the silent question. "Will it start, you ask? One of Otto's responsibilities, which he takes most seriously, is to start the Daimler twice a week and let it run."

"When did anyone last drive it."

"I have no idea."

"You cannot be serious. You mean to drive it not knowing whether it can travel further than the confines of your property?"

"I have absolute confidence that it is in perfect working condition. Otto may be a very simple man, but he is a born mechanic."

"What about having enough fuel for it?"

"I have been stock-piling."

She looked at him in amazement for she could see that he was relishing the whole adventure and did not seem the least bit worried. What she did not know was that Erich had spent many hours working on the details of his plan. The telephone was unreliable and not totally a resource he trusted. But he had contacted an old childhood friend who had a large property on the edge of the Black Forest, south of Baden-Baden. He was sure they would be welcome there.

Max stirred in his sleep, legs twitching as he lay with his great head close to Erich's feet. Their gaze focused on him and it was as though their thoughts became one.

A look of consternation crossed Madeleine's face. "What will become of Max?"

"He has been the source of much concern. He would sense any change in routine. He is apt to give us away by creating a devil of an uproar. I finally decided that it was too risky to leave him behind. We will take him with us."

She was astonished.

He smiled. "He could provide us with protection from inquisitive strangers."

She sighed contentedly. She was glad. The thought of leaving Max alone after the happy weeks of togetherness was more than she could contemplate.

"Maria will probably serve dinner a little earlier the evening of her meeting. We should have everything ready, so that as soon as we have eaten we can leave. I would like us to have a long start before our departure is discovered, just in case someone should take it upon themselves to investigate. I dare not tell Maria before leaving. I will have to leave her a note."

The next three days were spent in concentrated preparation. Most of the preparations were in the form of lists since they could not do too much for fear of arousing attention. Madeleine could not pack her bag until the last minute in case Maria should notice that her things had been removed. In any event, it would not take her too long. She had the same quantity of articles to go into her suitcase as had come out of it. Her main concern was a safe place to hide her passport. She mentioned her concern to Erich. He told her that he had given it much thought already and felt confident that a satisfactory solution would be found. It was decided to take a number of thick rugs and food and water for both themselves and Max. Erich's suitcase was already packed and placed in an inconspicuous place in his bedroom. He was taking relatively little and he doubted that anything would be missed.

Erich had decided that they should leave by a rear entrance to the property to avoid being observed. However, the gates were padlocked and he was concerned that the lock might be rusted. It would mean that Madeleine would have to go in that direction on one of her walks with Max and test the padlock to see if the key would turn. The gates were huge and it was possible that they might also have rusted in place.

As soon as she was able, Madeleine and Max made the long walk down the avenue of trees through the wood that led to the north entrance to the estate. It was a beautiful walk, but Madeleine was tense and worried at what she would find once she arrived at the gates. She had a small oil can and the key. She hoped that they would not have to formulate some other plan at this late stage. The south entrance to the property was much traveled and it would be impossible to leave it unobserved, especially since the Daimler was such an impressively conspicuous machine.

As she approached the far boundary of the property and saw the twelve foot high gates in front of her, her heart sank. They looked so forbidding and immovable. But she hurried forward, brushing aside her fears. The padlock looked brown and old with age, but it did not seem to be rusty, just discolored. She put the key in the lock and tried to turn it. Nothing happened. She got out the oil can and squeezed a little oil into the opening and rotated the padlock so that the oil would penetrate the different surfaces inside the lock. She tried the key again, gently, for Erich was fearful that the key might break in the lock. Again, she had no success. She tried a third time, a little more forcefully and it clicked easily and the padlock sprang open. They had decided that should this happen she should leave it open. As a precaution, she was not to try and swing open the gates, just in case she might be observed. Her relief was total and the walk back up the avenue of horse chestnut trees was as carefree as most of her daily walks with Max had been during these many weeks.

— 7 —

The day of departure dawned misty and grey. The morning passed uneventfully. But after lunch a visitor was announced. A representative from the village council come to pay his respects and invite Erich to supper in two week's time on the occasion of the Council's annual meeting. It was an irritating interruption, but one that Erich dealt with as patiently and calmly as he could. The visitor was not to be hurried. He had a sense of his own importance and wanted to make the most of his visit. Eventually, sensing that he was about to overstay his welcome, the visitor expressed profuse thanks and sincere wishes for a speedy recovery. With a sigh of relief, Erich ushered him out of the library and Maria closed the front door behind him.

Madeleine insisted that Erich spend much of the afternoon resting. It was going to be a long night. He told her that it was out of the question that she drive because if they were stopped she had no papers. The best that they could hope for was that she hide under one of the rugs and hope that no one look too closely. With Max on the seat beside her there was a good chance that they would not.

While Maria was working on the preparations for dinner, Madeleine packed her suitcase and took her passport from its hiding place. She could not risk forgetting it.

As expected, Maria served dinner early and they sat eating it in silence, both wrapped in their own thoughts. Finally, Maria departed. Madeleine verified this by watching from an upstairs window. They were alone.

It was not yet dark, and they did not wish to leave the house carrying suitcases until it was. In the meantime, Madeleine took Max outside with her and deposited some smaller items in the barn. She walked Max and then returned to the house to pick up one of the rugs and a small package of food. This time when she got to the barn, she loaded everything into the car, the rugs on the back seat, the food on the floor.

At last it was dark and they were ready to leave the house with their suitcases. They left appropriate lights on. Erich had written Maria a note and left it on his bed where he hoped she would find it the next morning when she came with his breakfast. Madeleine carried both suitcases and they walked slowly to the barns, careful of their footing to accommodate Erich's limping gait. They stopped occasionally to listen, but could hear nothing other than the sighing of the trees and the call of a night bird. The lights from Otto's cottage showed dimly through the trees.

Once in the barn, they groped their way to the car and opened one door whereupon the light sprang on. Max needed no persuasion to get into the back seat where he sat in eager anticipation. It was a long time since he had ridden anywhere. In earlier times, he had spent many happy hours being driven by his beloved master. Erich's suitcase was placed in the trunk; Madeleine's in a compartment behind the back seat. Her passport Erich placed in a slide-out drawer in the arm of the backseat. It was not a place that would be secure if the car were thoroughly searched, but it was a place that would not be noticeable to the casual observer.

Erich got in and started the engine. In that enclosed space the noise seemed deafening, but once the engine idled it did so almost silently. Madeleine opened the barn doors, having first looked in all directions and discovered nothing unusual. The car moved out of the barn and she closed the doors behind it. She slipped into the front seat and Erich drove the Daimler in low gear along the track to the woods. Once they reached the woods the track sloped gently downhill and Erich put the car into neutral and they coasted down towards the gate in silence, except for the odd crunch of the tires on pebbles.

A hundred feet from the gates, Erich braked the car and got out. Together they approached the gates. The padlock was as she had left it and it took only a moment to slip the chain off. They moved to the right-hand gate and together attempted to pull it open. It resisted their attempts, so Madeleine took the oilcan she had brought with her and applied some oil to the lowest hinge. It was perhaps a wasted gesture considering the size of the gates and the other hinges high above their heads which they could not reach. They tried again. It would not move. She had told Erich that the hinges on the gate had not looked rusted, but she was judging them from their outward appearance. They stood in silent frustration.

Suddenly, Erich grunted and bent down painfully and groped in the dark around the base of the gate. A murmur of satisfaction, a quick jerk, and he stood upright. He had forgotten the pin that held the gates locked in place. With it raised, the right-hand gate swung open easily, albeit with a certain groaning resistance. They only needed to open the one gate, so Erich walked back to the car, got in and eased it quietly down the slope and through the opening. Madeleine swung the gate back, placed the chain around both gates and snapped the padlock shut. Once in the car, they moved quietly forward and out to the road. It was very dark by now and with only the small parking lights to drive by it was going to be a very tedious journey. There was nothing coming in either direction and Erich swung the Daimler out onto the road and accelerated swiftly away. They had accomplished their departure without seeing another person. It was a minor achievement, but a satisfying one.

They drove for about two hours without encountering any traffic or roadblocks. Due to the lateness of the hour and the limited supplies of gasoline, the lack of traffic was not unexpected. Perhaps the number of roadblocks had been exaggerated. In any event, it was a relief not to have come across any as yet.

Erich sat erect, but relaxed behind the wheel, his cap on the seat beside him. He had looked even more handsome in his uniform than she had first remembered him. Perhaps he looked more rested now, despite his injury, or perhaps the uniform was fresh and uncreased, she did not know. They talked infrequently, both absorbed by their own thoughts.

Madeleine felt more vulnerable than she had in weeks. Now that she had left the sanctuary of Erich's home, she knew that her safety and her survival were in his hands and that they could hang by a thread if things got difficult.

Erich for his part was enjoying himself. He felt liberated. His convalescence had weighed heavily on him and although he knew that the longer he rested the stronger he would become, it had irked him terribly to be so idle and helpless. He really had welcomed the challenge that this beautiful girl presented. He was fairly confident that he could circumvent any roadblocks in one fashion or another, except for some unpredictable incident. Getting her out of Germany would be difficult, but not impossible. If they could avoid the big cities, it would be much easier.

For the first hour, Max had relished his new surroundings and sat erect and alert, but finally sleep overcame him and he lay down with his head on Madeleine's lap.

It was now close to midnight and Erich knew that soon they should be turning off the main road. Without lights, it was very difficult to make out familiar landmarks, to recognize some of the smaller towns they went through or to read any signs that still remained. He had brought a torch for this purpose. So far he had not had to use it. His night vision had improved as time passed, but there were moments when it was very dark indeed.

At a certain moment, he became aware of something different in the road ahead. He was glad that he was still alert for it was the first barrier of a road block and if he had been traveling faster he would not have seen it in time to allow him to slow down.

"Max, Max, up you get!" he commanded. And Max was sitting up in a flash, awake and tense as though he had never been asleep.

It was the signal for Madeleine to dive under the rug and curl up as best she could.

Erich slowed the Daimler still further and finally reached a barrier that completely closed the road in both directions.

A dark figure materialized, a torch in hand, which was flashed in Erich's face.

"Your papers, please."

Erich handed them to him and there was a long silence while they were being read.

Madeleine felt her heart beating painfully in her chest, her breath seemingly in gasps. Max had shifted slightly and had one leg positioned behind her knees. She reflected that this was probably to her advantage because in this fashion he must look as though he was taking up the whole seat.

"Where are you going, Herr Kapitän?"

"My destination is ultimately Bremerhaven, but I plan to stop somewhere for the night soon. Are there any decent hotels up ahead?"

"I have never had the good fortune to stay in any of the hotels in Stuttgart, but I am told that the Drei Koenig is the best by far. Do you always travel with your dog? He looks pretty fierce."

"He is a good companion, but he is not comfortable with strangers."

"I can see that," responded the soldier taking a step backwards as he handed Erich his papers, for a deep throated growl was beginning to come from Max.

"Alles in ordinung, Herr Kapitän."

"Can I expect many more roadblocks between here and Stuttgart, where I have an appointment?"

"I could not tell you for certain, Herr Kapitän, but I do know that some cars are being searched on the outskirts of the city. It has taken a lot of time and people have been complaining about the delays. I would not think anyone would want to search your car, they might loose a chunk of flesh," and he roared with laughter and waved Erich on.

"Many thanks and good night" and with that the car moved forward as the barrier was lifted.

"Good dog, good Max." said Erich with warmth as the car surged forward.

They had been moving now for ten minutes and Erich said at last, "I think that you can come out now. Good old Max , I think he is going to be very useful. We were not in too much jeopardy this time, but it was a good test."

Madeleine sat up and took some deep breaths and stroked Max. They were silent for a time and then Erich said, "I think that we should be able to leave the main road in a moment." He had no sooner said this than he turned off onto a smaller side road.

"We have about another hour before we reach our destination. It is a fairly direct road. Would you like to drive from now on? I am devilishly tired and my leg is throbbing?"

Her only surprise at this announcement was that he had not complained sooner, although she knew that he could not risk having her at the wheel when they came to a roadblock. He eased the Daimler to a stop, opened the door and slowly and painfully got out. Max leapt out eagerly, Madeleine more slowly. They walked up and down to loosen their stiff muscles while they waited for Max who was chasing a scent a short distance away.

Madeleine climbed behind the wheel and waited until Max and his master were comfortably settled. Erich had two of the rugs from the back seat wrapped around him, both to cushion and to warm him. She knew that this journey was a great drain on his stamina, that in truth it was far too soon for him to be doing something so energetic, but she was grateful that he had her safety in mind and recognized that he also was enjoying the excitement and challenge that it was presenting.

The road climbed slowly through a forest of pine trees, their fragrance enveloping them. It was intensely dark amongst them and she dared not drive too fast for fear of hitting some errant deer. Later the road began to twist and turn and she had to concentrate hard to see the way ahead. Eventually they broke out of the trees and there seemed to be a greater luminosity. It was very peaceful and she felt safe and secure in the darkness that surrounded them. Erich had told her that she should just follow the road for about an hour, at which point she should awaken him. They would come upon a small, white church. With that he seemed to go instantly to sleep, his head tilted away from her.

As she became accustomed to the Daimler, she was able to relax and enjoy the power of this beautifully engineered machine. It seemed to purr along effortlessly, regardless of the incline or the angle of the bend. She was amazed that it could perform so smoothly after such a long retirement. She wished that this were some special vacation they were taking instead of a reckless bid for freedom.

The clock on the dashboard told her that an hour had passed, but she was sure that her speed was much slower than in normal circumstances. She had seen no sign of a church and was not worried. She would not awaken Erich yet. She opened her window wider to let in the sweet, night air. They were on a steep incline swinging out and away to their right, when she thought she heard the roar of an engine above them to the left. It did not seem possible that someone should be out at this hour, the more especially when they had encountered so little traffic for the entire journey. But she was sure that she had not imagined the sound and it made her anxious. This was a narrow road and the visibility very limited in the dark. Two cars could meet with only seconds to avoid one another. She had to get off the road quickly. If her hearing was playing tricks no harm would be done, but if it was not, such an action could be life-saving. She searched desperately for a suitable place to pull over, but in the darkness it was difficult to see anything. She dared not risk the safety of the car by driving it into a deep ditch and breaking the axle. Then suddenly she picked out a shape, a lightness in the surrounding blackness. She slowed down and recognized a wayside travelers' shrine. There was a scooped out area, which she judged would be just large enough to park the Daimler. She braked and backed into the space, hugging the hillside so the car did not protrude into the road. She turned off the small parking lights, but left the engine running. She wound down the window. The Daimler engine hummed very quietly. She listened, but could hear nothing but the wind in the trees. Perhaps she had been mistaken and if so she was glad. She put her head back against the headrest and drank in deep breaths of the fresh, sweet-scented air. Erich slept,

The Kandahar Talisman

but Max had lifted his head in inquiry. She closed her eyes and stretched and tried not to think of what lay ahead. In some ways it all seemed so unreal. It was hard to believe that the two countries were at war and yet beside her was the proof that they were. She felt so relaxed and comfortable she thought it would be easy to drop off to sleep, but that could be dangerous and she must not let it happen

She had hardly opened her eyes, when there was a rush of sound, a deep roar and a squeal of wheels and a dark object rushed by and was gone. Its suddenness was shocking and left her shaken. She could hardly bear to think of the consequences had she not chanced to hear that far-off engine. Erich had moved his head, but did not wake. She sat paralyzed, so shocked was she by the unexpectedness of what had happened. Her confidence was gone and she felt vulnerable and undecided on what to do next. If the driver of that car was in such a hurry as to hurtle at breakneck speed down the mountain, was it possible that he was doing so to avoid another car which was in pursuit? She sat and listened, but could hear nothing unusual. She decided to get out of the car and cross the road. She would be away from the muffling shelter of the hillside. She stood and looked back and across to the Daimler. She could see its outline, but it was more like a black luminosity than a defined shape. She felt suddenly fearful and began searching hurriedly for some dead tree branches. She found only one, so she hurriedly picked fern that grew in abundance and ran across the road and carefully placed it on the shiny, polished hood of the Daimler. She went back across the road to view her handiwork. It had broken up the even contours of the Daimler and made it less conspicuous. She decided to pick some more, when she heard the even hum of a car engine. It was traveling fast, but in much more control. Her heart thumped as she lay down in the fern and peered towards the bend in the road. She was afraid to be separated from Erich and the Daimler. She prayed that Max would not be leaning out the open car window looking for her, perhaps choosing this moment to bark deeply and loudly. Or worse still, that Erich should awaken and get out of the car and start to call her or cross the road. But all other thoughts were swept away as the car came into view around the bend, traveling fast, but quietly, infinitely sinister. It was gone as soon as it had appeared. It left her feeling sick. She hoped that it had not noticed the Daimler. She was comforted by the fact that it was angled away from the Daimler as it turned the bend, and moved into the straight of the road. She was on her knees and getting to her feet, when another car came speeding around the bend, close on the heels of the one in front of it. She fell flat on her face and lay there. Now she knew that something was very wrong. Whoever was fleeing the two cars she had just seen, was fleeing for his life. They had been waiting for him. It was not a coincidence. This was not a group of friends leaving a late night party. Was her presence here putting her at great risk because of what had to be enemy-agent activity in the area? What of Erich? Could he be held accountable for having her with him?

She lay with her face in the damp earth, the smell of crushed fern pungent in her nostrils and waited for her heart to stop beating so painfully. Finally she got to her feet and stood and listened. She walked to the edge of the road and ran across it, a shiver running down her spine. She reached the car door and was back in her seat in a matter of seconds. Max was sitting up and leaned forward and put a cold nose on her cheek. Erich turned and opened his eyes and asked her why they had stopped. She told him what had happened. He was silent for a long time, digesting this information. Finally, he said, "I think that it is safe to drive on." She was relieved at this, eager to be moving, to get away from this place. She eased the Daimler back onto the road and accelerated up the steeply curving incline.

They came finally upon the little white church, nestled back from the road at the edge of the woods. It would have been easy to miss if one had not been looking for it. They drove on, this time more slowly. They were looking for a small track into the woods on their left. After half-an-hour, Erich told her to turn around. He felt sure that they had missed it. They drove slower still, Erich with his window open scanning the roadside. Finally, he told her to stop and he got out and walked back. She backed the car up and got out herself, much to Max's distress who started to whimper so that she had to tell him to be quiet. Erich had walked quite a distance and was walking back towards her when he stopped suddenly and bent over. He had found the track, which was almost entirely obscured by overhanging bushes. The ruts in the ground were still evident, but it would have been impossible to see them from the road unless one were crawling along. They got back into the car, backed up still further and carefully drove off the road onto the track. The forest swallowed them up instantly. Madeleine was concentrating so hard on the path ahead that she was unaware that a dark, silent car traveling in the same direction as they had been, passed the opening to the woodland track within seconds of their entering it. But Erich with his window still down, heard the car rather than saw it and wondered at their narrow escape. So much traffic on a country road at this time of night made him uneasy. He hoped it was not going to present difficulties for them whatever the reasons for such seemingly clandestine activities.

It was so dark within the forest that it was impossible to see anything but the outline of the nearest tree trunks. Madeleine had to drive by feeling her way along the ruts on the path beneath them. She tried to keep the wheels of the Daimler in the ruts, working her way back into them whenever she left them. It was very tedious, the ground uneven so that they were jostled hither and thither causing Erich to gasp in pain from time to time. On several occasions they came upon large tree limbs that blocked their way and they had to get out and move them aside. Fortunately there was nothing so huge that they could not tackle it. Surely this was not the normal entrance to his friends' estate, she had asked Erich, to which he replied that it was not, but that he thought it wiser to make an inconspicuous arrival. They gave up conversation and finally after a good hour had passed they came out into the open.

Now they could see the track clearly and were able to pick up speed. After a time, they turned off this track and began making their way towards an opening in the woods ahead of them. As they approached this, Madeleine could see in the distance the outlines of a big house. They had arrived at last at Lichtenfels.

— 8 —

Erich grunted in relief; he was not sure that his battered body could stand much more of the car's vibration and he felt sick with the strain of trying to brace himself against the jolts. He told her that they should make their way to a side entrance as they would probably stay in the west wing of the house so as to attract the attention of as few people as possible, including the servants.

They were much closer to the house now and the road divided, one branch led in a long curving sweep to the house, the other swung to the left through some trees. Erich suggested that they stop here briefly to let Max out. He was so happy to gain his freedom that he bounded hither and thither in great delight. In due course, Max came back to the car and leapt in, sitting erect and expectant. They then took the left hand road, which led them to a large arched entrance guarded by two huge, oak doors.

"There is a bell to the left of the door; we are to ring it four times," Erich told her. "Perhaps you would get out and do it, I do not think I can."

She got out and did as she was told, pressing the bell quickly and briefly between each ring. She could hear no responding sound beyond the walls of the house. It was about three-thirty in the morning.

After what seemed an eternity, one of the great oak doors swung inwards silently and the large silhouette of a powerful man stood observing them. When Erich saw him he said very quietly, "Is that you Reinhardt?"

"Mein Gott!" was the response, "I cannot believe that you are really here. Park in the old stable to your left. I will open the other door and you can drive through. I have left one door open."

"Madeleine, this is my very good friend, Reinhardt von Eschenbach. Reinhardt, this is Madeleine. She has been my guardian angel."

"I look forward to hearing more," responded Reinhardt, as he turned to open the enormous oak door.

Madeleine drove through the entrance and swung the Daimler to her left. She had a brief impression of an immense courtyard and then she saw the open stable door and drove through it. She braked the car and turned off the engine and sighed in relief. She felt exhausted.

"Congratulations, you did very well," Erich told her. "Now you will have to help me out, I am so stiff and sore that I can hardly move."

Reinhardt had closed the stable door and was walking towards them by the time Madeleine had reached Erich's side of the car and opened his door.

"My friend, how very good it is to see you." Reinhardt said as he grasped Erich's hand. "How are you?" he began, but then said, "you are not well, what is wrong?" as he saw Erich flinch with pain.

"I am not sure that I can get out of the car without some help. I seem to have developed a muscle spasm in my back and I can hardly feel one leg."

They looked at him in consternation for he looked terribly pale, dark circles under his eyes, his mouth contorted in a painful grimace.

"I do not think that we should move him. Why don't we let the back of the seat down. Perhaps in a different position the spasm will be released and he can rest there. If we do it slowly, in stages, perhaps it will not hurt. I know how painful such things can be. Can you go around to the other side?"

Madeleine did as she was told and between them they slowly lowered the car seat with Erich on it to an horizontal position. He groaned a few times, but they accomplished the task without compounding his discomfort. Madeleine took another rug from the back seat and covered him. She gently pulled out one of the rugs laying underneath him and put that on top too. But his legs needed to be raised to take the strain off his back.

"I will find something for his feet and perhaps a shot of whiskey might help too." With that Reinhardt was gone and they were left alone.

"Is it just the one leg you cannot feel?" she asked and Erich nodded, his eyes closed. "Yes, the bad one."

She hoped very much that this journey had not seriously jeopardized his recovery. She would never forgive herself for being the cause of such a mishap. The health of his leg was still very uncertain and its future mobility depended on a chance to heal well.

Reinhardt came back in due course with a small footstool and they eased Erich's legs onto it. Madeleine started to massage the good leg, but was fearful to touch the other at all. She massaged his arms and he said that he felt a little better. Reinhardt returned once more, this time with some hot lentil soup and a glass of whiskey. By the time Erich had consumed both of these, color had come back into his face and he claimed that the spasm was much less painful.

It was decided to take Max to Erich's room. Then they would decide whether they could get his master up there too or would have to let him remain in the car for the rest of the night, something that Erich did not relish. By the time this had been accomplished, Erich said he was prepared to get on his feet, so they raised the back of the car seat without provoking any grunts of pain. They swung his legs gently out of the car and after he had taken a few deep breaths they pulled him to his feet. He said that it felt much better to be on his feet. They walked him to a wide staircase inside the house. They waited at the bottom before making the slow and painful ascent, but up it they went, with Erich in the middle, his arms across their shoulders. They got him onto the bed and swung his legs onto it. Madeleine arranged the pillows behind him, removed his boots with some effort and covered him up. Another glass of whiskey was left beside him as well as a decanter of water. Madeleine was going to be two rooms away from him, so she left the door ajar and told Erich to call her if he needed help. He promised he would and with that closed his eyes. They left him then.

Madeleine hardly bothered to undress, she was so tired. She lay down and put her head on the pillow and fell into an exhausted sleep. She awoke as though surfacing from a deep dive from the bottom of the ocean. She had no idea where she was or what day it was. She opened her eyes to unfamiliar surroundings, a high beamed ceiling with beautiful moldings and leaded pane windows showing from behind deep turquoise velvet drapes. Her bed was draped in the same fabric. She closed her eyes and stretched. She felt stiff. She wondered what time it was. Then she remembered Erich, but even before she could open her eyes again, a cold, wet nose touched her cheek. So that was what had awakened her. She turned her head and saw Max standing there patiently expectant.

"Max, what a good boy. I am getting up right now."

She found that there was an adjoining bathroom and she quickly splashed water on her face, did her hair and tried to straighten her rumpled clothes.

She walked through the sitting room that separated their two rooms and peeked through the door to the adjoining room and saw that Erich had his eyes closed. She walked quietly up to his bed and bent over him. His color was much better. He looked more rested, although the shadows under his eyes were not entirely gone. She was about to move away, when his eyes opened and he smiled at her.

"Did Max awaken you? I sent him to fetch you."

"He did as you commanded," she responded with a smile. "How did you sleep?"

"Much better than I dared hope. I only awoke two or three times. I feel much better and my poor leg seems almost normal. It hurt like the devil." He grinned.

"You are disgustingly healthy. But I am relieved. I hope you will have the good sense to rest until it is better."

He grimaced and she wagged a threatening finger at him.

"I am going to take Max outside and feed him. He must be starving. It is way past his mealtime, I am sure. Do you know where I can find Reinhardt?"

"He said that he would leave you a message, He did not want you wandering about. By the way, I am starving."

"So who do I attend to first, you or your beloved, uncomplaining dog?"

"I think that I can sleep a little more, so please take care of Max." and with that he closed his eyes.

Outside in the long hallway, on a big oak table, she found a message from Reinhardt asking her to help herself to whatever she needed in the kitchen. He asked her to take Max for a walk in the woods and fields outside the kitchen door and to avoid the main courtyard of the house. He would see them at lunchtime. She stood still, looking about her. This was the wing of the house that was built near the stables and was probably reserved for visiting guests. The rooms were sumptuously decorated if one was to judge from the suite that she and Erich shared. Erich's room was twice the size of hers, his bed the largest four-poster she had ever seen, with the most marvelously woven tapestry draperies adorning both the bed and the long bay windows with their soft jewel colors.

She stood still trying to decide at which end of the long corridor were the stairs they had used on their arrival. As she walked down the long hallway, she looked out the window onto the courtyard of this immense house. It was a stone building of enormous proportions, with gabled roofs and ornate chimneys. Beyond in the distance she could see tree-covered mountains. There was no one in the courtyard although a horse stood tethered to a post, but as she watched, a groom came out with another horse, which he walked through an archway and out of sight.

She moved on and down the staircase, Max at her heels.

She found the kitchen without much difficulty. There was milk and butter, fresh bread and rolls, ham and cheese, preserves, tea and coffee. She put on a pot to make some coffee. Her next move was to find Max's food. She presumed that it had been left in the Daimler, which meant finding her way to the stables. She wondered about the source of so much food in these times of shortages, but concluded correctly, that a place of this size would have stored large quantities of food, long before the talk of war came about.

There was a lower, narrow corridor on this level and she followed it until she came to another door. She listened with her ear to the door and then turned the handle. She was in a stable but it was not the right one. She saw that a door was set in the far wall. It led to the next stable and so on down the line. She finally came to the one where the Daimler was parked, towards the farther and lesser-used end of the stable wing. It had been moved since their arrival. She assumed that the horses were housed in other stables, for these stables seemed to be used for general storage of different kinds.

She found Max's food and returned to the kitchen. By this time, Max was dancing in excitement and he almost knocked her over as she put his bowl down on the floor. He began gobbling up his food, but between mouthfuls took a moment to look at her and wag his tail as if to express his thanks. She had found the door which led out into the lane and as soon as Max's bowl was licked clean she led him out and he bounded off at full speed. They walked for about half an hour and saw no one. The air was fresh and sweet smelling, the hedgerows filled with wild flowers. The birds sang and rabbits scurried away at their approach. Max tore after them but they were too agile, despite his speed.

Back in the kitchen, Madeleine put together a breakfast tray and made the long trek back up to their suite. She set the tray down on a table in the window of Erich's room. His eyes opened as she came in. She had obviously awakened him. Max trotted up to the bed and Erich reached out and stroked his head.

"I have no idea what time it is. I think that it must be lunchtime."

"It is almost noon. You slept again. Do you want to get up to eat or shall I serve you in bed?"

"I think that I would like to stay where I am. Would that be asking too much?"

"I think that it is a excellent idea."

She had also found some eggs while making the breakfast and so she served him ham and eggs, with bread and preserves, and strong, delicious coffee. She had eaten her breakfast in the kitchen, but had brought an extra cup of coffee for herself.

"I do not think that breakfast has ever tasted so good," he said with a satisfied smile. "Thank you. I gather you have already eaten."

She nodded. "I could not carry it all on one tray. Will you have some more coffee?"

He nodded. She fetched his cup, poured some more and walked back to his bed. As she handed it to him, she said, "This is the largest bed I have ever seen."

"Yes, it is rather magnificent. But then it is a special kind of bed."

"What is special about it, other than its size and opulence?" she asked, falling into the trap.

"It is a matrimonial bed. It really is a waste to have only one person sleeping in it," he said with a provocative gleam in his eye.

She blushed and was angry with herself. "I am glad that you are feeling so much better. I see that you have eaten everything. Can I serve you some more?"

But she was not going to deflect him so easily.

"I think that my appetite is satisfied for the time being, but I think that I shall be hungry for much more very soon." He gave her a long look and she fumbled the cup and saucer he was handing her.

"It is easy to lie in bed and think you feel strong. It takes time to recover one's stamina. I hope you will do all things in moderation until your leg is truly healed," she said sternly and picked up the tray and left the room.

She was furious with him for taunting her and she was furious with herself for allowing him to see that he could affect her. Tears pricked her eyes. Damn him she thought to herself. There was an immensely virile quality to him, despite his gaunt features and fragile body. His eyes could be both gentle and penetrating. She felt he was not a man to be anything but straightforward and was not apt to lie or deceive without very good reason. She admitted to herself that she was attracted to him, but the circumstances were against any type of friendship. She felt guilt-ridden to be fraternizing with what any of her friends or colleagues would consider the enemy.

However, he was her only hope if he truly meant to help her escape back to England. She had to trust that this is what he intended. Did he expect her to repay him? She knew him to be a gentleman; but her heart told her that he was first of all a man. Tears rolled down her cheeks.

She was back in the kitchen putting away the last of the breakfast things, when Reinhardt came into the room. She had fortunately regained her composure.

"Good morning," he said. "I hope you slept well. And how is my friend? Did he manage to sleep last night?"

"He told me that he slept very well, although his leg was paining him. He looked much better and he ate a very good breakfast."

"That is good news. We have not had a chance to talk, he and I. What happened to his leg?"

"He was injured in an immense explosion in the station in Stuttgart. Workmen ignited gas or electrical wires which in turn set off ammunition which was in the area. It is a miracle that he survived. It was a terrible injury." She shut her eyes against the memory of it and shuddered.

"You were there when it happened?" he asked her in astonishment.

She nodded. "He owes his life to one of his men who acted so promptly and got him an ambulance and to Professor Schmieding who was fortunately at the hospital that day."

"You mean the renowned Professor Schmieding?" He did not try to hide his amazement. This beautiful girl was obviously no casual relative or acquaintance as he had first suspected.

"He really is not well enough to be bouncing around the countryside in such a fashion. He should rest until his leg is fully healed, otherwise he could jeopardize the amazing recovery that he has made. I cannot believe that his leg could be saved. I was afraid that he would bleed to death."

"Perhaps I can persuade him to stay here until he is fitter."

She shrugged her shoulders. "When he makes up his mind, he can be very determined, but I hope you are successful."

"Yes, my friend can be very obstinate when he wants to be. I shall try."

Erich slept most of the afternoon. Madeleine and Max went for another long walk. They both returned tired and happy.

"This fresh mountain air has given you a marvelous color," he told her in greeting. "You must be hungry."

"Yes, I am, the more especially since I missed lunch today because I slept so late.

Reinhardt tells me that we can have supper early. He apologizes for not being able to serve us in better style, but we need to keep a low profile. He told me to tell you that there is a dumb-waiter in the kitchen that services this wing. It would save you a long walk. I hope you don't mind looking after us in this way?"

She shook her head. "I will go down to the kitchen now."

A small stuffed chicken had been left in the oven with a selection of vegetables, a salad and an apple tart sat on the kitchen table. She set about making some fresh coffee and then loaded the dinner into the dumb-waiter.

Upstairs, she unloaded everything and carried it to the suite.

They were sitting at the table in the bay window. Erich said he could not stay in bed all day and that it would be good for him to get up. He limp was much less pronounced as he walked to the table. He always would have a slight limp. They had eaten well. It had been a splendid and satisfying meal in every way. He told her that he and Reinhardt had chatted for about an hour together. It had been many years since he had seen his old friend. He did not tell her that he wanted to be sure of his friend's political allegiances and was not disappointed. That he had asked him if he could provide Madeleine with documents since she was without any. She had lost hers in the explosion in Stuttgart. He had not elaborated on this with Reinhardt who had promised to see what he could do. Photos would have to be taken and reproduced.

They were sipping their coffee and looking out at the gentle contours of the distant tree-covered hills and the soft moving fields of grass undulating in the wind. It was such a peaceful scene, their surroundings so opulent and seemingly invulnerable, that Madeleine felt momentarily light-hearted and carefree.

"I cannot believe that I could have such an appetite, just lying in bed sleeping. That was a most delicious meal."

She smiled. "I think it is a very good sign. It tells me that you are mending."

"Reinhardt says that I should remain in bed for a week. I understand that there has been some collaboration on this matter between the two of you."

She smiled and nodded. "We were hoping to persuade you to let your body really heal. You had been doing so very well before we left Riquewihr. I fear that the journey was too much too soon."

He looked at her reflectively and nodded. "I did come out of it a bit battered and bruised. But I feel much better today and am confident that I will feel even better tomorrow. However, I am prepared to remain in bed for a week if that pleases you."

She looked at him in astonishment. "That would be wonderful."

"On one condition."

"What is that?"

"That you spend the week by my side."

She was taken by surprise. It took her breath away. She desperately tried to appear untouched by such a suggestion, but it was hard to quell her pounding heart. Although pale after such a long convalescence, there was still a sensuality about him that she had been aware of from the moment they first met. Of course, he was playing games with her. She would just have to play the game too and let him know that he could not win. She had nothing to worry about.

"So who will take Max for his walks? Who will bring you your meals? Your suggestion is not compatible with what we are trying to accomplish for you. We want you to rest, sleep and get well."

"You sound like my old Nanny, when I was ill in bed with a cold. How can you possibly know how I feel?"

"I know how you looked and felt yesterday."

"That was yesterday."

"I promise not to leave you alone and let you get bored, but I have too much to do to stay with you throughout each day.

What you suggest is out of the question." With that she got up and started to collect the dishes on the table. As she moved to pick up the plate in front of him, he grabbed her wrist and said, "I do not think it is out of the question at all, in fact it is a very desirable solution to what would otherwise be a very boring week."

She blushed deeply. "Stop playing games and be sensible. You must not overestimate your recovery. Tomorrow you could feel quite differently. It would be normal to feel energetic one day and tired and lethargic on another. Your body must be allowed to heal and overcome the terrible trauma it has been through. Anyway, I am afraid that you would soon get tired of my company."

"That is where you underestimate yourself."

Now she was furious with him and tried to wrench herself away, but he held on to her firmly.

"I think that I can help you change your mind."

"And what if I do not?"

"Then I will be forced to persuade you in a way that is quite irresistible."

"I am not that kind of a woman."

"You are a very desirable, attractive woman."

"You are taking unfair advantage of me. I had better pack my bag and leave." she said defiantly.

"And go where? You are lost without me," he said very gently and with much compassion.

He let go of her arm and she stepped back. She felt the tears well up in her eyes as she bent to pick up the tray of dinner things. She turned and hurried out of the room.

She had taken a long time to clear up the supper things. She needed to regain her composure. Eventually, she could delay no longer. She had to take Max for a walk.

When she walked back in the room, Erich was still sitting in the bay window. He was reading. Max sat at his feet.

"I think that I had better take Max for a walk."

Erich looked at her, noticed her puffy eyes, and nodded. He said nothing.

Max got to his feet and trotted to her and they walked out of the room together.

Max was overjoyed at being outdoors once more and they roamed even further afield than on the previous outings. Madeleine was reluctant to return to the house. She was confused and fearful. Erich was the most attractive man she had known in a long time. She felt that she knew him well in many ways, but a relationship, however casual, was impossible in the circumstances she found herself. If all went well and she got out of Germany, she was likely never to see him again. He must surely appreciate that. She was terribly indebted to him, and she could never repay him, but surely he did not expect repayment in the style that he was suggesting. It was far too calculating and she felt he was a man of substance, not one given to momentary flings. On the other hand, her mother had always warned her that women always looked for romance and men looked for gratification. She was disturbed by this remembered advice.

Back indoors, she found Erich with his light out, asleep. She was surprised, but relieved. She went to her room and sat reading, but with all the fresh air and exercise soon felt sleepy and went to bed. She eventually fell asleep.

The next day dawned wet and Max's morning walk was short. They came indoors and she rubbed Max down with an old towel. He nuzzled her appreciatively.

She set about preparing the breakfast.

Back in Erich's room, she carried the breakfast tray to the table in the bay window. Erich was up and reading, looking sophisticated and handsome in his navy blue, silk robe. He was enjoying being up for his meals again, and exercising, as he had done before leaving Waldesrauschen. He was determined to use his leg a little more each day. He greeted her, but went back to his book while she laid the table and poured the coffee. It disconcerted her to have him so distant. It was as though he were trying to make her feel like some disobedient child. It was an exceptionally dark and dreary day. It seemed like an omen and she was depressed by it. They spoke little.

She got up to clear away the breakfast things and had finished loading the tray, when he came up behind her and gently turned her towards him.

"I don't like this distance between us. You have been a great comfort to me throughout my convalescence and I think you are an extraordinary woman. I do not know what the future holds for either of us. These are very uncertain and perilous times. I want you to know that I do not wish to harm you, but find you immensely attractive. This might be the only chance for happiness either of us will ever have and I think it would be very sad if you denied us this moment," whereupon he drew her gently to him and caressed her hair.

She started to weep quietly and he continued to hold her and gently stroke her and then he lifted her face and traced her eyebrows, nose and finally her mouth with his long , slender fingers. He kissed her wet cheeks and her eyes. He gave her a handkerchief and she blew her nose and he continued to hold her and when she stopped crying he kissed her with infinite tenderness and she put her arms around his neck.

"I don't want to lose my heart to someone I will never see again."

"I understand, neither do I,"

This time he kissed her with a great yearning and she responded and knew that she was lost and that she did not care. She had not much hope for her chances of escaping from Germany, however optimistic Erich seemed about achieving such a goal.

He had told her that they could not move on until she had papers and that it could take some time to obtain them. He acknowledged that he needed to get stronger and promised to rest adding, with a wicked grin, that he had probably made a terrible mistake and that she was a very bad influence and that he would most likely have to stay two weeks in bed in order to recuperate. She aimed a light blow at him but he parried it and kissed her instead telling her that she was a most beautiful woman and that she had cast a spell over him.

Supper that night was a joyful celebration. They were in tune with one another, carefree and self-absorbed. He was careful to court her with words. He did not wish to rush their relationship and spoil the magic that somehow had been created.

The week passed uneventfully and their courtship was honed and enhanced like a beautiful jewel. Little by little, he grew stronger and with it, he encouraged her not to be fearful of him or his injury. Finally, the day came when they passed from courtship to lovers. And so the days passed in gentle and passionate love-making and he was surprised and overwhelmed by her seductiveness.

Reinhardt appeared infrequently, bringing news of one kind or another, as well as reports on the progress of the war. He sensed a change in their relationship and did not want to intrude. There was no news about her papers, but the photos which were necessary and had been sent might have delayed the process. It was a delicate and dangerous negotiation and could not be hurried. They were content for it to take time.

Erich's wound was beginning to heal. She was always fearful to touch his left leg and thigh. The once-flaming red scar that had encompassed his thigh and half his leg was beginning to fade but it was indication enough of a vulnerability that would threaten him for the rest of his life. She marveled at the medical skill that had accomplished such a miracle of healing. They must have used skin grafts in great number. From time to time, she would ask him if his injured side was troubling him. He would always shake his head and smile when she questioned him, but she was not reassured. He would never admit that he was incapacitated. Their premature departure from Waldesrauschen had been sheer madness in terms of his readiness to travel. However, she felt that he had done himself no serious harm except to delay regaining his strength and stamina.

Weeks had come and gone and they knew each other very well by this time. They had talked of their respective childhoods, their families and their hopes and fears for the future. He felt that her explanation for being on the troop train was plausible, since the requisitioning of the French train on the French-German border had been an unplanned and spontaneous maneuver by the army. That she was traveling as a journalist was not such an unlikely story. Anyway, Switzerland was a neutral country. Such a profession brought people to both interesting and dangerous places. If her explanation was not true, she certainly had a very small role in whatever exploit she had been involved in.

Their lives settled into a comfortable routine. Max got exercised several times a day, weather permitting. Madeleine seldom saw anyone on her rambles because she would wander the fields and woods and kept away from the tracks and paths. Mostly those she did see were on horseback, from the house, and they paid no attention to her. It was the servants that she needed most to avoid and they were obviously not inclined to walk the woods.

Erich's wound was no longer inflamed. He even took brief walks outdoors. Such outings helped him regain his strength. He slept more peacefully and his movements seemed less restricted. He limped, he always would, but walking produced only infrequent painful grimaces. He had to avoid precipitous movements, but in time he would probably have pretty good mobility.

She turned and opened her eyes and found that Erich was no longer beside her. She lay looking at the beautiful ceiling and the shafts of sunlight that had found their way through the heavy drapes. She could hear a chorus of birds chattering under the eaves, the distant sound of cows lowing. How peaceful it was. Was it possible that they were at war? Surely it could not last.

She turned her head towards the window and saw Erich sitting on the window seat.

"Good morning. Have you been sitting there long?" She sat up and stretched.

"I hope I didn't wake you. I couldn't sleep. I have been sitting here watching the dawn come up over the horizon. Such a tranquil scene. It gave me hope" He got up and came and sat beside her.

"I lay for a long time looking at you and decided that I have never known a more beautiful woman. I asked myself what I would do if I were never to see you again and I decided that I probably could never resign myself to such an eventuality." He leaned towards her and kissed her. Her took her hand and looked at her searchingly and finally he said, "Know that I shall always treasure the memory of these last few weeks. I have never been happier."

She knew by his expression that he was completely serious. He turned and looked out the window. When he looked at her again, it was with a faraway, wistful look, as if he was trying to see into the future.

"I cannot believe that this war will last for long. We must get you safely back to England. But once peace comes, it is my ardent hope that we can be reunited."

She flung her arms around his neck and said, "Dearest, darling Erich, if only that were possible. I cannot bear the thought of being separated from you."

He scooped her up in his arms and kissed her and then held her close to him.

They lay in each other's arms and whispered endearments and were at peace, happy in the shared knowledge of their infatuation.

They ate a leisurely breakfast and Madeleine cleared away the dishes. She was about to go out with Max when there was a knock at their door. It was Reinhardt. He came in flourishing some papers in his hand. Madeleine's heart sank for she was not prepared to face the next stage of her journey, to risk scrutiny at each roadblock, but worst of all to leave Erich.

The florid, tanned features in Reinhardt's rounded face were creased in smiles, the success of this difficult phase of their plan had been accomplished. They could leave. Reinhardt was an intrepid hunter and adventurer, but this present situation left him fearful for his family. He was convinced there must be something suspect about this beautiful girl and he was afraid that the repercussions for hiding a political suspect, if that were the case, would be swift and devastating. His relief at the prospect of their departure was considerable. He handed the papers to Erich.

"They have done a fine job, my friend. I hope that you will be pleased. Let me know if I can do anything else. I shall be gone most of the day. When do you think you might leave?"

"When would be the safest time for us to travel? When is the traffic heaviest?"

"There seems to be no difference, any more. All the roads seem to be congested all the time with military vehicles, especially outside the big centers."

"In that case, we shall leave tomorrow when we are ready. I have to fill up the tank of the Daimler. We only have two suitcases."

"I have already filled your tank. I thought you might need your extra reserves later."

"That is very generous. I don't know how I can ever repay you for all that you have done." Reinhardt waved away his thanks and smiled. "Then why don't you leave here at your convenience tomorrow, but I will move your car early tomorrow morning and park it down the lane. It will draw less attention from the servants."

With that he left, promising to see them later that evening.

The next stage of their journey was to take them south of Stuttgart in as wide a circle as could be negotiated and to an estate of another friend near Ravensburg, closer to the Swiss border. The cities were dangerous and papers were continually checked when one entered and left and many times in between. In any event, it would be difficult to accommodate Max in a city environment; not too many hotels had accommodation for dogs, only those in more rural areas. Max was going to be left with the friend from whose litter Erich had originally acquired him. He would be with other wolf hounds of his bloodline. Hopefully, he and his master would be reunited before too long.

The remainder of the day was spent discussing their plans. They tried to prepare for all unexpected eventualities, but knew that was really impossible. Erich did not tell Madeleine that he had asked Reinhardt to find out if there had been any unusual activity in the area. He had not forgotten the three cars that had hurtled down the hill in the dark. Reinhardt had found out that an enemy agent of unspecified nationality had been arrested hiding in a derelict barn. It was thought that there might have been an accomplice, but no one else was found. No radio or transmitter was found either.

The Kandahar Talisman

The day of their departure dawned grey with a promise of rain. Erich hoped that it would rain. Perhaps it would give them a better chance, possibly fewer inspections, although he felt that now Madeleine had her travel documents she was much less vulnerable, but you could never be sure of the whims of the military.

They had said their goodbyes to Reinhardt the previous evening. It had been decided that they should return by the road which had brought them to Lichtenfels. There was nothing but a maze of country lanes if they were to continue in the same direction and it would be longer. Also it would look suspicious to be found using them, since there was a better route. Once on the main road, they would drive for about 10 miles and then turn off to the right and drive east, thus avoiding Stuttgart altogether.

— 9 —

They set out at last and drove away from the beautiful Schloss that had been their home for such an important interlude. Max was the only one of the three that was content and happy to depart.

They returned the way they had come, driving along the narrow track through the forest until they reached the road that led down the hillside. They encountered no traffic, except a shepherd with his flock of sheep.

Once on the main highway, they made good progress for a brief period, but they soon saw that traffic was slowing to a crawl. It would be stop-and-go until they could turn off the main road. There was relatively little civilian traffic.

When at last they reached the crossroads where they were planning to turn east, they found it blocked by an armored vehicle. Erich stopped and enquired if they could pass and was told that no traffic could pass that way. There had been an accident. It would mean taking a turn further ahead. It would be inconvenient, but it would be only a slight detour. But when they came to the next intersection, there were barriers in the middle of the road. The traffic was being controlled so that vehicles were being funneled into the city. No one was allowed to turn and return in the direction from which they had come. Their hearts sank. It was not a good sign.

They negotiated two roadblocks without difficulty. It seemed that the police were only interested in inspecting people's papers. But at a roadblock outside the city limits, they met with a guard who was enjoying his position of power. He had scrutinized their papers carefully. He turned to Erich and asked him when and where he had purchased the Daimler. Madeleine could see that this annoyed Erich, but he answered calmly that he had purchased it some years previously. The response to this was that they were told to get out so that the car could be inspected. Madeleine's heart fluttered with fear, for she wondered where Erich had hidden her British passport. She knew he had removed it from the drawer in the back seat armrest. She had always felt a little uncomfortable that she might be deceiving Erich. Her passport stated that she was a journalist, not a courier. Her superiors felt that such a title might be too ambiguous in the wrong situation. They stood back a short distance whilst two of the sergeant's subordinates carefully and with great deliberation went over the car very thoroughly. In due course, they finished having found nothing. The sergeant was not satisfied.

"I am afraid that we will have to confiscate your car temporarily."

"You will do no such thing. How dare you insult my rank and my position with such a flagrantly outrageous suggestion,"

Erich exploded. "Such irresponsible incompetency is a disgrace. I have just recovered from wounds inflicted while defending the Fatherland and you have the effrontery to impede me from rejoining my unit. I shall have great pleasure in seeing that you are not only removed permanently from service, but that you are put in prison for unpatriotic conduct. I am sure the authorities will have a lovely time with you and be glad of the opportunity to make an example of you"

The sergeant was flustered by the fury of the attack upon him. He was not accustomed to being intimidated. He was used to having the upper hand. He started to stutter in self-defense. He said that they had been told to be suspicious of anything that seemed out of the ordinary in any way whatsoever. There was enemy activity in the area and promotions would be obtained for anyone apprehending suspicious persons. Erich's car was conspicuous by its elegance, there had been nothing like it all morning. He was only doing his duty. His voice faded away as he saw Erich's face.

"Are you suggesting that I might be an enemy agent, is that possible? Or are you retarded enough to think an enemy agent would use such a vehicle? Have you taken a good look at my papers? I think that there are some there that would be impossible for even a German to duplicate."

The sergeant by now was spluttering incoherently. Erich snatched their papers from him and stepped closer. Max by this time was growling threateningly and the sergeant stepped backwards as if ready to run for his life.

"I should let my dog make mincemeat of you, but I think the authorities will have more fun with you... and since you have delayed me unnecessarily and I am on business of the most urgent nature, have one of your men remove that barrier, so that I may make up for lost time and avoid this chaos."

With that he swung on his heel, steered Max into the back seat, guided Madeleine in to her seat and got in himself and slammed the door. The sergeant waved his arm abruptly at one of his subordinates and indicated that he should swing the barrier to one side. He had no sooner done this than there was an unexpected crunch and scraping of metal behind them. An army truck had run into the rear of a open wooden truck carrying large logs. Everyone was transfixed as the logs, beginning in slow motion, rolled with increasing speed off the back of the truck. The soldier who was about to remove the barrier stopped in mid-motion, his eyes bulging.

Erich leaned out of the Daimler and with frustration roared at the soldier to move the barrier immediately. The man froze for an instant and then leapt to do as he was told.

"Sehr gut." Erich growled. "Replace the barrier immediately and go and help the sergeant with that mess behind us."

They drove away sedately, speeding up when the roadblock was out of sight in a bend in the road.

Madeleine was awed by Erich's overwhelming authority. She had never seen this side of his character and knew that in battle he would be someone men under him would trust and obey unquestioningly. His self-assurance was impressive.

Erich, for his part, was unaware of the impression he had made. He knew the German character so well, that men such as the sergeant he had just encountered were not the least threatening to him. They were the backbone of the German army, fearless, obedient and unquestioning. Sometimes stupid, but more often cunning. But the scene that had just taken place had upset Erich for other reasons. If Madeleine should ever encounter such a man alone, she would be easily unmasked. She was no match for the dogged determination of such a man. It was even more important now that they get out of the city as soon as possible, but their exit would be surely more difficult than their entry. He hoped that on this road he could skirt it. Perhaps it was indeed a by-pass road and for this reason had been blocked. He was worried by the various challenges they had encountered, not for himself, but for Madeleine. He decided that he would have to find someone to help him.

They had not spoken since starting out again, but Erich finally broke the silence.

"We have to come up with a plan to get you out of this region. It is not going to be easy unless this road brings us to the main route joining Stuttgart and Munich. And there are no guarantees that we shall not have the same obstacles."

She did not respond. She had become very anxious, aware of her vulnerability, aware that Erich could at any point abandon her. There was so much at stake.

They drove on for a time until Erich drew up into a roadside lane.

"I think it is time we gave Max a walk. Would you take him for me. Don't be longer than ten minutes. I want to look at a map and refuel the car."

Max bounded off and she had to run to keep up with him. She felt heavy hearted. How could Erich possibly find a way out of their present predicament? There was so much activity on the main routes. The towns seemed just as threatening, if one took into account the volume of traffic. If she was honest with herself, she could not find a good reason why Erich should risk so much for her. It seemed like a mad game of chance. Anyone in his position would save themselves first rather than save a woman of suspect origins.

By the time she returned, Erich was again seated at the wheel. He looked relaxed. As she opened the door, he turned and smiled at her. She felt comforted by his smile. Max settled himself in the back seat. Madeleine closed her door and Erich started the engine.

"We will have to take the main Stuttgart-Munich road for a short distance and then, with luck, we will be able to branch off on to a lesser road that will bring us to Ulm. I have a friend of the family there, provided he is in residence."

She remained silent, not knowing whether to be happy or fearful. There were always so many unknowns.

They drove a considerable distance in silence. Amazingly, they had encountered no other roadblocks. Perhaps the one they had circumnavigated, had been meant to eliminate, in the minds of the authorities, the need of further controls. It was a great relief. Madeleine felt that Erich was relaxed and confident, despite his silence, as if he had known that their recent success at the last barrier would provide them with a clear road ahead.

In time, he was to confirm this. "In half an hour, we should reach the outskirts of Ulm. If I remember correctly, there is a hotel there where we should be able to find accommodation. I will leave you in the lobby. You can sit and wait for me there while I take care of some business. It might take me several hours.

We can have dinner together later. Be as inconspicuous as possible, I do emphasize that."

In due course, they arrived in the center of Ulm and found the Donau, the hotel which Erich had remembered from a visit many years earlier. It was obviously a popular place. The doorman was ushering in an army general and Erich urged Madeleine to slip in a side door while the general made his entrance. He was surprised at so much activity.

She stood to one side and took in the scene before her. The general was obviously expected, for an army of hotel personal were awaiting him. Hotel guests attracted by the commotion were pressing in to see the celebrity. There was much noise and chatter. Madeleine avoided the main entrance with its elegant columns which ran from the front lobby to the arched doorway of what seemed to be a large restaurant and took a back pathway behind a spacious open lounge to a palmed court in one corner. She hoped that no one had paid any attention to her. The palmed court seemed to be a secluded cocktail lounge. She found a seat just inside the entrance next to one of the palms. She was hidden from the main lobby, but not from anyone sitting in the cocktail lounge. It was the most secluded spot that she could find in the quick look she had taken upon arrival. The lounge was empty but for three couples. Everyone had been lured away by the hubbub in the main lobby. She had a limited view of the lobby through the potted plants that stood on the back of the banquette that divided the lounge from the lobby. She took a deep breath and tried to relax.

The restaurant swallowed up the general and his entourage and the lobby became a sedate and quiet place. A few people filtered into the lounge. Two waiters appeared and began to take orders. The hotel settled back into its routine.

Madeleine was happy to find that she could order a sandwich and coffee. She also ordered a sherry. She was very hungry and thirsty and hoped that the food would make her feel stronger. She was feeling on edge. The last roadblock had unnerved her. She could never have handled such a situation. The sherry made a warm path through her and she felt more relaxed. She knew that she might have to sit here a very long time. She was afraid that her inactivity would make her conspicuous. The guests would be less likely to notice than the waiters. That could be a problem.

The sandwich and coffee were long finished. She had found a paper someone had discarded and spent her time reading it cover to cover. Her spoken German had improved immeasurably under Erich's tutorship. Reading only helped to reinforce her general knowledge of affairs in Germany. What she read was devastating, even allowing for exaggerated reporting. She already knew that Denmark, Norway, Belgium and the Netherlands had been invaded by Germany, and that France had signed an armistice with Germany. What she had hoped to read was that the daily bombing of Britain had stopped, but according to the paper in front of her it was continuing uninterruptedly. It was reported that the skies over London were a crimson glow from the fires that raged out of control. She felt sick. Although her parents had a flat in London, they spent very little time there. Her parents lived in Dorset. However, her father, like so many others, often traveled there daily. How they must be worrying about her, too. They would have no idea what had happened to her. This was a war that would not be over soon. She felt very depressed.

As if to reassure herself, she unconsciously touched the Kandahar medallion under her blouse. She wondered what significance it had. She had been told to wear it when traveling as a courier on her various and regular missions for her agency. It was considered a unique form of identification if all else failed. Since their time at Lichtenfels had been one of seclusion, she had not chosen to wear it. However, the medallion was a gift from her father. Just to touch it gave her comfort, especially now in this time of great uncertainty. It was a rare gold coin with an exotic inscription fused together with soft green and lavender jade on a gold chain. It had been a souvenir her father had acquired on one of his expeditions into Kandahar in Afghanistan when he was on patrol in the Khyber Pass in India. He had told her that, on a rather long detour into a wildly beautiful lunar landscape, a savage dusty country, they had come upon a group of very colorfully dressed nomads. A young man in the group had fallen and badly broken his leg. One of her father's gun-bearers had stopped and skillfully bound the leg. In gratitude, the father of the young man had beckoned one of the women to him and had her remove several of the many coins adorning her costume. Her father had told Madeleine that it was the custom for the women to wear their wealth sewn into their garments. They were gold and silver coins that he had been given, mostly very old and thus quite valuable.

It had been almost three hours since her arrival at the hotel. She was beginning to worry. Perhaps Erich would not return, but surely that could not be after all that he had done for her so far? But why should he take such great risks on her behalf? Just his association with her would be considered treachery. She had no doubt that were she arrested she could be easily unmasked by the authorities, especially the Gestapo. She shivered and felt nauseous at the thought.

The waiters had changed shifts, which was a relief to her. But during all the time she had been sitting there, she had noticed in the main lobby a man who had remained in his seat as long as she had in hers. He was dressed as a civilian. He gave the impression that he missed nothing. There was no doubt in her mind that he was scrutinizing everybody. Because of him, she had remained in her seat, afraid to move about as she longed to do, for fear of catching his attention.

A voice behind her caught her by surprise. "Do not move, do not look at me. But when you have the opportunity to leave this lounge with a group of people, do so and go to the reception desk and check into your room here. Then go upstairs and I will contact you again." Her relief was overwhelming. It was Erich. It was evening now and there was much more activity. The majority of men in the hotel seemed to be in one uniform or another, but there were a lot of well-dressed woman too. They wore well-tailored suits or elegant cocktail dresses, some with stylish little hats. There came a moment when two groups came to the cocktail lounge and filled the entrance. Madeleine took this moment to slip out. The reception desk was similarly busy and she waited for her turn. The clerk had her reservation and took her papers, promising to return them shortly. Would they be returned to her in time for her to go out to dinner in about an hour? She was assured that they would. The procedure completed, Madeleine stepped away from the reception desk, key in hand, and realized in horror that she was quite alone, that the rest of the crowd around her had left. The sinister man in the lobby was probably totally absorbed with her. She felt like a fish in a fish-bowl. He must not see her face. So as she moved away from the desk, she turned her head and spoke to the clerk over her shoulder. It was not much, but at least he had not been able to have a good look at her.

She lay in the bath and tried to let the tension flow out of her. The relief to be away from curious, probing eyes was immense. The strain of waiting had been much harder on her than she had imagined. She knew that she could never feel safe until she set foot once more on English soil, but for the moment it was comforting to feel that she was out of sight and out of mind.

She was lying on her bed with her eyes closed, when there was a knock on her door. Her immediate reaction was one of joy at the prospect of seeing Erich again. She sat up and was about to call out when it occurred to her that it might not be Erich. Perhaps it was the clerk returning her papers. No, that did not make sense; so much easier for people to go to the desk and collect their own. What if it was the man in the lobby who, having scrutinized her papers, had come to ask questions? She felt sick with fear. If it were Erich, he would call her by name or use his own, surely. The knock came again and she shrank back on her bed and tried not to breathe.

Someone tried the handle, but finding it locked, did not try again. She trembled at what might happen next. However, half an hour passed and nothing more happened. Her fear receded somewhat. But now she was in a dilemma. How would Erich contact her? She doubted that he would use the telephone. She had no sooner come to this conclusion than it rang. She was too paralyzed to act. She lay back on her bed in a misery of indecision. The phone stopped ringing. Her heart was racing and she felt that she could not breathe. Fifteen more minutes passed and the telephone rang again. She had to act. She picked it up but held it to her ear without speaking into it. There was no voice on the other end. She replaced it carefully. There was no doubt now that she was under surveillance. A tap on the door brought a stab of fear. She was trapped. Another knock and quietly, "Erich." At last his familiar voice!

She flung open the door and he stepped into the room and closed the door behind him. He saw her deathly pale face and asked her what had happened. She flung herself into his arms and quickly told him of all that had happened, as well as the telephone calls. She was launched into a description of all her fears, but he stopped her hurriedly.

"We must leave here immediately, but first wipe all surfaces that you may have touched."

She rushed into the bathroom and picked up a towel, wiping doorknobs and faucets and finally the telephone.

"Be sure to leave nothing behind."

She shook her head. Her suitcase was still in his car. She had everything on that she had worn.

They left the room and were walking down the corridor when they heard the lift doors open around the next corridor. Erich grabbed her and told her to run back down the corridor and meet him at his room. Her gave her the number of a room two floors below. She fled as fast as her legs would carry her.

— 10 —

When Erich left Madeleine at the Donau, he had been uncertain of what to do next. There were several possibilities. He had quite a few friends in both Stuttgart and Munich, but he was reluctant to get in touch with them. They would ask too many questions. He did not have a good reason for being where he was. He was still on sick leave. Also they were not in the immediate vicinity and communications could be haphazard.

He thought he would get in touch with the nearest naval representative in the area and find out what had happened to his unit and what, if any, plans were being made for him. They would be surprised to hear from him, but it was also possible that they had no knowledge of him at all. It all seemed a bit chaotic at present...

This proved to be the case and he could not get satisfaction from any of the people with whom he spoke. He telephoned Berlin in due course, but no reply had come through and Erich, after spending two hours waiting for something to happen, had lost patience. While sitting and watching the confusion around him, he had made an important decision and he wanted to pursue it.

An old family friend was Bishop Rudolf Steiner. His residence and administrative offices were in a large and beautiful house not far from the center of the city. Erich had telephoned the Bishop's residence while he had been waiting for news from Berlin. He had been told that the Bishop was in residence, but had a full day of appointments. Erich was delighted to find that Bishop Steiner was in Ulm. The fact that he did not have an appointment did not worry him at all. It was a small detail. He climbed back into his car and set off again. Max was happy to see his master and nuzzled him over the back of the seat.

"I am sorry, old fellow, to leave you cooped up like this. We will take a walk very soon."

Erich reached his destination and drove down the wide, tree-lined street bordered by immense and stately baroque mansions. He parked the Daimler, got out and let out Max, whom he put on a leash. They walked for ten minutes. Erich put Max back in the car and told him he would get a longer walk on his return. With that Erich limped up the front steps of the Bishop's residence and rang the bell. After a long wait, the door was finally opened by an elderly cleric who squinted painfully into the light at Erich.

"Good day. I am Erich von Brandenburg and I have an appointment to see Bishop Steiner."

There was a silence while the old man digested this information. "I do not recall seeing your name in the appointment book. What time is your appointment?"

"I have just spoken to the Bishop's secretary. I am being squeezed in as he sees fit. Perhaps you would be good enough to let me in so I might sit down. I am on sick leave and have not yet recovered from my injuries."

With his aristocratic bearing, Erich was an impressive figure at all times, being tall and very handsome. In uniform, he was the epitome of everything the Fatherland would wish of a naval officer. His demeanor was imposing and that together with his unassailable self-assurance generally enabled Erich to get his way more often than not. It was thus not surprising that the old cleric bowed to this demand, despite an aptitude for turning away unwanted visitors. It was not every day that a man of Erich's rank and stature turned up on the Bishop's doorstep.

Erich stepped into the lofty, paneled hall, from which a wide staircase rose upwards. The old cleric ushered Erich into a large reception room which led from the center of the hall and asked him to make himself comfortable. Erich sat down in a large soft armchair and looked around him.

There were seven other people in the room. There were three elderly men sitting together, an elderly couple and a middle-aged woman with a young man of about 12 years of age. They all stared in unabashed curiosity at Erich. He was probably the most exotic personality they had ever encountered. Erich addressed the room with a "Guten Tag" that was meant to encompass everyone and settled back in his chair, his bad leg stretched out in front of him, the other braced beneath him. The room responded with respectful nods and bows. A clock ticked on the large marble mantle above a huge fireplace. Two large landscapes in oils hung one on each side of the mantle. The adjacent wall was taken up with three immense windows, draped in rich crimson velvet. They looked out onto a walled garden with a screen of trees at the end. To the left was a large double mahogany door which was the entrance to the Bishop's study.

Twenty-five minutes had passed when the cleric was at Erich's shoulder. He whispered obsequiously into Erich's ear. He was very regretful, indeed he was most embarrassed to have to inform Erich that he had no appointment. There must be some mistake, he could not understand how such a thing had happened. If Erich would be good enough to make another appointment with the Bishop's secretary before he left....

He was interrupted in the middle of his apology, when the door to the Bishop's study opened and the silhouette of a short, portly man was revealed as he backed through the opening, still talking to the Bishop who faced into the room.

"We are most grateful, Herr Berger, indeed we could not be more appreciative for all your helpful suggestions. I will certainly have my secretary inform you when we propose to proceed."

It was at this moment that the Bishop looked over Herr Berger's shoulder and addressed his cleric, "Father Schwenn, as you show Herr Berger out would you kindly give him the latest copy of our ecclesiastical calendar for the Advent season. Thank you." He was about to turn back into his study, when his eye fell upon Erich. His face reflected his astonishment.

"Can I believe my eyes? My dear Erich, what a joy to see you, pale but alive. Your parents were distraught about you," at which the Bishop stepped into the room and walked to where Erich was seated. Erich struggled to his feet, and was embraced warmly by the Bishop.

"How good it is to see you. Come, come we have so much to catch up on. Father Schwenn, please see that we are not disturbed. And could you bring us some small refreshment?"

The cleric beamed and smiled at this turn of events. It was a relief to be free of the embarrassment of having to turn away such a prestigious personality. He winced at the thought of it. It was fitting that he should be a close friend of the Bishop. He bowed and herded Herr Berger out of the room and to the door, before that gentleman had time to continue any further conversation. The old man knew Herr Berger well and it was a penance to have to deal with him. Words poured out of him. But now he had an errand and could graciously excuse himself.

They were settled in the Bishop's study, a book-lined room with a huge desk and a comfortable sofa and chairs. They spoke of Erich's parents and the evening that Bishop Steiner had spent with them and of their concerns for Erich. How they had learned so belatedly of his injury and how weeks later they had managed finally to speak to Prof. Schmieding and receive a prognosis for his recovery. They had been unconvinced by Erich's reassurances. He had been in hospital too long. They spoke of mutual friends and the progress of the war. By this time, tea on a silver tray arrived together with some fruit.

"So tell me, why are you in Ulm? I thought you were still convalescing. You do not look yourself. You parents told me what happened to you. It sounds as though you were very lucky to survive. The Lord obviously has other plans for you."

"I want to get married and wondered if you would do me the honor of performing the ceremony?"

"Oh, my son, what a pleasure that would be. When are you planning this happy event?

"I want to get married tomorrow. I know that it is very short notice, but there are extenuating circumstances."

The Bishop looked surprised. "That *is* very short notice. There is always the usual paperwork to be processed. I am afraid you are asking for the impossible. Anyway, I have quite a busy day tomorrow. Could you not arrange for it in a week or so?"

Erich shook his head. He was not surprised, but he was deeply disappointed. He struggled to his feet and let out a small gasp as a muscle spasm ran the length of his injured leg.

"My dear young man, you are far from well. You must take care of yourself." observed the Bishop as he saw the moist pallor of Erich's face. His heart was full of compassion for this wonderful young man whom he had known all his life. He stood looking at him thoughtfully and finally said. "You know, my secretary is a resourceful man. We will let him worry about your paperwork. Can you be at the Münster tomorrow morning at eleven? I will perform the ceremony before the High Mass being held at noon. This must be a most exceptional young lady."

"I cannot thank you enough. We are very indebted to you. And yes, she is a most exceptional lady. She helped save my life."

The Bishop's eyebrows arched in query, but he said no more.

"Well, well, there is much to be done then. Go and see my secretary on your way out and give him all the details. I will prepare him so that he does not throw you out the door." He smiled, pressed a button and spoke into his telephone. He embraced Erich and opened the door.

"I will see you tomorrow morning then."

Erich limped across the reception room and into the hall. The Bishop watched him thoughtfully and sighed. What a tragedy and a waste war was when young men such as he had to risk and lose their lives.

Back in the street, Erich walked Max with a light heart. He could hardly believe what he had accomplished. It really was against all odds. The Bishop's secretary had frowned at him when he presented himself. But Erich had never given up the idea of marrying Madeleine. He felt that the only chance he had to get Madeleine out of Germany, was to have her papers linked with him. It never occurred to him that he was taking an enormous risk.

"Very irregular," the secretary kept repeating, as he wrote down the details he was given by Erich. "Very irregular...." But he became aware that the young man was in considerable pain and he held his peace. Finally he asked if there was anything he could do to help him. Erich shook his head and said instead how grateful he was for the secretary's assistance. He could not emphasize enough the urgency of his mission. Whereupon the secretary concluded that this young man was off to the war again, despite his frail appearance.

Indeed, Erich was off to war, but a slightly different one than he had most recently left. He got back to the hotel in due course and parked the car. He went straight to the reception desk and confirmed his reservation made earlier by telephone. He was told he was lucky to have one of the last rooms available. He had had the foresight to make one for Madeleine from the Bishop's residence. In that way, no connection could be made between them. As he waited for the clerk to complete the details, he casually looked around the lobby and almost instantly identified a man he was sure was a member of the secret police sitting in a far corner.

As Madeleine fled down the corridor, she prayed that she would not bump into anyone. But she was lucky and as she turned the corner into the adjoining corridor, there was no one in sight. She stopped running and slowed to a brisk walk. Now the question was whether to make a circle back to the lifts or to take the stairs. It would be more normal to take the lift. There were three people waiting when she arrived, a man and his wife and an elderly woman. Madeleine tried to take a deep breath, but her heart was racing. The lift came at last and she got in only to find that it was going up instead of down. She prayed that it would not stop at all the floors. Finally, it began its descent and she got off at Erich's floor. She hoped she could find his room quickly and not waste any more time. She found it at last and knocked. She was about to knock again when the door opened and there was Erich with a smile of greeting. She stepped into the room and he closed the door behind her. He swept her up in his arms and kissed her.

"I was beginning to worry," he told her. "The two men that got out of the lift were an unsavory pair. I am sure that they were on some official business. I could not turn my head to see which way they went, but I was very glad that you had left your room."

"Oh, Erich, what are we going to do? How can I possibly leave here without their seeing me?"

"I think that I have a perfect solution. We will get married."

"Erich, be serious, don't joke. You are too cruel. We know it is not possible."

"But that, my most beautiful Madeleine, is where you are mistaken. I have arranged everything. We will be married tomorrow morning at eleven in the Münster. It is not far from the hotel. You will have only a short walk."

"But what if those men sitting in the lobby see me?"

"It should be easier than you think. Tomorrow there is going to be a special funeral service at the Münster. A lot of people will be attending. I think that you will find the lobby quite busy and congested."

She shook her head and looked up at his earnest face and knew that he had no fear.

"Now, stop worrying. We will have dinner together here. You will stay in this room for the night and I will go and stay elsewhere. The less we are seen together the better both our chances."

It was a quiet meal; Madeleine had to force herself to eat. They were both preoccupied with their own thoughts, but Erich did his best to lift her spirits for he realized how very anxious she was about her chances of leaving the hotel unobserved the next day. She tried to console herself that all of it was her imagination, that the knocks on her door had been in error, but the law of averages were against two phones calls being made in error in such a short space of time.

Erich had brought her suitcase so that she had a change of clothes. He would take the suitcase when he left. That would be very helpful.

She clung to him when he left, fearful that she would never see him again. He comforted her and kissed her and said he would see her in the morning.

She did not expect to sleep, but she was exhausted from the strains and stresses of the day and eventually slept. In Erich's room, she felt that she was protected by an invisible cloak.

They had discussed at some length whether she should pick up her papers at the reception desk. To do so would attract attention; to leave them would be confirmation of her illegal status and make her a marked suspect. Much depended on how busy it was in the morning. She might be able to do it easily and leave immediately. She would have to wait and see.

She awoke the next morning refreshed, but her first waking thought was of the risks which lay ahead of her and she felt exceedingly depressed. She had packed her suitcase the night before. Her wardrobe had been a simple selection of skirts, blouses and sweaters, none of which had taken much room in her suitcase. She had the suit which she had traveled in and an elegant dress for the one official evening that had been planned for her stay in Switzerland before this whole nightmare began. She put it on now and viewed herself in the mirror. It was a lovely lilac silk. The shape and color of this simple, elegant dress was very becoming. Erich had not seen it. She hoped it would be a surprise. She quickly ate some fruit left over from the previous night's meal. It was enough. She checked the room for any forgotten possessions. There were none.

She stepped out into the corridor and closed the door behind her. As she turned, someone bumped into her and she dropped her key. She bent to pick it up and was surprised to see the young man who had obviously knocked the key from her hand still standing in front of her staring in amazement at the Kandahar medallion, which had fallen out from under her dress.

"My God," he said in German, "What luck!"

She was too mesmerized to act as he stepped forward and whipped the medallion off over her head and fled down the corridor.

Her first reaction was to chase after him. Instead, she started to walk down the corridor, her mind racing. She must remain calm. She was outraged at the theft of her medallion. It was precious to her in all sorts of ways. Her good luck charm. This brusque encounter had unnerved her. Did this man she had so unexpectedly encountered have some authentic connection with the associates in her agency? He was obviously on the run, which meant she was at risk too. It made her feel ill. Her greatest asset was that she was elaborately dressed, not looking like some hounded escapee. But she did not have her papers should they ask her. She could hear laughter and chatter coming from around the corner of the next corridor and she hurried towards the sound. As she approached the corner, she heard behind her a shot and a cry and she went cold with fear. In an instant she was around the corner and was astonished to see a group of about a dozen nuns laughing and talking excitedly together.

A couple of them saw her, as she leant up against the wall, her knees weak beneath her, feeling faint and nauseous. They hurried to her and took her by the arm and walked her slowly into one of their rooms. They sat her in a chair and gave her a glass of water. She took some deep breaths and tried to pull herself together. They fluttered over her and peered at her anxiously. She decided finally that she had nothing to lose by telling them a bit about herself. So she told them that she had heard a shot and a cry and thought it came from a young man who had bumped into her running down the corridor. He had stolen her necklace. She was very afraid that he was a very suspicious character and that if she reported the theft of her necklace she might be detained and delayed. That today was to be her wedding day and she was afraid that the authorities would start questioning everyone and she would be prevented from walking to the Münster, where she was to be married shortly. It was a very sketchy explanation, but the nuns were filled with awe and consternation by what she had told them. Two of them had gone to see if anyone had been injured. They returned quite soon to say that they had seen no one, but that there were bloodstains on the wall and carpet. It was evident that they were very upset by their discovery. At this piece of news, Madeleine's nerves were so shattered that she burst into tears. She was convinced that she would be connected with the death of the young man she had collided with in the corridor. Soon the whole hotel would be swarming with police.

The nuns were chattering and conferring together until finally one of them came and sat next to Madeleine and took her hand. She asked at what time the wedding was planned, who was the groom and who would be officiating at the ceremony.

When Madeleine told them that Bishop Steiner would be officiating and that she was to marry a naval officer, recently wounded, they nodded with satisfaction. They seemed reassured.

They left her sitting in their small reception room and retired into one of the two bedrooms. They were obviously staying in a group of rooms because one nun hurried by her and out the door.

Madeleine was anxious and upset. There was plenty of time before the planned ceremony, but how could she ever manage to leave the hotel after the furor of this recent incident?

The young nun returned with an older one at her side. The two disappeared into the bedroom and the door was again closed.

Madeleine got up and locked the door to the small suite of rooms. It was not much protection against unwanted visitors, but it gave her a little comfort. A strong man could shoulder the door open in an instant. She brushed the thought aside.

The nuns had just begun to filter out of the bedroom, when a loud pounding on the door Madeleine had just locked froze them in place. One of the nuns grabbed Madeleine and pushed her into the cupboard in the second bedroom, motioning her to kneel down in one corner behind some hanging robes. She left the door slightly ajar. Madeleine's heart was pounding. She could hardly breathe.

The sound of men's voices reached her in the confines of the small space. She could not understand anything that was said, but the low tone of the words were infinitely sinister.

One of the nuns entered the room and was speaking. "We have several rooms in this corridor to accommodate our group. We are about to leave for the cathedral where we are singing at a funeral today. We have very few possessions with us, but perhaps you would like to look under the bed and in this cupboard." She swung open the door but stood in such a fashion that the corner where Madeleine crouched was hidden by the nun's habit. Madeleine was sure that the pounding of her heart must be deafening to all present.

There was a shuffling of feet which indicated that several others were in the room with the nun. Someone came close to where she lay shaking because the man cleared his throat and then, as abruptly, she heard him walk away.

The Kandahar Talisman

The nun, who had obviously not moved, spoke again. "We are sorry that we can be of so little help to you. We have been practicing our singing and have heard no noises in the corridor outside."

The room sounded empty, but Madeleine did not move. Suddenly, the robes were swept aside. Her heart lurched sickeningly.

"You may come out," a gentle voice told her. "They have left."

Madeleine got slowly to her feet. An older nun was looking at her appraisingly.

"You have had a nasty shock, my dear. Come and sit down and have something to drink."

Madeleine nodded weakly.

They sat her down in a chair and grouped themselves around her. They handed her a glass of wine. It surprised her, but she drank it gratefully.

They told her that one of their number was sick in bed and would not be able to sing at the funeral to be held at the Münster that day. They thought that in the circumstances it would be advisable if she were to dress as a nun, so that she could leave the hotel in their company. They were not required to show their papers. Sometimes a head count was made when they came and went.

Madeleine was awed by this act of faith in her for she was convinced that they were taking a big risk on what she felt was a very flimsy story. But once the decision was made, they set about dressing Madeleine with great enthusiasm. The habit did not need to fit her well and in fact was much too large. But it helped hide her handbag and shoes which had to be attached to her person. The old nun's shoes which she was obliged to wear were too large, but the nuns stuffed them with paper and she was able to walk without their falling off.

At last she was dressed and ready to leave. The nuns, instead of being fearful of the masquerade, seemed stimulated and excited as if they were taking part in a school play. Madeleine was astonished at their lightheartedness, but she had to remind herself that they lived on a different plateau of faith.

As Madeleine turned to leave the room, she noticed one of the nuns take Madeleine's medallion out of the pocket of her robe and place it on a near-by chest of drawers. She gasped and asked where it had been found. She was told that one of the nuns who had gone to investigate the incident in the corridor had found it near a chest by the window at the end of the corridor. Madeleine felt a sudden surge of hope flood through her. She picked it up. Perhaps things would turn out well for her after all. She explained that it was this piece of jewelry which had been stolen, a gift from her father, and how upset she was at its loss. The nuns smiled, pleased at her happiness. Madeleine realized that such worldly things had little significance to these religious women.

They set off down the corridor and waited for the lift. It took several lifts before all twelve of them arrived at the main floor. Once arrived in the main lobby, they had to struggle through the tremendous crowd which was milling around in the confined space. The ceremony at the Münster had drawn people from all walks of life. But there seemed an agitation about the crowd which could not be explained and one of the nuns asked a waiter walking by what all the excitement was about. He told her that a suspected enemy agent had been shot, but that he had escaped down the laundry chute and into a waiting van.

When this piece of news reached Madeleine, she felt an enormous elation, not only because the young man had escaped, but because she felt that it was an omen for her own escape from the hotel. They had reached the hotel entrance, the nuns laughing and chattering amongst themselves. No one seemed to pay any attention to them and they started across the road. They had got half way across when a sharp bang split their ears and they all turned in surprise. Madeleine's nerves were so fragile that she started in fright, but it was only a truck backfiring, and they all laughed and had soon reached the other side in safety. They had only a short distance to walk before they came to another intersection, across from which stood the Münster. Madeleine had scarcely any time to drink in the magnificence of this Gothic cathedral. Its enormous and graceful spire seemed to reach to the heavens. She was not aware that it was the tallest in Europe, but she would never forget it.

— 11 —

Erich rose early from a fitful and restless sleep, but with no sign of the throbbing pain in his leg and side that had disturbed him the previous evening. His initial mood upon waking had been one of excitement. But this mood was soon replaced by a sense of foreboding. He could not shake off the remembrance of Madeleine's terror at the unexplained knocks on her hotel room door and the telephone calls. He remembered grimly the various sinister characters he had seen in the hotel the previous day.

He had awoken hungry but his appetite had disappeared as concerns clouded his mind. He took Max for a walk and upon his return forced down some breakfast.

Intent upon avoiding the crowds who would be coming to the Münster, he left the hotel much earlier than needed. He managed to park in the small, private entrance to the cathedral. The old custodian had not challenged him; the mention of Bishop Steiner's name seemed passport enough. He had walked through the vestry and spoken with an old priest who was in charge of all things administrative. It seemed that Erich was expected and that some of the excitement of the wedding had spilled over into the somber interior of the cathedral's offices. There were several choir boys, with robes over their arms standing and chatting. There was to be a choir practice before the mid-day service. Erich had waited until all was in order, the papers on the Bishop's desk, before entering the vastness of the Münster.

Erich was seated in the left front pew of the Cathedral. It was still very early. It was very peaceful sitting under the fan vaulted ceiling which covered the four aisles of the old church. Great shafts of multi-colored light came through the huge windows, leaving the rest of the interior in shadow, except where large stubby candles lent their mellow flickering light. He remembered being told that the elaborate and unique pulpit was 16th century. Erich was not a particularly religious man, although his upbringing had included regular attendance at church on Sundays. But the majesty of this place impressed him and brought a tranquility of spirit to him that he had not felt all morning. He could not help but reflect on the incredible odds against his having survived the explosion. Those had been long, painful weeks and he knew that if he had not had the hope of seeing Madeleine again, it would have been a very dismal period indeed. He realized that he must have lost his reason to fall in love in these circumstances, but comforted himself that love had nothing to do with logic or wisdom. It was an overwhelming force, far more compelling than anything he had ever encountered before. He could not get over the magic of the weeks he and Madeleine had spent together. She was as enchanting and intelligent as she was beautiful. It really was hard to imagine that she would be his wife in a little over an hour from now. He resisted any negative thoughts other than it might be months or years before they could contemplate life together. The war news had not seemed good in the sense that Hitler was extending his frontiers and escalating the offensives. It meant that an end to it all could not be in sight for a long time to come, unless some miracle were to happen. He considered that this moment in time was a miracle in itself. He felt himself relax.

He reviewed his plans for leaving the city. He had armed himself with extra passes before leaving Lichtenfels. He had not told Madeleine but he had arranged for another set of papers be made for her, the second set in her new married name. He had gambled that he could accomplish this. He hoped that these passes would be protection enough until he could get her out of the country. He hoped that he had covered all the eventualities for the time being. He was counting on the surge of visitors to make Madeleine's departure from the hotel a simple one.

It was nearing eleven o'clock and Erich was restless and uneasiness began to creep through him. The cathedral was beginning to fill up. He turned around to look at the main entrance way behind him but could not see a familiar silhouette in the milling throng. He now was anxious and his earlier fears and concerns began to haunt him, but knew there was nothing he could do. What if she had been arrested? There would be no way he could save her. No explanation he could give that would clear her name without the right papers and credentials. Despite the fluency of her German, it would not be good enough under the stress of a severe interrogation. He closed his eyes and took a deep breath. He was interrupted from this depressing reverie, by a soft voice at his side.

"Herr Kapitän, would you kindly follow me. We are almost ready."

He looked up in surprise at the young nun looking down at him and got to his feet. He could not find an explanation for this, but followed her back to the vestry. The Bishop was waiting for him there surrounded by a group of nuns who sighed in quiet admiration at the sight of the handsome young officer.

"Erich, my son, there you are. We are nearly ready. Your fiancée will be with us momentarily. The sisters have told me that they would like to sing for you. I think that this whole ceremony will be truly memorable. That such an event could have worked out as well as it has at such short notice is truly remarkable. The ways of the Lord never cease to amaze me." He beamed at Erich, who was suddenly feeling terribly nervous.

"Let us go ahead, your fiancée will follow with the sisters."

It was a beautiful ceremony. They seemed to be surrounded by music. The nuns, standing under the ornately carved 15th century choir stalls and the carved figures of the Old Testament, sang an "Ave Maria." Off in the distance, the choirboys were practicing and when the nuns were not singing the young voices could be heard, clear and pure, a magical sound. Erich was mesmerized by Madeleine's loveliness. He had not seen the dress she was wearing before, the color and softness of it was wonderful. She wore a rich and intricate lace scarf on her head which allowed wisps of soft curls to escape and gave her a medieval beauty that he had not noticed in her before. She smiled at him softly as she joined him at the altar. He felt his heart bursting with love and saw his happiness reflected in her eyes.

Their vows exchanged, the ceremony over, the Bishop congratulated and embraced them both, the nuns tittering and giggling in shy enthusiasm. They walked back to the vestry and shared a glass of wine in celebration. The Bishop wished them long life and happiness and then excused himself. There were last minutes details he needed to oversee before the next service. They thanked him warmly and then they were left alone.

Erich took both of Madeleine's hands and, holding her at a distance, said "Madeleine von Brandenburg, you have promised to love and cherish me, so now I want my first kiss as your husband."

She laughed lightheartedly as he pulled her towards him. He kissed her long and tenderly. Finally, he said, "It is time to leave. We have a long journey ahead of us."

Out in the church courtyard of the Münster, Max pranced in excitement. Erich looked out the gate. Traffic was heavy, mostly army vehicles. He wanted to time his departure so that he did not get sandwiched between convoys. The old custodian fluttered over them. They were all settled in the Daimler. Finally there was a break in traffic and the custodian opened the gates and the Daimler eased out onto the road.

Progress was slow. They were stopped several times, but their papers seemed in order and they were waved on. She wondered what Erich had done with her passport. She was tempted to ask him, but felt that perhaps it was safer if she did not know its hiding place. Madeleine was anxious. She could not forget the young man. The memory of that encounter made her feel terribly vulnerable. She felt that her face revealed all that she knew and felt. She had not told Erich about the incident. How could she explain it? It was a random encounter. She still did not understand its significance. If that young man was an agent on the side of the British, she hoped fervently that he had managed to escape.

They were nearing the outskirts of the city. They could see another roadblock ahead. Every vehicle was being thoroughly searched. They were asked to get out. Erich had told Madeleine to walk Max on his leash, but not to go far from the car. They had completed the search and Erich was standing near the driver's seat. A guard was approaching Madeleine as she walked back to the car.

"I want to ask you a couple of questions," he said to her. Max stood rigid and growled deep in his throat. Madeleine felt an icy finger of fear run through her. She felt that her German was good, but she knew it would be easy to trick her into a false reply.

Then suddenly the guard said to her in English, "Behind you!" But at the same moment, Max tugged on his leash and Madeleine was given a few seconds in which to hang on to her wits. She was horrified at the trap she had so narrowly escaped. Without Max she knew that she would have turned her head. She swallowed and in as unemotional a voice as she could muster she asked the guard what he had said. He began to respond, but at this point Max reared up and the guard changed his mind, and waved Madeleine to the car. She got in and sat shaking until the roadblock was well behind them.

"You were superb," Erich told her.

"No," she responded, "I was very lucky. Without Max, I would have turned my head."

"I blame myself. I never thought to warn you that they could possibly use such tricks. But even a trained person is apt to fall for something like that. It is a reflex action to respond and very hard to control."

They were now on the open road and making good speed. Soon they would turn off the main highway and would be less conspicuous. The Daimler was impressive and had given them a right of passage where others would be questioned. But Erich recognized that it could also arouse suspicion in others and that he would be wise to change cars at some point.

It was good to be away from the roadblocks and military vehicles and in the sweet scented pine forests. They began to relax and talk. At one point, they stopped and let Max romp through the woods, while Erich refilled the tank with one of his reserves of gasoline. Erich had brought a modest picnic. They left the car and walked to the top of a gradual slope and found before them a marvelous vista of the valley below. They sat with their backs against a pine tree and ate a simple meal of sausage, cheese and fruit. A bottle of Rhiesling to quench their thirst. A glint of water could be seen in the far distance and beyond, still further, the misty blue outline of mountains. Madeleine had been ravenously hungry. The simple fare had refreshed and renewed her.

They had met no traffic as they had driven through the forest, so it was a surprise when they saw a sleek, black car speeding along the road in the direction they had come. Erich made no comment about it, but his resolve to switch cars was now much firmer. It resembled too much an official car, so like the sinister ones which had passed them on their way to Reinhardt's home. He was glad that the Daimler was parked in the forest and behind some bushes which had hidden it from the road.

Their destination was an old and lovely country inn lying between the Swabian Jura and the Black Forest. It had once been an hunting lodge. Now it catered to people seeking peace and fresh, mountain air. It was owned by Helmut and Matilda

Ziegler, an elderly couple who had once worked for Erich's parents. Erich had often visited there in his youth.

It was going to be a long journey, especially as they worked their way up the winding and steep slopes through the mountains. But Erich told her that the views would be spectacular at times and they should enjoy it all and make a leisurely trip of it. For reasons both of convenience and caution, they stopped the night in a little inn poetically named "Am Weissen Schwann," the White Swan. Here they ate a simple but tasty meal and retired early. Erich hoped that this might avoid any encounters with official cars. They would turn off soon on to a smaller road and one which he hoped would be less traveled.

The air was invigorating and the views of mountains, sky and valleys, throwing together all the colors of a painter's palette, stimulating and soothing. They could almost forget where they were and the purpose of this particular journey.

By late afternoon of the second day, they came upon the hunting lodge at last, nestled at the end of a winding lane, set snugly into the craggy hillside behind. Pine trees seemed to embrace it on either side, the mellow timbered structure blending so comfortably with its surroundings. An arched entrance led to a small, inner courtyard. It was here that Erich parked the Daimler and got out. He was about to turn and let Max out, when a heavyset man in his early sixties came out of a side door. His weatherbeaten wrinkled features wreathed in smiles as he saw Erich.

"Welcome, welcome. I cannot believe that you are here. It has been so many years since we have seen you at Grünewald.

What a fine young man you have become. My dear wife is going to weep at the sight of you. Matilda, come and see who we have here," he called over his shoulder.

A few moments later, a round and smiling Matilda came out of the kitchen, brushing flour off her hands, laughing and exclaiming at the sight of Erich. He strode towards her and embraced her in a bear-like hug, while she giggled and clucked. She had put flour on his uniform and he laughed with her. He shook hands warmly with Helmut and they embraced.

At last they had finished with their greetings and Erich turned to help Madeleine out of the car. He introduced her and they smiled and nodded in approval at his new bride.

There were no visitors staying at the inn. They would have it all to themselves. Erich asked Helmut if he had a place where he could leave the Daimler for an indefinite period, a place where curious eyes would not see it. Helmut thought for a moment and then nodded. He had an old barn out in the far meadow. It would be safe and dry there. He would have his son take it as soon as he had finished milking the cows.

They removed their few possessions from the car and followed the farmer and his wife into the inn. Max was left in the kitchen where he was to have his long-awaited dinner. Matilda led the way through the huge, cobblestoned kitchen to the staircase in the raftered hall. She puffed up the staircase ahead of them, chatting and laughing all the way. She was full of memories of Erich's childhood visits. They walked along a wide passage and when they came to the end she flung open a door into a spacious sitting-room.

"It is our favorite suite and one that your dear parents often used to occupy, if you remember." She walked into the room, closed a window, and adjusted two others. The sweet smell of the forest filled the room. They walked through a connecting door into the spacious bedroom. A large canopied bed stood in the middle, a window with a balcony overlooked a small flower garden with a pond, where a family of ducks were foraging. It was a very tranquil scene.

"I hope you will be very comfortable and happy here," she smiled. "I have baked an apple tart and we have a choice of venison or trout for dinner."

"Matilda, it sounds wonderful. What a luxury in these hard times. We are starving. Would it be an imposition if we had dinner in our sitting-room?"

Her shiny, red face glowed with pleasure. "I was hoping you would decide that," she responded. "The dining room would be full of echoes with just the two of you." She told them she would serve dinner at seven o'clock if that suited them and with that bustled out of the room.

"This is such a wonderful place," exclaimed Madeleine as she leant out of the window and looked down at the pond below.

"Yes, it is. In high season, it was impossible to get a room for months. People would sometimes come for a few days and end up staying for a week or more. Matilda and her husband have worked very hard and done well. They also have a small farm which is run mostly by Helmut's sons, so it helps them to be self-sufficient in times such as these. He stretched and yawned. "I cannot wait to get out of this uniform and into some comfortable clothes. Would you mind if I took a bath first. I want to go and chat with Helmut. You can then take as long as you want to bathe." She nodded in assent and he turned and walked into the large bathroom and turned on the tap to the oversized bath.

His bath had refreshed him and soothed his aching side. Despite some of the long days on the road, his injured leg and hip seemed to be healing well. He had dressed again in a soft, thick sweater that had all the colors of the woods in it. He looked much younger out of uniform. It changed him. It seemed to reveal a softer, more intellectual personality. He looked very much the country gentleman, Madeleine thought, as she sat looking at him. His shoulders had filled out again and he looked less gaunt. He crossed the room and bent and kissed her.

"I will see you soon. If you cannot wait for dinner, I am sure that Matilda will have some tasty morsel for you in the kitchen," and with that he was gone.

Erich was relieved when he got to the kitchen to see that the Daimler was no longer in the courtyard. Instead he saw Max bounding up and down chasing a boxer who seemed to be enjoying a game of tag.

Helmut was sitting at a large kitchen table drinking a mug of ale. He got to his feet at the sight of Erich who waved him back into his chair and sat down beside him. It was good to be back in the familiar surroundings of this wonderful old kitchen. The huge table sat in the middle of the room. Behind it in the middle of one wall was a large potbellied stove with a saucepan simmering on it. Behind, blue and white tiles made a splash of color. Over in one corner was a large pine armoire and on another wall a dresser filled with multi-colored plates. Matilda was standing at a sink preparing vegetables. The cobbled floor sloped slightly towards the fireplace at the far end.

They relived those summers of years gone by. How much Erich's parents had loved this place. How much his father had enjoyed the wonderful trout fishing; his mother the serenity of the surroundings and the opportunity to write. Of the elegant caravan of families who would wend their way through the forest to this peaceful oasis. The same families would come year after year and many of the children, when they had come of age, had married the childhood sweethearts that they had met at Grünewald Inn. They spoke of their respective families. Helmut and Matilda had three sons and a daughter. Two of the sons were away at the war. The third had a disability which made him exempt from military service and he spent all his days helping them with the farm, as did his wife, their daughter and her two younger sons. It was hard work for everyone, but they managed.

Erich told them that he had not seen his parents in nearly a year; that he spoke to them infrequently as the telephone service was unreliable and that the postal service was even more erratic. He knew that this was very hard on his parents, the more especially since his injury.

They spoke of the war, their hopes and fears. Erich asked Helmut if it had touched them at all at Grünewald. Helmut told him that in a way it had isolated them from the rest of the world because so few people were able to travel any more. Most of the visitors that came to them now were in the military. In a way, it was very peaceful, but it meant that they now lived on a very limited income. There had been an unexpected visitor this afternoon. He seemed like some sort of official enquiring if they had any guests. It was obvious that they had none. He did not seem interested in the lodge, but he did inspect all the barns. Before leaving he had told them that they were looking for an enemy agent who had been wounded during his escape. A handsome reward would be available to any one handing him over to the authorities.

Erich digested this information thoughtfully. He knew that a suspected enemy agent had escaped from the hotel in Ulm. He wondered if there was any connection with this visit. He hoped that the official would not return to the inn. He had planned to stay with the Zieglers for four to five days, but now wondered if it would not be wiser to remain with them for only two or three. He had not forgotten the sinister little man sitting in the hotel lobby scrutinizing all those coming and going. There was no doubt he was a member of the secret police. He knew that Madeleine had found him frightening. Due to his presence, she might have had difficulty in getting back her papers. He reflected on Madeleine's encounter with the nuns. How she had accomplished masquerading as a nun he could not imagine, but it might have been all for the best.

He brought up the subject of using other transportation to their next destination which was still a good day's journey away. Helmut said that he had an old truck which could be used, but he was always short of fuel. Erich decided that perhaps it was wiser not to leave the Daimler. If found, it was very out of character in these surroundings, whereas at his next destination it could easily be left without arousing comment. They left the kitchen and took the dogs and walked across the open pastures.

When Erich got back to the inn, he found that the table in their sitting room had been laid with a white lace and linen cloth. A vase of wild flowers sat in the center of the table with a large candelabra to one side. It looked immensely elegant and romantic. Madeleine was sitting in a chair reading a newspaper. She had on a soft blue sweater that matched a skirt of similar color. Her outfit intensified the blueness of her eyes as well as accentuating the pinky white luminosity of her skin. She was infinitely desirable. She smiled at him, glad to see a little color had crept into his cheeks.

A knock on the door behind him announced Matilda. She came into the room carrying a large tray. She had fresh rolls, butter and two plates of homemade duck paté. A wine bucket held a bottle of champagne. Helmut had sought out his oldest and best vintage for them. As self-sufficient as they were compared to city-dwellers, Erich felt sure that the Zieglers were using up the last of their stock-pile of reserves. But he knew that if he remonstrated with them at their indulgence, he would offend them deeply.

They had eaten marvelously well. It was a leisurely meal. They thanked Matilda for giving them such a memorable dinner. She had smiled shyly and responded that they were grateful at having the opportunity to participate in their wedding celebration.

Madeleine looked up from her coffee and saw Erich gazing at her. She blushed, feeling guilty at the secret she was hiding from him. She felt that his searching gaze was an indication that he suspected her. She was unhappy at deceiving him and decided that she would have to tell him about the possible enemy-agent.

She put down her cup and stood up. His gaze never left her as she moved towards him. She was so fearful of what she was about to tell him that she could hardly breathe. She was only a few steps from him, when he got to his feet and caught her around the waist.

"It was a most superb wedding dinner, and I was very hungry. But I have spent the whole evening looking at you and thinking of how good you taste and how soft you feel and I cannot wait another moment to hold you, and kiss you."

He took her hand and led her into their bedroom, picked her up and gently put her on the bed and then sat down beside her. He kissed her then with a desire that he had not shown before and she responded with immense longing that surprised him.` He ran his hand up and down her back, slowly exploring all of her until neither of them could stop the momentum of their need. Satiated and limp, they fell asleep in each other's arms. Their garments lay scattered like wind-blown leaves.

Their stay at Grünewald was one of great tranquility and happiness. Madeleine's resolve to tell Erich of her encounter with the secret agent melted. She would wait. They walked the woods and meadows, with Max bounding ahead of them. Matilda prepared them wonderful meals. But Erich was eager to move on to their next destination. He did not like to contemplate his separation from his beautiful bride, but he knew the longer she remained in Germany the greater her risk of discovery. He had no idea how her escape could be accomplished but that it could be worked out he never doubted. She did not share his optimism and tried not to let the shadow of fear and uncertainty that hung over her cloud their happiness.

At last it was time to leave. It was impossible to thank Helmut and Matilda sufficiently for their hospitality and generosity, but Erich knew that their visit had brought much happiness to a loyal and special couple. Max was sitting in the back seat. Their two suitcases in the trunk. Matilda handed Madeleine a picnic lunch and they were on their way, waving a last farewell as they turned onto the road and accelerated away.

They drove a long time in silence, enjoying the beauty of the countryside. There was hardly any traffic, only a few farm vehicles, mostly horse drawn carts. They went through numerous little villages for they were keeping to all the back roads. They stopped for lunch by a stream and watched the fish come up to bite when they threw a few crumbs in the water.

They talked of where they might live after the war. Erich thought that he might want to spend his time running his parent's farm and stables in which case they would perhaps live in a house nearby. Madeleine asked him how many children he wanted and his face clouded and he became silent. Finally, he turned to her and said that he hoped she would forgive him but that it was unlikely that they could ever have children. He had been very ill with mumps at a vulnerable age and the doctor had told his mother that he probably would never be able to conceive children. It was a shock, but in the circumstances, it was no time to contemplate family life and she leant forward and kissed him and told him that she did not mind. He was very relieved and infinitely grateful to her. He had dreaded telling her. It had been very difficult for him to accept this in himself. He knew that it grieved his parents for he was their only child. But he knew that they loved him and only lived for his happiness.

— 12 —

They came at last to Langenhof, the residence of Count Anton Wolfgang Casimir. Madeleine was awed by the immenseness of this country estate. When she had seen Lichtenfels, Reinhardt's lovely home, she had thought never to see a larger estate.

They drove down a long avenue of trees and came to rest at the bottom of a large half-moon staircase which led up to an enormous front door. They had hardly got out of the car when a liveried servant came down the steps to take their luggage. He led them into a spacious hall with a stone staircase leading upwards. He asked them to wait in the library while he found their host.

Erich had told her that his friend, Anton, did not know the purpose of their visit, but that he was confident that Anton would support any daredevil plan that they might devise for her escape because he had an infinite capacity for adventure. She was not reassured by this, for people's political allegiances could often take precedence over everything else, and Anton might very well feel that he had no obligation to help out his old friend, but in fact felt it his duty to hand over to the authorities someone who might be a threat to the Fatherland.

She sat looking out over the glorious view of manicured flowerbeds and shimmering lake in a mood of deepening anxiety. She could not see how a plan for her escape could be devised without entailing great risk to all concerned. She felt her eventual capture was inevitable; the consequences she hardly dare contemplate. But her most immediate preoccupation was her overwhelming sadness at the prospect of being separated from Erich. She was deeply in love with him and the thought of not seeing him for possibly months or even years, was more than she could bear. That she might never see him ever again had her mind teetering on the edge of an abyss that she found more threatening than anything she had ever known.

Anton swept into the room like a mountain breeze. He was as fair as Erich was dark. His blond hair and tanned complexion gave him the air of a Viking. He exuded vitality and strength. His face broke into an enormous grin at the sight of Erich and the two embraced each other with noisy gusto. After an exchange of masculine banter, Erich turned and with outstretched arm called to Madeleine who was standing by the French doors overlooking the park.

"Anton, I want you to meet my wife."

The introductions were made and Anton bowed and kissed Madeleine's hand. Anton stared long and appraisingly at Madeleine. "You have chosen a most beautiful woman to be your wife, my friend. How did you manage to be so fortunate?"

"I hardly know myself," was Erich's response.

"Well, we must celebrate together. How long can you stay at Langenhof?"

"Not too long, I fear, but we will speak of that later."

They were shown to an enormous apartment hung with tapestries at the center of which stood a bed canopied with blue satin. On the floor was a huge oriental. The floor to ceiling windows which were draped in matching satin, overlooked the immense park and lake. In the distance stood the woods like a backdrop. The servant who had brought their luggage went into the bathroom and drew a bath. He told them that dinner would be served at eight o'clock, but that the Count would meet them in the library for drinks whenever it was convenient. He bowed stiffly, for he was no longer young, and left.

"I want to have some time with Anton alone," Erich told her. "I need to be sure of his political allegiances before asking for his help. So I will go down to the library ahead of you. Give me forty-five minutes. That should be enough." She nodded but did not smile. A tight band of fear encircled her chest.

When Madeleine entered the library, both men were laughing heartily at some shared experience and she felt like an intruder. But at the sight of her they both leapt to their feet and made her welcome. She took the sherry that was brought to her and leant back into the cushions of the overstuffed armchair. She surveyed the beautiful room about her. An intricate molded ceiling with gold and blue detailing fanned out above her head. So many shelves of books some, it was obvious, of great age. The muted, soft colors of their exteriors gave the room a warm and companionable atmosphere, as though the spirit of all who had leafed through their pages still lingered there.

Madeleine had not being paying attention to the conversation until now when she caught the word "unorthodox," at which point their was a pause in the conversation and she found both men looking at her.

"I was telling Anton that your situation is somewhat unorthodox and that we have to take steps to protect you from getting into trouble with the wrong people."

"How unorthodox would that be?" Anton asked with a smile.

There was a long pause before Madeleine finally found the courage to say, "I am English."

"Engländerin!" exclaimed Anton in astonishment, his eyebrows shooting up.

The band of steel around Madeleine's chest had tightened and she felt as though she could not breathe. Anton was staring at her. She felt nauseous. She took a large swallow from her glass and felt her hand shake as she raised it to her lips. She did not want to believe that Erich's old friend would betray their friendship by informing the authorities about her, but these were strange and desperate times.

"You are in a very dangerous situation, however good your papers are," commented Anton. "We live very near to the border with Switzerland here and so far we have not been subjected to any searches, but I do anticipate that happening. We can hide you, if necessary, but not indefinitely."

The band of steel felt a little less restrictive, but Madeleine could not be sure that Anton was not just playing for time.

"I was hoping that some way could be found to get Madeleine over the border into Switzerland," Erich said very quietly.

There was a silence as the words hung on the air and the two men looked thoughtfully at one another. Another ripple of fear ran through Madeleine. Could Erich trust Anton, she wondered.

At last, Anton broke the silence. "I think that it can be done, but it will need a lot of thought. Let us now go to dinner and speak of other things." He got to his feet and crossed the room to a bell-pull which he rang.

It had been an elegant meal served by white gloved servants. The candlelight had reflected off the crystal chandeliers that hung unlit above the table while the paneled walls that surrounded them glowed softly. It was a huge and lofty room, but Madeleine felt they were sitting in a small cave, for the shadows held back the true dimension of the spacious interior.

The two men did most of the talking and reminisced about their youth. It was light-hearted enough, but Madeleine felt a great weight on her shoulders, a great fear in her heart. Fear for the future, her future, but mostly a fear at the prospect that whatever happened, she would soon be separated from Erich. She could think of nothing else, but the pain of not being with him, not being held by him. She could not imagine how she could escape from here. It was a truly insurmountable problem.

As she lay in Erich's arms, back in their room, surrounded by the blue satin curtains of their huge mahogany bed, she expressed her fears.

"Erich, how do you know that you can trust Anton? You have not seen each other in several years. These are strange times, how can you know what he truly feels about the war, about the future and about housing someone who at best is from the other side, at worst is an enemy agent?" It took courage to say that, but it gave Erich comfort that she was able to say it. There were certain aspects of Madeleine's behavior which did not add up.

"Anton has not changed," Erich assured her. "He has never been someone very interested in politics. He has always been a free spirit, an adventurer. Now, he has become a little more serious. His family has connections with an old aristocratic line in Poland. When Poland was invaded, it killed a measure of his patriotism. He is the heir to a great estate which he does not want to see become part of the spoils of war."

"Or to risk losing because he is harboring the enemy"

"Have faith in my friend, dearest, I think he will not disappoint us."

She finally slept, but in her dreams she was being chased by a dark, threatening, faceless shadow which slowly came closer and closer.

They had been staying at Langenhof for two days. Both men had spent the afternoons out shooting together in the woods. It had been invigorating weather and Erich had come indoors with a warm glow in his cheeks that Madeleine had never seen before. It made him look vibrant and more attractive than ever.

Nothing had been said about the possibility of getting Madeleine out of Germany, which made Madeleine intensely uneasy, but Erich reassured her that a great deal of thought was required to work out the details of such a plan.

They were sitting on the terrace overlooking a beautiful vista of descending pools and waterfalls which stretched before them ending in the green expanse of a meadow. It was a very soothing, tranquil sight. They were having tea. Madeleine was the designated hostess and had filled their cups and was offering Anton a selection of cakes from a filagree porcelain dish that had to be something a museum would covet.

He smiled at her as he selected a small Napoleon. "I think that I might have found a solution to your travel plans."

Her heart constricted as she held her breath.

"We have a twin-engine plane which we used to fly on a regular basis for both business and pleasure, but I discarded the idea of using it, because even if it were possible to fly it across the lake into Switzerland unobserved, it would be much more difficult to return unseen. If I knew that it could have a safe haven until the war was over, I would be willing to part with it, but I have no way of making such an arrangement. There is also the possibility of using a boat, but the lake is patrolled on a regular basis and I think that it would be difficult to avoid capture, except if one were very lucky. My solution is that we use a hot air balloon."

Erich and Madeleine stared at him in astonishment and Anton roared with laughter at their surprise.

"The advantage of a hot air balloon is that it is virtually silent. Once high enough, it might never be observed. The disadvantage is that it is very difficult to predict exactly where it would land. One is at the mercy of erratic winds."

"Do you have a balloon, Anton? And who would navigate it?"

"My brother, Fritz, and I used to do a lot of ballooning. We actually own two. They are different sizes. That is not a problem. The difficulty is finding someone who would have the knowledge to undertake such a journey and who would not be opposed to remaining in Switzerland. I do not think it would be possible to make the return journey."

They were all silent while they digested this suggestion. Madeleine had never flown in a balloon. The concept did not frighten her nearly as much as the possibility of never seeing Erich again.

"Well, my dear Anton, I should have known that you would come up with some daredevil plan. I would not be worried at all if I knew that you were the navigator, but my peace of mind will depend on whom we can find to act as pilot, if that is in fact possible."

Anton smiled. "All things are possible."

They were interrupted at this point by a servant who approached Anton and whispered something in his ear. Anton frowned, gave some reply, whereupon the servant disappeared through a door nearby.

"We have visitors, I am afraid. The authorities have come on official business, whatever that means. Why don't you both leave me here to take care of things?"

"Certainly not" responded Erich. "I think that you, Madeleine my love, should leave, but I will remain here with you, my friend." Anton nodded, satisfied. "Madeleine, if you will take the door at the end of the terrace, it will bring you into a salon which leads to a staircase in that wing. If you go up it you will hopefully find your apartment. I am afraid there is not time to give you better directions. Go now, quickly.

She ran lightly down the terrace and entered through the door he had indicated.

Madeleine had not been gone more than a few minutes, when two officials were ushered onto the terrace. They clicked their heels and saluted and Erich and Anton rose to their feet and responded.

The Mayor of Ludwigsburg was a man of large dimensions who took his position seriously. When the army asked him to provide a list of all the large buildings in his jurisdiction, he unquestioningly set to work. His diligence was rewarded by the promise of special favors. It came as a shock to him when he discovered that the army proposed requisitioning the listed buildings. It became his uncomfortable task to visit the various property owners in question and inform them of the army's proposed intentions. He was accompanied by an army lieutenant whose main purpose was to give credence and support to the mayor's role.

Franz Kiesel could not have been more uncomfortable in his present surroundings. He had never been inside Schloss Langenhof and he found it more imposing than his most vivid fantasies. It had been his hope that as one of the more important officials of the community he would be invited as a guest at the Schloss. He knew his present task would leave that hope in shreds. With Lieutenant Hellmann at his side, he could not disclaim responsibility. His discomfort and nervousness was causing him to perspire profusely. He wiped his face with his large handkerchief before launching into his speech.

Anton and Erich had observed the Mayor's embarrassment and were somewhat comforted by it.

"My apologies, Count Casimir, for interrupting you on such a beautiful day," began the Mayor. "You have such a beautiful view from this terrace. It is enviable..." he stopped short, confused and dismayed at his choice of words.

Lieutenant Hellman cleared his throat and Herr Kiesel stumbled on.

"I have been designated in the name of the Führer to inform his patriotic citizens that the army has a need, might have a need, at some unknown point in time for additional housing for its soldiers. That any property owner who has additional residential space available will be asked to give it to the army, temporarily of course. This will be considered his patriotic duty for which he will be handsomely recompensed. Your most spacious residence has been listed as a probable," at this point, the Mayor stuttered, "possible, possible property to be requisitioned."

Anton was on his feet, his face inflamed with anger.

"Have you any idea what you are saying? You would intend allowing an army of peasants to roam this property? It would take an army to repair the damage they would inflict. Is the Führer prepared to finance such a project? Has he not more important things to do?"

Lieutenant Hellmann cleared his throat. "The army understands that this could be a considerable sacrifice on the part of property owners and plans are being made to recompense all those concerned. I have a paper here to that effect, the details of which will be supplied later." The Lieutenant proffered a paper but Anton ignored it.

"I think you had better leave," he said in a voice that suggested, another word and he would not be responsible for his actions.

The servant who had announced them appeared as if on cue and ushered the Mayor and the Lieutenant from the terrace.

Anton was pacing up and down the terrace. He was speechless with fury and Erich knew better than to open his mouth.

Instead he helped himself to another cake and dwelt mournfully on the loss of peace and tranquility in all of their lives.

"How can we protect ourselves from such bureaucrats, they will destroy us all?" Anton had ceased to pace and had flung himself into a chair next to Erich.

"I doubt if we can. We can only join them, possibly."

Anton snorted. "If you mean that we should pander to them, I would rather see myself in hell first."

You may well, my dear friend, thought Erich, but he remained silent. Instead he offered the plate of cakes to Anton, who took one and ate it in one mouthful and leant over and helped himself to another.

"Try to put this visit out of your mind. The war might be over before we know it. Anyway, you are not likely to be in the center of activity here. It is possible that the Führer will forget all about Langenhof.

Anton looked at Erich thoughtfully and a smile slowly crept over his face and he relaxed visibly. "You are right, of course. I will try and forget about it. Let us go inside. I have things to do. Can you amuse yourself until dinner time?"

"I don't think that will be difficult" was the response and Anton grinned and said. "You lucky devil. I wish that there were such a beautiful woman in my life."

"I have never known you to be short of beautiful women. You must not let yourself be depressed by the recent visit."

"True, but I suspect that your Madeleine is not only beautiful but special in ways we do not know."

Erich's eyebrows arched in inquiry but he said nothing.

Madeleine had found the staircase leading to the guest wing, but it had taken her some considerable time to find their apartment. The immense size of the Schloss was staggering and she had wandered up and down corridors and into dozens of rooms before finding her way at last to their apartment.

She wondered about Anton. He was an immensely attractive man. Quite a different type from Erich. But she had to wonder about his willingness to risk so much in order to help her escape across the Bodensee to Switzerland. Did friendship extend so far?

Now there was this official visit. What did that mean and how would it affect his attitude to her. Would he feel that she was a liability he could not afford?

She was lying on their bed looking at the beautifully decorated ceiling when Erich came in. She raised her head and he smiled at her and she felt reassured. He came to the bed and threw himself down beside her.

"I thought you might be sleeping."

"No, I was worried about the visitors."

He smiled down at her and told her what had transpired.

"How terribly upsetting for Anton" she said. "This is a museum. I cannot imagine having the army taking over such a place."

"Yes, he was pretty angry, but I think he does not have too much to worry about for the time being."

He leant over and kissed her. "Anton asked me if I could amuse myself until dinner and I said that I thought that I could."

She laughed and playfully poked him in the ribs.

The hours melted away as they lay in each other's arms and Madeleine was able to forget the fact that in a short time she would probably be separated from this overwhelmingly handsome and interesting man forever.

Dinner that night was a more boisterous occasion. Perhaps because they all knew each other better, but it was also due, Madeleine thought, to the fact that both men drank more than they had the previous evening. They were certainly not drunk, but they were more relaxed and they all laughed at the many stories and jokes with which both men enlivened the evening.

At last the meal was ended and they got to their feet. They walked through the adjoining salons with their beautiful pictures and wonderful artifacts until they came to the salon that led out to the terrace. They went outside and watched the moon play hide and seek with the clouds.

"The wind would be right for the trip tonight," said Anton. "It would not take long to cross the lake. However, the visibility would be too good. I would rather have a cloudier night." He turned suddenly to Madeleine and said to her. "I want you to be ready to leave at any time so have your things packed. I do not anticipate it being possible for another day or so but you never know. I am sorry to leave you in this uncertainty, but I shall probably be gone most of tomorrow and the next day."

Madeleine's heart sank and the light-heartedness of the evening evaporated.

The next two days Erich and Madeleine spent walking in the woods. They had to keep active and the Schloss, despite its size, was confining.

That night at dinner, Anton told them that he had completed his plans and now it was just a question of the weather. He did not elaborate and they knew better than to question him in the presence of the servants.

Later he told them that he had found an old gentleman, a member of his original ballooning team, who was originally from the small village of Herbstein in Switzerland. He had lost his wife and had been intending to move back and go and live with his daughter. He was no longer a young man, but he was worried at being separated from his daughter and was prepared to risk the journey.

The following evening found Madeleine sipping sherry in the library as she browsed through an old pictorial magazine on Africa. She was absorbed in pictures of elephants, rhinos, lions and cheetahs. She had visited Africa with her father when she was younger and had fallen under the spell of the bush and the wild animals she had seen. She had never found a more stimulating environment and had loved finding herself in remote wilderness with only the wild animals as company and no human being within hundreds of miles.

She was so preoccupied with the pictures that she jumped when Anton looked over her shoulder and said, "Have you ever been to Africa?"

She nodded. "Yes, it was some years ago, with my father. We were on safari in East Africa for a month. It was a mesmerizing experience. I would love to live there."

"You are full of surprises" he told her. "You look much too fragile for such a primeval environment."

She blushed at his appraising gaze. He sat down in the chair opposite her. "I think that tonight might be the night."

Her heart skipped a jump and she swallowed hard.

"Johann is not young any more, but he has had a lot of experience flying with me. I think that I could not find you a better pilot for the balloon. Anyway, so much is up to the vagaries of the wind currents. I will provide you with as many cylinders of gas as the balloon can carry, so that you can go almost as far as you wish. I hope that you will have a good landing. Then it is up to Johann to hide the balloon. You can perhaps travel together to his daughter's. The only other problem is the question of money. I don't know how you will find your way to England without it."

This was a difficult moment. She did not want to divulge the fact that there was money in an account for her in Switzerland. A provision made in case of an emergency. There was no satisfactory way that she could explain it.

"I am hoping that the British Consulate might make arrangements for me."

His searching gaze made her uncomfortable. She felt he could read her mind.

"We will have to take up a collection for you." She blushed deeply and stood up abruptly.

"I don't think that is necessary. Where do you want me to be and at what time."

"If Erich were not my most respected friend, I think that I would make an assignation with you to meet me in the stables."

Now she was furious, for not only was he laughing at her but she was angry at herself for reacting as she did. She would have liked to remain coolly aloof. But despite her love for Erich, there was the lithe power of a beautiful animal in Anton and he knew that women were irresistibly attracted to him.

He was suddenly serious. "Be ready to leave for the far meadow in four hours. If the weather changes, I will let you know. Most balloon launches are at dawn. A night flight is more challenging."

He bowed slightly, his face serious, and turned away and left the room.

She took a deep breath. It was not welcome news. Another journey into the unknown. She got to her feet and made her way back to their apartment. Erich was sprawled in a comfortable armchair reading, his legs resting on an elegant footstool. He beckoned to her and she bent down and kissed him on the forehead. "I have something for you."

She looked puzzled as he put his hand in his pocket and slowly pulled out her passport. He handed it to her, his face expressionless. She stared at it in amazement. She had not seen it since leaving Waldesrauschen several months ago.

"Where on earth did you conceal it in the car?" she asked, her eyes wide with surprise.

"Where it was safest; next to my heart." He smiled softly at her.

"Erich, be serious. I want to know. I was terrified every time someone came near the car or decided to search it. I could think of no possible place where it could be hidden. I decided that even a secret compartment was something the police would eventually find."

"My darling Madeleine, I could not be more serious. It was next to my heart inside the pocket of my uniform jacket."

Madeleine sat down opposite him, shaking her head in amazement, her eyes wide with disbelief. "But what a risk you took to do such a thing."

"It was not the least bit risky. Who would have the audacity to search me, a wounded naval officer?" He looked slightly affronted at her suggestion.

She burst out laughing. He really had not worried in the least about its discovery, whereas she had been worried to distraction about her passport and her inevitable arrest had it been found. He was a man of immense self-assurance. He smiled, obviously pleased with himself and at her reaction to his audacious act.

She stood up and bent to kiss him. He pulled her down and she sat on his lap and laid her head against his shoulder. "You are absolutely amazing. You do not seem to be afraid of anything or anyone. I truly envy you." Her stroked her hair and buried his face in it.

"I shall always worry about you," he said with great seriousness. She sighed deeply. If only they could slow down time, their parting indefinitely delayed. But she had to change and put the last of her things in her suitcase. Had she remembered everything? Her thoughts were interrupted by a servant who came to announce dinner.

Dinner that night was a much more sober affair. They spoke of the war, the different rumors that were circulating. Both men spoke of their hopes for the future. But Madeleine could not concentrate on the conversation; she was far too occupied with her own thoughts and fears.

They retired to their apartment after dinner and lay on the bed, fully dressed, waiting for the time to leave. Madeleine was infinitely sad and could not be consoled. Erich tried to comfort her as best he could, but it was not possible. They knew that it might be months, perhaps years before they could be in communication again. The future seemed to hold such fragile hope.

At last there was a knock on their door and Erich got up and answered it. It was Anton. The wind was fair. They should hurry.

They left by the terrace, using the back staircase so as to avoid seeing any of the servants.

There seemed to be no wind as they walked along the path that paralleled the descending fountains, but every so often the trees would rustle gently as if a giant hand had brushed them. Anton was leading the way, striding purposefully ahead of them. As they approached the meadow, they became aware of more movement in the woods behind. They were higher here, the meadow more exposed. It was still quite light; the sky a greyish blue.

Madeleine was introduced to Johann and had a sense of strength in his gnarled, old hand. She judged him to be in his late sixties. She had not expected him to be so old, but she was not disconcerted. She could just make out his features and she got a sense of confidence in what she saw.

The three men set to work to lay out the balloon that had been rolled up and lying beside a woven wicker basket. They worked hard and quickly. Air was pumped into the balloon and it slowly began to inflate. The smaller balloon had been chosen, not for its size but for its color. It was a deep, sky blue. The other balloon was in brighter colors.

Finally the balloon floated above its basket, tugging at its ropes. The extra cylinders were loaded aboard, as were Johann's and Madeleine's suitcases.

Erich kissed Madeleine's hand and stepped away quickly to man one of the guy ropes. They had said their farewells, but the abrupt separation was wrenching.

Johann was in the basket and Anton was giving him last minute instructions. He turned to Madeleine. "Now it is time to leave. I have made a small contribution to your treasury. I hope that it will be enough." He was perfectly serious. He took her hand and kissed it. "I wish you luck."

She was terribly indebted to him and wondered how she could thank him.

"I can never ever thank you for what you have done for me." she said with great sincerity

"Hopefully we will meet again and you can thank me in the manner that I am accustomed." He bent forward and picked her up in his arms. He stood a moment, looking at her, holding her tightly to him. She could just make out his wicked grin.

"You are incorrigible,"she responded.

"I know" he said in her ear and with that thrust her upward so that her legs were over the side of the basket and she was being pulled into it by Johann.

Johann was playing with the burner. Madeleine was straining to see Erich, but she could only dimly see his outline. Tears poured down her cheeks.

They were suddenly floating at the level of the treetops. She had no sense of motion or movement. It was the strangest experience to be moving upward and yet have no vibration, no sense of having been separated from the earth, only a feeling of weightlessness. They were rising quickly, she could see the outline of the Schloss dimly below her as they floated over it. They seemed to be gathering speed for the Schloss was now well behind them and ahead was the dim glint of water.

It was a warm, cloudy night, with no sign of a moon. The clouds above them seemed to be scudding at a greater speed than their balloon at a lower elevation. Now they were out over the lake and she caught her breath. It seemed darker now. There was no turning back. It seemed the final separation. She was too fascinated by this new experience to be fearful of the possibility of discovery. As heavy-hearted as she felt, it was exhilarating to be suspended between heaven and earth in a silence unlike any she had ever known. Only the occasional ignition of the burner above their heads reminded her that she was standing in an airborne craft. They traveled without conversing. Johann was constantly checking the balloon above them and making observations of their course.

It seemed scarcely any time at all before they were over land once more and speeding towards the black outline of the mountains in the distance. It had been decided that they would travel as far as their cylinders permitted, provided the wind was not pushing them off course. It was going to be difficult to make out where they were, for it was going to be a dark night. However, Johann had told Anton that he thought he could steer by the outline of the mountains.

They had been traveling for about an hour and it was time to change cylinders. The terrain below them was changing and they needed to fly higher. There was a lot of weight in the balloon and Johann knew that it would be difficult to reach the elevation they needed without off-loading some weight. Luckily they could drop off the empty cylinder. It would mean losing some altitude so as not to off-load the cylinder in a populated area. It proved to be a difficult manoeuver because of the trees and buildings, but they accomplished it finally and immediately noticed a response in the balloon.

They crossed a body of water and then another. At one point, Johann grunted in satisfaction and Madeleine assumed that he had somehow found a landmark and recognized their location. He finally spoke and told her that they were beginning to move off course, but that he was expecting the wind to blow them back in the direction they wanted to travel.

Another hour had passed and another cylinder had been dropped over the side. They had tried a different altitude and found a current that blew them in a more southerly direction. Johann seemed relaxed and satisfied. There were moments when the moon peeped from behind the clouds and Johann was able to make some better observations.

They had been traveling for nearly four hours and would soon be out of fuel, but they were close to their destination and must make preparations to find a good landing place. Their altitude made the terrain below deceptively flat. What looked a smooth place could be quite hilly or rocky.

They were flying very low now, a few hundred feet above the ground and descending. The wind at this altitude was freakish, one moment strong, another no wind at all. Johann had told Madeleine that he was looking for a pasture.

They came over a slight rise and found the ground beneath falling away from them. In the distance a river.

"This must be the place, we do not want to be on the other side of the river."

Johann allowed the basket to travel about 50 feet above the ground. The field below looked smooth and was beginning to flatten out. Now they were only a few feet above ground and Johann told Madeleine to sit down and grasp her knees in preparation for landing. They hit the ground with a big bump and then another and another and then they were being dragged along the ground until they came to a stop. They were down, safe and sound, and with no broken bones.

They crawled out of the basket and got to their feet, stretching stiff legs and body. They ran ahead to the still inflated balloon and began to flatten it so that it no longer rippled in the breeze. They rolled it up as best they could and surveyed their surroundings. There were some bushes about a couple of hundred yards from them. It would be a less conspicuous place to leave their balloon if they could manage to drag it there. They disengaged the basket from the balloon and dragged the two parts separately and left them sitting in a small clump of bushes.

They gathered their personal possessions and looked around them. Johann said they would make good time if they could find someway to travel by river. He told her to wait for him by the river bank. He left his possessions with her. She made several trips to the river's edge, found herself a rock and sat down to wait.

Two hours had gone by and she was beginning to get worried that she was not going to see Johann again, when she heard the splash of oars and a small boat came into sight. It was Johann.

He said that he had "borrowed" the boat and would make sure that it was returned. She climbed in, after stowing their possessions, and he turned about and they began to make their way downstream. The current was with them and they made good headway.

They had been traveling for about an hour when they saw in the dark the outline of a bridge. Johann grunted and drew the boat into shore. They found a place to tie up and stepped ashore. He told her that from this point they were about five miles on foot from his daughter's house. It would begin to be light in about half-an-hour.

They started to walk. It proved to be far the most tedious stage of their journey. They did not have a lot to carry, but their possessions were awkward as much as heavy and they were now getting tired after a sleepless night. They left the road after about an hour and the rest of their journey was on a cart track which was rough and uneven.

It was broad daylight by the time they stopped in front of a small cottage on a hillside. It had a small fence around it. Smoke was coming from one of the chimneys. They opened the gate and walked up the path. Madeleine put down her suitcase as Johann walked up to the door and knocked. It was several minutes before it was opened. A young woman, a long apron around her waist, stood there, her cheeks burnt a glowing honey color from the fresh mountain air.

She stared in disbelief and amazement at Johann. Then burst into happy laughter and ran into his arms and embraced him. They were ushered into a cozy kitchen and sat at a scrubbed pine table. They were not hungry as they had eaten well on their journey, but they were thirsty. They were served hot chocolate and fresh rolls. Johann and his daughter chatted animatedly while Madeleine sat quietly. All she really longed to do now was sleep. She was both tired and drained. It was a small house with only two bedrooms. It was decided that she would be more comfortable and less disturbed if she slept in one of the barns. So she found herself lying on the fresh, sweet-smelling hay covered with two woollen blankets. She heard briefly the twittering of the birds under the eaves and the scratching of the hens in the yard before she drifted into oblivion.

— 13 —

She awoke to find the sunlight creating patterns on the ceiling of her bedroom just above her head. How cozy and friendly was this room compared to those special, elegant places she had occupied all those years ago. That had been another world, another era. Imposing and beautiful. But this was her home and she felt safe in it.

Birdsong seemed to surround her. She could see the sky was blue and clear. A perfect English morning. She dressed and went downstairs. The table had been laid for her. Madeleine sat down and sipped the tea she had made for herself. She looked out into the garden, unseeing. It seemed she had lived many lifetimes since then.

It was very much like that first morning, over three years ago in 1941, when she had awoken in her own bed after her escape from Germany. She had gone downstairs in her old, soft robe and let her mother fuss over preparing breakfast. Her mother had smiled at the sight of her, trying to control the emotion she felt at having her beloved daughter safely home once more. She remembered that her mother had left for the Institute once the breakfast had been served, with instructions to take any telephone messages. She knew that her mother had deliberately forced herself out of the house, not only to disguise the overwhelming emotion she felt, but so as to allow Madeleine the time for private reflection. Her daughter had been very grateful. She needed time to adjust and accept all that had happened to her.

She could not believe that she had made the journey safely from Germany to England. The odds against escape had been great, but she had been lucky and Erich's friends unbelievably loyal to him.

The journey from Switzerland to England, had been tedious but not particularly difficult. She had traveled via Portugal but there had not really been any complications. Once she had reached Bern and the Bank there, it was a matter of waiting for a seat on a plane. She had been very touched that Anton had slipped a solid gold cigarette case into her bag. It was his contribution towards her travel expenses in the absence of any useable currency.

Her parents had met her at the airport. Seeing them again had been an emotional moment. It had taken her two days before she could bring herself to tell them about Erich, about their marriage, that she truly loved him. She was not sure that they understood. She was pretty sure that they did not approve, although nothing was said. They were far too happy to have her safely home.

Left alone on that morning so many years ago, she could still see Erich on that last evening. He had been a dim shape as the balloon had risen aloft over the fountains and park at Schloss Langenhof. But she could not bear to remember Erich that way. Instead, she had relived their last night together at dinner. His deep blue eyes had rested on her with great longing and sadness. She had tried to eat her dinner, but her throat was constricted with sadness and emotion. He had smiled at her across the dinner table. She had struggled not to weep and had smiled weakly back.

After a period of adjustment at being safely back in England, Madeleine had joined the Wrens. It was good to have a focus, to be able to help the war effort and, most important of all, to be busy. At first, she did not get leave very often, but she was assured that once her training period was over, she would get a regular assignment and with it a regular schedule, although she soon learned that a regular schedule in wartime England was anything but regular. Her parents had been ambivalent about her new career. They were proud that she should be as motivated as she was, but felt both fearful and deprived to be separated yet again from her. However, they realized that her new career provided her with a much-needed occupation. The fact that Madeleine was a member of the armed forces would help minimize any particular curiosity in her. Nowadays, people's lives were very much disrupted and erratic. At some point, it would help explain her marriage to someone now "missing in action." Madeleine's mother shrank from dwelling on this fact of life. She was aware of the pain her daughter was suffering from this impetuous romance. But with no solution in sight, it was possible to push it to the back of her mind. And because the war had escalated and months had become years, it became easier and easier to forget.

Madeleine made herself some toast. Somehow, the act of getting up and moving about the kitchen had broken her reveries of the past and brought her into the present.

There had been a lull in the bombing and Madeleine decided that this would be as good an opportunity as she might have to go to London for a few days. She had a few day's leave. Her parents were in Scotland taking a short holiday. The house was rather quiet. She had been traveling down to Plymouth to her present assignment and had been returning home at week-ends, when possible, for the last three months.

London had changed since her last visit so many months ago. The sandbagged entrances to buildings and bomb-shelters alike, which had been such a shock at first, looked even more dilapidated and time-worn, though such changes had been depicted over and over in the newspapers and newsreels. It was hard to accept what had happened to London. Luckily she had not had to be in London during the Blitz although her father had traveled there every day and had remained there many nights taking his turn voluntarily on fire-watching duty. On other occasions he had helped man a battery of guns, despite his age. He had been in the artillery during the First World War. He realized the fear and strain this put on his family, but he felt compelled to do his share for the war effort. So many had given their lives already. The London blitz had left that great city a shambles of bombed-out buildings. For a year the sky had glowed red from the buildings that continued to burn after the nightly bombing raids. Would this madness ever end?

The scars of the bombing, however, were not too evident in Kensington and for that she was grateful. Their former residence had been demolished early in the War, during her absence. Luckily her parents had not been there. Sadly, some of the other residents had. She walked from the tube station and felt immediately comforted at the sight of the classic square with its elegant facades and private gardens where they now resided when they came to London. She had felt instantly at home in her parent's new flat the first time she saw it.

The pillared portico entrance to their period house seemed unchanged and she was warmly welcomed by Mr. Johnson, the caretaker. He was a Lancashireman, solid and reliable with a sense of humor as keen as any cockney's.

The southern exposure of their flat gave it a bright and cheerful feeling even on a dull day. She loved the high, elaborately sculptured ceilings. It was not a big place, but it was spacious and elegantly decorated with a collection of well-worn and much loved pieces, some of which she suspected were of great value. She had never consciously made a study of period furniture, but instinctively recognized the good pieces when she saw them.

She carried her small suitcase to her bedroom and hung up the few clothes she had brought with her. She kicked off her shoes and walked to the kitchen and put on a kettle for tea. She sat at the old, scrubbed pine table and drank her tea thoughtfully. After she had finished her tea and washed up her cup and saucer, she picked up the telephone and rang several of her friends. After several conversations, she had managed to fill the next few days with social engagements.

Before changing out of her uniform to go out, she decided that she had better go downstairs to the basement and check the condition of their simple bomb-shelter to which her father had given some considerable thought and attention. The caretaker lived in the basement in a spacious and comfortable flat. There was also a rabbit warren of storage rooms belonging to the various residents in the house. Madeleine unlocked the padlock on the door, swung it open and turned on the light. She was surprised at the spaciousness of the room she had remembered as a dark, unattractive cubicle. The walls were painted cream, two narrow bunk beds sat on each side with a small, narrow table separating them. Some new shelves had been installed and they were filled with boxes of tinned food and other necessities. One could have a sense of security in this room she thought. It was nevertheless a very claustrophobic space. She pushed aside all other thoughts and locked the door.

She enjoyed a simple dinner her first night at her friend's house. They had not seen each other in many years. There was much to learn about mutual friends and it was possible for Madeleine to avoid any excuses she might have to manufacture about the time she had spent in Germany.

She slept well that night. She was relieved that it had been a quiet night, although wet and windy. Perhaps the Germans had been deterred by the weather or perhaps some coastal, naval shipyard had been the target instead.

This evening she was invited to a dinner party. Her hostess said that it would be a mixed group, various couples whom they both knew and then a sprinkling of friends of her husband's from the armed forces. She welcomed the distraction. Her thoughts dwelt far too often on Erich, on his safety and on how much she missed him.

The party was an entertaining interlude. Madeleine received a lot of attention as an unaccompanied woman. She was always surprised at this because it was unexpected. She had forgotten what a sense of urgency the uncertainties of a war-time existence had instilled in everyone. The mood seemed almost frenetic, from drinking to dancing to conversation itself. She finally excused herself for she suddenly felt tired and made as an inconspicuous exit as she could manage. It was not easy for there were two young army officers vying for her attention. It was a clear night and the stars showed brightly between the scudding clouds and the many barrage balloons littering the sky.

As she closed the flat door behind her, the air-raid siren sounded. Her heart skipped a beat, as it always did. She took a deep breath. She stood still and listened, but as yet could not hear the throb of engines. She hurried about the flat, gathering some personal belongings together, pulling closed the black-out curtains as search-lights swept across the sky. She had set everything she needed on the kitchen table and was walking down the corridor from her bedroom when she heard the first sinister throb of German aircraft engines. It was such a distinctive sound, different from those of British planes. In any other circumstances, she thought, it would not sound sinister, but now London waited and wondered if they would survive another night of bombing.

She closed the flat door behind her and walked down to the basement of the house. She could hear voices down one of the corridors, but chose not to go and see which of the other residents it was. She set her belongings on one of the beds in their basement shelter and then sat herself on the one opposite. She felt very alone. She must have been sitting there ten minutes when she became aware of the distant hollow reverberation of guns, which grew louder as the wave of bombers grew nearer. Then came the crump-crump of bombs falling and as they grew nearer, she was conscious of the earth responding with increasing shudders. She felt very afraid. She hoped that she was not going to die that night, alone in a small basement room. It was a fear one never could overcome although, as it became a part of everyday existence, she found she dwelt on it less. It was a fact of wartime life. All the images of bomb victims she had seen in newspapers and newsreels rose before her. She knew that she was safe enough unless the building sustained a direct hit, but the thought of being buried alive held all the horrors of the worst nightmare.

Suddenly a very loud explosion rocked the earth beneath her feet and the lights went out. She sat gripping the edge of the bed, waiting, a feeling of suffocation enveloping her. She thought of her parents, her friends and all that was dear and precious to her. Most of all she wondered about Erich. It was a never-ending cycle of hope and despair. The next bomb did not seem to be as near, nor the next. She relaxed a little, but felt instantly guilty that she should be relieved, when surely so many others were lying injured.

She heard a voice call out, echoing down the corridor outside the door. She got up and groped towards it and opened it.

"Hello," she responded.

"Ah! is that you, Miss Devaux?" A flickering candle outlined the features of Johnson, the caretaker. "I wanted to be sure that no one was left stranded in the dark." She could feel his smile, rather than see it and felt instantly comforted.

"How kind of you" she replied. "We do have candles somewhere, but it would have taken me a long time to find them in the dark."

"You are there all alone, are you?" he enquired.

"Yes, yes. Just for a couple of nights."

"Well, Miss, if you would care to join Mrs. Johnson and myself, we would be happy for your company. Jerry got a little close tonight."

She did not hesitate. "How kind. That would be lovely."

There were two waves of bombers and the raid lasted what seemed like half the night. But there was no way Madeleine could have slept and she welcomed the cheerful company of the Johnsons. They brought her up-to-date on all the residents in the house, on the activities of other residents in the square known to them all and on the neighborhood tradespeople. It passed the time and Madeleine found herself relaxing despite the constant threat above her head.

"How I wish that I could make a real contribution to the war effort," sighed Mr. Johnson. "Much of the time I feel that I am useless, that I could be doing something much more worthwhile towards the war effort."

"But, Mr. Johnson, you do your share of fire-watching duty. Think how invaluable that is to the survival of London and the lives of people."

"Yes, yes, I know, but I want to be able to hit back. I am too old to be more active. I have always had a hankering to raise carrier pigeons."

Madeleine laughed. "Surely London has enough pigeons soiling our buildings and monuments." Mrs. Johnson nodded in agreement.

"But my pigeons would be a different breed. They would be trained to return home, carrying messages between two destinations. Life-saving information for those hiding undercover and for our secret service who are doing their best to combat the enemy. You may not know it, but pigeons can fly at remarkable speeds, at least 60 mph for long periods, covering hundreds of miles in a day without ever stopping to take food or water. They are truly unique. It is something that soldiers cannot do in challenging situations when other forms of communications are interrupted."

"I can understand how exciting and important that could be."

"Where would you keep them?"

"The most convenient place would be the roof of this building."

Madeleine and Mrs. Johnson giggled. "Would that not be rather unpopular with the residents?" commented Madeleine.

Mr. Johnson nodded. "It would probably not be allowed and anyway I would have to have special clearance and training for such an occupation and I am sure the War Office would have their own ideas, but I still would love to give it a try." He smiled nostalgically.

"Well, I do wish you well, whatever you decide to do about it." Madeleine smiled.

At last the All Clear sounded. The tension that had built up in Madeleine suddenly fell away and she took a deep breath of relief. She did not realize how taut with apprehension she had been. She thanked the Johnsons for their thoughtfulness and made her way back up to her flat. She went straight to bed and fell into an exhausted sleep.

She awoke late the next morning. She was due back on duty the following day, which meant she could return home first.

Her parents were returning from Scotland and the plan had been to pick them up at the station at home. She wondered now whether she should wait and meet them at the train in London, but finally dismissed the idea. Trains no longer ran on time anymore. It would be good to get home and take a rest before going to meet them. If they were late they would surely ring the house. She also remembered her father saying that he was planning to drop off and pick up papers from his office before catching their train from Waterloo.

Brigadier General William Devaux and his wife, Claudia, emerged from the station with their porter and a trolley of luggage. It was a small holiday crowd, with a few mothers with little children, balls and toys, the odd balloon. So many of the older children had been evacuated. The larger percentage of travelers were from the armed forces. There were people everywhere coming and going in every direction. Trains shunted, whistles blew and the loud speaker announced departures in a tinny voice. It took all the presence he could muster for the General to attract the attention of a porter. They were in short supply. But porters were pleased to be hired by the General. He was obviously a VIP and they anticipated a good tip and were rarely disappointed. In due course, he and his wife were safely installed in a taxi, the luggage, golf clubs and fishing tackle stowed as well as possible.

The run to his office was a relatively short one, depending on traffic. They had plenty of time and the General sat back comfortably in his seat and closed his eyes.

It had been a wonderfully relaxing holiday. Good trout fishing and some invigorating rounds of golf in that marvelously bracing air. Claudia loved to paint and had not minded his absences. They were very compatible and understood and respected each other's needs. For the last several years they had rented a very beautiful stone cottage high on a cliff above a small fishing cove. It was remote and off the beaten path. They both loved the seclusion it afforded them. They had lived much of their lives in the limelight.

They had wished that their beautiful daughter, Madeleine, could have joined them, but she had other plans and in any event did not have any leave due at the present time. Their holiday this year was shorter due to the uncertainties of the times. The General knew that Madeleine wanted to spend a few days in London. The idea made him very nervous but he felt that he could not interfere with her plans when he himself traveled there so regularly. But he had lived a reasonably full life. She was really only just beginning hers.

He had lived in a unique time-frame, a time when the British Empire was, for the most part, in its zenith. He had lived in India when the Raj was at its pinnacle. He had played polo with some of the most illustrious names in the field. His string of ponies were the envy of the regiment. He had proved his manhood hunting tiger. It had to be the perfect shot for he was only allowed one bullet. Some had gone out with bow and arrow and not returned. Those odds were not for him.

He had patrolled on the Northwest Frontier and the Khyber Pass. One dark morning, he had slipped his feet into his boots and been bitten, some thought, by a black mamba. His leg became so black and swollen his pyjama leg had to be slit to the thigh. A runner was sent for a doctor - a four-day journey away. His life hung in the balance. By the time the doctor arrived the swelling was receding. He had been lucky. If medical attention had been instantly available his leg would have been amputated. He had fought alongside the Ghurkas, among the world's most fearless and intrepid warriors. His admiration of them was beyond measure. He had dined with rajahs and princes. It had been a magical world for a single man.

But then he had met Claudia while on leave in England and they had married. The focus of his life had changed. They had traveled the world together, but life had become a bit more sedate. Indeed, another generation would not witness such times again. It might be better, but it would certainly not be the same.

He had been fortunate enough to pursue his love of polo. He had been Captain of the Hurlingham Club for many years. He had recently declared himself ineligible for reelection. He maintained that younger men than he could bring new life to the position. He had in any event taken an advisory post with the War Office. He anticipated spending much more time in London. Anyway he did not like the way things were shaping up in Europe. It looked as though they were in for a long siege.

He counted himself very lucky to have found such a rock as his life's partner. At least his wife would stay at home and serve as an anchor and pillar to the community during these unsettled times, not off doing some frivolous job, like others he knew. She was a marvelous organizer. She had the women at the Institute organized into industrious, hardworking groups, providing food, blankets and other necessities to bomb victims. They knitted squares for blankets and socks for the armed forces. They manned canteens and provided tea for all-comers during the daily air-raids. You could count on her to be an enormous example and comfort to those in need, whatever the circumstances or situation. He smiled quietly to himself.

Claudia noticed her husband's smile, as he sat with his eyes closed in the corner seat of the taxi. She could not guess its source, but thought perhaps he was reliving one of life's pleasurable experiences.

What an extraordinary life her husband had led. As a young man he had spent some years in Africa where he had worked on an uncle's estate in the Aberdares. There had been enormous freedom and a certain amount of adventure. She had heard a lot of tales about those times, but none from his lips. It had been a wonderful place to live. But in his early twenties he had been forced to face the fact that he had to earn a living. He decided to join the army. It was a nomadic life and suited his nature.

Thus when the first World War broke out, he was one of the first officers to be shipped to France. He served his country valiantly. It was the grimmest of battles, waged under conditions of extreme deprivation and hardship. There were long periods when he and his men were up to their waists in freezing mud and water. At times, severely short of food and drinking water, they fought on despite hunger and exhaustion. The casualties were staggering with many dying for lack of accessible field hospitals as much as from the severity of their wounds. William had suffered the nightmare of mustard gas poisoning - his gasmask blown from his face. He was left blind for weeks. He lost the lining of his throat and lungs. Each breath was an agony. But he recovered enough to return to combat, where he distinguished himself at the Battle of the Somme and was subsequently awarded the Victoria Cross.

Claudia had been born and raised in Dorset where her father occupied most of his time supervising a large and beautiful estate. As the only daughter in a family of four sons she was indulged. She had received a good education, but she was not expected to make a career. So when she announced that she planned to marry William Devaux, ten years her senior, no one objected, despite her young age. He was after all from a good family and had a promising career ahead of him.

They had met and married after the War was over. Madeleine had been born in England. It had been considered more sensible for Claudia to have her baby in England and later make the long journey to Bombay when mother and child were strong enough. Once in India, their life proved to be one of considerable comfort. They always moved up into the hills to Simla during the monsoon season. Contrary to expectations, it had been a fairytale place to raise their daughter. They had found a wonderful amah and with a house full of servants, life had been very comfortable.

Claudia had very much enjoyed her short holiday in Scotland. It had been both relaxing and invigorating. She loved to paint and had very little opportunity to do so when at home. She always seemed to be involved in charitable works. She enjoyed her responsibilities in this field, but there were times when her co-workers could be very tiresome and very demanding. They never seemed to be able to do things without her. She smiled. She was probably too good at what she did whether it be to organize a village fair to support the church renovation or to supervise bridge parties to raise money for the local orphanage. Now, of course, all her energies were devoted to the war effort. She sighed. It was time to go home, but the best part would be seeing their beloved daughter again. She could not tell anyone this, but she thought Madeleine, with her blond, curly hair, pale pink complexion and lean, athletic build the most beautiful young woman anywhere. She knew her husband felt the same. For, although William had dearly wanted a son, he had always told Claudia that he would not trade Madeleine for a whole stable of sons. He was absolutely infatuated with her. She was glad. They had never been able to have any more children, the difficult birth had precluded that.

They had been stopped in traffic for some considerable time, but the General had not seemed to notice. Claudia had looked at her watch and was not worried. It was not a long journey and they were still early. They began to move forward slowly and she noticed now that this was not a normal traffic jam. There were too many policemen about. It became evident that the cause of the delay was bomb damage from the previous night's raid. An enormous crater had taken a large bite out of the road and traffic was maneuvering this unaccustomed obstacle. As they edged their way forward, she noticed now that several buildings had lost their facades and rubble lay all about.

They had stopped again. William opened his eyes and became aware of his surroundings.

"Another raid. Did Madeleine say that she was coming up to London?"

Claudia nodded. They were both silent, their minds holding but a single thought.

Madeleine reached home finally, after a series of delays. What a joy it always was to see their beautiful 18th century thatched house in its velvet green hollow of land. Somehow the natural stone of its exterior always looked warm and welcoming even on the greyest of days. She loved the smell of beeswax that always greeted her as she entered the much-loved interior. Mary, the housekeeper, was so faithful in her attention to all her mother's wonderful oak antiques. You could see your reflection in all the waxed surfaces. It was an interesting house, not only for its age, but for its design. It was really only one room wide, for the entrance hall, sitting room, dining-room and kitchen had windows that looked out in both directions. This gave the house a light and airy atmosphere despite the lowness of all the ceilings. Where there were ancient beams, some taller guests had to bend their heads to avoid a collision.

Mary opened the door to her, beaming from ear to ear. Her relief was evident. News of another raid on London was on the morning news. She had fussed over her as though she were visiting royalty. Madeleine felt very pampered and coddled. The fact was that Mary had no children of her own and had been happy to play the role of nanny and great-aunt as was needed. She had missed Madeleine very much during her adventures in Europe and had worried silently about her well-being.

After lunch, Madeleine settled down in a chaise in the garden. She had a book, several magazines and the Sunday Times beside her. It was a beautiful afternoon, with a dry heat and an almost cloudless sky. The bees humming in the rose bed behind her made her feel drowsy. She had enjoyed Mary's lunch - a light quiche, a salad and strawberries. A perfect summer's afternoon and a delicious lunch, but she could not help but feel depressed.

The war news was very pessimistic. It seemed that hostilities were escalating. There were fewer bombing raids now because Hitler was launching first his V-1 and then the V-2 rockets at Britain. There was something infinitely sinister about the manless aircraft better known as Doodlebugs. She remembered standing in the kitchen one morning and hearing the familiar pitch of a doodlebug's engine and seeing it come into her range of vision. Then, not more than a few hundred yards away, its engine had cut off and she knew that before she could finish counting to ten, there would be a most ear-shattering explosion. She had been too mesmerized to move, knowing that she did not have time to save herself, so powerful would be the blast. But as she watched, transfixed, the wind caught a wing and it turned ninety degrees to fall 400 yards further away. She had gripped the edge of the sink to steady herself, she was shaking so violently. She had raced out of the house and run all the way to the bomb site. She could not believe the devastation. The doodlebug had leveled almost a complete street of houses. She stood at a distance and just shook. Fire engines, police and home-guard were already arriving at the scene. A crowd had gathered, held back by the police, and they had stood there watching as the rubble was inspected for both victims and survivors. Amazingly, there had been very few fatalities, as most of the homes had been vacant, the owners having gone to work, shopping or to school.

Her thoughts moved, as they so often did, to Erich. Would she ever see Erich again? So much could happen to both him and his family. The thought brought tears to her eyes. Now she was trapped in a country at war. They were two star-crossed lovers on opposite sides. It was all so senseless. She did not for a minute regret marrying Erich and she could wait forever if need be to see him again. But to be so totally out of touch was unbearable.

She was an adventurous type by nature. She loved to travel. But one had to have a destination or a purpose. She was not one of those people who were content to drift along with the tide. That was no doubt due to the structured, albeit, nomadic life, which her parents had led. In each place, there had been a solid foundation, an established social circle. How difficult it was going to be to re-enter the circle of her friends and have to hide from them all knowledge of Erich. She did not know how she could possibly keep up such a charade. At least while she was serving in the Wrens, she would be free of many explanations. At home, she knew that her friends who knew her well would intuitively know that she was hiding something.

She forced herself back to the present. Her parents would be home soon. She looked forward to seeing them, although she had enjoyed this brief interlude alone, both at the house and in London. She forced herself not to think about the raid. One had to remain functional and it was better not to dwell on the chaos that now filled everyone's lives. In fact, this barrage of suffering and destruction at times numbed the senses.

— 14 —

The telephone rang. Mary came out onto the veranda and announced that Madeleine's parents had arrived safely in London. They had missed their train and would be arriving in Sherbourne an hour later. Madeleine looked at her watch. She had plenty of time. She closed her eyes and inhaled deeply. The perfume from the roses was intoxicating. She felt herself slowly drifting off to sleep.

Madeleine met her parents at Sherbourne station. They embraced her jubilantly, they were so relieved to see her. They looked tanned and rested, the sea air more than the sun having given color to their complexions.

Their arrival at the house was one of noisy confusion. Their beautiful Labrador welcomed everyone with uninhibited joy, racing up and down the driveway and trying to retrieve any article which had been laid down. Finally, to satisfy his need to please, he was given an old cloth golf hat which he accepted with great dignity. It remained in his mouth until they were all settled quietly on the terrace waiting for Mary to serve tea.

General Devaux surveyed his garden with approval.

"George did a good job on the beds this year," he commented with satisfaction.

"George always does a good job on the flowerbeds," responded his wife. "As much as I am grateful to have a garden full of vegetables, I shall never quite resign myself to the loss of the sunken garden and pond, which you had George dig up and replace with a Victory Garden."

"Yes, yes, I know that I cannot compensate you for such a deprivation, my dear. But I do promise you that when the war is over - and one day it will come to an end, although God knows when - we shall build you another sunken garden."

She sighed. "Yes, I know. Thank goodness we kept all those wonderful pieces of sandstone. It was such a pretty place with the lilies on the pond and those wonderful irises and the aubretia dripping over the walls. I do realize that we could not dig up the lawn and have the vegetables right outside the window and that we could not cut down the trees in the fruit orchard, but how I do miss it." She sighed. Claudia always complained about the loss of her sunken garden when she was depressed. She was depressed now because she knew she had to pick up the threads after her holiday and start coping with the everyday frustrations of running the house in wartime, with its shortages of food and the long hours spent queuing for it, and the eternal waiting for simple services because all the tradesmen were now short-handed with so many away at the war. The daily stresses of worrying about the safety of loved ones. She knew that she was being ungrateful. They were altogether at this moment in time, but nothing lasted and Madeleine would soon be leaving. That really was the source of her depression. She looked at her daughter and saw her smiling.

"You know, mother, the garden has never looked lovelier." It was true.

The garden was an absolute picture. Tall and elegant purple and blue delphiniums contrasted with a waterfall of orange lilies and masses of white daisies. There were pink and red geraniums in pots mixed with rich blue lobelia. Purple and lavender aubretia had bloomed earlier. Climbing roses covered one facade of the house. To one side was a separate rose garden. The profusion of colors, the hum of bees and the gently scented air were like a balm that overcame the insecurities of the past. They drank it in. Madeleine was to remember it always. It became indelibly printed on her mind and was to sustain her during the months and years to come.

The magic spell was finally broken by the telephone.

It was for the General. He returned with a somber expression. "Very unsettled times," he growled. "We are about to have a visitor. The last person I would expect to visit me at my home, so it means something is up and obviously it must be pretty urgent and important. When he arrives, I will see him in my study. I had better go and see that it looks half-way respectable. By the way, his name is Roberts. Colonel Roberts."

"What a pity to have to interrupt this peaceful interlude," his wife sighed. "Still, dear, I know you love to be involved."

He gave her a sharp look to see if she was teasing him. She was not.

Colonel Roberts arrived within the hour. He had flown down to a nearby airfield from where he had been driven over to the Devaux's residence. Claudia ushered him into the General's study and there they remained cloistered for several hours.

He left and the General returned to his study.

Claudia was not a particularly curious person, but this visit was unusual and she could not help wondering what part her husband had to play in it. Where she was concerned, her husband was not a particularly secretive person, but she realized that where national security was concerned, even he would not divulge any information which might risk reaching the ears of those not sympathetic to the British war effort. It seemed hard to believe that there could be, indeed were, people of British nationality who espoused Hitler's cause.

The General finally appeared and announced he was going to have a sherry and would anyone like to join him? They gathered in the lovely living room filled with flowers that Mary had picked from the garden to welcome them home.

"You know," began the General, "the war has managed to unite the British in a way that no other event ever could and yet we have squabbling in the ranks. No one really contests Churchill's ability, charisma and instincts, or in fact his incredible intellectual knowledge and strategy. However, amongst just a few men in the lower ranks there is a tremendous power struggle. I don't want to get into the details of Roberts' visit. It is in fact not terribly interesting. However, we have a situation where something has to be done about one such rebel in our ranks and the question is what and how. Roberts knows that I know the fellow in question quite well and wants my advice on how to approach him and talk sense to him. Very difficult, but I think something can be done to smooth things over."

Claudia cluck clucked sympathetically.

They sipped their sherry in silence.

"You know," the General continued, "the most interesting thing that came out of our conversation was a piece of information that has nothing to do with me, although it does fall within the jurisdiction of my department at the War Office. Apparently the French Résistance has been contacted by a man claiming to be British who said he had some vital information and wanted to be brought out of France. They get dozens of these types of messages. They are always suspicious that they are bogus claims by the enemy in an attempt to infiltrate the ranks of the French Résistance. Then, in what seemed to be an unrelated incident, a French agent was shot while escaping from the Germans. Somehow he managed to make it back without being captured. He was found by his own people, but he died without being able to give them any information. By some strange coincidence, they found a Kandahar medallion clasped in his hand. Now, we might never have been informed of this but when they inspected the medal closely, they found it could be opened and inside was a piece of microfilm. The film revealed a British document that our fellows say is authentic. It was also a very secret document that had no place being where it was. I would never have paid any attention, but for the fact that Madeleine wore the Kandahar medallion that I once gave her when she went on those assignments in 1938 and at the beginning of the war. However, this was not hers. It was a good copy but not gold, of course. It rotated open, so there was no conspicuous clasp and it had a slight hollow inside. Madeleine's was a old Persian gold coin fused with a piece of carved jade, not a simulated locket like the one they now have. I do hope you still have yours safely, my dear?"

Madeleine had gone white. It was just one of life's strange coincidences, but she could not help but feel shaken at the memory of that anguished face in the hotel in Ulm. His blond hair dark with perspiration on his forehead, his breath coming in gasps, his face tense with anxiety. There had been a moment of immense relief in his eyes as he had seen the medallion around her neck, before snatching it from her and fleeing down the corridor. It had all happened so fast, but the sound of gunshots still rang in her dreams at times, before she herself had fled down the corridor and into the arms of the nuns, who had surely saved her from a terrifying confrontation.

"Are you feeling unwell?" her mother asked looking at Madeleine.

Madeleine picked up her cup and saucer and sipped her tea, not only to give herself sustenance but to gain time. She had never mentioned the incident in the hotel with the medallion. In fact, there were many things that she had not mentioned. None of it seemed to have any relevance any more and, knowing her mother, she knew that she would have been lectured on all the risks she had taken. But they were all risks that for the most part she could not have avoided.

She took a deep breath. "While I was in the hotel in Ulm, I had a strange encounter. I collided in a corridor with a young man who was obviously being pursued. He saw the medallion around my neck, muttered something, snatched it from me and ran away as fast as he could. It was only minutes later that I heard gunshots. I do not know if he was shot or someone else. I only know that someone had been shot and had escaped. However, I did get the medallion back. He dropped it."

"How perfectly dreadful. I am so relieved that I had no idea that all this was happening to you, darling. I really feared for you, but I truly tried to convince myself that you were not in any danger." Her mother stood up and poured herself another cup of tea and stretched out her hand to take her husband's cup.

Madeleine's father said nothing, but sat looking thoughtfully into his teacup.

"When is your train, darling?" Claudia tried to sound casual. She was upset, but trying to sound matter-of-fact

"I will have to leave in about half an hour. I have packed. I have nothing to do. Perhaps I could take the rest of the sandwiches with me and some fruit cake. I can probably get something to drink on the train."

Her mother got up and took the sandwiches into the kitchen. She was glad for something to do. Departures unnerved her, but she always wanted to appear calm and unruffled.

She kissed her daughter and Madeleine stepped out onto the driveway and got into the car beside her father. They drove to the station in silence, each thinking of the moment of separation. It seemed as though this war was a time of continual separations and all of them painful.

The train came at last. It was only a few minutes late, which meant that there was a quiet night in London. The General embraced his daughter with more affection than usual and stepped back from the carriage door as he slammed it shut. Madeleine placed her case on the rack above her head and sat by the window smiling out at her father. The train jerked slightly and they were moving. They waved to one another and suddenly he was gone. She leant back in her seat and closed her eyes and for a brief moment she was back in that fateful train all those years ago. She took a deep breath and opened her eyes. This was an English train with English passengers. She must let go of the past, but she knew that it had come back to haunt her with the mention of the Kandahar medallion.

It was an uneventful train ride down to Portsmouth. With the blackout regulations, it was not possible to read, but she was feeling tired and so was content to sit with her eyes closed.

Back at the naval base, life took on its accustomed routine. There always seemed more than enough to do. There seemed fewer raids than earlier in the war. The Germans, however, were now having to fight on more than one front. The RAF carried out regular bombing raids across the Channel and not infrequently both crippled bombers and fighter planes limped homeward to crash-land both on and off runways. Miraculously, some of the crews escaped from their burning planes unscathed, but far too often some of the pilots were terribly burned. Many planes ended up ditching in the sea and highly trained and organized sea rescue teams would work around the clock ferrying survivors ashore. When able, the pilots released carrier pigeons to notify the naval stations of their location. It was a method of communication that saved many lives. Madeleine was to wonder often whether Mr. Johnson had been able to fulfil his ambition to rear these valiant animal war heroes. There seemed no end to the death and destruction that filled their everyday lives. Mined ships were another aspect of daily warfare. For some servicemen, a certain desensitization took over. A few went to pieces and had to be hospitalized, suffering from the type of shell-shock that hit men in the field after a particularly horrific military engagement. Some recovered and returned to duty, but most of them were discharged and returned home, never to be quite the same again.

Madeleine was never immune to the trauma that surrounded them, but her exposure was remote. Her duties were mostly of a secretarial nature, much to her disgust. Occasionally she would be asked to ferry a high-ranking officer from one location to another, when personnel were in short supply. This did not happen too often to her, but the chance to get off base was immensely pleasing.

Today was one of those days. She was to drive a naval intelligence officer to London. The train service to the city had been interrupted due to an overnight raid on London. He was immensely attractive in his uniform, dark-eyed and sallow skinned. One had to wonder if his ancestors were not part of the survivors of the Spanish Armada. For the first hour, they drove in comparative silence. But soon traffic became heavier and it began to be more difficult to make good time and Commander Melville was anxious to make his appointment at the Admiralty. They discussed the route and possible shortcuts to avoid bottlenecks. Slowly the conversation became more personal and relaxed.

He was from a naval family and was following in his father's footsteps. He had a sister. She was still living at home. His parents lived in Wimbledon, within walking distance of the All England Lawn Tennis and Croquet Club. He was unmarried. He was afraid that his visit to the Admiralty was going to add extra work to what was already a very busy schedule.

She duly delivered him to the sandbagged entrance of the admiralty building for his appointment, with the understanding that she should await his phone call at her flat. If she heard nothing, he had given her a number to ring and a person's name. He apologized for the vagueness of it all. That was war-time England. He smiled warmly at her and his deep-set eyes showed that he was not immune to her fair, blond looks.

Back in her flat in Kensington, Madeleine was able to pick up the phone and fill her time trying to speak with those friends with whom she had been out of touch. She hung up from an unsuccessful attempt to reach one of her old school friends when the telephone rang. She was surprised. No one knew she was here, not even her parents. It was Commander Melville. His appointment had been canceled due to more urgent business and had been rescheduled for the next morning. Would Madeleine be free to join him for dinner?

Madeleine hesitated. She did not want to remain alone in the flat tonight. Her social life had been very limited and she was tired of having too much time to dwell on the uncertainties of war. She accepted and it was arranged that he should pick her up at seven-thirty.

It was a very pleasant evening. They dined at his Club. The warm, paneled bar had set the mood and Madeleine felt cosseted. They ate simply, but well and she wondered how the rules about ration cards were handled in such circumstances. From the club they moved on to a smoke-filled nightclub. There, the noise level grew as the evening lengthened. An air-raid siren went off, but no one made a move to leave. Madeleine had not really spent many nights in London. She realized that by long exposure to the nightly bombing a fatalistic attitude had been reached. If the bombers and their bombs seemed to be closing in then people would move to the bowels of the earth, but otherwise they were not going to move unless the enemy was right overhead.

The crump, crump of exploding bombs could be heard above the din. It seemed to be getting closer. Suddenly, the earth heaved under them and people dived under tables or knelt hugging their heads with their hands. Madeleine and the Commander dived under their table and he cradled her against him as they held their breath. Minutes passed and nothing more happened. People began to get up from the floor and conversation was renewed.

"That was a little close," he said to her.

"Yes and thank you."

"For being protective? It was an unexpected pleasure," He smiled wickedly and she blushed profusely. "And my name is Ian. I think it would be difficult to remain formal after such a heart-stopping moment." She could not tell whether he was being serious or just provocative.

The evening became more raucous after the All-Clear, a release of tension, another night survived.

He dropped her off at her flat and saw her safely in the door. He would telephone her after his meeting and then hopefully they could drive back to the base.

She awoke the next morning, feeling sluggish. She had not drunk much the night before, but the cigarette smoke always seemed to give her a headache. Her clothes reeked of it.

It was just before lunch that she heard from the Commander. He was to lunch at the Admiralty. Could she please pick him up at three o'clock.

Their journey back to Portsmouth was uneventful. He had been annoyed to be detained so long in London. One seemed to spend so much time sitting and waiting to see people. Appointments were rarely on time. There were so many unanticipated events and one had to patiently await one's turn.

As they approached the base, he asked her if she would dine with him at the week-end.

"I have to tell you that I am married." He was silent. She went on. "He is missing in action. It has been several years."

"I am sorry," was his response. "So you do not know if he is dead or a prisoner of war." It was a statement rather than a question. She shook her head.

"I would still enjoy having your company at dinner. I promise to return you home to your nanny safe and sound."

She knew he was teasing her, but at the same time she knew he meant it. It was for her to set the pattern of the relationship.

She was looking forward to her dinner with Ian. She had made a few good friends on the base. They were mostly women of her own age, although not all of them of her same background. Most of them had boyfriends or family living near, so the weekends when she was not on duty were lonely times.

Her parents rarely telephoned her while she was on duty, so she was surprised one morning to receive a call from her father.

"You know, my dear, that story I told you when you were last home. Without getting into details over the phone, I feel that you should know that those who are interested in such things will be contacting you."

Her heart sank. Would she never be free of those memories? There was so little to tell. It surely had to be a coincidence, although in her heart she felt this was just another step in her destiny.

"How I wish that I could be allowed to forget the whole thing."

"You know, my dear, there is just the chance this could be a piece of vital information involving national security as well as the means to save precious lives."

"I am sorry if I sound unpatriotic, Daddy. I am tired and dispirited. I know you are right."

They had spoken briefly of other things and then hung up.

The week-end arrived at last and Ian picked her up and they drove out into the country to an old pub which had a reputation for good food. They sat in companionable silence until they had placed their order. He wanted to know about her and her family and what her hopes and aspirations were. The evening passed very pleasantly and it was over all too soon. He had just learned that he had to go up to London again in the coming week. Unfortunately, his regular driver would be available if trains were not running. He smiled at her. "I am truly sorry about that." And she knew that he meant it.

It was a few days later and Madeleine was working her way through a pile of files when she was called to the office of the base commander. It both surprised and frightened her. This had never happened to her before and she worried that something might have happened to one or both of her parents.

"Please take a chair," the Commander gestured with his hand. "I will come to the point right away. I understand that a few years ago, at the beginning of the war, you were in Germany and had an encounter with a young man. It may all be a red herring, but the powers-that-be at the War Office would like to have your first-hand account of this incident. We would be happy to cooperate with them. Would you make the necessary arrangements to take a day's leave and travel to London for this purpose.?"

"Certainly, sir," she responded, as though she had any choice in the matter. "When would they like to see me?"

"Tomorrow," was the prompt reply.

She was surprised. It might be something of far greater importance than anyone could suspect. But after all these years...

At the War Office in London, she was ushered into a spacious and beautifully paneled room in the middle of which stood a large oval table and about twenty chairs.

"Please take a seat, Miss Devaux," the young man said. "I don't think the Brigadier will be long."

She sat down and felt ridiculously nervous all alone in this large conference room. It was as though she were sitting for an oral examination.

The door at the far end of the room opened and a very tall and somewhat portly, florid gentleman with very bushy eyebrows walked in with a file under his arm. He was followed a few minutes later by a much younger man not in uniform.

"Miss Devaux, how good of you to come. I am Brigadier Quinn. This is Carter who will take notes for us."

"Could you please tell me exactly what happened on the day you encountered the young man who snatched the medallion from around your neck. I would like to have every possible little detail. I know you were debriefed by M.I.5 upon your return to

England three years ago, however, we now need to be sure of all the details as a result of this new development."

She nodded. Slowly and carefully she repeated her story. Brigadier Quinn did not interrupt her until she had finished.

"Now repeat again, as you remember them, his exact words."

"He said," repeated Madeleine, "'My God. What luck.' He spoke in German."

The Brigadier was silent while he digested all that he had heard. He questioned her on the appearance of the man. He asked her if she thought he was German or of some other nationality. He repeated some questions several times. Instead of making her nervous, the repetition relaxed her. The scene all those years ago was still amazingly vivid in her mind. She did not feel threatened by the questioning.

Satisfied at last that he had cross-examined her thoroughly, and that her story was consistent, the Brigadier sat back in his chair and thoughtfully surveyed the ceiling above his head.

At last he said, "Could you describe this man to an artist sufficiently well that he could sketch a likeness that you could recognize?" She nodded without hesitation. His face had appeared to her so often that it was indelibly imprinted on her mind.

"Well, let's give it a try." With that the Brigadier got up from his chair and went out of the conference room. He returned a few minutes later.

"We will be joined by a police artist shortly. Would you care for a sandwich and some coffee, Miss Devaux, while we wait?"

She nodded. "Thank you. I am quite hungry."

It was a fascinating process. She quickly described the most distinctive features that she remembered and the artist almost as quickly reproduced them. Slowly, feature by feature the portrait was refined until the artist sat back and asked if there was anything more that he could add or subtract?

She sat quietly studying it. Something was missing, but it evaded her. She could not have seen him for more than a moment and then her attention was not entirely on his face, which had seemed so stressed and haggard. She closed her eyes and relived those brief moments, trying to reenact the surprise she had felt in finding someone bumping into her as soon as she stepped into the corridor from her hotel room. She tried again to hear the sounds. The noise of the elevator, a door that was opened in another corridor, voices and laughter which she knew were the nuns. Think, think she said to herself. What is there about his face that is missing? She opened her eyes and looked again at that now familiar face.

"I know what it is," she said. "He had a slight separation in his left eyebrow, as though he had a scar where the hair no longer grew. It was not large, but I do remember it."

"Well done" exclaimed the Brigadier. "Small details can make a great difference when there are hundreds of photographs from which to pick.

"Also his eyes were slightly lighter, although his anxiety made them look darker."

The Brigadier grunted and waved the artist out of the room.

"You have been invaluable, Miss Devaux. If this is someone in our files, he will be found. If not, then we have a challenge on our hands, but we have solved greater puzzles. Thank you very much, my dear young lady. I hope that this has not been too tedious for you, or too painful." She saw he was looking at her closely. Did it show how much she hated to relive those few moments?

There was not time to get back to Portsmouth and so she stayed the night at the flat. She indulged in a long, hot bath and spent the rest of the evening curled up with a book, a sandwich and a glass of milk.

A week had gone by since her trip to London, when Madeleine received another request to present herself in the base Commander's office at eleven-thirty that morning. She sighed. It seemed as though her past would not go away.

When she was ushered in, she was surprised to see not only Commander Hawkins, but Brigadier Quinn and, her heart skipped a beat, Commander Melville.

"Welcome, Miss Devaux. Please sit down. Will you have some tea or coffee?" Commander Hawkins was obviously the host.

"Some tea, please." Madeleine responded. Then impishly, because she knew that they were beholden to her and not she to them, "I would love some biscuits too."

Commander Melville tried to control a smile. Commander Hawkins smiled graciously, but he was obviously surprised and trying hard not to show it.

"Brigadier Quinn. Would you like to conduct the meeting since this is in your particular field?"

"Miss Devaux, since we last met, we have made an extensive search of our files but cannot find a match for the sketch which was drawn up of the man you ran into in Ulm. But we have not exhausted all the sources available to us, so there is still hope. We have a file covering defectors, agents, double agents, previous employees for whom we do not have physical descriptions, but who do have a psychological profile. There are also other agencies whom we can approach. However, we have reason to believe that he might be British, not German, and, without going into details, someone we would very much like to contact. We have a proposition to make to you. You are under no obligation to undertake the assignment that we have in mind, but we would like you to know that in the event of a successful outcome, it might make an enormous difference to the outcome of the war in a particular arena. We wondered if you would be willing to go to France and try and locate our mystery man?"

Madeleine gasped. "It would be like looking for a needle in a haystack. Why on earth would I risk my life for such a dangerous assignment?" She was furious at the casualness with which they had presented their proposition.

Brigadier Quinn cleared his throat before speaking. "Yes, it is a lot to ask of you, we do realize that. Again, you are under no obligation. But you are the only person who might be able to identify him. As you might imagine, the world of espionage and counter-espionage is a highly complex one. We are continually bombarded with information that has to be deciphered, decoded and analyzed. At times there is much confusion and those in charge are often only able to make an educated guess as to the true facts. However, I am told that for some considerable time they have suspected a serious leak. They would give a lot to find the source. It is intolerable to imagine traitors in our midst."

He concluded, "Please tell us how you came to be wearing the medallion. It is on record in your dossier, but not everyone present is familiar with the details."

"In 1938, before the war broke out, I answered an advertisement describing a position for a young, well-educated, dignified person willing to travel extensively to interesting places in an executive capacity. When I went for the interview, it turned out that the position was with an agency which provided private couriers for companies. I had just completed a university degree, I had no commitments and really enjoyed the prospect of traveling. I was offered the position. My job mostly involved the delivery of documents, but sometimes I was asked to deliver or pick up small artifacts or jewelry. In point of fact, I was really a well-paid postman. It was a very remunerative job. I was constantly criss-crossing the Channel. I would travel both by air and train, or by whatever method brought me to my destination as speedily as possible. Sometimes I would get a few extra days between assignments, so then I was able to be a tourist and visit some of the places that I had always wanted to see."

"You have not explained about the medallion," the Brigadier objected.

"Initially the medallion had nothing to do with my job. It was a gift from my father. The medallion was an old gold coin from Afghanistan with a decorative piece of jade bonded to the back of the coin. I was very fond of it. It was my good luck charm."

"But you did begin to use it on some of your assignments?" prompted Commander Hawkins.

"Yes" responded Madeleine. "There were occasions when a delivery was particularly urgent and, to save a few hours, I would be met at an airport. Of course, neither party knew the other so we had to have ways of identifying each other as well as verifying that we were who we were supposed to be. The medallion was useful as an initial identification; not easily reproduced like an identity card. At the beginning, I generally wore it even if I was expecting to be met at an airport by someone I knew, just in case that person, at the last moment, was unable to come."

"Did you ever part with it, or lend it to another courier?" This was the first time that Commander Melville had spoken. She was afraid that she was about to blush and was annoyed at herself. She hoped that she had managed to hide her face behind her cup of tea.

"No, I never lent it to anyone. One company asked if they might photograph it. They were diamond merchants. It was considered a reasonable request. I did not always wear it. Later the idea of using it was discarded because it was thought wiser to have one identification for all couriers, as well as their individual passwords."

"Did you ever have an assignment when you were not met as had been arranged?"

"Perhaps twice."

"Was there anything particularly unusual about either of those occasions?" Brigadier Quinn was frowning.

Madeleine paused, trying to recall the sequence of events.

"The first time it happened, I was upset. I was meeting someone I knew and in his place was a stranger who claimed to be a chauffeur who would drive me to the company offices. He gave me a telephone number so I could verify this. When I got the receptionist at the company in question, I asked to speak to my opposite number. I was told he was in bed with the flu, but I was given his home number and I spoke to him. It all checked out. I happened to be carrying a small bag of diamonds. I had no problems."

"What about the second occasion?" The Brigadier had been scribbling on his notepad.

"That was strange. I arrived to find no one there to meet me. I telephoned the company and asked for the man I was to meet. Neither he nor a second man with whom I had spoken was there. It seemed as though I was not expected."

"Where were you on that occasion?"

"Paris"

"What did you do next?"

"I telephoned my agency. They told me to stay overnight and they would contact me the next morning. In the end, I returned to London. I was carrying documents. I was told there had been a mix-up. I never heard anymore about it. Neither did I get another assignment to that company."

What few knew, including Brigadier Quinn, was that a second medallion had been duplicated and used by M.I.5 and that Madeleine's seemingly failed assignment was as a result of a trial run by counter-intelligence.

"Well, Miss Devaux, I think that we have covered the subject fairly thoroughly for the time being. Thank you very much." This was Commander Hawkins' way of dismissal.

She got to her feet, smoothed her skirt and picked up her shoulder bag and gas mask and left the room.

She had been unnerved by the experience, not only because she had been forced to relive some memories she would prefer to forget, but also because she was annoyed at the casualness with which they had suggested she should be dropped into enemy territory on a wild goose chase.

A week went by during which time she heard nothing more. Neither did she hear from Commander Melville. She felt very much in limbo. There were times when she ached in loneliness. Would the war never end? Would she ever find Erich again? Was he still alive?

In many ways, she was bored with the repetitive monotony of her job. She had to be grateful that the bombing had eased up. She was angry that she was being held hostage by a war that was so disruptive and destructive. She wanted to be free to go forward with her life.

At last came the call to present herself to the base commander's office. She was surprised to find that Commander Hawkins was not present. Brigadier Quinn got to his feet as she entered and waved her into a seat. Another man was seated at the table. He eyed her critically. He was not introduced to her and he did not speak during the brief interview. She presumed he was from one of the intelligence gathering agencies.

"We have not been able to identify your mystery man. As I have said before, he is most likely British, probably not German. He is certainly not French. We would very much like to find out who he is, whether he is friend or foe. We think he is probably not a friend. We have been having some trouble with our agents in that area. The French have one person they suspect, but they have been unable to substantiate their suspicions. To discover his identity could be dangerous. We have good communications with the French Résistance in that region. We would very much like you to consider accepting this assignment. We cannot offer you any particular incentive for undertaking such a risky venture, other than, as has already been stated, that you would be doing your country a great service. If you were to accept, you would be given some basic training. We would plan to deliver and pick you up by submarine. Commander Melville would coordinate the operation. Do you have any questions?

"How long do I have to think about it?"

"I think three days should be enough. In my experience, the longer the time for a difficult decision, the more ambivalent one becomes."

"If I were to accept, how soon after would I be sent over to France?"

"Since I understand you are a quick learner, I would say you would have grasped the essentials of what you would need to know within a two week period."

"Am I allowed to consult with my parents on this?"

"Your father is already aware of our intentions."

"It was he who set this in motion?"

The Brigadier nodded. There was a pause. He stroked one of his bushy eyebrows as if debating what he would say next. There was a pause before he continued. "Well, Miss Devaux, think about it and give us your answer as soon as you are able."

She was walking back to her office when the air-raid siren went off. She hurried to the shelter and took her place on the wooden bench, her gas-mask at her feet. She hated the damp, musty smell of the shelter, the restriction of space with so many people sitting shoulder to shoulder. The low murmur of voices as people recognized their friends in the crowd. The familiar crump,

crump of the anti-aircraft guns could be heard above their heads. Then came the louder, greater vibration of bombs dropping. It came slowly nearer and all conversation stopped. People held their breath and, she knew, most silently prayed. There was the high-pitched whistle as a bomb dropped very near them and dust, earth and some planks showered down on them. The noise retreated and soon there was silence from the guns. The electricity had been knocked out and someone had called out that they were looking for the candles. Someone had a flashlight and the candles were located. The dismal light lit up a few faces, but most of the shelter was in darkness. Madeleine had been sitting clasping her hands tightly together. She took a deep breath of the turgid air. She thought back to the meeting she had just had and thought how much better she would feel if she could be doing something, anything, rather than sitting in a bomb shelter praying that she was not going to be buried alive. At this particular moment, she was inclined to accept the assignment to go to France. She was angry that she had spent all these years feeling both sorry and guilty for someone who might turn out to be a traitor. She would like to put the record straight, as much for her peace of mind as for any other reason.

The All-Clear had gone off and they slowly scrambled up the staircase to the fresh air above them. It seemed as though a number of buildings had been hit and smoke and flames were belching around them. It was a mess, but they had lived through worse. They all hurried to their respective posts to do what needed to be done there or to help those in need elsewhere.

It was not until the next day that Madeleine had the time to telephone her parents. Her father answered the phone.

"You must have known that I would be asked to undertake this assignment" she said without any preliminary greeting.

Her father sighed. "Yes. I happen to know how desperately important it is to them to try and discover the leak they suspect. Your man could be the source. What have you decided, if you have decided anything?"

"I think that I would like to take it on."

Her father grunted. "I was hoping you would, although you know that your mother and I will be very anxious for you. But it is what I would do myself in your shoes."

She knew he was proud of her, and she suddenly felt lighthearted, which in the circumstances was not logical.

"Is mother there?"

"No, but I think that we will not tell her about this until a little nearer the time. She worries enough about you without prolonging the ordeal. Give us a ring and try and come home before you leave."

She hung up and made her way to Commander Hawkins' office. It had escaped the brunt of the bombing, but some windows had been blown out and a man was sweeping up the glass into little piles

She found Commander Hawkins, looking more gaunt than usual, picking pieces of glass off his desk and dropping them into a waste basket. Other pieces lay scattered on the floor and he stopped what he was doing as she stepped into the room.

"Do be careful where you walk. Would you like to sit down?" He looked around him.

"No, thank you, sir." she responded. "It won't take a minute. I just wanted you to know that I have made a decision about the assignment we have been discussing. I am prepared to take it on."

She was surprised at his reaction. He beamed at her. She had never seen him smile before. She realized then what a burden and responsibility his job must be. Not only did he have to oversee the running of the base, but it fell to him to inform families when there were casualties. "I am so very pleased to hear you say that." was his response. "We seem to be making so little progress with this bloody war. I understand that this is considered to be a very vital and important mission. Every time we eliminate an infiltrator, it is a step closer to bringing the war to an end."

She was surprised at the speed with which she was removed from her post and put into a special training class. Physical fitness was of the utmost importance. She was encouraged to run laps around the track, swim lengths in the pool and repeatedly scramble through the obstacle course. She was also instructed in the art of self-defense. Commander Melville reappeared into her life and was responsible for teaching her the subtle and sophisticated art of intelligence work. This was the most fascinating of all and she enjoyed it immensely.

The days seemed to race by and she knew that it would not be long before she would be told the expected date of her departure. Much, of course, would depend on the weather. She was told that it would be better if she did not go home. It could be too upsetting. She wondered if they considered it a security risk. She did not try to speculate. Her mother, she knew, was desperately unhappy at this course of events. Her father was matter-of-fact. It was a good facade for what he really felt.

She would be leaving in three days. At night. There would be no moon. The plan was for Commander Melville to accompany her and put her into the hands of the Résistance. He was known to them. They wanted her to identify the man from Ulm if he was to be found. They did not want him to recognize her. To this end, it had been decided that she should dye her hair. She was aghast at this desecration. She enjoyed her beautiful blond, curly hair.

"So what color would you like to have it?" Commander Melville had asked her when they were discussing the subject.

"I think that I would like to be a red-head."

"Out of the question," had been the response. "You would be much too conspicuous."

So she had become a brunette. She was amazed at the change it made in her appearance.

Her wardrobe had to be adapted for wartime France; no give-away labels. False identify papers had been created. Her French was impeccable. It was for this reason as much as any other that the powers-that-be in M.I.5 had given their blessing to Madeleine's selection. Her ability to identify the suspect would have been useless without a supremely good working knowledge of French.

— 15 —

The night of departure had arrived. There was a breeze and a small chop on the sea with a promise of rain. It was perfect weather for the mission.

Madeleine had never been in a submarine and did not really relish the prospect after so many years of bomb-shelter existence. She was surprised to find the sub much less claustrophobic than she had expected. It might have been her high state of anticipation, but she enjoyed the journey across the channel to France. There seemed something warm and secure about her environment. She did not even think about the possibility of mines or enemy submarines. They surfaced about a mile off-shore and a rubber boat was dropped over the side. She was lowered into it. She wondered how such a maneuver was accomplished in rough weather. Before she knew it, they had left the submarine behind. It was hardly visible from a few hundred yards. Commander Melville was rowing evenly through the swell, looking occasionally over his shoulder, although she could not see any landmarks by which he must be steering. They bumped softly on the sand and she hopped out as the sea receded. They dragged the boat onto the beach and stowed the oars inside. They walked quietly towards the trees and sat down on a flat rock. The Commander was looking towards the left end of the beach. They had arrived ten minutes early for their rendezvous. They sat silently, not speaking. This was a dangerous time in such an operation, when they might be observed by unfriendly parties.

Finally a blinking light was to be seen at the end of the beach. They got to their feet and walked towards it. At a certain moment, Ian Melville touched her arm and indicated that she should stand still. He continued forward. She felt alone and vulnerable, but the understanding had been that he should first identify their contact. She doubted that if things were to go wrong she would have the time to run back to the boat and escape out to sea. But that was what she was to attempt in that eventuality.

Soft crunching footsteps came towards her and Ian was once more at her side. She was surprised at how relieved she was. She had not realized how very taut her nerves were.

"All is well," he whispered in her ear. "Now Devaux, try to remember all we have taught you. Most important of all, please try and look a little disheveled, even scruffy. That glowing peaches and cream complexion of yours is too attractive by far, even though you are now a brunette, and no longer a smashing blond."

She could feel his smile and knew that he wanted to lift her spirits.

For himself, Ian Melville had no fear in the role he was playing. But he felt sick with anxiety at leaving this beautiful girl in enemy-occupied territory. He had grown very fond of her in the few weeks they had been together. The primitive man in him lusted after her. The intellectual side of him was in love with her. He spent his quieter moments of solitude writing poems about her. She had shown no fear throughout this period of training and had been a quick learner. But he instinctively knew that, when he left her alone with a stranger and returned to the submarine, she would be overcome by a moment of panic. Her escape route to England perhaps severed forever. He swallowed hard and cleared his voice.

He took her arm and gently moved her forward.

"Madeleine, this is Jean-Yves. You will be as safe in his hands as it is possible to be in these uncertain times. Good luck to you all." With that he turned and left them.

"Follow me," murmured Jean-Yves, and set off towards the trees. They reached a small track. Jean-Yves had left two bicycles hidden in some bushes. He handed one to her. As she sat on the saddle, she wondered what he would have done if she had been unable to ride it. She smiled to herself. They rode in silence for about half an hour.

They had left the sea behind. She could no longer hear it. In front of them was open sky. She presumed they had reached a road, for Jean-Yves dismounted and was walking his bicycle. He waved for her to stop and wait for him.

He returned. He told her that they had to travel down the road a brief distance to another cart track which would lead them to their destination. He told her that if she heard an approaching vehicle which would mean a German patrol, she was to throw herself and her bicycle into the nearest bushes.

They set off. Jean-Yves approached the road cautiously, then, obviously satisfied, he waved to her and set a fast pace along it. Madeleine followed him a little more slowly. She was unfamiliar with her steed and did not want to risk falling off it and incapacitating herself so early in her mission. She reached the entrance to the narrow cart track and found Jean-Yves waiting impatiently for her. It was a very bumpy track, until she learnt to stay out of the ruts. Although it was a cloudy night, the air was fresh and invigorating and she felt very much awake despite her lack of sleep. She had a hard time believing that she was actually in German-occupied France. It all seemed very peaceful.

The track came to another road which led to the beginnings of civilization. She saw the large outline of a barn, with a house in the near distance. A denser collection of buildings lay beyond.

"We want to reach those buildings in the far distance. There is another barn there where you will sleep. I have some food in this bag that I will leave with you. I will come back around midday to fetch you. It is a busy time when everyone is going home to lunch. Remain hidden in the barn until that time. I will be whistling a few bars of Edith Piaf's 'Un Monsieur me suit dans la rue.' I do hope you know it." He whistled a few bars.

She smiled. "Luckily, I do. I love all her songs. I just hope that the title is not significant. I do not want to be followed by anyone except you."

A glimmer of a smile showed briefly on his face. "Good. Do not show yourself to anyone else for any reason at all unless you hear that tune."

"Entendu," she replied.

They set off again and Madeleine almost enjoyed the ride along the deserted street, although she told herself she must not relax her vigilance for a moment. They saw no one along the route, although at one point they were surprised by the sudden barking of a dog who must have heard them as they passed the gate of a small house. He stopped almost as soon as he had started and they rode on undisturbed.

They reached the barn where she was to stay. She was surprised when she looked at her watch to find that it was almost four-fifteen in the morning. How quickly the time had passed. People would soon be getting up. There was no time to waste. Jean-Yves must be on his way before it was discovered he was somewhere where he should not be at this hour of day.

He unlatched the huge barn door and pulled it open just enough to let her and her bicycle pass through it. He handed her the bag with the food in it. He told her it also contained a flashlight. With that he was gone, latching the barn door as he left.

She opened the bag and took out the flashlight. She was amazed at the size of the interior of the barn. There was an old tractor to one side and a variety of farm implements, as well as an old wooden cart. Ahead of her were piles upon piles of hay. She moved forward to find herself a place to sleep and hide. The bales were stacked so high one upon another that she thought at first she would not find a way to climb up and out of sight. But to her left, the bales of hay were unevenly stacked. She presumed that these were older and that they were being used first. In one spot, they lay like stepping stones so that she was able to climb them easily. She found herself a place in a far corner, high up near the rafters. No one from the ground could see her there and no one who started loading the hay would reach such a distant place. She had left her bicycle half hidden behind a collection of pitch-forks and other implements and hoped it seemed a natural place for a discarded old bicycle.

She was grateful for the food and wine that Jean-Yves had thoughtfully provided. She was extremely hungry. She ate the cheese and sausage and drank some rough-flavored wine. It had begun to rain. That might also be providential. Perhaps the farmer would not be outdoors working tomorrow. She was so glad to be in a dry, safe place for the night. There was something very soothing about the patter of the raindrops on the roof of the old barn. She arranged her bed of hay with enough to cover her and gratefully lay down and fell sleep.

The rain continued all morning, so that it was not until nearly eleven o'clock that Madeleine was awoken by the opening of the barn door. She was immediately alert, refreshed from a deep and uninterrupted sleep. She lay quietly listening. It was difficult to tell what was happening below her. There was a rattling noise, then silence, and then a bang. Another silence and an attempt to start an engine. Someone was working on the tractor. It was proving stubborn. She began to fret that this would go on much longer than was convenient for her planned departure. The intermittent banging, rattling and low muttering went on for what seemed an eternity. The attempts to start the tractor proved futile and finally, whoever it was, gave up in disgust, swearing loudly. Another thump; had he actually kicked the miserable beast? Then the barn door was shut with a loud crash and finally silence.

She sat up and opened her bag of food and ate what remained. She drank sparingly of the wine.

She lay back and looked at the rafters and pondered on the next step she was about to take. She wondered how unnerving it might be to step out into the daylight. Would people seem curious about her. She wore dark clothes. She had a head scarf. She hoped that she would look pretty nondescript. It was also still raining. She had a navy-blue raincoat that looked as though it had seen better days.

Suddenly, the door of the barn was opened and somebody had entered. There was no sound other than the soft padding footsteps on the floor below. She held her breath. The steps receded, but the door was not closed. She lay still, her heart beating a little faster. The footsteps returned and someone began to whistle erratically, but it was not the tune she was listening for. More rattling noises, silence and then the roar of an engine as the tractor sprang to life. She signed with relief and hoped they would drive the wretched vehicle away. But instead, the ignition was turned off. More footsteps and the barn door was closed once again.

It was after midday. Now she began to fret again. What if Jean-Yves could not return. What would become of her. She had no other contact than him. At best, she might have to wait another 12-24 hours. At worst... but she stopped herself from thinking further.

Someone else entered the barn. They shut the door behind them. They were moving about. They stopped. She then heard the familiar tune being whistled. Her heart beat faster. All should be well, but what if it was just a coincidence? Then again, she could try and catch a glimpse of whoever it was, but in the dark she had not really had a very good look at Jean-Yves. There was nothing for it, but to show herself. She climbed down the way she had come and stepped out onto the floor of the barn. Jean-Yves turned as he heard her. She sighed with relief.

He looked much younger in daylight. His sallow complexion and sparse frame gave him a gaunt appearance. His beard showed dark on his chin and there were circles under his eyes. She realized that he had probably not slept, or very little, since she last saw him. She judged him to be in his early thirties.

He was appraising her, as though he were summing her up. What faith to risk his life for an unknown stranger.

"We have to hurry. We are a little late. I was delayed. I want to make the journey to my home while the streets are still fairly busy. Just follow me. Where is your bicycle?"

"Over there." she pointed.

He nodded. "I will let you know if it is safe to leave. Then just follow me." He was about to turn away from her, when she reached out and touched his arm. "Thank you, for giving me shelter. I hope that it never puts you or your family at risk." He shrugged. "Some of us would do anything to be free again," and with that he turned and stepped out of the barn.

"Come now. Do not look around. Just follow me,"

She had her bicycle and pushed it through the barn door. Jean-Yves closed it, mounted his bicycle and started to peddle quickly away towards the gate. She got onto her bicycle as quickly as she could and followed him.

Her heart was in her mouth, but she had to concentrate so hard on where she was going and on following Jean-Yves, that she was really unaware of the passage of time. The streets became busier the longer they traveled. People on foot, a lot on bicycles, not many cars. At one heart-stopping moment she saw a German army vehicle, but it passed them by. Jean-Yves kept up a steady pace, but nothing too fast to cause them to be conspicuous. He had only once turned to see if she was behind him and that was when they had first set out.

He began to slow down and turned down what seemed to be a small, grassy alley between two rows of houses. About half-way down this, he dismounted and turned. He waved her to follow him. He walked his bicycle through a small wooden gate and propped it against the wall of an outhouse. She was through the gate and he took her bicycle from her and put it into the outhouse. He led her through the back door of the house.

Jean's parents acknowledged her solemnly. Jean-Yves took her raincoat and scarf and her shoulder bag and told her that lunch was ready to serve. Jean-Yves looked even younger without his black beret, almost vulnerable. She wondered if he got enough to eat. His parents were far less gaunt looking. However, she was convinced that his mother would deprive herself of food for his sake. She suspected that Jean-Yves's gauntness was due more to lack of sleep, because of his activities with the Résistance.

They sat at table together. Jean-Yves' mother had prepared a soup, which was thin but flavorful. She apologized for the lack of bread, a rare commodity which they were seldom able to obtain despite their bread coupons and the hours standing in line whenever the baker had some to sell. It was possible for some people to obtain bread on the black market. One had to have money or goods with which to bargain. However, the soup was warm and tasty and there was paté to go with it, which was very sustaining. Madeleine was amazed that she should be served such a luxury item. She was to learn later that some luxury items did not require food coupons.

Very little was said during lunch and Madeleine was grateful at not having to make conversation. She was feeling very drained. She was aware that Jean's parents were very relieved to discover she spoke fluent French. It meant that she could be much more easily assimilated into her surroundings.

With lunch over, Jean-Yves led Madeleine up to the attic which contained a bed, a small table with a lamp, a chair and a small chest of drawers. There was no window, but light filtered through several roof vents. The door to the attic was a bookcase which swung out when a small lever was released.

"I am afraid that you will have to spend much of your time here," he told her, "until we can move you again. We do not wish you to remain in any one place for more than three days. Since it is not possible for you to attend our meetings, as much for your protection as ours, we hope that we can arrange for you to be able to observe them unseen, in the hope that you may recognize the person you are seeking."

She nodded.

"I have left you a selection of books to help pass the time. I will also give you a bowl so that you can wash your clothes. They can be hung on a line that I will put up for you. We are rather short of soap, so use it sparingly. I will come and get you at supper time." With that he left her.

The next few weeks were to pass in similar fashion. She moved from attic to basement, to barn, to workshop, wherever the host family felt that she was inconspicuous or hidden. She was often chilled by the dampness of her hiding place; at times too cold to do anything but shiver all night, unable to sleep. She always felt hungry and tired, drained by the strain of her unaccustomed surroundings and lifestyle. The constraints of being so confined and not being able to wash her clothes or herself on a regular basis made her depressed. She was uniformly courteously received by each host family, but she felt that a great reserve existed between them. She could understand their sincere reservations about her presence, about her threat to their safety. It meant that conversation was very limited and even stilted. She admired them enormously for their courage and faith in taking her in and giving her shelter.

Late one night, at one of the homes where she was given refuge, the Germans came knocking at the door. Everyone had been in bed for some hours. The husband, an elderly man, went to answer the door. She heard German voices and heavy boots. There were two Germans and they climbed down into the cellar after having searched the rest of the house. She lay stricken with terror convinced that at any moment she would be dragged from her hiding place and driven away for interrogation. How many stories had she heard like that? The beams from their flashlights penetrated the cracks of the false wall of her hiding place. For a heart-stopping eternity, she cowered under her blanket and tried not to breath loudly. But she had a nasty cold. She prayed that she would not sneeze or cough. The soldiers kicked over furniture and old crates and, in general, made a lot of noise. She blew her nose quickly and hoped that it would not be heard above the noise being made. Anything to prevent an unexpected sneeze. They muttered to one another, but she could not make out what they were saying. There was a long silence and she presumed they were just standing and listening. She felt sure that they would hear the pounding of her heart. Then, with a few muttered curses, they stomped back up the cellar steps. After pacing to and fro above her head, obviously interrogating her host, the Germans finally left and the house had lapsed into silence. Her hosts had never chosen to discuss the incident and she had not enquired. But she marveled at their composure and courage. She was moved the next day.

She had much time to dwell on the irony of her situation. That she should be married to a German, and yet be in France trying to outwit the German regime on behalf of the British and bring about the ultimate defeat, as she hoped, of Germany, was a flagrant contradiction. She tried to analyze her feelings. She had no doubts about her love for Erich. She also believed that he had loved her, for he had done the unthinkable, in the eyes of a German. He had helped her to escape back to her own country. She could not think of him as a German of the type so often depicted in press coverage and newsreels. He seemed more like the gentleman soldier of ancient times. But so much time had passed since they were last together that she could not help but feel anxious that he might no longer feel the same ardent longing for her as she did for him. Then, of course, there was the possibility that he had become a casualty of war and was dead. She tried not to dwell on this aspect, but it kept creeping back into her mind. She had far too much time to think. If only she could be doing something, anything, that would involve physical activity, but she realized that in this particular environment she had to be very circumspect in her movements. It was too small a town, and although not everyone knew one another, eventually someone would notice that she did not belong. She wished that she could go to Paris. At least she could get lost in that city without too much difficulty. If she were there, she might find some way to learn whether Erich was still alive. She would not be able to contact him, but if she just knew that he was alive, it would be such a comfort. The thought made her heart beat faster.

She had so much time to fill. She had forced herself to think of ways to keep her mind busy. She relived her childhood over and over again. She thought of the many years that she had accompanied her parents on the family holiday to Cornwall. It was a place they all loved for its rugged, unspoilt beauty. They always rented a delightful thatched cottage high on a cliff above a small fishing cove near the Lizard's Head. The sound of the sea was always in their ears, especially at night. The smell of the sea filled their nostrils and the brisk, clean air colored their cheeks. Her father had been accepted by the local fishermen, despite being an outsider by their standards. They would take him fishing with them, when they went out to sea to inspect their lobster pots, or to fish for mackerel. Madeleine would swim in the cove. The sea was warmed by the gulf stream along this coast, but the temperature was still fresh and she would come out, her skin a bright pink glow.

She loved the cliff walks, where the tufty grass was springy to the feet and filled with every variety of wild flower. They would sit and have picnics looking down on the sea, the powerful waves crashing and seething against the rough and jagged cliffs below. The gulls and other seabirds would circle and sweep above them in raucous glee at the prospect of the odd scraps that would be thrown to them.

Then on other days, perhaps when the weather was wet and windy and too uncomfortable for cliff walks, they would drive to a nearby village and have a crab sandwich lunch in a small café or a strawberry cream tea.

Such day-dreaming helped Madeleine to pass the time, but it also succeeded in making her immensely lonely and homesick. It made her even more determined to complete her mission, given luck, and return to the embrace of her family.

── *16* ──

She had been able to attend a number of meetings, hidden in whatever way was appropriate. So far, no one had been present who resembled in the slightest the man she remembered. Jean-Yves told her that she had seen almost all members of their particular group. A few were absent and, although he did not elaborate, she assumed that they were on some mission.

During this period of intense boredom, Jean-Yves was the central figure in her life. It was always he who shepherded her to whatever hiding place she was destined to stay in. She got to know him better. He was a most solemn young man. She could not make him laugh. He did not talk about himself, but she did extract a piece of information from him which explained much about him. She asked him why he had chosen to take up such a risky career with the Résistance. He replied that he had been riding home one day from work, when a German truck had pulled up and stopped some few hundred feet from him. A number of Germans had jumped out and rushed up to the door of a nearby house. They had knocked and got no answer, whereupon they had broken the door down. A few minutes later they had reappeared with an old man, probably in his seventies, whom they hustled into the truck. A young girl had rushed out of the house a few moments later and run up to the truck. She was weeping and crying out to her grandfather. One of the soldiers had leant out of the truck and hit her on the head with his rifle butt. She had fallen to the ground, bleeding profusely. The truck had driven away. Everyone had rushed to the aid of the young girl, who was probably only sixteen years of age. She had been rushed to a doctor and then to a hospital. She had survived, but had lost an eye. It had left her face very unsightly. Madeleine surmised that this was a young woman that Jean-Yves had known and possibly loved. It had sowed the seed in him of a passionate hatred of the Germans.

On days of light drizzle, Jean-Yves gave Madeleine permission to go riding on her bicycle. With a head-scarf and raincoat, she looked like most of the other citizens. The only danger she ran was to be stopped by a German patrol. For this reason, she only knew the first names of anyone she had met. It was a small protection should she ever be interrogated. However, it was an imperfect system because she sometimes overheard names of people she knew. She enjoyed this break from the long periods of forced seclusion. There was little chance that she would come upon or be recognized by the man she sought, especially since everyone was muffled and protected from the weather. It was much more important to her to get the exercise and fresh air.

On one of these outings, she was tempted to stop and visit an old and lovely church. She propped her bicycle behind a stone staircase. She hoped that no one would steal it. She felt it was a small risk that she could afford to take. It was cold and damp inside the church, but the air of peace and tranquility that emanated from it filled her and lifted her spirits. She walked down a side aisle and a few pews from the altar rail she sat down. There were a few elderly people scattered around her.

She meditated on her life since returning to France. It had been a very reflective time for her. She could not help but have enormous admiration for the French, who continued to live their lives as normally as possible despite the ever present vigilance of the Germans. There seemed to be daily incidents. People were regularly stopped to show their identification papers. Some were taken in for interrogation and still others were arrested and taken away. There were reprisals for sabotage, for clandestine operations, for stealing, for false papers, for no papers. Some people were taken away for no apparent reason and some never seen again. Men were taken and shot in a street, in the main square. Worst still, some were tortured and, if they survived, were left to languish and suffer or, later still, shot.

When the Jewish population were forced to wear yellow stars, many of their non-Jewish friends wore yellow stars in support. They would risk being arrested and questioned for doing this, but were generally freed. However, the process of identifying those of Jewish origin preceded the collective arrests and deportations which later were to follow. Thus singled out, they were soon shunned. Since many Jewish families owned valuables of varying importance, denunciations began to accelerate out of jealousy and for reasons of gain, in the hope of acquiring possession of the boutique, apartment or property of the family in question. She shuddered at the stories she heard.

Then there were other members of the population who joined the Résistance and the Maquis. They lived in barns or huts used in summer to shelter cattle or in caves or tents made out of parachutes. From these hide-outs, they made daring raids on German and French supply depots. She had been told tragic stories where family members had been tricked into joining the Maquis to revenge themselves for the massacre of their family by the Gestapo, only to find the German SS were lying in wait for them. Conversely, many Gestapo tried to infiltrate the Maquis.

But the majority of French went about their business, trying to make ends meet, despite the shortage of food and other daily necessities. But it was mostly the women who kept life in motion as best they could, for so many of their men were gone - imprisoned or working in Germany keeping the German army supplied with munitions, tanks and aircraft. Many of the men who refused to leave were executed.

Madeleine was becoming increasing more homesick for England, despite the bombing, and was extremely motivated to try and accomplish something meaningful and worthwhile towards the war effort. She really doubted that her present mission could have any positive outcome. The odds of ever seeing the man she had encountered in Ulm were so unlikely. Also there was no proof that the medallion found here in France on the French agent had been brought here by the man in Ulm, even if there was a connection. Jean-Yves had assured her that some of the meetings had been attended by key members from far-flung districts in France, when circumstances necessitated it.

She sat quietly in the pew and tried to focus, not on the war, but on her parents, her friends and on Erich. She prayed for patience and courage and for an end of the war.

She stood up and turned out of the pew and walked straight into the arms of the man she was seeking.

Her reaction was one of overwhelming shock. She felt the steely cold blade of fear run through her. She was like a rabbit caught in a trap, unable to move. He was dressed as a priest, which somehow made him infinitely more terrifying.

"Are you ill?" he asked, as she staggered against the pew.

"No. Just a little dizzy." She sank back into the pew and took a deep breath hoping it would help calm her and clear her head.

"I will get you a glass of water." With that he left her. Her first instinct was to get up and run out of the church, but she really did feel dizzy. She knew she was hungry. It had also been a terrible shock. He had changed since she had seen him in Ulm. Perhaps it was more a question of demeanor than appearance. He was in a position of authority in the church, not an agent on the run. His physical appearance was not much different. His hair looked lighter even in the dark interior of the church, possibly in contrast to his black robes. His eyes were a steely, penetrating blue. The only difference was a scar from the outside of his right eye to the jaw line. It had faded, but it had not been there when they had collided in the corridor of the hotel in Ulm. Perhaps that scar was the source of the bloodstain on the carpet and wall.

She was about to get to her feet when he was back and offering her a glass of water.

She drank it all slowly and thanked him. She hoped that he had not seen the shock and fear in her eyes. It could have only been a fleeting moment before she had turned away from him. She was not too concerned that he could possibly recognize her, but that she should show fear at seeing him, would certainly arouse his curiosity.

"I feel better," she said, "I am afraid that I am hungry."

He nodded understandingly. "So many are nowadays," he said, with a semblance of sympathy.

"Thank you, again, Father." She turned to go.

"Do you live near here?" he asked.

Her heart sank. She wanted desperately to leave, to escape from his presence.

"No, not far. Why do you ask?"

"I don't remember seeing you before."

"I work all week and some week-end shifts at the factory, so I am rarely able to attend Mass. I come at odd times, like today."

He contemplated her thoughtfully and her heart raced. But she tried to return his gaze, calmly and with a slight suggestion of resignation.

Finally, he said, "I am very short-staffed. Is there any possibility that you could come and help in the church office from time to time? I realize your work hours must be long."

She relaxed slightly. "I do not have a lot of free time. I also help out on a farm, but the next free day I have, I will let you know. Would that be helpful?"

It obviously satisfied him for he responded, "There is no immediate hurry, but it would help me catch up on a large accumulation of paperwork. I shall need time to prepare for your coming." He smiled.

She got up and turned to leave, saying, "Then perhaps I shall see you later on next week. What time of day would I find you here?"

"My hours are very erratic, I am never sure where I am going to be needed. But generally, I am here for early morning Mass, say between seven and nine. You could always leave a message and tell me where I might reach you."

"That will be fine." She started to walk away, feeling his eyes following her. She did not look round, but walked slowly as though in no special hurry. She reached the heavy oak door and pulled it open. She stood at the top of the steps for a few moments and took deep breaths. Her body was quivering. She was much more tense than she realized. She had an enormous urge to run, to forget her bicycle and just run as fast as she could, but she resisted. She walked down the steps to the bicycle which remained where she had left it.

She wondered whether he was standing somewhere watching her departure. She would like to ride away out of his range of vision. She might get lost doing that but it would give her a greater sense of security to mislead him, however slightly or fleetingly. There was a lane behind the church which separated two rows of houses, one back garden from another. What lay behind the windows on that side of the church she could not tell, but she was pretty sure it was not possible to see out of them, they were situated high in the wall or seemed shuttered. She shrugged and climbed onto her bicycle and pedaled briskly away. She was now between the houses and out of sight of the church. She raced her bike twisting and turning, always trying to keep her sense of direction, until she felt she could slow down and concentrate on finding her way home, the one of dozens she had lived in. It was getting dark and it was raining again. She was beginning to worry that she would not find any familiar landmarks, when finally she saw a building that told her she was not far from her destination. She arrived at the little house on a back street, got off her bicycle and quickly went through the back gate and into the garden.

Once in the house she collapsed into her chair at the kitchen table where the family was assembled for dinner and found she was shaking. They stared at her in silence until the husband pulled himself together, coughed and asked her if she would like a glass of his homemade wine.

"I would love one," she responded, "but I have not eaten since breakfast and have had a rather stressful afternoon. I think it better that I eat something instead. I do apologize for being late, Madame."

Madame Boiseau responded in a thoroughly motherly fashion by hurrying to the stove and ladling out a hot, brimming bowl of thick garlic-flavored soup. She placed it before Madeleine and told her that it would put the color back in her cheeks. As vegetables were almost impossible to obtain, Madeleine wondered at the contents of the soup or if the family were drawing from their precious reserves on her account. Robert, their son, handed her the basket of a dark, coarse substance that passed as bread. Madeleine realized what a sacrifice it was for them to share with her this precious staple. Bread was one of the most sought after and difficult commodities to find in occupied France. Women fought one another in queues for it; they exchanged and bargained for it. They stole for it. Food cards were stolen and false cards were printed. It was a dangerous game for all involved.

Monsieur Boiseau rose from the table and returned with a glass of red wine which he placed in front of her.

"Later, drink that and you will sleep like a baby." He smiled kindly at her. He was a short, thick-set man with the ruddy complexion of a farmer. He had lost two fingers in an accident. This misfortune had spared him from being shipped to Germany, like many of his compatriots, to work in a German munitions factory.

They had told her how the Germans had published articles in the newspapers on the great advantages to be found for Frenchmen who went to work in Germany in the factories, aerodromes and submarine bases. They were promised good wages, good food and 15 days vacation every 10 months back in France. Letters published in the papers spoke of better conditions in Germany for workers. But the French were not deceived by propaganda in these articles which sounded too seductive to be true. The result was that once the campaign against Russia was launched, the Germans needed workers in great numbers and although some French did volunteer, most were forced or taken prisoner and sent to Germany.

The simple meal proceeded in silence. When Madeleine had finished her soup, they passed her some more bread and the plate of cheese. She helped herself and returned the plate. How could she ever repay them for their generosity?

"I need to get a message very urgently to Jean-Yves. Do you think that would be possible tonight?"

Madame Boiseau shook her head vehemently. "Pas possible," she said abruptly, her mouth drawn down in disapproval. Madeleine sensed her fear of involvement in Madeleine's affairs and her heart sank. Speed was of the essence.

"You must understand our fear of the corbeaux," Monsieur Boiseau said in a tone of apology. "Corbeau?" queried Madeleine, puzzled at this reference to black crows.

"Yes, that is our name for informers. We are surrounded by people who are prepared to write anonymous letters, denouncing Nazi supporters, denouncing those collaborating against the Germans. People will write about anything."

Madame Boiseau was nodding her head vigorously. She took up the conversation.

"People will write about people being given special favors by the baker, the butcher, by anyone. It is terrible how jealous, envious and desperate people have become. We are almost in as much danger from our neighbors as we are from the Germans."

They both shook their heads sorrowfully.

"It is a very short, very simple message." She waited.

The husband cleared his throat, as if ashamed of what they had just admitted. "I think that could be arranged. Do you wish to write it down?"

"No, that will not be necessary. I can tell you it."

"No, no," the wife almost shouted.

"Jeanne, let me be the judge of this situation," said the husband with some impatience. "What is the message, Mademoiselle?"

"The message is 'I understand the weather will be fine tomorrow'."

They stared at her in astonishment, but she sensed that the tension had melted away at such an innocuous sounding message and everyone was inclined to smile. Madame became suddenly cordial and bustled about bringing fruit to the table and a cup of tea brewed from old tea leaves to her husband, having first offered one to her guest.

"That is the complete message?" questioned the husband.

"Yes," responded Madeleine.

"We could send one of the boys, if that is acceptable?"

"I would prefer it. It would also look more natural if he could be delivering something, fruit or vegetables perhaps."

They smiled, seemingly much relieved that the message held no threats to their safety.

"He had better leave at once if he is to avoid the curfew."

"Yes," responded the husband to his wife.

Their sixteen year old son was instructed on where to go and what to say should he be stopped. He was to carry a basket with half a dozen eggs. He was also to bring it home with him. If stopped he was not to mention the message.

Madeleine marveled at the matter-of-fact way the parents handled this errand, knowing that, as simple as it was, it still held unknown risks. She felt very guilty at exposing them to the possibility of their son getting arrested. She wondered why Monsieur Boiseau should have chosen their younger son instead of his 18 year old brother.

"Does he have far to go?" she asked anxiously, once he had left the house by the back door.

"No, no distance at all. He will return before we know it. Please do not fret, Mademoiselle. I am glad that my son has a chance to learn the responsibilities of a man." With that, the husband lit up a foul-smelling cigarette and took refuge behind his newspaper.

It was obvious that his wife did not share this view of her son's errand, but she said nothing. She began to clear the table and encouraged her older son to bring in more firewood for the stove.

With the old pot-bellied stove the kitchen felt like a haven of comfort and safety. Madeleine attempted to read, but she was too tired to concentrate. Instead she watched the flicker of fire-light through the little door of the stove and the drifting spirals of smoke from Monsieur Boiseau's cigarette, which smelt like burnt rope. It was a very comfortable room with its cobblestone floor and heavy oak table, the center of family activity.

She had obviously dozed off for she awoke abruptly at the sound of the back door closing. It had taken young Robert less than an hour to return to the house, much to the relief of everyone.

"Did you see Jean-Yves?" asked his father.

"No," was the response, "but I was told that the message would reach him this evening and to expect a reply soon."

"Is that satisfactory?" asked Monsieur Boiseau.

"Yes, indeed," responded Madeleine. "I am very pleased. I cannot thank you enough for your hospitality and support. I shall never forget the great risks your family took to help me. I have enormous admiration for all of you."

Monsieur Boiseau nodded solemnly in acknowledgment.

— 17 —

With dinner over, Madeleine retreated to her refuge in the attic. It was bleak having to spend the rest of the evening in the dark, but they had done their best that she should not be cold. She got herself comfortably settled under the many covers of her makeshift bed and tried to focus her mind away from her present uncertain destiny.

The weather had been bitter and she wondered at the fortitude of the French who were without heating fuel, gas and electricity so often. People had found creative ways to insulate themselves against the cold by lining their shoes and clothes with newspapers. She had been told that the elderly would put on hat, gloves and scarves and remain in bed all morning.

One of the sadder aspects of the occupation was the separation of family members one from another. At the beginning the French had fled in front of the German occupying armies, seeking to distance themselves as much as possible by hiding in the countryside or with relatives in another town, or near the border with Switzerland or Spain. It took seven days, she was told, for a particular relative who was a refugee from Paris to get by train from Le Havre to Brest. The Germans did not permit circulation by road or rail at night when they needed to move their own troops. In June 1940, France found itself plunged into the Middle Ages; vast areas were out of touch and silent. Slowly the population began to filter back to their homes, only to find their towns and villages almost unrecognizable as a result of bombing or looting. Then came the arduous task of trying to locate loved ones, especially children separated from their mothers. Many children had just been handed to strangers in a desperate attempt to save them from the Germans. The papers were filled with heart-rending stories of lost children, lost relatives, lost luggage and possessions.

Slowly the French had begun to regroup. They made it a habit, when it was safe, to listen to the BBC transmissions in French. There were twelve daily, although the Germans did their best to jam them. "Ici Londres" was a means of passing messages to the Résistance and others. They had their own clandestine newspapers to combat the German propaganda. These clandestine printing operations also produced false work permits, identity cards, food cards and food stamps. Banks and security trucks were robbed as well as trains to fund these operations. There were many reprisals and the penalties harsh when French citizens or members of the Résistance were discovered in such activities. Madeleine shivered at the thought of discovery.

So it was with a sense of shock that she heard Monsieur Boiseau calling her from the bottom of the attic stairs. "Mademoiselle, could you please come downstairs right away."

Had her presence in the house been discovered? Had she been betrayed? She descended the attic stairs fearful and shaking.

She was back standing in the cozy kitchen, reassured by the tranquility of her surroundings.

"Jean-Yves is in the garden and asks that you go out there to speak with him." said Monsieur Boiseau.

She nodded and moved towards the door.

"Put this coat over your shoulders," said Madame Boiseau, handing her a dark woollen overcoat.

Madeleine stepped outside and stood a moment adjusting her eyes. Jean-Yves materialized out of the shadows of the garden shed.

"Am I to understand from the message we agreed upon that you have completed your mission here?"

"Yes," she whispered in reply. "I saw him earlier this afternoon. He is masquerading as the priest at St. Xavier's."

She heard the young man's indrawn breath and waited. He was obviously having to digest this information and plan his next move.

"Then we should try and get you out of here as soon as possible. Can you describe him to me, to be sure we are speaking of the same person."

She gave him a careful description.

He responded immediately. "No, that is not the priest whom I have known for the last three years. He was much, much older and was due to retire, but we could not find a replacement and had asked him to stay, which he was content to do, having nowhere else to go. One has to wonder what has become of

Father Bartholomew? The important thing now is to move you. Be prepared to leave at very short notice."

"My suitcase is always packed."

"Good. Then give it to me now. I plan to leave it in the same barn where you began this journey."

"In which direction does that lie?" she asked.

"About two kilometers in that direction." he pointed over the garden gate. "I want you to leave here tomorrow and to move back to the barn. If no one can come for you, I will let you know. You will have to make your own way. You will have directions to memorize. We are moving one other person and you can join them. It is the best I can do, but the Germans have been more vigilant of late and we cannot take the risk of their finding you. Do you think he recognized you?"

"No, I do not. But he was careful to see if I was in the church for innocent reasons. I felt he detained me deliberately to test my reactions."

"He is particularly dangerous in that disguise."

Madeleine slept well that night, as much from the fatigue she felt from the stresses of the day, as for her relief to be finished with her search. There had been many sleepless nights during the months of her mission, due to worry and the discomfort of her surroundings.

The morning dawned grey and misty. She ate a substantial breakfast, uncertain when and where her next meal might come from. The hours passed slowly and no word came. She became very anxious and for the first time in months began to worry that she might not be able to escape back to England. Perhaps this hurdle might prove the most difficult of all. She lay in her attic room, her ears alert to every sound in the house. This had become a routine for her because it had been considered wise that she spend as little time as possible with her host family. In this fashion, there would be fewer risks of discovery or of giving away critical personal information that could be used against her or the family with whom she was living.

She could hear Madame Boiseau in her kitchen preparing the midday meal. The back door slammed, which meant that one family member at least had arrived home for lunch. The door banged again and a few moments later young Robert was calling her to come down for lunch.

By the time she joined them, all four family members were gathered in the kitchen. Bowls of soup lay steaming at each place and they took their places and began to eat in silence.

They had almost finished their meal when a knock came at the door and Madeleine leapt to her feet, ready to run up to the attic and her hiding place. But Monsieur Boiseau motioned her to wait as he glanced through a window to see who was standing outside. Seemingly satisfied, he motioned everyone to sit down and opened the door. It was Jean-Yves. Monsieur Boiseau let him in and waved Madeleine to join him just inside the back door. He looked more fatigued than usual and Madeleine's heart went out to him. How could he keep on leading this double life, with not enough sleep, probably not enough to eat and far too many stresses and burdens and responsibilities on a daily basis?

"There is no one to lead you back to the barn. I am very sorry. But we have a lot to do in a very short time to prepare for the pick-up which is to take place tonight, by plane, weather permitting."

Her heart flip-flopped

"So I am going to have to give you all the information I can now. First of all, I think you should leave near the end of the normal workday, as it begins to get dark. That way, perhaps you will not be easily identified leaving here and can reach the barn without being observed. The Germans have been making house-to-house searches in different parts of the town today. I hope you do not run into them. We have discussed what your position is should that happen to you. Here is the map giving you directions to the barn. Learn it by heart and destroy this piece of paper. Promise me that."

She nodded.

"Your suitcase is already in the barn, also some food."

"You are depriving yourself because of me, I feel terrible. How can I possibly repay you?"

He smiled for the first time in all the months that she had known him. "By not getting caught and by telling them in England all you know of this traitor in our midst. He has cost us many lives." He was serious again.

"For instructions to get you to the field where the plane will land, I have not had time to work that out. I did not want to leave them in your suitcase for fear of their discovery."

"Suppose no word gets to me in the barn, what am I to do?"

He pondered that for a moment. He knew how anxious she would feel if no word came and how helpless also. "How well do you remember the barn?" He asked finally.

"I remember all the tools, the tractor, the great pillars supporting the roof."

"Let us decide now where a message should be left," he said. " I really do not like to leave written messages, but in this case I am not sure there is a quicker or safer way."

They discussed it briefly and agreed on a hiding place.

"There will be one other person going out on that plane. It will be nobody you know. We prefer it that way, much less temptation to converse." He paused in thought. "Well, I think that is everything. Bon chance, Mademoiselle."

"I thank you for everything you have done to protect me, at great risk I suspect to yourself."

Another fleeting smile, as he shook her hand, and then he was gone. She felt a genuine sense of loss. He had been her lifeline.

The light was beginning to fade and it would soon be time to leave. She asked Madame Boiseau to look down the lane and see if it was quiet. At the same time, she asked her to leave her bicycle against the wall next to the gate.

Earlier, they had removed all signs of her presence in the attic. She would be carrying very little with her.

She had on her coat and a scarf covered part of her face. She stood in front of Madame Boiseau and thanked her most warmly for her hospitality and for all the risks she, her husband and her family had taken on her behalf.

"We wish that we had the courage and the means to do more. We hope that your stay in France will be rewarded by every success and bring us all a little nearer to peace and freedom." With that she embraced her and Madeleine stepped out into the garden.

She looked out into the lane. There was no one around. She took the bicycle, pushed open the gate and rode slowly away. She took the first turning on the right and was now on the street. She had learnt the directions by heart and then burnt them in the kitchen stove. She was to take a twisting, zig-zagging course, until she reached the outskirts of the town. There were more people now, as people began to leave work and find their way home. The further she traveled the more people she encountered which made her feel much safer, much less conspicuous. She had been traveling for about half an hour, when she heard the screaming, hollow wail of sirens. Everyone scattered to either side of the road at the approach of German military vehicles. They screamed passed and came to a screeching halt, the last vehicle stopping level with Madeleine as she stood frozen to the ground gripping the handle bars of her bicycle. Soldiers leapt out and ran in all directions, entering the gardens of the houses nearest them and pounding on their front doors. Madeleine was conscious of the driver of the vehicle nearest her staring in her direction. She resisted the temptation to look at him, but instead kept looking at the door of the house opposite her. Before long two soldiers came out dragging a woman who was weeping and screaming for some one to help her. They half carried her to the vehicle in front of Madeleine and pushed her in. Others were similarly being forced from their homes and shoved into the various vans.

Madeleine had taken a quick look at her surroundings to see how far she was from her next turning. It was a good 150 yards away, too far to make a dash for it. Her heart was pounding. She felt that she was doomed if she stayed there too long. It was then that she noticed a small footpath on her left that paralleled the backs of some houses. She was within 10 feet of it. She edged towards it. The driver now was busy with his passengers. She moved closer. The others on the street were like frozen puppets. No one moved. She reached the path, took a deep breath and turned into it, getting on her bicycle in one fluid movement and pedaling for her life. There seemed to be a lot of shouting behind her, but she did not look back and prayed that they would not shoot her in the back. There were the sounds of shots, but whether they were directed at her or not, she would never know, for she escaped unharmed. The sounds behind her began to recede and she could breathe more easily despite the pace she had set for herself. She came at last to the end of the path and turned in the direction she needed to go. She realized that she had actually come closer to her destination by taking this shortcut. She pedaled on. Now she was reaching the outskirts of the town and there were fewer people and fewer vehicles. It made her feel rather vulnerable. But it was also much darker. It took another twenty minutes and at last she saw the outline of the barn. She had met fewer and fewer people and no one seemed the least bit interested in her.

She had reached the gate to the lane leading to the barn and she stood there hesitating. She opened the gate, walked her bicycle through and closed the gate behind her. There seemed to be no one around. She rode the rest of the way until she reached the barn door. She propped her bike against the barn and carefully eased the door open. It was very dark inside. She passed through with her bike and closed the door behind her. She stood and listened for a long time. There was no sound, except for the intermittent rustling of straw - small animals, she surmised, nothing larger. She had taken the precaution of bringing a torch with her. She turned it on. Everything looked much the same as it had all those months ago, except that the tractor was gone. She put the bicycle back amongst the tools where it could hardly be seen. She then slowly made her way around the large stack of baled hay. It was much as she had left it. Only the other side of the barn had been partly cleared. She found her staircase to the roof of the barn and was astonished to see that Jean-Yves had put her suitcase in the far corner, just in the place she had described to him. What an incredible young man he was. She sat down next to it and sighed with relief. She was totally exhausted. He had left her food as before and a bottle of water. She drank and ate a little. She moved a bale of hay to make a screen for herself, lay down and tried to sleep. But she was too tense and it seemed a long time before she slept.

She awoke slowly and naturally from a twelve hour sleep, for nothing had disturbed her throughout the night. She lay there looking up at the rafters not far from her head. She was suddenly aware of a pair of unblinking eyes looking at her. It was a barn owl. How handsome he was. He closed his eyes. With his mottled coat of feathers she would never have noticed him but for his golden flecked eyes. She stretched and sat up slowly. It was a little after eight o'clock in the morning. She opened her suitcase and reviewed her limited wardrobe. She was utterly tired of everything she had. Tonight, she would wear all black. It had been decided that she should somehow discard her suitcase and its contents, keeping only her shoulder bag. She ate and drank sparingly, fearful that the food she had might have to last her longer than just a day. She wondered if it was too soon to see if a message had been left. She knew that it was going to be difficult to cope with the possibility of not finding it. She decided to wait.

It was midday and no one had come near the barn. In fact, there seemed to have been no activity in the general vicinity. She climbed down from her perch under the rafters and quietly inspected her surroundings, being always careful to have a place to hide should someone enter the barn. She made her way to the pillar where the message was to be left. She inspected all four sides of it, carefully moving the straw from its base, but she found nothing. She checked three others at the same end of the barn. Nothing there either. She was not surprised. They were taking enormous risks daily, these heroes of the Résistance. Last night was obviously one of turmoil in the town. Not the time to be wandering off the beaten track.

The hardest part of her mission was entertaining herself on those days when no reading material was available or when she could not use a light for security reasons. She had taken to writing stories in her head, reciting poetry she had learnt, composing short rhymes. She had found that to relive her past became depressing; it only emphasized her aloneness. She did not regret her decision to take on this mission. She truly felt that she had accomplished something very important. But she did worry about her chances of making it back to England. If she was caught there was no doubt in her mind that her family would never see her again.

The day wore on slowly. It had rained a little. She thought again, as she had so often done, of her parents' garden in summer and how incredibly beautiful it had looked when she had last seen it. The marvelous palette of colors that surrounded the house, the soft perfume that floated on the air and the hum of bees as they foraged in that magical place. She thought of the mellow warmth of the setting sun as it washed the natural stone of the house and blurred it together with the gentle contours of the thatched roof. The lawns had looked like soft green velvet. The outlines of the surrounding trees etched and darkened by the brilliant crimson of the sun as it slowly sank behind them. It filled her with a longing that was almost overwhelming. But it also filled her with a resolve so strong that she was surprised, for with it came courage and determination. She must succeed.

She ate another small snack. She wished that she could find a source of water to refill her large jug later. Jean-Yves had given her a smaller one, something suitable for travel. It was going to be more important than food should she not make contact for the intended departure later that night.

The light was beginning to fade when she heard the sound of the barn door opening. She lay still and held her breath. The soft crunch of footsteps and then silence. The same footsteps receded, the barn door opened and closed, and then there was silence.

She waited a considerable time before descending to the floor of the barn. She went straight to the pillar and found the thin, rolled slip of paper taped to the base. She removed it and quickly climbed back up to her rooftop eyrie. She took out her torch and read the instructions. When she had memorized them to her satisfaction she tore the paper into the smallest shreds, rolled them in her fingers into little pellets and scattered them in all directions. It was now a matter of waiting. She was very relieved that contact had been made. She prayed that the weather would not force cancellation of the pick-up.

It was very dark outside the barn, a windy night, with rain threatening. It was perfect for concealing her activities, but she wondered if the plane would be able to fly in these conditions or if they could even hope to find the landing site. She was to meet someone at the end of the lane where it joined a footpath through the woods. Could she find it in such blackness? She hoped her eyes would adjust and she would begin to see better.

Identification would be made by a special combination of long and short calls of an owl. She smiled as she thought of her barn owl and what he would make of that and whether it would set off an explosion of owls hooting. She almost laughed aloud.

She found the intersecting lane and path. She paced up and down seeking some suitable hiding place. She could see much better now, but it was still very dark. She finally found a thick bush that provided good coverage, not too far off the footpath. She settled down to wait. She was deliberately very early. She felt both tense and excited. Inactivity was very depressing and diminished one's reflexes. Except for the bike rides she had taken, she had not had much exercise during these months. She hoped that if she was forced to sprint for the plane she could do so without collapsing.

Over an hour had passed. She sat up and started to concentrate on the sounds around her. There were all sorts of noises, but the predominant sound was the wind sighing in the trees. She was listening for something else, the soft pad of footsteps, a cracked twig, something that would indicate a human presence. Then she could concentrate on the bird calls. She had been told not to reveal herself if the calls were not in the order given. She hoped her memory would prove reliable.

There it was. An owl hooting. She waited and started to count the sequence. It was not correct. Again, different and still not correct. Her heart started to flutter and pulsate in her throat. Now silence. She thought the strain would suffocate her. She wanted to move her straining muscles, but dared not. The wind seemed to be gathering in force and the trees lashed out at one another in odd spurts of violence. Then there were moments when it seemed almost silent. There it was again, but it was wrong. Was it perhaps a real owl? Had she remembered the sequence incorrectly? She was beginning to feel panic. Then suddenly there was the outline of someone walking stealthily along the path not ten feet from her. She almost squealed in terror, even though she knew someone had to appear soon if they were to meet. No sound. Another fifteen minutes must have elapsed when the hooting began again. She counted and counted a second time. Both times correct.

With her heart in her mouth, she rose slowly to her feet and waited for the circulation to return to her lower limbs. She stepped slowly and carefully through the vegetation to the footpath. She stood there, uncertain what to do next. Her instructions had not mentioned any responding call, but to just show herself and stand and wait. This was the most difficult moment of all. She felt very vulnerable. She felt afraid.

One moment she was alone, the next he was standing beside her.

He whispered the password in her ear and she responded. All was well.

"Stay about five meters behind me. We will be walking for about 45 minutes." With that he set off at a slow, but steady pace. She followed behind him, infinitely relieved to be moving, so grateful to have made contact.

She thought his pace rather slow when they first set out, but she soon realized that with such poor visibility it was all she could do not to trip, between the unevenness of the path and the various tree roots that waited to trap her. There was very little light, she could distinguish the spaces between the tree trunks that stood near the perimeter of the path, otherwise all was blackness. Overhead the tree branches slashed at each other and the noise totally obliterated any sound of their progress. There were times when she could hardly see the man in front of her. Like herself, he was dressed in black from head to foot. She had put a ski hat on her head that partially covered her nose. Her forehead which was still exposed she had rubbed with earth and hoped she had not left any white spots. He had obviously done something similar for she had only seen the whites of his eyes. She would never be able to recognize him dressed normally in daylight.

She realized that they were walking in the direction of the sea for the smell of salt was strong and fresh on the wind. There were times when they seemed to break out into the open before being enveloped by the trees again. She had begun to relax and enjoy her freedom, and the exhilaration of walking in the fresh air. She no longer feared that a German was hiding behind each tree. She began to hope that she might truly be able to get home to England. If only the plane could fly in this weather, could find the landing field. Then suddenly she found he had stopped for she almost bumped into him. There was a lightening in the sky ahead. She realized that they had probably come to their destination. He motioned her to join him. He told her that he was going to leave her at the perimeter of the field. He would rejoin her before the plane's arrival. If this should not happen, once the plane had landed and turned around for take-off, she was to run as fast as she could and climb in. She was to take no notice of anyone else.

They scrambled through the undergrowth. It was difficult going. Small branches slashed her face and body. Roots and vegetation tried to trip her. At one point she lost her footing, but managed to catch hold of a tree trunk. He had stopped again and he put his hand on her shoulder and pushed her down, and then he was gone. She was sitting in the middle of a dense clump of bushes. She did not dare move. She guessed she was probably 30 feet from the edge of the field. She could not tell how much scrub and low-lying bushes would present an obstacle when it came time to break into her race for the plane.

Her watch told her it was about forty-five minutes to the hoped-for arrival of the plane. Her eyes adjusted to her surroundings. It seemed lighter. She hoped that was a good omen, that the weather was moderating.

She had been sitting with her head on her knees, relaxed but alert to the sounds around her, when she was aware that he was back with her. He made no move to speak to her or touch her. She wondered how they would know when the plane might be approaching, when they should light the flares that would be needed to guide it in. She wondered how often they had done this. How often they got caught. She must not dwell on that.

The expected arrival time had come and gone. She became aware of the accelerated beating of her heart. The man in front of her had hardly moved. If she had not known he was there, he would have been virtually invisible. She hoped that was true for her too. She had not even thought of what she would do should this pick-up not materialize. It had not been discussed. Go back to the barn, perhaps. At least she could find her way there alone, if needed. But what then? More weeks, or even months of hiding. That would be unbearable.

The wind seemed to have dropped, the trees sounded less angry and the noise of their frenzy to have abated. Suddenly, at the other end of the field, far too close it seemed, the landing lights flared up and traveled towards her. Her heart was in her mouth, not so much for what was expected of her, but for this terrible illumination that seemed to light up the whole world. It made her feel naked. The man in front of her moved to her side. He put his hand on her shoulder to indicate she should not move. It seemed an eternity and then it was suddenly there, a thundering noise and a great bulky shape tearing towards them. He hauled her to her feet and shoved her forward. She hesitated, only uncertain which way to run because the bushes in front of her blocked her view of the terrain, but before she had made up her mind, he pushed her to the right and she was off. She was leaping bushes and running as fast as she felt she had ever run. The plane, because of its size, had seemed so close to her, but it was at least 100 yards off. It was turning now and she tried to increase her pace. It had completed its turn and the engines were revving up and she began to panic. Please, please wait for me, she cried silently. It sounded as though more than one person was behind her. She resisted the temptation to look over her shoulder. She must not fall. She was at last gaining on it. She had reached its tail, but it was moving forward. She was gasping for breath, her lungs feeling as though they would burst. How to climb aboard? She reached the wing and saw a step. She struggled to find a handhold, her foot was on the step, she struggled to haul herself upwards and went into the plane head first. She lay there with her chest heaving too exhausted to move, but aware of the vibration beneath her. She got herself upright and strapped herself into the seat and realized they were picking up speed, bumping over the uneven ground beneath them. Then suddenly they were airborne. She looked over the side, but could see no lights beneath her. Were they already extinguished or had they banked away so the lights were no longer in her line of vision? She worried about those brave men and women below her.

It seemed no time at all and they were out over the sea. It was a bumpy ride and she feared that the wind would flip them over. The pilot seemed to struggle to keep them level. She could just see his shoulders and the back of his head. She turned to look behind her. Whoever was seated behind her was hunched forward and she could only see the top of his head.

If the journey across the channel, with the erratic, buffeting winds had made her fearful, it was soon forgotten in the aftermath of their dramatic landing. As they approached the airfield, it was obvious that all was not well. Orange patches of illumination showed through the patchy cloud cover. As they approached, it was apparent that the airfield was a hive of activity, as trucks, vehicles and planes came into view in a disorderly array. It looked as though they had just suffered a bombardment. For as they came closer, men were running in all directions. They slowly came lower and lower, until they were soon at treetop level. The wheels had touched down with a brief squeak and she heaved a sigh of relief. But suddenly an ear-splitting roar enveloped them and a plane came down upon them, catching their wing and sending them careening in circles until they finally came to a crunching stop a few hundred yards from the Spitfire that had crashed off the runway and was now resting belly down, one wing tipped skyward.

The pilot scrambled out of the cockpit and came round to help her out. She felt dazed and shaky, but he put a firm hand under her arm and steered her towards one of the buildings situated on the perimeter of the field.

"If you can make it the rest of the way by yourself, I will join you as soon as I can. Just sit on the steps and wait for me." Then he was gone. A fire-engine roared over to the crippled Spitfire and she could see the outline of men running around it, but it seemed that if there was any fire, it had been quickly contained.

She did not know how much time had elapsed, but the pilot was beside her and helping her up the steps into the prefab hut that served as the nerve center of the airfield. The bright light after the hours of darkness blinded her and she raised her hand to her face as if to protect herself. Her escort led her to a chair and gently seated her in it. She was shaking quite violently. He left her, but was back in a few moments with a hot cup of tea with lots of sugar.

"Drink that, it will make you feel better."

The warm liquid coursed through her and was very comforting. She felt stiff and very cold from her flight across the

Channel, but especially from the shock of their near-fatal landing.

The door opened and a group of men, still in their flying gear, clumped in and seated themselves in one corner of the room. They were greeted with much banter. It was obvious that the rigors of war had created a strong bond between them all.

Madeleine and her pilot had not been seated long, drinking their hot tea, before a door opened and the base commander stepped into the room and called across the room, "Wing Commander Hazlett, how very good to see you. Sorry about the messy welcome. Can you spare me a moment?"

The wing commander got to his feet and beckoned to Madeleine. She got to her feet. The room was totally silent as they were drinking in the image of Madeleine, black from head to toe, her face streaked in mud. Her thinness after the months of deprivation did nothing to detract from her femininity. As the door closed behind them, the room exploded in conversation.

"What a sight for sore eyes, mud and all! Some blokes have all the luck. Blimey, who'd have thought it was a bloody wing commander in that old tin can," commented someone, and there was general laughter all around, for word traveled fast on such occasions.

It was a few days later and she was seated back in Brigadier Quinn's office. Was it possible that it was all those months ago when she was last here? In some ways it seemed like a lifetime. Certainly she felt a changed person. She had been told that they were awaiting the arrival of Wing Commander Hazlett. She had been brought tea and biscuits on a tray. She felt very relaxed.

Wing Commander Hazlett arrived just as she was finishing her second cup of tea. The Brigadier entered the room less than five minutes later.

"Thank you both for coming. I realize a trip to London is not easily accomplished nowadays."

He had a file in front of him and he was turning the pages. There was no sound except the sound of traffic outside.

"First, let me congratulate you, Miss Devaux, on the completion of a difficult mission. We are very appreciative of the risks you took. However, the final outcome of the mission is rather extraordinary. Truly rather a mystery. May we go through it step by step? I have on record here what you reported to the base commander. Firstly, Miss Devaux, you state that you only looked over your shoulder twice during your flight and on both occasions observed that there was someone seated behind you. You landed at the airfield, narrowly missed being killed by a crippled Spitfire which crash-landed with perforated fuel tanks and inoperable landing-gear. However, once Wing-Commander Hazlett had helped you safely out of the plane, he found that his other passenger was missing.

"It seems," continued the Brigadier, "that no one who was questioned, the ground crew or any of the members of the crippled Spitfire, had seen anyone occupy that rear passenger seat. We have to conclude that at some point he jumped out, perhaps that he was prepared to jump out and had a parachute."

"It is the only logical conclusion, sir." observed the Wing Commander.

"But you tell me that you were aware of three people running out of the woods to your plane, one of whom was, of course, Miss Devaux?"

"Yes, sir, definitely."

"And you, Miss Devaux, never looked over your shoulder as you approached the plane?"

"No, sir, but I had the impression that two people were running behind me."

There was silence as the Brigadier pondered these facts.

"We are still awaiting some word from France, but they might not be able to give us an explanation either."

"You were not expecting three passengers?"

"No number had been specified," responded the Wing Commander, "but it is generally known that a Lysander does not carry more than two passengers comfortably."

"It is all very puzzling." grumbled the Brigadier. "In fact, very irritating. I don't like unanswered questions."

As if he had pressed a button, the door opened and his secretary walked in and handed the Brigadier a sheet of paper.

There was a long silence. Finally, the Brigadier cleared his throat and said, "Bad news, I am afraid. A decoded message from France says that the agent trying to board the plane three nights ago was stabbed in the back and killed. So who in heaven's name was your second passenger? Now that little mystery has me very worried."

Madeleine was given two weeks leave. It was with immense gratitude that she returned home at last where her parents received her with great jubilation. It had been a very long and stressful three and a half months for them. They were shocked at her thinness, but said nothing. For Madeleine, the inactivity and uncertainties of her many enforced confinements had nearly exceeded the stress of her mission.

Mary was preparing tea and Madeleine wandered out into the garden. How often she had thought of it during the long and tedious days of waiting. She had treasured the memory of this beautiful garden and it had helped sustain her through many dark and dreary days. The summer was over and the garden was now no longer the vibrant and vivid picture it had been. But she looked around her at the many familiar sights, like the old garden seat, weathered a soft grey and the apple tree which became a little more bent and gnarled each year, and she sighed with contentment to be standing under it once again. It seemed so very safe here and she realized that she had not felt truly safe all those months she was in France. For despite the best efforts of her French hosts, her hiding places had been primitive at best and would never have withstood intense, professional scrutiny.

A bell tinkled from within the house and she was brought back to the present.

— 18 —

It was Sunday. A heavy mist shrouded and obscured everything. There was no sound. It was as though the whole world still slept, although the hall clock had just struck nine-thirty in the morning. Madeleine hugged her knees as she sipped coffee from a mug. The war had been over for three years, but it was still hard for Madeleine to believe the freedom from fear that she now enjoyed. There were mornings when she awoke with the lingering memory of all those occasions when she had opened her eyes in strange surroundings, wondering if she could survive another day without discovery and capture by the Germans and the horror of possibly ending up in the hands of the Gestapo.

She sat musing about the party of the previous evening. It was one of those noisy, tiring affairs. As the evening progressed the noise level rose, clouds of cigarette smoke enveloping them, leaving the clothes she wore smelling stale and acrid. It was the usual crowd. She knew most people there. Friends from both the tennis and hunt clubs. The core of the village elders sat in a group, no doubt critical of the younger generation and their wild ways. For some, every party was like an extended victory celebration. It was as though they could never catch up for the time lost.

One person stood out. He was of medium height and slender build, sallow complexion and dark reflective gaze. He was the guest of the Hunt Club's president, who had ambitions of making the club famous not only for its annual hunt, but also for its superior class of polo.

Sir Francis Winterbottom was meticulous in his introductions. No one was excluded from meeting the renowned polo player from Paris. Even Mrs. Russell, President of the Woman's Institute, was introduced to the Comte, despite the fact that she was considered by some the scourge of the Village Council in her anti-cruelty campaign and opposition to fox-hunting.

Madeleine had turned away from the hors d'oeuvres table and as she did so she caught Sir Francis' eye.

"Madeleine, my dear, you must meet Comte de la Croix. He is captain of one of the most illustrious riding teams in France. We hope to entice him and his team to play us here in Dorset."

He introduced them and made a point of telling the young Frenchman that in his opinion, Madeleine was one of their most promising riders, having won three blue ribbons in recent dressage events. She remembered the slight leap-frog her heart had taken as he had bowed over her hand. His English was very halting and she had suggested that they might converse in French. His relief was obvious and Sir Francis smiled like a Cheshire cat, as much as to say that this might be rural England, but they were as cultured as any Frenchman. They had conversed at some length and then Sir Francis had come back to claim his guest of honor.

Something glistened and sparkled outside the window and caught her eye. It was a perfect spider's web, pendulous with large drops of moisture which threatened to destroy its fragile beauty. She wondered where the architect of this elegant and subtle trap was hidden. She was suddenly depressed, as though a shadow had fallen upon her. How could such a small thing have any significance? As though to fend off a premonition that had crept unwanted into her mind, she drank deeply from her coffee mug and took a large bite out of one of Mary's marvelous, fresh almond turnovers. Mary's turnovers - and she produced them in various flavors - were the prize attraction at all the village fairs. Locals scrambled to purchase them. Even Mrs. Caldwell's lemon curd took second place to the turnovers Mary made.

Restored by breakfast, Madeleine dressed and walked to church at St. Christopher's across from the village green. The rector, as always, gave a good sermon and she felt renewed and reassured. As they processed out, she saw Mrs. Phillips hand a mug of steaming coffee to Sam Brown. Sam had just handed a biscuit to his yellow Labrador, sitting sedately next to him on the floor of the pew. They were regulars at St. Christopher. No one quite remembered when they first started coming together, or why indeed the dog was permitted when his master had no special impairment, such as poor vision or hearing loss. But come they did every Sunday and no one ever contested it.

Outside, the mist had lifted and a hazy sun suggested that the day would be hot. Whickham was a classic village with a duck pond, village green and church. The post office also sold newspapers, stationery and sweets, which were sometimes still in short supply. It seemed as though rationing would never end. There was a grocer's shop, gift shop, butcher's and a bank. There were two pubs, one of which dated back to the twelfth century. Half-timbered brick houses encircled the green where cricket matches would be played during the season.

Madeleine had been invited for drinks at the Stephensons, who lived in a large Tudor mansion on the outskirts of the village. Madeleine was a familiar guest at their house. They had a clay tennis court and Madeleine was an accomplished player. Julia Stephenson was a matronly woman with a kindly nature and greying hair. Her husband, Nigel, looked younger with his slender build and now sandy-grey hair. He was a very successful businessman and owned his own company. He could be the most gracious host and very amusing. But there were those who could be the butt of his humor and avoided him. Julia was an active member in the community and much liked.

Madeleine rang the bell and waited for the door to be opened by Elsie, the maid. She was ushered through the hall towards the drawing room. The volume of sound swelled as she approached. The large and elegant room was filled with a crush of familiar faces. Madeleine hoped she would have a chance to chat again with the French guest of the previous evening. But she saw no sign of him. She managed to work her way to the doors leading out onto the terrace. She stepped outside, relieved for a breath of fresh air. A croquet lawn adjoined the terrace and Madeleine sat on a garden bench contemplating it.

"May I challenge you to a game?" She turned and smiled at the sound of Guy Hamilton's voice.

"Whatever makes you think I would accept yet another defeat? I never ever come close to beating you."

"That is where you are mistaken. Each time you narrow the gap."

"Well, Guy, I think that today I would rather be lazy. I am still feeling a little jaded from last night's party. I never really drink all that much, but somehow the cigarette smoke gives me a hangover."

He smiled and sprawled himself across an armchair facing her. "I saw you yesterday evening being very charming to that debonair gent from gay Paree. What was he trying to sell you?"

"Don't be unkind. You're just jealous. He was very gracious. We talked about the various horse trials and events we had attended or participated in this year. Our views about horses in general. He also reflected on France's chances of beating Argentina in this year's polo cup."

"So what are your plans for yourself since being demobilized from the Wrens?"

"I don't know. I have no immediate plans. The summer is slipping away in a series of boring cocktail and dinner parties.

"Now don't let our gracious hostess hear you say that!"

"I like Julia. She is a good friend and a great hostess. No, I feel restless and unsettled. It's just that I need a change of scene. Some new faces in my life."

"Like Monsieur le Comte."

"Now stop it. I found him refreshing."

Guy laughed. "I have not seen you so animated in a long time. Refreshing is it? Not attractive or seductive? Alright, I'll stop."

He saw her stiffen as though in irritation.

"How about having an early supper with me before I return to London tonight?"

"That's nice of you, but I can't. My parents are having friends to dinner and I am expected to help and provide dazzling conversation."

"Well, what about next Friday?"

She smiled. "I would love to."

"There you are," boomed a familiar voice. "I thought I caught a glimpse of you." It was Sir Francis.

"My dear girl, might I intrude a moment?" Sir Francis plonked himself down without waiting for a reply. He settled his large form comfortably into a cushioned wicker armchair. His size was deceptive. The crumpled clothes which he tended to wear disguised the fact he was careful to train daily to keep his muscles in optimum condition. Only his hands, on closer inspection, might have given away the measure of his strength and fitness. He was a talented observer. There was little that missed his seemingly random gaze. He had a very keen mind and he rarely allowed himself to relax from his professional responsibilities.

Guy winked at Madeleine as he got to his feet and made his way back into the house.

"I was so delighted that you could put our guest at ease last night. I had forgotten you were fluent in French. Marvelous. Bloody marvelous. I never could get the hang of it myself."

Madeleine laughed. "Well, I fancy you perhaps did not try very hard. You are much too British."

Sir Francis beamed. "Well, my dear, I see you understand me. I have always felt that they should learn our language." He waved a vague hand at the croquet lawn. "After all, why have an

Empire if you have to spend all your time at the books learning to speak umpteen different lingos. But I did not come to talk about British rule overseas." He settled himself more comfortably and took some moments to light a pipe.

"Can't smoke this in there," he grunted and took a big draw which he exhaled slowly. "Did I hear you mention last night that you were planning a trip to Liechtenstein?"

"Yes," she replied, "My cousin is getting married at the end of November. Why do you ask?"

"Just an idea that I have. I was wondering if you would mind including Berne and Paris on your itinerary?"

She raised her eyebrows in surprise.

"If we could manage to get a team entered in the Paris horse trials, it would be a stepping stone to a few individuals connected with the polo circuit. I cannot go myself, but I could give you all the necessary introductions. You could lay the groundwork. It would not be very arduous and possibly very interesting socially. What do you think?"

She shook her head. "I have no experience in such matters."

"My dear, you speak superb French. I will provide the rest. I need to involve a few illustrious names. By the time you leave, I will have the cream of the equestrian world here involved. But I can hardly put that in writing or over the telephone. It is much better to do that in person. All you will have to do is a bit of name-dropping, set the scene, so to speak." He smiled, well pleased with himself.

As she sat up and opened her mouth to speak, he raised his hand, his hazel grey eyes suddenly seeming more penetrating than usual. "No objections. I have made up my mind. You will do very well. Also, Marc de la Croix will be delighted to see you in Paris, of that I have no doubt."

She blushed and was truly aggravated with herself and Sir Francis.

"A pity that de la Croix had to leave this morning. He had to dash back to set in motion arrangements to ship his ponies to an up-coming event. You know he had not planned to visit us here. We were very lucky to have him drop in on us." He chuckled, stroking his elegant military moustache, as he contemplated the success of his recent social coup. "Of course, we will talk about all this later in greater detail, but I am counting on you, I want you to know that."

"I think you are overestimating my ability to influence anyone in this matter."

"Now my dear, stop fussing. You will see, it will all work out very satisfactorily."

He suddenly seemed to become aware that Guy Hamilton had left.

"Did I interrupt something between young Hamilton and yourself?" he asked contritely.

She smiled and shook her head. "No, not really." She liked Guy, but there was something about him that she could not define. Was it lack of chemistry or something more than that? Some character flaw, or void, which as yet had not really shown up? A blank page which could not be explained?

She turned to the large and affable gentleman at her side. "Sir Francis, I have to go home. Mary will have my lunch waiting."

His face lit up. "What a joy to have someone like Mary in your life." He patted his well-padded stomach. "I know that I do not look deprived, but what I wouldn't give to be able to indulge myself daily in some of Mary's wonderful meat and fruit pies. As for her cakes..." he left the sentence unfinished.

"We will have you over to dinner one day soon," she responded. He was a kindly, gentle soul and she liked him, even when he had pompous ambitions for his precious club. She liked his courtly ways and his dry sense of humor.

His smile became beatific. He lumbered to his feet and kissed her hand. "My dear, that is music to my ears. I will not come empty-handed. I will have something for Mary's larder that I have bagged when out shooting."

He let her go with a few more courtesies and a promise to keep in touch with her as to his progress.

— 19 —

It was a few days later. They were having tea indoors as it had started to rain.

"Well," sighed her father, "if it stops when tea is over, I am going out to see how the vegetables did in my absence."

"The rabbits have been feasting." responded his daughter.

"You're joking, I hope."

"No, George has been very busy devising deterrents."

"Well, resign yourself to lots of rabbit pie." He helped himself to one of Mary's bakewell tarts and bit into it with determination, as though sending a message to the delinquent rabbits.

He turned his attention to Madeleine. "So where will you be staying for your cousin's wedding?"

"Before going to Lichtenstein, I will stop first in Berne. I will stay with the British Consul and his wife there. He is a friend of David Knight who is Captain of the British equestrian team. It seems as if the wedding is to take a back seat to all things related to horses. Another of Sir Francis' social manipulations."

Her father laughed. "When Francis gets a bee in his bonnet, he is a hard man to turn. Anyway, the whole thing sounds rather fun. I think you need a change of scene. When you return, you can get down to some serious job hunting. So where will you stay during the wedding celebrations?"

"I shall be staying at Schloss Schönhof, in Liechtenstein. Yvonne's grandmother offered to accommodate most of Yvonne's university friends. Really very kind of her. Luckily there are not too many of them. Apparently, she loves young people, is a great supporter of the arts and has endowed several orchestras with a view to encouraging young musicians, penniless as they usually are."

"Splendid," responded her father. "Did you know all about this, Claudia, my dear?"

"Yes, William, I did. But I also mentioned it to you. But half the time you don't seem to be listening to me. Off in another world." She smiled indulgently, even though his absentmindedness infuriated her at times.

"Well, sounds like our beloved daughter is going first-class." With that he got to his feet. He was still trim and an imposing figure at six foot three inches. His head had hardly a grey hair in it and at 58 years of age he looked much younger.

"Don't worry," her mother said as the General stomped out into the garden, despite a gentle rain. "He does not have time to sit out there and wait for the rabbits to turn up for target practice. George will build a fence, if necessary."

"So did anything exciting happen while we were away in Cornwall?" her mother enquired.

"No, the usual round of parties with the same old people."

"Well then, dear, your trip to Switzerland and Liechtenstein is going to be a nice change," her mother responded briskly.

"There was an attractive Frenchman whom Sir Francis was romancing. He would love to have their team come and play us here in Whickham."

"That would certainly cause quite a stir here..." Her mother smiled, envisioning the social implications.

"Yes, everyone would vie with one another for the right to entertain them. Sir Francis wanted me to go to Paris and plead his case."

"Is that necessary?"

"No, I don't think so."

"Good. I need you to help me with the Christmas Fair. With you away an extra week or whatever, I cannot imagine how I shall manage." Her mother got up. "I must go and talk to Mary. Do we have any prospective guests in the next week or so?"

"Sir Francis would love to be invited to dine."

Claudia smiled. She knew Sir Francis would turn cartwheels if need be to sample one of Mary's more elaborate meals. He was a dear man and it pleased her to see him so appreciative of Mary's culinary talents.

"Then he shall be."

"He promised to bring something with him. I imagine a duck or a pheasant from one of his trips out with the dogs."

"How kind. Mary will be thrilled. Such a treat."

The following week was taken up with preparations for the wedding in Liechtenstein. The wedding invitation had not yet arrived, but Yvonne had told her cousin of all the parties and special functions that were to take place the week before the wedding.

"You must bring with you all your best party dresses," had been her advice. "It will be a glorious opportunity to dress up."

Madeleine had serious misgivings as to whether her wardrobe, so depleted as a result of wartime stringencies, could measure up to the occasion. Her clothing coupons in those stress-filled times had been used for the barest of essentials, shoes, sweaters and a warm coat. Never anything fancy.

She had set about shopping frantically for suitable fabrics. She had made several trips to London for this purpose but there was such a limited selection, although things were slowly improving. There was a woman who lived in the next village who was a magician with a needle and could copy anything without the aid of a pattern, if necessary. Her name was Madame Fez. She was a petite, bird-like woman with dark, enquiring eyes. No one had ever seen her without one of her small and elegant head-hugging hats, indoors or out. She seemed to have plenty of hair, for she wore a chignon and small silvery-gold curls always framed her much wrinkled face. She claimed to have lived in Paris most of her life. No one had dared ask her how Monsieur Fez, deceased, had come by such a name. Suffice it that she had a very French accent and that her creations were envied by all who saw them. She lived in a small thatched cottage at the edge of the next village. Piles of fabric and many outfits in various stages of completion lay scattered in a seemingly haphazard manner about her living room. But it was a warm and inviting place that never failed to intrigue visitors. Madame Fez seemed to have a limitless selection of material and it was from this pre-war collection that Madeleine was able to complete most of her shopping list.

Madeleine was having a fitting for a long ball gown. It was of crimson brocade embroidered with small birds of paradise. The brocade was a gift from her uncle who was much traveled and had purchased this and other lengths of dress material on pre-war visits to Hong Kong.

Madame Fez was fussing over the hem. She could not pin it correctly until Madeleine had the shoes that she planned to wear with the gown. But Madeleine did not yet have a pair of shoes for this particular gown, despite having spent many arduous afternoons looking.

"Ah, my dear young lady, you do not seem to be very organized." was Madame's comment. "You could have a pair made to match this beautiful gown. That would be perfect."

"Yes, it would, Madame Fez, but it would exceed my budget."

"A pity. How many dresses and gowns are you planning to take to Switzerland?"

"I have not decided," was Madeleine's reply, knowing that Madame would be even more convinced that she was obviously not used to coping with such complex social engagements.

"You need someone to help you plan everything. This could be the most important social occasion of your life. You might meet the man of your dreams. Ah, if only I could go with you, all would be well," sighed Madame. "But I cannot, such a pity."

"Yes, it is," responded Madeleine rather wistfully.

"Well, do not distress yourself, my dear young lady, We shall find a way of working out everything together. It will be perfect.

You will see. Since I cannot work on the hem today, then I will work on the train and such a beautiful train it is."

Madeleine almost giggled. Between her accent and her French way of pronouncing words, there were times when it was very difficult to know if she was speaking French or English.

The fitting over, Madeleine pulled on her skirt and sweater and began to gather her things.

"Next time you come, I want you to bring a list of all the dresses you plan to take with you. Then we can discuss what else you may need to complete each outfit. Then you will not have to make any decisions once you have arrived in Liechtenstein, it will all be decided." Madame smiled broadly, nodding her head in approval of the whole plan.

"I will do that, Madame. Thank you," murmured Madeleine.

Once back on her bicycle riding home, she sighed in resignation. Getting ready for this wedding was proving to be much harder work than she ever imagined.

Friday came and with it Guy Hamilton. Their dinner together was enjoyable. Guy was an entertaining and lively companion. He liked Madeleine immensely and so made every effort to please her. She knew this. She wished she knew what it was about him that bothered her. He was immensely handsome. Black wavy hair, very dark eyes and white complexion, He did not play tennis, but was a good squash player. The closest she could come to putting it into words was that he was obsequious and it irritated her.

"You are leaving soon for Europe." It was more a statement than a question.

She nodded, sipping her coffee which had followed a very good meal they had shared at a local pub.

"After the wedding, Sir Francis is trying to persuade me to go on to Paris to negotiate arrangements for a possible series of polo matches to be held here."

Guy's eyebrows arched in surprise. "Do we qualify for such an honor?" he asked smiling.

"No, of course not, even though we have a couple of outstanding riders who are members of the British equestrian team. However, Sir Francis seems very determined to make it happen, so perhaps it will."

"Do you think you will get to represent the Club at the horse trials to be held in Devon next year."

She laughed. "I really don't know. I have had some success recently at a few of the shows, but there are quite a few other riders who are far more experienced…

"To my unskilled eye, you look marvelous astride a horse. I have always enjoyed watching you."

"It is kind of you to say so, but dressage can be boring, unless one is a participant."

"You could never be boring." His face showed his sincerity.

To Madeleine's relief, the waiter came to refill their coffee cups and they began to talk of other things.

She was back at the dressmaker's for a final fitting of her ball gown. There was a knock at the door and Madame Fez went to answer it. Madeleine surveyed herself in the mirror. The dress made her look positively regal. It was a fitted sheath with a short train. She was pondering what accessories she would wear with it, when a horrified scream from Madame Fez made her jump.

"Quel horreur! C'est térrible! What am I going to do?" Madame Fez continued her exclamations in a stream of uninterrupted French, wringing her hands in despair.

"Madame, what is wrong? What can I do to help you?" responded Madeleine, who without thinking was also speaking in French.

"It is the cleaners, the imbeciles. They have completely ruined this most beautiful velvet evening coat." She pointed to the collar and to the large imprint of an iron on the middle of the coat's lapel. It can never be removed."

Madeleine looked at the beautiful coat and then at the poor little woman in front of her and felt a flood of sympathy.

"What a terrible thing to happen to such an elegant coat. Is there nothing that can be done?'

"Nothing, absolutely nothing. It is ruined."

"It would be a lot of work, but could you replace that part of the coat?"

"Yes, yes, normally, I could, but I do not have any more velvet. If I buy some more it will not match. It never does."

"I am so very sorry, Madame. How can I comfort you?"

The little woman stopped wringing her hands and looked at Madeleine in amazement. "You speak the most beautiful French, Mademoiselle. How is that possible?"

"I was taught it at school and made to speak it regularly."

"Amazing. Oh, Mademoiselle, you do not know how much pleasure it gives me to be able to speak my own language. That is comfort enough. Somehow, I will have to find a solution for the coat. Luckily, I have another week before it is needed. Now we must not waste another moment on that disaster. We must get you ready and make you the most beautiful guest at the wedding." Madeleine was impressed that Madame Fez was once more in charge of her emotions.

The fitting was finished in silence. Madeleine was dressed and ready to leave the small, cozy cottage with its attractive disorder.

"Mademoiselle, I have been thinking. We have listed your wardrobe and you know what items remain to be purchased. Would it be helpful if I came and packed your dresses for you? I am very experienced with folding clothes. It would give me great pleasure to help you. I know you still have a lot to do."

"How very kind and thoughtful of you. That would be such a great help. But don't you have a lot of do, especially now that you have the problem of the velvet coat?"

"Do not worry yourself. I am quite expert at juggling my time. It is a normal part of my routine." She smiled brightly.

"Wonderful. Then we will set a day when I can pick up my gown. I will fetch you in the car."

"Perfect, Mademoiselle. I look forward to it. I do not often get out. I always seem too busy."

The day finally dawned for her trip to Switzerland. Her parents drove her to the station and saw her off with smiling faces and every encouragement for a happy and successful trip. It was decided that she should break her journey in London and stay overnight in the flat. She had left her luggage at the station so that it would not entail much labor when she came to catch the boat train the next day. In the meantime, she could speak to all those friends whom she might find at home later that evening.

Madeleine was happy to have the opportunity to travel again. She had become more and more restless in recent weeks. Not having a job or a routine anymore, left her without direction.

She could not believe that Erich was dead. She knew he had been imprisoned, but clung to the hope that he could survive whatever rigors he might have to endure. When they had first set about tracing him after the war, she had hoped that each day would bring news of his survival. Finally when the letter came, she had been in the garden reading. Her mother had sat down beside her and waited while she opened it. She had cried out in anguish, but there had been no tears. They had come much later. It seemed that the authorities could find no trace of him. How could that be? Perhaps he was in East Germany, which might explain the lack of information. She was terribly upset and frustrated, but she was not prepared to give up hope. How often she had relived their time together. He still seemed to be a living presence in her life. He always would be, even if she might never see him again. She had truly loved him and believed that he had loved her. To be cherished, however briefly, was perhaps the rarest gift of all. Something that not everyone experienced.

— 20 —

The journey to Berne was uneventful. She enjoyed immensely being back in peacetime Europe. The war had left its mark, but there seemed a new vitality everywhere. The Swiss countryside, of course, was untouched, the scenery as always glorious and pristine.

Madeleine was met at the station in Berne by one of the consulate's chauffeurs and driven to the Morrisons' residence.

Angela Morrison met her in the high-ceilinged vestibule of the spacious house and welcomed her warmly. She was a middle-aged woman with greying blond hair. She had a wonderful honey-colored tan which spoke of time spent in the mountains. Her good deportment hid a slightly thickened waistline.

"I do apologize for having so much luggage, but it seems as though each gown needed a suitcase all to itself. Despite elaborate details about the different functions being held and the dress requirements, I was still uncertain what I should wear to what event. I am sure that I have overestimated my needs."

"Don't worry a bit." responded Angela. "We are used to it. Let me take you up to your room. I can then tell you all about our social schedule. You can take a bath and have a rest."

They had reached a wing of the house which was for the exclusive use of the Morrisons' frequent visitors. Madeleine was surprised at the very extensive guest quarters of the consular residence. There was a light and spacious living room with a grand piano in one corner and many potted palms. Off this room, on both sides, were several bedrooms. There was also a small kitchen.

Angela had selected the rose guest room for Madeleine. The large, double bed was covered in a rich rose and cream woven linen depicting pastoral scenes of trees, animals and ladies in long dresses. A thick, deeper rose rug on the floor complemented the fabrics of the curtains and the bed. It was a warm and inviting room.

"Tonight," began Angela, "we are holding a fairly large cocktail party for the diplomatic community. All the various consulates will be represented. I will try and remember to show you the guest list and give you some background on a few of the more interesting people. Then tomorrow we have a dinner party. I understand your French is fluent. That will be so helpful. Two of our guests have only a smattering of English. Do forgive me, but I must rush away. I have a busy afternoon. If you need anything, just press this bell. If you want something to eat the cook will be pleased to make you anything. The guests are invited for six-thirty this evening. You need not appear until then." She smiled and was gone.

Madeleine took a long and luxurious bath. Wrapped in a thick terry robe, she pulled back the bedspread to reveal the softest sheets of high quality cotton. She climbed into the bed, lay down and was soon fast asleep.

It seemed as though most of the ladies at the cocktail party were dressed in black. Madeleine had chosen a very fitted black woollen dress with a short jacket for the occasion. It was another selection of Hong Kong's finest, a high quality woollen material with a silver thread that gave a very soft glint to its surface. The visual effect was one of great richness and elegance. She always received compliments when she wore it for nobody had ever seen anything quite like it. It also flattered Madeleine with her blond, curly hair and flawless complexion.

Angela, in a black moiré skirt with a black velvet top, was the perfect and thoughtful hostess. Always on the move, introducing guests to one another. Moving people from one group to another, although so many of those present knew each other well.

Madeleine was standing with a group of the British members of the community, mostly business officials. She had turned away to help herself to some hors d'oeuvres from a tray being circulated by a waiter. As she turned back to the group, the gentleman on her left addressed her saying, "Miss Devaux, I do not believe you have met Peter Weiss. He is the liaison here with Cadbury in Britain."

If she had not been munching on the last mouthful of a smoked salmon canapé, Madeleine knew she would have gasped out loud. Instead she hastily put a napkin to her lips, before responding to the introduction. In front of her stood an all too familiar face, a face that had haunted her dreams in days gone by. The man from Ulm. The priest from France. The incision in his eyebrow was hardly visible but it was still there, as was the long, light scar on his right cheek.

"Mr Weiss, what an enviable job you must have, for surely most of the world is addicted to chocolate." There was an appreciative murmur from the group at this remark. She went on. "So are you able to spend a lot of time in this beautiful country?" She was back in control.

"Yes, at least a week every month."

His blue eyes were lighter than she had remembered. There was a steely quality to them. How could she have ever seen a look of distress or fear in them in Ulm?

"Do you get a chance to ski during your visits?"

"Quite frequently. I am fortunate enough to own a small chalet in the mountains not far from here. So what brings you to Switzerland, Miss Devaux?"

"The wedding of a friend." She had no intention of elaborating on her plans. She was frantic to discontinue her conversation with him. It was then, to her great relief, that Angela came up to her, taking her arm and saying to those present, "Please forgive me if I steal our guest away from you. I have a friend whom I want her to meet."

Angela led her across the room. Madeleine was angry with herself that she felt slightly weak in the knees; she told herself that it was ridiculous to have reacted in such a fashion. But it had been an unexpected shock. There was no likelihood that he would ever recognize her and even if he did, what did it matter now? What should she do next, if anything? But she had no more time to dwell on it, for Angela was introducing her to an elegant and attractive man in his early thirties.

Like all cocktail parties, it seemed to go on too long, be too noisy and result in a series of fractured and unfinished conversations. Through Angela's industrious efforts, she had probably met half the people in the room. For the most part, all the men she met were solicitous, interested or calculating. Some were even interesting and entertaining. The women were mostly formal, polite and distant, depending on how much they felt threatened by Madeleine's fresh beauty.

Madeleine needed to escape from the cigarette smoke. She wandered down the corridor to the library in the east wing. It was a spacious and comfortable room. Books lined two walls. A beautiful natural stone fireplace was the focal point of the third wall. French doors led out to a terrace. She sat herself in a comfortable armchair and put her feet up on a convenient footstool. What a relief. She closed her eyes.

She had liked the elegant young man whom Angela had introduced as a member of the Swiss equestrian team. They had talked at some length. She spoke of her mission in Paris and he had told her that he would give her an introduction to some friends of his there who might have some influence. But then they had been interrupted and she had not seen him again.

Someone had come into the room, very quietly, very stealthily. She opened her eyes but saw no one. So she closed them again. But she felt a presence. She sat listening intently with her eyes closed. Her heart was pounding in her ears. For a few seconds she could hear nothing else. She forced herself to concentrate on the room. A cold shiver ran up and down her spine. She knew that she had to leave this room as fast as she could and return to the cocktail party. She took her feet off the stool and positioned them so she could get to her feet quickly and easily. She felt for her evening purse and gently eased it into her hand. She was ready. She opened her eyes and saw that she had a clear path to the door, except for one armchair. She would have to go around it. As hard as it was, she forced herself to sit there a little longer, in the hope of putting him off guard if he was watching her closely. She could stand it no longer. She had to move.

She was on her feet and running in one fluid movement. Something touched her arm but she did not turn and then she was through the doorway and into the corridor, where she ran straight into the arms of her newly-found equestrian friend. She stared at him in surprise and relief and then swung round to look back into the library. Someone was hurriedly leaving through the French doors. She could not tell who it was, but her instincts told her that it was Peter Weiss.

"I am so sorry," she gasped up into the face of the young Swiss man. "Someone was hiding in that room, but I could not see them. I had to get out as quickly as possible."

"You could not recognize who it was?" She shook her head.

"Perhaps we should mention it to our host."

"Yes, but not now. I will do it later."

"Then perhaps we should close the doors in the library." The young man strode into the room and closed the door to the terrace that was ajar and locked it.

They walked back to the party in silence.

"Are you all right?" he asked with concern. "Would you like a drink?"

"Yes, a glass of Dubonnet would be perfect."

He waved to a passing waiter and ordered her the drink.

When she had taken several sips from her glass, he told her that he had to leave, but that he would telephone her and give her the information that he had promised. He led her to the center of the room where he introduced her to a group discussing the schedule of Christmas concerts. With that, he left her and went to see his host and hostess, before leaving the party.

Madeleine surveyed the room to see if she could see Peter Weiss. There was no sign of him.

Finally the last guest had left and she was alone with John and Angela, sitting and sipping a coffee.

"That seemed like a very successful gathering," Madeleine remarked.

Angela smiled. "They all end up being very much the same. The only way I can remember one from another is if someone gets drunk, says something outrageous or wears a ghastly outfit." Angela laughed, "We have seen a few hilarious costumes in our time, haven't we dear?" Her husband nodded.

Madeleine took a deep breath. "John, I had a very strange experience in the library this evening. I think you should know about it." She related her story and waited for his response.

John Morrison was not a man with any particular presence, but he had a quick and able mind and it had served him well in his career.

"You say you never saw his face, only his back as he left the room? Could he have been a guest."

"I rather thought he might have been from the way he was dressed. If it was someone planning a robbery, I imagine they would dress in such a way as to blend with their surroundings."

John digested this and was silent. Finally he said,"Do you think it was someone who might have followed you to the library?'

"It is possible.

"Have you ever met any of our guests before?"

How should she answer that. "No." She hoped that she had not hesitated too long.

"Well, he has gone now. I will have the house and grounds searched, but I am sure he is no longer anywhere near the property. I am really sorry if you were frightened."

He got up and went to his office where he made a telephone call.

Angela tried to comfort her guest by enumerating all the security measures that surrounded the consulate. While she was speaking, a guard with a dog came into the house and systematically went through all the rooms, including the guest wing.

The Morrisons escorted her to her room and saw her safely into it. She was exhausted. She undressed, but was so upset she could only pace restlessly up and down. Eventually she climbed into bed and pulled the covers up to her chin. She fell asleep, but dreamed on and off all night of being chased by someone whose face she could not see.

The next day she asked if she could be driven into the center of town. She had two small errands to do. Also she wanted to go to the post office. The Morrisons' chauffeur took her into the center of Berne. He dropped her at the main post office and arranged to pick her up there again an hour later.

She had decided to ring Brigadier Quinn and tell him of her encounter. Perhaps he was no longer interested in their mystery man, but she needed to know if he was a threat to her. It was possible that Quinn would not tell her anything.

She wondered if the telephone number she had memorized all those years ago was still operational. She realized how much she needed to be able to talk to someone who would understand her predicament.

The operator had finally connected her and the number was ringing. She gripped the telephone fiercely. A woman finally answered the telephone on the other end and her heart sank.

"Is this the office of Mr. Quinn?" she asked hesitantly. Considering the nature of her telephone call, she felt she should be a little circumspect and not give anything vital away to a stranger. "No, it is not." was the curt reply.

"I have had this number for quite a few years, so I suppose it might have been changed. I will repeat it in case the operator has made a mistake."

"That is the number you have dialed" said the voice, a little less curtly. "It has been in operation for quite a few years."

Madeleine thought she would try another approach.

"Is there anyone by the name of Quinn at this number?"

"Yes, but it is not Mr. Quinn."

"Brigadier Quinn, perhaps?

"Yes."

Madeleine sighed with relief. Now if only he was in. She used her old identification and code name and explained that it was very urgent.

"He is in, but in a meeting." Madeleine groaned. There was a pause. Then the voice continued. "I will put a note in front of him. Please hold on."

She turned and looked out the window of her telephone kiosk at the people milling outside. There were lines at all the counters. They were doing a brisk business. Then suddenly she saw him. He was in profile, but she would recognize him anywhere.

She turned quickly to face away from him. She pulled her scarf over her head. Had he seen her she wondered? Was he waiting for her or was it just coincidence? "Oh, please, please hurry," she prayed silently. "Please, please answer the phone, Brigadier."

She waited tensely, expecting any moment for the door to be opened. Finally, the familiar voice on the other end of the phone boomed into her ear.

"What a pleasant surprise. What can I do for you?"

"There may not be much time," Madeleine began in a rush. "The man from Ulm, the priest from France, is standing only 20 feet from me. I am in the central post office in Berne, Switzerland. I am staying tonight at the British Consul's residence. Is he still of interest to you? Is he a threat to me?"

A whistle vibrated in her ear. "My dear young lady, are you perfectly sure?"

"I have absolutely no doubt. He was introduced to me last night at a cocktail party given by John Morrison, the British Consul, as Peter Weiss. He is supposed to be the liaison for Cadbury in Switzerland."

"Amazing. We never did identify him. It always remained an incomplete dossier. Congratulations. We will take it from here. Try to get away unobserved, but if you are not able to do so, the less said the better. You don't happen to have a camera on you?"

"I do not." Madeleine responded curtly, for now she was furious. "And if I did, the answer would be, no, no, no. Also, I think you owe me the full story one day." She disconnected abruptly but hung onto the telephone as if she were still talking. She needed time to think.

She truly believed that he had not recognized her from the two brief encounters after all these years. In Germany, he had not really looked at her, he was so much more interested in the medallion. In France she had worn a scarf and all he had seen was her eyes and face. Perhaps it would be better to remove the scarf, however, so that there would be no association with her conversation with him in France. She hung up the phone and stood thinking. Why was she in the post office? She must have a logical explanation. Someone knocked on the door behind her and her heart jumped. She turned slowly and went weak with relief to see a large Swiss matron making faces at her. She opened the door. She stepped out and took a deep breath.

She looked casually around and there was no sign of him. She attached herself to a line, feeling very conspicuous. She bought herself a dozen stamps suitable for postcards. She put them in her bag and went through the door into the open air.

"Miss Devaux, what a pleasant surprise." Peter Weiss was smiling at her.

"What a small world it is," responded Madeleine more irritated than afraid.

"What brings you into town this morning?"

"Very little that would be of interest to you." In any other circumstances, she would have smiled broadly. As it was, she felt greatly cheered that she had spoken to the Brigadier. But she knew that she was playing a dangerous game and must be very careful. He was a few inches taller than she, probably five foot ten inches. The dominant feature was his eyes. She hated his eyes, which were somehow accentuated by the whiteness of his complexion and the red fullness of his lips. She did not like his lips either. There was an unpleasant sensuality about them. He had told her at the party that he had been educated at Cambridge, but there was something crude about him that set him apart from such a background. There was a lot about him that probably no one knew. She, for one, only wished to escape from his presence as soon as possible.

"I would have thought the consular residence could supply its guests with all their needs."

"Yes, we are very pampered."

"So where are you going from here? Perhaps you would care to have lunch with me?"

"I just want to purchase some postcards and then the Consul's chauffeur will be here to pick me up. It is very kind of you to invite me to lunch, but I am not free to accept."

"How about tomorrow?"

"Mr. Weiss, you are very kind as I have already said, but I have a very full schedule which was planned weeks ago." She started to move away, but he grabbed her arm and when she looked into his face, she saw something in his eyes that turned her heart cold.

"I never take no for an answer. I will telephone you at the Morrison's tonight and you will find some way to excuse yourself. I will pick you up there and we can go to dinner."

She did not respond. She knew it would only inflame him more if he got another rejection.

"I have to go so as not to be late."

"I will telephone you at six o'clock this evening."

She nodded and walked away from him.

She managed to find a newsagent near the post office and went in and purchased 12 cards. She walked briskly back to the place where the chauffeur was to meet her and waited. She was early and he had not arrived yet. Please come soon, she whispered to herself. She resisted the temptation to look around to see if he was watching her.

She had been standing only a few minutes when the consul's Mercedes drew silently up to the curb. The chauffeur got out and opened the door for her. She got inside and sighed with relief. She looked casually out the window. He was standing at the top of the steps to the post office. There was something infinitely sinister about him.

Peter Weiss stood contemplating the Mercedes as it drew into traffic, accelerated and disappeared to view.

A flicker of anger coursed through him. She was going to be an elusive quarry. It was an unfamiliar sensation for him to find that he was not in control; that the outcome of the situation was not his to make; that his influence was superficial. He lusted after her and the fear that she might not respond to his insistence that they meet and dine together only accentuated his anger. His hurried and undignified escape from the Morrisons' library only added fuel to his growing obsession about Madeleine.

His previous evening had been one of supreme frustration. Once back in the center of Berne, he had picked up a voluptuous barmaid from the bar where she worked. She wanted to go and eat in a small café that she liked. He realized that he had to go through the charade of showing interest in her. He was convinced that she had a minimum of intelligence. But then most women's minds were focused on domestic issues and the acquisition of a partner. Such a waste of time.

He thought of his own parents. He had loved his mother once, but he felt that she had deserted him, as had his father. It was a betrayal. He especially hated his mother for turning away from him and going back to her career on the stage. He wanted to be her entire focus. He realized that she did not understand him or his attraction to learning. She was not bright enough.

Peter Weiss had the misfortune to be born of parents who were not a compatible couple. Oscar Weiss, his father, met his mother on a visit to England. He had been on business and had chosen to spend a week-end in Blackpool. He had bought a ticket to a vaudeville production and had fallen in love with Gladys the instant he had laid eyes on her. She was a well-endowed, buxom girl of 19 years with a limited education, but she was witty and bright and her slight crudeness had amused Oscar.

Every time Oscar traveled to England on business for the Swiss pharmaceutical company he represented, he and Gladys had been inseparable. Within two years, they were married. When Oscar was transferred to London by his company the newly-weds settled down in a flat in Golders Green.

It seemed as though all went well for a year or so. Young Peter was born and was the apple of his mother's eye. But soon she began to miss the limelight of her short-lived stage career. Oscar traveled a lot. Gladys consoled herself with gin. As much as Oscar was obsessed by Glady's physical attributes, her uneducated mind irritated him. By the time young Peter was eight years of age, they had agreed to separate. Peter was sent to a good boarding school. Gladys returned to the stage. Oscar continued to travel.

Thanks to his father, Peter Weiss was well-educated, eventually obtaining a first in political science at Cambridge. But his growing years had been lonely and although his mother loved him, she did not know how to nurture him and give him the attention and affection he craved. She could not understand how he could be so absorbed with books. She never read anything, except occasionally one of the daily rags when some sensational event made the headlines.

Peter's preoccupation with torturing small insects and animals made her fearful. She thought it was a boyish trait that would disappear once he got interested in girls. It did not.

Peter had contemplated the girl he had picked up as she sat in front of him that previous evening. She had downed three quick beers in a row. She was thirsty after a long evening on her feet, she had told him, in a simpering way that irritated him further. She was not supposed to drink while working in the stube. Judging by her condition, he knew that she had not abided by the rules and was well on the way to getting drunk. He had ordered dinner and had hoped it would have a benign affect on her.

He had left the table to make a telephone call. He wanted to be sure everything was arranged for his appointment at the bank the next day. He had reveled in the thought of collecting so much money. He had enjoyed his assignments, but now he had other plans.

Upon his return to the table, he had found his Swiss pick-up downing a second whiskey. He had rebuked her, but had kept his temper with difficulty. She had reminded him of his mother. He had yanked her to her feet and propelled her into the fresh air. She had leant against him and giggled. He knew it was a waste of time to try and sober her up. Too time consuming. Very little satisfaction.

He had walked her away from the café and down towards the older part of town. There had been fewer people about there. She had started to get fractious at having to walk in her high heels. He had told her that they would arrive soon at his apartment. At last they had come to a deserted street. There was a dark alley to his right and he had steered her into it. She had giggled in contemplation and leant against him. He had liked her soft, full body, but now he had lost patience and was disgusted with her. So he quietly strangled her. He left her lying in some weeds and walked away.

Once back at the Morrisons', Madeleine went to her room and changed for lunch. She hoped this lingering menace would soon be removed from her life. She had great confidence that Brigadier Quinn could muster the necessary manpower to overcome such a challenge. She yearned for peace of mind.

She was reading in the library when Angela came in. "There you are," she said rather breathlessly. "John has just received a communication from London which concerns you. Apparently someone rather important wants to speak to you. You are to take the call on the private line in his study. Why don't you bring your book and come and wait for it there?"

Madeleine followed her. The study was a high-ceilinged room, not unlike the library with two walls of books. A big desk occupied one end of it, several chairs and a sofa the other.

"This is the telephone you should pick up when it rings. It is a secure line. I will have some tea sent in to you. It could be a while." With that, ever the discreet diplomat's wife, she left.

Madeleine was drinking her second cup of tea, when the telephone rang. She jumped. Although she had been waiting for it, she was tense. She was hoping that it was good news. She was very eager to be liberated from her preoccupation with Peter Weiss.

"Hello," she said.

"There you are, Miss Devaux." A rather long pause as Brigadier Quinn debated how best to present his unpleasant proposition. "It looks as though your Mr. Weiss, as he calls himself, is not going to be an easy fish to catch. However, what we know so far is that his arrival at Cadbury coincided rather neatly with your return to England and the disappearance at the same time of the priest in France, who we are pretty convinced was the passenger riding behind you in the Lysander."

She gasped.

"According to the people we spoke to at Cadbury, Mr. Weiss always makes his own arrangements in Switzerland. The telephone number he leaves takes messages but otherwise is untraceable. He has also told them that he has a chalet in the mountains, but so far no link to such a place has been found yet. He is not registered at any hotel under that name."

Madeleine's heart sank. She said nothing but waited for him to continue.

"The dossier that we are building up on him leads us to believe that he is responsible for the death of a large number of our agents. We have too many agents who have been eliminated.

I will not elaborate on all the information that I have. Another time. But the most important fact of all is that you are still our only link with him. His profile does not match any living person's dossier on file. We need you to help us one last time to catch him."

"What is the profile of the deceased agent that he most resembles?"

She had taken him by surprise. For he cleared his throat several times and seemed uncertain of his response.

"Someone has suggested, goodness knows why, that his profile resembles that of a very dangerous executioner for hire who worked for the Gestapo and who somehow infiltrated the French Résistance. He was known to have been responsible for the death of 38 of our best agents. But there can be absolutely no connection because that man's death was witnessed by several people."

Madeleine's heart flipped and she was filled with an ominous premonition.

"No, no, my dear, take no notice of that speculation. It does not hold water. However, we want you to do one last mission for us. We want you to find some way to meet him so that we can set a trap to catch him."

"No, no, I won't help you anymore." The anguish in her voice vibrated through the phone. "He was waiting for me outside the post office this morning. He was very angry when I would not accept an invitation. Insisted that I accept. Is telephoning here tonight at six o'clock. What I saw of him today made me terribly afraid of him."

He was silent at this. Then asked her to describe the encounter in detail.

"From what you have told me, my dear, I think you are in some sort of danger until he is captured. You are the only person that can identify him for us."

"You cannot make me do this."

"No, I cannot force you to do anything against your will. But do you want to spend the rest of your holiday looking over your shoulder? We may never get a better opportunity to catch him. Whatever his interest in you - and like you I do not believe he associates you with the other encounters - it has something of an obsessive nature. He is not going to give up. Will you think about it and ring me back?"

"Yes," she replied very quietly and put down the phone.

She paced the study floor for nearly half an hour. She had never been so tormented. Finally she picked up the telephone and got through immediately to the Brigadier. He had obviously been waiting.

"What do you want me to do and how will you protect me?"

"I did not think you would let us down." She could feel him smiling through the telephone. "Accept an invitation for a drink somewhere. You choose the location and do not deviate from it. Do not let him pick you up, but meet him there. On no account get into a car or a taxi with him. When you have chosen the location, let me know immediately so I can put a team in place. Perhaps Mrs. Morrison can help with the location." He elaborated on what would be the ideal location. They rang off and Madeleine hurried off to find Angela.

Peter Weiss rang promptly at six o'clock and Madeleine was called to the phone. He told her that he had made reservations for dinner in a country inn and that he would pick her up at seven-thirty. She told him that she really was very busy and that it would be difficult to have dinner with him. Perhaps they could have a drink instead. She told him that she was meeting friends who were staying at the Schweitzerhof in the center of town and that perhaps he would not mind meeting her in the lobby. She heard the anger in his voice when he thought she was going to refuse him, but he became calmer when he realized that she was willing to meet him the following evening.

He had rung off and Madeleine hoped that she had given the impression of someone who was not very sophisticated, a slightly dizzy blond with a busy social schedule. She fervently hoped that he did not realize that he had been manipulated.

The Brigadier and she had spoken again, trying to cover every aspect of the meeting. He gave her examples of situations and how best to respond, but so much would depend on reflexes. He assured her that there would be adequate agents in place to protect her. She asked how many? He told her that there would be more than four. She seemed reassured. In fact, he hoped to have ten undercover people, but thought telling her that would frighten her. She would then know how dangerous they considered her assignment.

A room had been arranged for her at the Schweitzerhof. She was to get there an hour and a half before the rendezvous. There would be two agents assigned to her in the room. She had their names and a code word. The Brigadier had provided this for reassurance, not because he thought it necessary. There was no question in his mind that Peter Weiss was a lone operator.

The wait in the hotel room was a long and tense one. She had a book with her to read, but she could not concentrate. The agents assigned to her looked rather nondescript. A man and a woman. They talked about what she was going to do. It was a second floor room. She was going to take the staircase down to the lobby. She was not to take the lift. She had on a black woollen suit with almost flat heels. She wore a little more makeup than usual. She was sure she would look white as a sheet if not. She began to feel nauseated and short of breath ten minutes before she was due to leave the room. She complained of this to the two agents and they told her she was only hyperventilating. They helped her work through it and she soon felt a little better. But the fear that held her stomach in an iron fist would not go away.

It was time to go. She walked out of the room and down the corridor to the staircase. It was two short flights and a large mezzanine and then a longer flight of stairs. It was a very obvious route for her to take, but the Brigadier felt that all Weiss wanted to do was to get Madeleine out of the hotel and into his car.

It was a spacious and elegant lobby with a large circular marble table in the middle, topped by an enormous Chinese vase filled with flowers. Sofas and chairs were arranged in groupings. Most of these were occupied. There was a continuous flow of traffic through the lobby.

When she looked over the balustrade of the mezzanine, she could see no sign of him. She was deliberately ten minutes late by agreement with the Brigadier. Standing at the bottom of the staircase in the lobby, she scanned the reception area, but could not see him. She saw an empty pair of chairs a third of the way down the lobby towards the main door. She decided to go and sit there.

She feigned making up her face and scanned the room again. He was not there. She wondered which of the people in the room might be there on her behalf. It was difficult to tell. She could make educated guesses, but that was all. It all looked pretty innocent.

Twenty minutes had passed. They had discussed the possibility of his not showing up. Also the possibility of his waiting outside and forcing her into his car. She was not to leave the hotel alone. She was to leave it with him by her side. She wondered about the subtleties of this difference.

Thirty minutes. No one. What was he thinking, she wondered. Why would she wait for a man she did not know, when she had announced how busy she was that evening? Would he not be suspicious of this behavior? Guess that it was an entrapment? Thirty-five minutes. She uncrossed her legs and picked up her book that had slid to the floor. She sat up and he was standing in front of her.

"You are still here. How kind of you to wait for me." But his eyes were cold as ice.

"I was a little late in arriving too. I was just about to go and telephone the chauffeur who is supposed to pick me up to see if he could come earlier."

"That will not be necessary. I can take you back right now."

"You do not have time for a drink?"

"No, I have had some business come up."

"Well, please do not let me interfere with your plans." She stood up and made to walk around him. "I don't know why you invited me in the first place."

He took her arm. "I find you fascinating."

"You amaze me. We have hardly spoken." She was genuinely angry. It had succeeded in overcoming her fear.

"Please forgive me by letting me take you back to the consulate."

"I had better ring and let them know, so the chauffeur does not make an unnecessary journey."

"We will be home before he needs to leave."

He started to steer her towards the door.

They were within a few feet of the door when he stopped and turned to her. "I think that I am not being very gracious. Let us go and have a drink before I take you back to the consular residence."

"That is not necessary," she responded. "I am perfectly happy to leave now."

"No, I have made up my mind." They walked into the bar and found two vacant stools.

"What will you have?'

"A Dubonnet, with a twist and no ice, please."

Her gave her order to the barman and asked for a whiskey and soda for himself.

"So what do you do when you are not on holiday?"

"I am job hunting at the present time. I was recently demobilized from the Wrens."

"Did you see any active service?"

"I had a shore job. But the bombing kept us pretty busy at the base. What did you do during the War?"

"I was in a parachute regiment."

"Were you dropped into enemy territory?"

"Quite a few times. We were often sent in as reinforcements."

"Pretty dangerous stuff. Did you see a lot of action?"

"Enough to get invalided out halfway through. Then it was more or less office work."

"So you must speak German?"

"Yes, my father is Swiss German."

Their drinks had come.

He pulled a handful of change out of his pocket and laid it on the counter in front of him. There lying amongst the coins was a plaster impression of the Kandahar coin. She could not believe her eyes. She was completely mesmerized by it. She was taken back to the hotel in Ulm. She saw again his face in the moment before he had snatched it from around her neck. She had been mistaken. The look in his eyes that she had thought to be one of anguish was one of intense concentration, even one of ferocity. The sort of ferocity to be found in someone who risked all, but was unafraid. He was not capable of fear or anguish.

She suddenly noticed that he was watching her with a strange look in his eye, a look that told her that she had triggered something in his mind. She had no idea how long she had been looking at the plaster impression, but she was certain it had been too long. But it was a reproduction of her medallion, there was no question in her mind. It seemed a lifetime ago since he had snatched the original from around her neck. What possible explanation could she have for her interest in it?

"You have seen something like this before?" he asked in a voice so controlled and quiet that the menace in it took her breath away.

She shook her head, more to clear it and give her time to think than to deny it, although deny it she must. "I have a friend who collects coins. I have never seen anything like it. It is so unusual and very beautiful. What is it?" She hoped that her voice did not shake or her tongue sound thick for her mouth was parched. She picked up her drink and took a sip.

"I think you are lying." was his response. "I think you know much more than you care to admit."

She was now forced to look at him. She must show no fear.

"What more is there to know about it other than its country of origin? What a very strange thing to say." How could she ever have thought to see anguish in those eyes. He was incapable of such an emotion. He was not capable of any feeling, save perhaps sadistic pleasure. She shivered involuntarily. He revolted her. There was some terrible, mad quality about him. She thought about the agent described by the Brigadier who was supposed to have died. A man who obviously enjoyed killing. She knew instinctively, was convinced that this man sitting beside her was one and the same man. Give me courage she prayed. Please help me to escape from him.

She took another sip from her drink. Now there was silence between them. She could get up and run out of the bar, to hell with her mission. It was as though he read her thoughts.

"If you get up and leave me I will shoot you."

She felt sick with fear, but her next emotion was of overwhelming anger. She had lived with this menace in her life, both consciously and unconsciously, for years. There must be an end to it soon. How dare he threaten her.

"That sounds a little dramatic? Why do you feel so threatened by me?"

She had angered him, for she saw the change in his eyes, those soulless eyes. "So do you plan to shoot everyone else in the room too?" She had gone too far, but she had provoked a reaction and distracted him.

"Drink up your drink so that we can leave."

"I really think that I have had enough."

"Drink it." It was an order.

He took her arm and she got off her stool. His grip hurt her. She was no longer afraid. Illogical. But she knew what she had to do.

They walked out through the hotel entrance into the open-air. They had walked about 20 feet when she dropped her book. She bent down to pick it up. As she did so, he released her arm slightly. Before she knew what was happening someone had knocked her over. She lay sprawled face down on the paved entrance to the hotel. At the same moment, she was aware that two men had knocked Peter Weiss down. Two other men materialized and handcuffed his arms behind him. As they walked him away from her, he swivelled around to look at her and she saw the intense look of hatred in his eyes. An icy finger of fear ran down her spine.

It seemed a long time before someone put a firm hand under her arm and pulled her to her feet.

"Are you hurt, Miss?" a very British voice enquired.

"No, no," she replied a little breathlessly, despite a grazed knee and hand.

"Well, then, it is time that we got you home."

She was back at the consular residence. The Morrisons met her as she crossed the entrance hall and as she was about to make her way to the guest wing. They were very solicitous of her. She wondered if there was something in her appearance that suggested that she had lived through a dramatic, life-threatening experience. She was sure that the Brigadier had not divulged the nature of their telephone call. However, John Morrison must have guessed that something was amiss. They hastened to assure her that she should not attend their dinner party later that evening. She reassured them that she wanted to be present. With that they returned to their guests.

Madeleine drew herself a hot bath and lay in it for a long while. What had happened to her earlier that evening all seemed a little unreal. She felt a little light-headed. Whether it was caused by stress, euphoria at her liberation from fear or the Dubonnet that she had drunk in one gulp on an empty stomach she did not know. She knew that she could not lie down and sleep, so the dinner party would provide a much-needed distraction.

The dinner party was a success for her hosts. Madeleine herself floated through it rather like some disembodied person. She spoke French with both of her dinner partners. Afterwards she scarcely remembered the conversation. She was aware of the elegance of the dinner, but hardly noticed what she was served. After the guests left, her hosts thanked her for her contribution to the evening. They discussed briefly her plans for her morning departure. With that she retired to her suite. She climbed into bed, feeling both exhausted and tense. It was a restless night, filled with strange people and sinister shadows.

— 21 —

She felt enormously liberated to be in motion once again. Liechtenstein, a principality of castles and alpine villages, lay some four hours drive from Berne. The Morrisons had insisted that she use their chauffeur. She was infinitely grateful to them. It simplified what would have otherwise been a tedious journey. There were no trains to Vaduz, the capital of Liechtenstein. She sat back and drank in the passing countryside. How she loved the mountain scenery and the clear, pristine air. The sky was a brilliant blue with puffy white clouds scudding across it.

She had one last conversation with the Brigadier before leaving. He had congratulated her upon the success of the mission. Had thanked her for all she had done and had promised when she returned to England to tell her the whole story. She was content. It was wonderful to be free at last.

She began to relax. She realized how much she was looking forward to her week at the Schloss. The invitation to the wedding had also included details of the various parties and celebrations that were to be held. She hoped very much that her wardrobe would be adequate.

They had just spent the last half hour following a winding road that snaked its way through a majestic forest of deep green pine trees. As they reached the next bend the trees separated and she saw through the opening a deep valley through which ran a narrow river. Beyond, on a bluff on the opposite side of the valley, stood a spectacular castle, nestled beneath the mountain and in the shelter of another forest. That was Schönhof her chauffeur informed her. Her spirits soared.

They crossed the rushing waters of the river and were now slowly ascending the road that disappeared through the forest ahead of them. She wondered how much farther it would be before they came upon their destination. It had seemed much closer, but distances were deceptive in the clear mountain air.

They were enveloped in trees once more. She loved the sweet strong smell of the pines. It was so fresh and clean. A movement on her left caught her eye and she saw a small herd of deer foraging. The Mercedes was slowing down and suddenly they were turning off the road between huge moss-covered stone pillars into a long tree-lined avenue.

Then suddenly there it was, a classic castle with turrets and gables and an imposing series of terraced gardens with a magnificent view of the valley beyond. The driveway swung in a steep curve through an archway into an enclosed courtyard. The Mercedes stopped in front of a shallow flight of steps leading to massive oak doors. The chauffeur had scarcely started to unload Madeleine's luggage when two of the staff came down the steps.

The entrance hall to the castle was a vast room with several massive dark oak tables and equally massive oak chairs placed along the walls upon which many pieces of armor and weapons were displayed. She was led through several reception rooms and finally asked to wait in a small sitting room filled with comfortable chairs and sofas covered in pretty soft colors. Definitely a woman's touch. She sat down and contemplated a portrait over the fireplace of an older woman, dressed in a gown of royal blue silk. A huge sapphire pendant surrounded by smaller sapphires and diamonds hung from her neck. An intricate diamond brooch adorned her dress. At her feet sat a hound. In the far distance was the outline of a castle with a crown of elegant turrets. She wondered if this was the mother or grandmother of the present châtelaine of Schloss Schönhof. It was hard to tell from the classic design of her dress the vintage of the oil painting.

"How wonderful that you are here," exclaimed Yvonne, who bounced into the room and flung her arms around her cousin.

"It is wonderful to be here. What a beautiful place."

"Yes, it is. I cannot wait to show you around. I will take you first to your room."

They set off making their way along a series of corridors and staircases, passing through several reception rooms as they went. Every now and then, Yvonne would stop to knock on a door and introduce Madeleine to the occupant. Friends from her university days and various young relatives were scattered throughout the Schloss. They came at last to the spiral stone staircase leading to one of the tower guest rooms. Madeleine was amazed at its spaciousness. A magnificent four-poster bed with floral tapestry hangings dominated the room. A sofa and two comfortable armchairs were angled in one corner. An ornate carved oak armoire took most of the space against another wall. Persians rugs covered the floor. A few small landscape oil paintings decorated the walls. It was a room filled with sunlight. A room of great charm and warmth. It was such a contrast to the contemporary style of the Swiss Consulate. She was momentarily back in old world Germany, but immediately closed her mind to those memories. The views from the window were quite breathtaking, overlooking the valley far below in one direction and the forest in the other.

"This is my favorite guest room. I wanted you to have it." Yvonne was delighted at the pleasure she saw in her cousin's face. "I am sure your luggage will arrive soon. We are all gathering for lunch in the terrace room. You will see grandmama then."

"What an exciting time this is. You have so many wonderful parties planned. When do I get to meet Charles, your fiancé? Has he already arrived and where is he staying?"

"Yes, he arrived yesterday from Salzburg and is staying a few miles away. I'm so sorry, but I must go now. Your maid will help with your unpacking and press your dresses. This is the bell. Is there anything else I can do for you?"

"No, it is all perfect. I will see you at lunchtime. I will try not to get lost!"

It took her half an hour to find her way to the terrace room where lunch was served at little round tables. She came upon the great hall of the castle with its enormous beamed ceiling. There were huge fireplaces at either end and much armor and weapons of all kinds decorating the walls. This was where the ball was to be held. She stood and thought of all the many colorful and splendid celebrations that had taken place in this historic hall.

Yvonne came to meet Madeleine as she entered the terrace room, overlooking the gardens and the valley beyond.

"Come and see grandmama. She has been asking after you."

For all of her seventy years, there was a quality of great vitality and youthfulness about the Countess Elisabeth von Altenburg. She was tall and slender and very upright. Her hair was a glorious silver and her complexion a soft and delicate pink. But possibly her most outstanding feature was her eyes for they were a startling periwinkle blue.

"What a pleasure to see you, Madeleine my dear. It has been far too many years. How well you look. You have grown into a woman since I last saw you." She kissed her on both cheeks and stood back and looked her up and down.

"You look wonderful, Aunt Elisabeth. How do you manage to look so young? You never change."

"It must be the mountain air and the quiet life I lead."

"It is very kind of you to have me. Yvonne tells me you have planned so many exciting events for us all this week."

"I have had a very happy time planning Yvonne's wedding. It has been too long since we have done much entertaining here. Except for family parties at Christmas and Easter, I have not entertained since my husband died. A place like this comes to life when it is filled with family and friends. Now come and have some lunch. Later we will find a quiet moment to talk. I want to hear all about what you have been doing since we last saw each other."

Lunch was a light-hearted occasion and Madeleine met all of Yvonne's university friends and the family members who had arrived.

Weather permitting, a walk through the forest and up a mountain trail was planned for the next day. Lunch was to be served in a small guest cottage which apparently had a wonderful view overlooking a mountain stream and waterfall.

Friends of Countess von Altenburg had invited all the guests to a dinner and dance that evening. The ball at the Schloss was to be the evening of the following day. There was also a luncheon to be given by other friends. Finally, the eve of the wedding an intimate and relaxed dinner was planned at the Schloss.

The wedding was to be at eleven on Saturday morning.

Back in her room, Madeleine pulled out her invitation and reread the instructions.

Dress for the gentlemen: White tie or full-dress uniforms and decorations and ribbons: ladies, decorations, without ribbons, without tiaras.

Madeleine did not have a tiara. She smiled. It was not likely that she would ever own one.

Her luggage had been delivered to her room during the time she was taking lunch. She rang the bell for the maid and began to remove the dresses which Madame Fez had packed so beautifully for her. She selected first her most romantic dress which was a deep lavender chiffon. She was still unfolding it, when there was a knock on her door and the maid entered. How did she manage to get here so quickly Madeleine wondered, remembering with a smile the time it had taken her to find her way to lunch.

"Mademoiselle rang for me?"

"Yes, please come in. I have just started to unpack."

"Please allow me to do it for you, Mademoiselle."

An hour later all the dresses were hanging in the enormous armoire across from the four-poster. The smaller items were neatly folded in their drawers.

"I think that the only dress which needs attention is the lavender chiffon. My seamstress said that it would be impossible to have it arrive without creases, although I think she has done a marvelous job."

"What a beautiful dress that is, Mademoiselle. I will take it and do it now. Is there anything else I can do for you?"

"No, thank you very much. That really is all for today."

Everyone became more familiar with the floor plan of the Schloss. Yvonne's fiancé arrived and was introduced to all the guests. He was a tall, fair-haired young man who looked much younger than his years. He had a very boyish quality about him and seemed amazingly at home with everyone. But perhaps that was not so surprising. He was one of eight children. His father was Austrian and his mother Italian. Madeleine liked him immensely. Charles was not staying at the Schloss. This meant that Yvonne was able to be with her friends. They spent a lot of time giggling and laughing together at the beginning of each day and sometimes before retiring at night. It was a very happy and carefree time.

No one chose to dress and take breakfast in the Morning room next to one of the smaller dining rooms. Instead they breakfasted in their rooms.

The trek through the forest and up the mountain trail to the guest cottage by the waterfall was an interlude that was obviously enjoyed by everyone, even those who were less than athletically inclined. The luncheon was spread out, buffet style, on a long table covered in a blue and white check cloth. There were a selection of breads and patés, cheeses and salads, cold chicken, ham and turkey. The dessert consisted of a selection of fruit. Champagne was served in abundance, as well as fruit juices, tea and coffee. Some guests chose to eat outside in the sun and brisk mountain air, sitting on the steps of the guest house or on a collection of brightly colored picnic chairs. Others lounged indoors, sitting on pillows on the floor or at little tables. It was an animated party.

Tea was always taken at the Schloss at four-thirty every afternoon in one of the main sitting rooms, a glorious, spacious room filled with antiques, sofas and chairs covered in soft pastel silks. The Countess's collection of art was to be envied. Madeleine knew that among the paintings she was looking at there was a Gainsborough, a Monet, and a Degas, with many lesser known artists of great distinction.

On their second day, Yvonne invited all her friends to come and see the display of wedding gifts. It was an amazing collection of china and crystal and silver. Enough to fill a whole room at Asprey's, Madeleine thought.

It was after one such tea party that Countess von Altenburg invited Madeleine to stay and chat with her after everyone else had left. They spoke of Yvonne and Charles and how happy they were and how suited to each other. Then the conversation changed course and focused on Madeleine. It was not possible for

Madeleine to be evasive with someone whose intense gaze seemed to monitor every passing thought and emotion. She spoke of her wartime experiences, leaving out the most sensitive parts which might still be considered confidential. She told her great-aunt how she met Erich and the sequence of events that led to their marrying and her eventual escape back to England. How difficult it was to believe that she had ever met Erich. It was like an encounter in another life, a very beautiful dream. Yet in so many ways, it seemed impossible that someone who still seemed so real might no longer be living. There continued to be no definite word from the authorities. It was assumed that he was still imprisoned somewhere in East Germany. She did not feel that she would ever meet anyone else. Now, that the War was over, she felt directionless. She mentioned her mission for Sir Francis in Paris and the plan to meet with de la Croix.

"My dear child," smiled the Countess, "As unsettling as it may seem to you, it really is a time to reflect and plan for the weeks ahead. You cannot remain paralyzed by past events. You may find each other eventually, but if that should not happen you should be prepared to go forward. There are so many possibilities for you, so many eligible young men. I realize you do not believe that now, but I can help you to meet one or two of them during this week of social events."

"That is very kind and thoughtful of you, dear Aunt Elisabeth, but you are much too busy to concern yourself with me. I am just so happy to be here. I am looking forward to meeting all of Yvonne's friends. Everyone is having a wonderful time in these beautiful surroundings. Thank you for making this wedding truly memorable, not only for Yvonne but for each one of us."

"My dearest Madeleine, what a sweet thing to say. It gives me immense pleasure to be part of such a special celebration. Now, dear child, off you go. We shall see each other at the dinner-dance tonight at the Remingers'. They have a very lovely house. You will enjoy seeing it."

Madeleine wore her lavender ball gown. She received many compliments. She had many dance partners. Countess Elisabeth, true to her promise, introduced several young men to her. She returned to the schloss with tired feet and legs. She soaked in a bath and went gratefully to bed.

The ball at Schönhof was a magical affair. The great and lofty beamed hall steeped in memorabilia of ancient times was a magnificent backdrop to the colorfully gowned ladies and their elegant escorts with their medals and vivid uniforms, some of whom could have stepped out of the portraits surrounding them. Added to this visual panorama were the liveried footmen in their deep periwinkle blue uniforms with white lapels and trim and gold buttons.

The dinner was sumptuous. Courses of smoked salmon, crab cocktail, salmon en croûte, venison, lamb ribs that melted in the mouth and a selection of desserts that included a raspberry bavaroise, gâteau St. Honoré and profiterole. To Madeleine, even though the war in Europe had been over for several years, such sumptuous fare was an overwhelming vision after years of deprivation. However, she realized that so much could be provided through local sources in these untouched surroundings, the more especially if one had the connections which would be the case of her great-aunt.

The engaged couple, seated on the dais with their families, were obviously absorbed in each other. Yvonne wore a pale pink gown of rich taffeta and layers of chiffon that enhanced her coloring and gave her the appearance of a Dresden shepherdess. The orchestra played until four in the morning. Some of the older generation had left at midnight, but most of the guests had remained for the entire evening. Countess von Altenburg looked regal in a rich blue silk gown with a short floating train. It matched her eyes. Around her neck she had worn the sapphire and diamond pendant necklace that Madeleine had seen in the portrait upon her arrival. All the young gentlemen as well as the older guests had invited their hostess to dance. Madeleine was amazed at her stamina. But the Countess had paced herself well and had only danced one dance out of each set.

Madeleine wore the deep crimson brocade gown with birds of paradise on it. Around her bare shoulders was draped a soft pink and gold scarf which was held in place by a magnificent multi-colored butterfly brooch. When she danced she carried the train over one arm. She was quite unaware of the many admiring glances. Her hair was swept on top of her head, so that the curls hung down and framed her face.

Madeleine enjoyed her dinner partners. One was a retired elderly colonel in the French army, who entertained her with stories of the French Foreign Legion. On her other side was a young man who was a botanist who had spent some years in the Amazon. He regaled her with his adventures with unfriendly natives, wild animals and insects. Only the flowers and fauna had seemed benevolent, and some of those were poisonous he had told her.

The pre-nuptial dinner at the Schloss was another elegant evening made memorable by music and many speeches.

The wedding day dawned fine and clear. It was a busy morning, with the girls popping to and fro between rooms to be helped with buttons and fastenings and coiffures.

The ceremony and the music touched Madeleine deeply as she remembered with both pain and pleasure her own wedding in Ulm. How many lifetimes ago that seemed. Not nearly such a carefree and sumptuous occasion as this day, but still one filled with love and hope. The sermon was long, but eloquent and filled with many historical references concerning both families. The bride looked like a fairytale princess in a rich peau de soie gown with mutton-chop sleeves, reminiscent of medieval times, and a twenty foot train. Her veil was held in place by a simple diamond coronet. Her bouquet was a profusion of flowers in pink, lavender and white. There were a dozen attendants, which included a flower girl and two pages. The bridesmaids wore pink chiffon dresses and coronets of flowers. The bride and groom processed out of the church to find the sun breaking through the clouds as they climbed into their horse-drawn carriage for the ride back to the Schloss. They were a handsome pair and Charles suddenly seemed older and more sophisticated in his white tie and tails. The church was several miles from Schönhof and so a procession of cars and carriages followed them back to the Schloss where a luncheon was served.

— 22 —

Madeleine was at last seated on the train to Paris. It had been a tedious journey so far, as much for the quantity of luggage as for the various changes to be made from car to train to yet another train. She was tired. It had been a very strenuous week. She had enjoyed herself immensely, but she was short of sleep and she had eaten too much rich food.

Once the newlyweds had departed on their honeymoon in the Greek Isles, the house party at the Schloss had slowly begun to break up as individuals took their leave and returned home. Madeleine had remained one more night at Schönhof because there were no train connections so late in the day. She had been fortunate enough to be given a ride in a car driven by another guest, so that she did not have to take the bus to make her train connection.

She sat back in her seat and closed her eyes.

The wedding luncheon had been elegant. A small orchestra had played background music. There had been many speeches and toasts. Her table companions had been polite and courteous, but not particularly interesting. Perhaps she had been tired, but she had reached a point where she had begun to feel a little deflated. She realized that with the festivities drawing to a close she had to face the next stage of her journey and she was not looking forward to it. She was sure that she would feel awkward presenting Sir Francis' request that polo matches be arranged between the two clubs. She could not believe that the French would be the slightest bit interested.

The train picked up speed and settled down to a repetitive rhythm. It lulled her to sleep and she slept deeply, her head resting against the padded window seat.

The carriage was still empty when she awoke. She felt much refreshed and looked at her watch. Another hour and she would be in Paris. It had been arranged that she stay at the Prince de Galles. Luckily she was not paying for her accommodation, but Sir Francis insisted that since she was representing them she could not stay in some smaller hostellerie. It was a question of appearances.

The train journey to Paris was comfortable, even luxurious. Now that she no longer felt tired, she realized that she loved being in limbo again, loved the exhilaration of speed, the feeling of anticipation at the sights and sounds awaiting her arrival.

But when she arrived at the Prince de Galles she found that no reservation had been made in her name. They would be very happy to provide her with a suite, but the hotel was very full due to a special assembly of UNESCO. When the receptionist quoted the price for the suite, she knew it was out of the question, appearances or not. She had the number of a small hotel in St.

Germain and asked that they telephone and see if she could have a room there. This was accomplished without any difficulty.

A taxi was called and her luggage was once more stowed aboard it.

She was deposited in front of the black oaken door of the Relais Fleuri which stood on a side street in St. Germain. A small door with a latch was set inside the larger one which had at one time, when opened, admitted coaches. She stepped across the threshold into a flagstone passage and thus into a small inner courtyard. Here a flight of steps led into the hotel's foyer. At the reception desk, Madeleine asked for the room which had recently been reserved in her name.

The receptionist, an elderly lady with a grey chignon, consulted her book and looked up, shaking her head.

"I am sorry, Mademoiselle, but there is no reservation in your name. I have been here nearly all morning. I certainly did not receive a telephone call on your behalf. Besides which, we have no vacancies."

Madeleine sighed in frustration. "How annoying," she exclaimed. "This is the second time this morning that I have found my reservation has not been made. I have so much luggage. Could you recommend another hotel nearby?"

"Perhaps we can find a solution for you here. We have a very large and lovely bedroom with a sitting room on the top floor which is in the process of being redecorated. If you would not object to a room which has only half the wallpaper up, you could take that," said the receptionist smiling.

"That sounds wonderful," responded Madeleine, "but it sounds rather expensive."

"Please, Mademoiselle, do not concern yourself. I should be very happy to let you have it for a very modest amount. I would normally never make it available, but the painter had to leave Paris for three days on family business."

"It sounds perfect. However, I was planning to remain longer than three days."

"Will you want to spend a lot of time in your room?"

"No, I think that I shall be gone most of the day."

"Since there are two rooms which he has to complete, I am sure it will work out. Possibly, I can move you to another room if it becomes inconvenient."

"Madame, you are too kind. I will do whatever is necessary to accommodate your painter."

"Then all is arranged," smiled the receptionist. "Now where is the luggage you speak of?"

Finally, Madeleine and her luggage were installed in her suite after the bellman had made several journeys up three flights of stairs.

When Madame Fauberg saw all the luggage that Madeleine had left sitting inside the front door of Relais Fleuri, she smiled broadly and said that one room would certainly not have been enough for her newly-arrived guest.

Madeleine walked into her suite to find a step ladder and bucket sitting in the room. One half of the bedroom had bare walls. The remainder of the walls were covered with enormous grey and pink cabbage roses. The sitting room walls were still bare. The smell of paint was rather suffocating.

A maid appeared at the door. "Madame Fauberg has sent me to tidy your room, as we were not expecting to use it. I will try not to get in your way."

The view from her suite was quite spectacular. A sea of roofs and spires stretched as far as the eye could see. Although the gentle hum of traffic reached her ears, the Relais Fleuri was insulated from the more raucous sounds of the city,

The maid had left, having swept the floor and dusted the room and opened the windows to let some of the paint fumes escape. Even without the wallpaper, it was an elegant suite and she would be very comfortable. It was too early for dinner, so she took a long, leisurely bath in the enormous, claw-foot bathtub. She emptied a small phial of bath oil into the water. Its perfume enveloped her as she lazily floating in the scented water.

Dinner was equally pleasing. A four course meal, impeccably served. No portion was too large. The dessert was unusual; poached prunes stuffed with almond paste served with a vanilla cream custard. Superb. She lingered over her coffee and thought about her reason for being in Paris.

Sir Francis had told her that he would inform Comte de la Croix of her errand so that she would be expected. All she had to do was to telephone for an appointment. She had the telephone number. She was still puzzled by her experience at the Prince de Galles. It was so unlike Sir Francis to forget to make her reservation. Then there was that same experience on arriving at the Relais Fleuri. She had heard the concierge make the reservation. She pulled the slip of paper he had given her out of her bag. Hotel Malesherbes. She looked at it in surprise. He had written a different hotel and address on the paper. The two pieces of paper had become switched. At least that explained why the Relais had no record of her name and reservation. She felt relieved. She did not like too many coincidences.

As she walked out of the dining room, she stopped at the reception desk. She did not want to oversleep the next day. There was so much to see and do. She asked that her breakfast be delivered at eight.

She slept well that night and awoke refreshed a little before eight. She lay contemplating a sunbeam that lit up the ceiling above her head. She had learnt during dinner the previous evening that the Relais was a converted priory. That explained the beautifully beamed ceilings in many of the rooms. In places, the walls were three feet thick. It was a very old and historic building.

After a breakfast of deliciously fresh brioches and croissants and coffee, she went for a short walk. She passed a news stand and purchased a paper. When she got back to the hotel, she placed a call to the Comte's residence. When she got through, she was told that Monsieur le Comte was not at home. It was not certain when he would return. She could not find out whether he was out for the day or out of town. She was disappointed and puzzled. Would Sir Francis not have informed her if de la Croix was away?

She shook off her frustration and decided to explore the city. She had never been here alone. She walked for miles. She explored Montmartre in depth, lingering inside Sacré Coeur. Its peaceful, shadowy interior soothing her. She contemplated the great stained glass windows and marveled at them.

She found a little bistro tucked down a side street. It was crowded and noisy and the smoke and scent of Gauloise cast a haze through which people's faces became muted and subdued, rather like some old and faded painting. She had a salade Niçoise, crisp, fresh bread and butter and coffee. It was the perfect lunch. She was crushed in between two groups at a long trestle table. There was a lot of hilarity between the waiter and his customers. Obviously, they were mostly regulars and knew each other well. She reveled at the flow of French conversation around her. Her ear always became attuned effortlessly.

She lingered over the many paintings displayed in the narrow streets before eventually wending her way back to the hotel. She was pleasantly tired and feeling more alive than she had felt in months.

She picked up her key from the desk clerk and as she was about to walk away, he called her back and told her that someone had enquired about her earlier in the day. Surprised, she asked if they had left their name. They had not. It had been a telephone call, so he could not describe the person. She was slightly puzzled. Surely if it had been de la Croix or Sir Francis they would have left word.

Back in her roof-top room, she decided that she would ring Sir Francis. She wanted reassurance that she was not on a wild goose chase. As much as she was enjoying being in Paris and could easily entertain herself indefinitely, she did not have unlimited funds at her disposal, nor did Sir Francis, she felt sure, want to underwrite an extended holiday without some results of interest to him.

She placed her call to Sir Francis and hoped that it would not be delayed and interrupt her dinner. It did not.

"How good to hear from you, my dear. All is well I hope?" boomed his voice over the telephone.

"Yes and no," was her reply. "I was so surprised to arrive at the Prince de Galles and find that there was no reservation in my name."

"How can that be? I arranged with de la Croix that he should make the reservation for me."

"But do you know if he did so?"

"Yes, my dear, he did. He confirmed it in writing. So where are you staying?"

She told him. Then, on an impulse mentioned the strange repetition of circumstances in which she had arrived at the Relais Fleuri to find no reservation there either. Due to an error, a reservation had been made at Hotel Malsherbes.

There was a long silence on the other end and she wondered if Sir Francis had put down the phone. But he had not. It was a different man who was speaking to her now. The somewhat pompous and jocular personality was gone. This was a man who spoke with authority; a man used to giving commands and being obeyed. He asked her to tell him all about her arrival in Paris, to leave nothing out. She was reminded of Brigadier Quinn and sighed in resignation. Why was he being so strange and fussy all of a sudden?

She recounted everything in sequence. She ended by expressing her irritation at the fact that de la Croix seemed not to be aware of her arrival or had been called away so precipitously as not to have left instructions should she call. That someone had called her but not left a name.

Sir Francis was as mystified as Madeleine. She could sense a real concern in him. In fact, Sir Francis was very concerned. He felt guilty that he had somehow put this innocent, inexperienced young girl in jeopardy, for he had no doubt that these different coincidences were in fact deliberate acts against her safety. He was using her for his own purposes, albeit seemingly innocent, but how had anyone known that? A lucky chance, or the same leak he was trying to uncover? He had not intended that she should become a target, only an innocent decoy.

"The arrangement was for him to collect you soon after your arrival and show you around. Then, as you know, you were possibly to attend the Horse Trials at Longchamps next week. I really cannot understand what has happened."

"Would you like me to return to England," she asked.

There was a silence. Finally, Sir Francis responded with a return to his more jocular self. "My dear, you have not accomplished your mission. I am sure de la Croix will show up tomorrow. But one thing you must promise me, that you will contact me tomorrow and let me know that he is back in Paris."

"Yes, of course." She found his concern comforting. She was relieved. Now she could enjoy herself without feeling guilty that she was spending his money, more correctly the Club's money, under false pretenses.

— 23 —

The next day dawned sunny. Following much the same pattern of the previous day, she set out and took the metro to her furthest destination, working her way back towards her hotel. Her wanderings encompassed the Opera, the Champs-Elysées, Place de la Concorde. Despite the deprivations of the War, the Parisians seemed to have a vitality about them that was contagious. The boutiques were enough to make her envious of anyone who could afford to indulge themselves. She had lunch in a small café not far from the Georges V. It was a more sedate place than the bistro of the previous day. The food was superb. It was a place that she felt tourists rarely discovered.

It was late afternoon before she returned to Relais Fleuri. She walked up to the reception desk for her key. As the desk clerk handed her the key, he pointed over her shoulder and told her that someone was waiting for her. She followed his finger and saw a man seated in one corner reading a newspaper. As she stood there, he lowered the paper and their eyes met. He was an older man, probably in his mid-fifties, with slightly cropped greying hair. He wore a moustache. He had the look of a military man. She hesitated, reluctant to break the spell of a carefree day.

He came towards her. "Mademoiselle Devaux, I am Luis Brazzini. I am Comte de la Croix's manager. May I invite you to sit down with me for a moment?" He spoke in French, but with a slight accent.

She sat down in an armchair. He in another with a small table between them.

"Monsieur le Comte has been unavoidably detained on business. He very much regrets not to be here to receive you. He has delegated me to offer you any assistance that may make your stay in Paris a most pleasant one until he returns."

"Please thank the Comte for his courtesy. Perhaps I do not need to await his return. I can complete my errand by entrusting you with the information that I have brought with me."

"My dear Mademoiselle, the Comte will be returning in the next day or so. I think that the information you have should be given to him in person. In the meantime, please consider yourself his guest during your stay in Paris."

"I could easily post the information to him," she said, not to be deterred. "It might save time and be more convenient."

"No, no. Please do no such thing. If you could just be a little patient and give it to him in person. That would be much more satisfactory."

She shrugged, a little mystified by his insistence.

He was silent for a few minutes, seemed about to speak, but changed his mind.

"I really would enjoy the chance to explore Paris for a few days," she said in an effort to reassure him.

"Bien, bien," he responded, getting to his feet. "Then that is settled." He seemed relieved.

The following day she spent exploring the Louvre. It seemed to be in a state of some disorder, as though she had interrupted them in the process of moving. However, she concluded that all museums spent a lot of time rearranging their exhibits. It would also be important to have the many artifacts brought back to Paris from their various wartime hiding places in the country. Much restoration and repair would be necessary. She knew that many works of art had been stolen and secreted out of France and listing those still missing would be time-consuming.

On her way back to the hotel, she stopped at the news stand to purchase a paper.

She unlocked the door to her room and stepped inside and was astonished to see a man in silhouette clambering out of the window. She ran and leaned out and watched him hurrying along the ledge of the roof, only to disappear around the corner gable. She had glimpsed his face, but it had looked an eerie green color. The adjacent hotel's neon sign cast a strange light on the facade of Madeleine's room and that side of the hotel. She wondered if she could recognize him again because of this distortion of his features.

She rang down to the front desk and explained what had happened. It was only a few minutes before the assistant manager was knocking at her door. She relayed to him what had happened. He was as shocked as Madeleine. He assured her that nothing similar had ever happened at the Fleuri before. He was as mystified as she. Nothing seemed to have been touched. After securing her windows and drawing the curtains, he left her. He had regretted that he could not move her because they had a full house. But she reassured him that she was not concerned and would call if she needed anyone.

She took a long bath and changed for dinner. She picked up her unread newspaper and went down to the dining room. The staff were most attentive to her throughout dinner. She assumed that word had circulated on the incident in her room. She was content with the attention she received. It was not intrusive. She was served coffee. She picked up and unfolded her newspaper. She skimmed through it and was about to return to the front page when a small paragraph caught her eye. It was the name of Hotel Malesherbes which had somehow jumped out at her. She read the paragraph. A guest had died at the hotel under suspicious circumstances. The victim's room had been ransacked. No name was mentioned. It was under investigation. A slight shiver coursed through her. She wondered again at the coincidence that she had been booked into that hotel and not the one she was now in. She got up from the table and walked out of the charming, beamed dining room. It was small and intimate and there was a good crowd, although not all the tables were filled. Once back in her room, she picked up the telephone and placed a call to England. She had tried to reach Sir Francis the previous evening, as promised, but he had been out. His housekeeper had taken her message that she still had not seen de la Croix.

Sir Francis sounded like his old cheerful self. She told him of her meeting with Luis Brazzini. Sir Francis responded with warmth. They had met. Fine military record. Very accomplished horseman. An excellent man to have running one's stables. They conversed a little on the subject of horses. They were about to hang up, when Sir Francis asked her, as an afterthought, if she had enjoyed her day. She responded with enthusiasm.

"I even walked into my room and found a man exiting by the window. Never a dull moment."

Sir Francis could hear the smile in her voice, but his heart sank.

"Was anything taken?" he asked sharply, no longer jovial.

"Nothing at all. I have nothing of interest to anyone. I did bring a little jewelry but I was carrying it with me."

"You are also carrying that envelope with you?" He sounded solemn.

"No. I left it locked in my suitcase."

"Is it still there?" He sounded severe, as though she were some delinquent pupil.

"I will go and look."

Sir Francis sat and waited. He decided that he must be getting old, for he found that the suspense of waiting for a reply was almost more than he could stand. In the good old days, he was able to handle the strains and stresses of his work and even relished the dangers. Times had changed. Also, it was one thing to be directly involved and quite another to have others involved, especially someone like the lovely Madeleine who was quite unaware of the part she was playing. She did not know that he was a member of M.I. 5. She must never know that. Few people did. He had had her medallion duplicated so that the duplicate could carry both false and authentic information. They had a particularly elusive mole in the organization and by inserting misleading information into the duplicate medallion they hoped to give a false sense of security to the mole and lure that person into revealing themselves.

Sir Francis found it exhausting nowadays playing the dual role of the courteous and sometimes bumbling cocktail-goer, while part of his razor-sharp mind could not rest for a moment trying to juggle the complexities and challenges of his immensely demanding job.

"Yes, the envelope is still there. In fact, I have it in my hand."

His grunt of satisfaction and relief was audible.

"Does it look at all as though it has been opened?"

She turned it over in her hand and inspected it carefully.

"There is nothing unusual about it. I think it has not been opened since it was sealed."

"Good. Now I have to go. My dear young lady, guard that envelope well. Give it to no one, except to de la Croix. Continue to ring me until you meet with de la Croix. Now I have to go." And he was gone.

She sat digesting this conversation. Why was his polo team list of so much concern? He obviously felt he could not entrust it to the postal system. Why entrust it to her? She only knew de la Croix from that one encounter. He was a terribly attractive man and she would be glad of the opportunity to see him again. But there was still something distant and aloof about him that made her hesitant to push the polo match question. It made her feel uncomfortable.

She awoke the next morning to the clatter in the next room, which announced the arrival of the painter. She had slept longer than usual, but she felt refreshed and eager for another day of exploration.

When she was dressed, she went into the sitting room and met the painter. Alphonse was a large and jovial Frenchman of uncertain years. He apologized profusely if he should be inconveniencing Mademoiselle.

Madeleine reassured him that she would be gone most of the day and that he should not change his plans because of her. She had obviously said all the right things, for Alphonse was effusive in his wishes for her to have a very enjoyable day.

She picked up her bag from her bed and was about to leave when the telephone rang. She picked it up.

"Marc de la Croix, Mademoiselle Devaux. Please forgive me for being absent upon your arrival in Paris. I returned late last night. I do hope that you have been able to entertain yourself."

"I have had a most pleasant few days. I was only concerned that there might have been some misunderstanding."

"Would you be free to join me for lunch today?"

"Yes, I would." Her heart did a small skip.

"I have a terribly busy morning. Would it be an imposition to ask you to meet me at Taillevent, let us say at one o'clock?"

"Of course not. I will be there at one o'clock."

She stepped into the bathroom and surveyed herself in the long mirror. Could she wear what she had on for lunch or should she change into something else? She was wearing a navy suit with a bright multi-colored scarf at the neck. The navy color was rather severe but the scarf added life and was flattering to her fair complexion. If she added a brooch to the lapel, it would certainly be dressy enough for an elegant lunch. Satisfied with her appearance, she waved to Alphonse and stepped out into the corridor.

The luncheon at Taillevent was a euphoric experience after three days in Paris alone. Marc de la Croix was awaiting her arrival at the restaurant. They were seated in a secluded corner of the restaurant. There was a brief lull in the conversation as the capacity crowd drank in their meeting. Once they were seated, the wine waiter took their order and in due course they were given menus.

"Shall we decide upon our luncheon first before doing anything else?" he asked.

She ordered a crab bisque, sole and salad. He ordered hot leek and potato soup, filet mignon and a salad. This accomplished, he turned to her.

"I do want to apologize again for not being here when you first arrived. Something quite unexpected turned up. It was too late to contact Sir Francis for you were already en route. I left word at the Prince de Galles. But I see that you did not stay there."

"No. When I arrived there, I found that they did not have a reservation in my name. The hotel was full, except for some suites which were rather too expensive.

"How strange, I made the reservation myself."

"I am very comfortable at the Fleuri. Although that was rather strange too." She told him about arriving at the Fleuri and finding, for the second time, no reservation in her name.

"Before, we talk of other things, I want you to have this envelope which Sir Francis Winterbottom asked me to give you. He was very particular that you should have it and that I should not give it to anyone else. I assume it is not just about polo." She smiled rather archly. He took it from her and thanked her.

"I am very grateful to you for bringing this. I hope it will give me the information I need." He did not choose to elaborate further and she wondered if she had offended him by being inquisitive.

At this point, the waiter returned to serve their first course.

"So, tell me what have your been doing since your arrival in Paris?"

She told him briefly. They then went on to speak of the horse show which was to begin the next week and of his involvement.

"I want to make amends for my absence. First, I wondered if you would like to visit my stables in the country?

"I would enjoy that very much indeed. Is it far outside Paris?"

"It very much depends on the time of day and the traffic. It can take from an hour and a half to two and half hours. But it is well worth the effort." He smiled at the pleasure it gave him to be there. "Then I wondered what you had decided about the Dior Fashion Show tomorrow?"

"I know nothing about it."

"They never gave you that message either then at the Prince de Galles?"

"No."

"I have been given a pass to the Dior Fashion Show and wondered if you would like to go? Even if I were free, it is not something that holds great interest for me."

"I would love to. What time does it begin?"

"I forgot to bring the ticket with me but I will have it delivered to the Fleuri first thing in the morning. Let us have dessert and then I must go."

"Just coffee for me, please. The lunch was delicious."

He smiled at her and she felt a ripple of pleasure.

They took a taxi and he dropped her off near the Place de la Concorde. He promised to telephone her later. He hoped that they could dine together that evening.

They did dine together. This time he took her to Maxim's. The maitre d' ushered them to their table and waved imperiously to the wine waiter who glided across the room to them. It was obvious that Marc de la Croix was not only well-known to the staff at Maxim's, but also to many of the patrons who acknowledged him in various ways. It was an immensely pleasurable evening. The food and wine were superb. However, for Madeleine it was just very stimulating to be with such an attractive and interesting man. Marc for his part was enchanted with the lovely girl at his side. She seemed so fresh and unworldly, something that could not be said of most Parisians. They talked at great length about horses and the world of competition, what it took to produce a champion. Marc maintained that they were born not bred. It was something they debated at length. Finally it was time to leave and he deposited her at her hotel. He had remembered to bring the ticket to the Dior Show. He left her holding it in her hand as she walked through the oak door of the Fleuri.

Once back in her suite, she was impressed with the progress that Alphonse had made in her absence. The wallpaper had been completed in her bedroom. It made an immense difference to the appearance and mood of the room. It seemed both sophisticated and intimate. She looked at her invitation and saw that she was expected to arrive promptly for the Dior Show at eleven. She was thrilled at such an unexpected opportunity. She could not wait to tell Madame Fez.

The following day, a Friday, dawned bright and clear. She had dressed and enjoyed a leisurely breakfast by nine-thirty. Alphonse was in full swing and working on the second wall of the sitting-room. She had complimented him on her finished room. He was obviously pleased by her comments.

Nothing about the fashion show was as she had anticipated. First of all the salon was much smaller than she expected. She did not know how many it held, but she felt it was not over a hundred people and some of those were standing. It reminded her somewhat of a small salon that one might find at Versailles. Pastels with gold leaf accents. She was sitting in the fifth row. It seemed surprisingly intimate. When the models came out, she was shocked at their gaunt appearance. What also surprised her was how soon she got used to this long and lanky gauntness. The clothes looked marvelous on such shapeless forms and were for the most part stunningly simple in design. Perhaps it was the pastel colors after so much somber, wartime apparel, but even the outfits that had a certain avant-garde look, were nevertheless most appealing. Madeleine could imagine herself in many of the more classic designs. She gasped with pleasure as the last model paraded out in an extraordinarily beautiful and classic wedding gown and was then surrounded by the remaining models attired in evening gowns. It was a splendid and luxurious interlude and she sighed contentedly as she got to her feet after the last bow had been taken by Christian Dior himself.

— 24 —

Back in her room at the Fleuri she found Alphonse just returning from a late lunch. He had nearly completed the sitting room and he seemed well satisfied with his progress.

She kicked off her shoes and flung herself on her bed and contemplated the ceiling. The fashion show had been enormously enjoyable and entertaining, but it had left her feeling adrift. Here she was in this beautiful city, having accomplished her mission, to all intents and purposes, with the prospect of returning to England and another new beginning. She was again in limbo. It seemed that it was a continual repetition. It left her feeling very unsettled. Marc de la Croix was a very attractive man, but there was a remoteness about him that she felt was not meant to be overcome. She was not sure that he was a person that she could ever get to know well. She was not sure that it was important to her that she did. When he left her at the hotel the previous night he told her that he wanted to leave early on Saturday and would ring and let her know what time he would pick her up. She closed her eyes and listened to the faint sounds coming from the next room where Alphonse was preparing to hang the paper on the last unfinished wall.

The sound of a door closing awoke her. It must be Alphonse who was leaving. She was not aware that she had fallen asleep. It had only been about half-an-hour. She felt refreshed. She got up and splashed water on her face and combed her hair.

The telephone rang. It was Marc. There had been a change in his plans and he wanted to leave within the hour and drive to his farm in the country. Would it rush her too much to be ready to leave so soon? She could stay in the guest cottage which was not too far from the main house. She would need only her riding clothes and possibly one other outfit.

She thought a moment and decided that there would not be any great risk at accepting such an invitation. When she thought of all the risks she had taken during the war, she almost laughed.

So it was, that within the hour, they were seated in his Citroen and wending their way through the Friday evening traffic in Paris. It was a pleasant drive, despite the initial congestion. At first they spoke little for Marc was concentrating on making as much time as he could and wove his way dexterously through the endless bottlenecks. But finally, the traffic began to thin and they made better speed.

He told her of some of the problems he was having with the organization of the horse shows. He had 23 horses in his stables and there were five of them that were not well. One of them he suspected had colic, but he was afraid that one of them had something more serious. It was a valuable horse and he was worried. The conversation then drifted to post-War France and then finally to the War itself. Marc had been disgusted that the French had been forced to fight two enemies, the Germans and the Vichy government. It had split France into two camps and left many loyal Frenchmen vulnerable to betrayal. For this many had lost their lives. She could hear a certain bitterness in his voice and knew that he must have suffered some personal loss. He told her that the War was over for most people, but there were some for whom the memories were far too painful to ever forget. That for some there could never be peace until justice had been done. The hunters in some cases had become the hunted. He turned to look at her, at that moment.

"The information that you brought with you might help us equalize some of the terrible injustices and crimes that were perpetuated during the War. For that, we are truly indebted to you, Madeleine." He had not ever used her first name. She was taken aback at what he had said and found no words to respond. No wonder Sir Francis was so anxious about the envelope. He was the last person she would have suspected of possibly working for a branch of intelligence. But perhaps that was the genius of those in charge of counter intelligence and internal security. They could find men with special gifts willing to risk their lives for their country, who at the same time would be unlikely to cause suspicion.

They had been driving in silence for some time. Madeleine was sifting through her Paris stay and realized that, knowing what she did now, none of the unexplained things that had happened to her were likely to be all coincidences. It shocked her a little and she felt anxious that she could not pick up the phone and tell Sir Francis of the incident at the Malesherbes. She had not mentioned it because she thought it of no consequence. She shivered at the idea that she might have been staying at that hotel.

She looked sideways at Marc and wondered if she should confide in him. She hardly knew him, but obviously Sir Francis must trust him. She decided to wait.

They did not stop for dinner, but drove straight through, arriving in the dark. He stopped first at the guest house and led the way in. The lights were already on and it was obvious that she was expected. He told her that he would be back in less than hour and they would dine together at the house. He wanted to go and check on his horses and with that he was gone.

It seemed strange to awaken the next morning in unfamiliar surroundings. She had hardly had time to inspect her lodging the previous evening. It was a one-storied building, as was the main house, both of them designed in the style of South American haciendas. Several doors gave off the natural stone passage way. Her suite formed part of one corner of the building. It was a high-ceilinged room with an enormous beam running its length with several supporting struts. A chandelier made from antlers hung in front of the large fireplace, where last night she had found a fire burning. Comfortable stuffed chairs and a sofa filled most of the sitting room. Beyond this, through an open arch, sitting in its own alcove was a spacious bed with an ornate oak carved headboard. It was a marvelously comfortable bed and she suspected that it had a horsehair mattress.

It was a beautiful clear day and Madeleine was able to see out of her window the uncluttered landscape surrounding the farm. The rounded outlines of woods dotted the skyline. Horses grazed in various paddocks.

She walked down the winding path which led to the main house. The brick facade had mellowed over the centuries and the result was a warm and pleasing combination of faded pinks and browns. The kitchen stood at the end of a long and covered arched passage way. It was empty. It had a very high ceiling which must have kept it supremely cool in summer with its two foot thick walls. It was a room of considerable size. The ancient pine trestle table that sat at one end could seat sixteen persons. This was where all the farm hands would take their meals. A pot of coffee stood on the stove, several loaves of fresh bread and a dish of butter stood on the enormous table. There was also a bowl of fruit. In the middle was a very large ceramic jug of mixed dried wild flowers. A woman's touch. Madeleine had not been seated more than a few moments, when a woman entered from the back of the house.

"Bonjour, Mademoiselle. My name is Jeanne. May I serve you some coffee. It has been freshly made. Please help yourself to anything on the table. The stable hands have already eaten."

"Thank you. I would like that. By the way, did you make that most delicious stew which I had last night?"

Jeanne nodded. "I am glad you enjoyed it." She bustled around the kitchen, washing some dishes in the sink and putting them away. Finally, she picked up a large basket and left by the kitchen door, saying that she was going to collect the chicken's freshly-laid eggs.

They had eaten alone in the kitchen the previous evening. Marc had been entirely preoccupied with the health of his horses and they had spoken at length of their physical well-being.

As she cradled her morning coffee, she was suddenly aware that she was no longer alone. Marc was quietly staring down at her. She felt disconcerted by his unexpected appearance. She had not heard him enter the large kitchen. She hoped that she did not look too rumpled by sleep. As though reading her thoughts he said, "You look well rested."

"So do you." The fatigue of yesterday had left his face.

"I am going to be busier than I expected this morning. Why don't you enjoy this beautiful day. It is going to be unseasonably warm. There is a lovely spot down by the river where there is an opening in the trees. It would be a peaceful place for a picnic lunch."

She brightened. "I wish I had a sketching book. It sounds like a beautiful place."

He smiled. " We might be able to provide some basic materials. I will ask Jeanne to pack a lunch. She is busy now. Someone can bring it down later, if you are serious about the sketching."

"Yes, yes, I am."

In due course, she set off. It was a most idyllic spot. A bend in the river which in summer was shaded by an old willow tree, underneath which was moored an old wooden boat, long discarded. There was a family of ducks foraging at the water's edge. Reeds dipped in the breeze and rippled away in the distance. Woods crested the hills beyond. The colors were beautiful and she wished very much that she had her watercolors with her. She would do several sketches. On her return to England she could introduce the watercolors.

She completed several compositions and then lay back in the sweetly scented grass and watched small, puffy clouds ride slowly across the sky.

She heard the sound of slipping feet and sat up abruptly. Her heart skipped a beat. It was Marc, a basket in one hand.

"So there you are. I was afraid that you had changed your mind and left."

She smiled, "This is such a beautiful spot - an artist's dream."

"May I see what you have done?"

She shrugged. "I am not sure you can tell much without any color."

He looked over her shoulder. "I think you have captured the essence and mood of the place. I like it very much."

He sat down beside her.

"I thought I deserved a break. I hope you don't mind if I join you." His eyes drank in her fresh and youthful countenance.

She smiled, too self-conscious to respond.

"Perhaps you would unpack the basket while I open this bottle of Pouilly-Fuissé."

Jeanne had given them each a fresh baguette, butter, tomatoes, cheese and a delicious farm paté. Dessert was fruit.

Madeleine laid this out on a cinnamon floral cloth. It looked very appetizing.

"Will you hold the glass while I pour." His fingers touched hers and she felt a tingle of excitement.

It was a delicious meal.

Marc spoke of his morning in the stables with the vet and his assistant. They had operated on a hernia. He had sat on a bale of hay and waited until his colt had come round from the anaesthetic. They had levered him up into a sitting position until half an hour later he had scrambled to his feet and stood swaying shakily in much bewilderment. Then there were two lame horses. It was a time consuming process to cut through the rock-hard sole of the horses hoof until the site of the infection was found and pressure from the abscess relieved. But the results were satisfying. Much harder was sitting through the delivery of a foal from a famous mare. After a long struggle, she had given birth and everyone had rejoiced.

The meal over he lay back and closed his eyes.

Madeleine picked up her sketch pad, but finally put it down. Marc was asleep. She lay down herself and listened to the sounds around her. The gurgle of the river. A woodpecker seeking insects in a dead branch nearby. The twittering of birds.

She awoke suddenly. Nothing had changed, the same sounds surrounded her. She had slept deeply. She opened her eyes and was startled to see Marc on one elbow studying her. She blushed deeply, feeling vulnerable and self-conscious. She thought he might kiss her and half hoped he would, but knew it might spoil what was an uncomplicated relationship. But he did not. Instead he said, "You looked so tranquil and serene. I wish that I had the talent to capture you on canvas while you slept."

She sat up, brushed the grass and dried leaves from her hair.

He got up and offered her his hand. She took it and he pulled her to her feet. He let go of her hand. She was both relieved and disappointed.

"We had better pack up the basket," she said, busying herself with the remains of the meal. He picked up the glasses and the empty bottle.

"I have to get back to work. If you like to walk, there are the remains of a château a few miles from here. It might make a good subject for another sketch."

"It sounds interesting. How do I find it?"

He gave her directions. He left her at the entrance to the farm. She watched him walk briskly up the slope, the basket swinging from his hand.

It was several miles to the château, but once she reached the crest of the small hill behind the farm, she had a clear view of it in the distance.

It stood at the end of a high bluff, which was a natural fortress in itself. The château was in a much better state of repair than she had expected. She explored it thoroughly. She climbed three flights of stairs in the main tower and peered out of the narrow slits which were the only sources of light. Back on a lower level which adjoined the tower was a large open space with crenellated walls. This had once been the great hall. There was a marvelous view in all directions. She could see two villages in the distance, neither within miles of the farm. Its remoteness was unique.

She climbed the other tower and then clambered into the main body of the château. Except for one end, where a corner of the roof had caved in, it seemed much as it might have been several hundred years before, with only the debris of recent times to remind one that this was the twentieth century.

It was a peaceful and serene place with swallows circling and diving around its grey battlements. It seemed a place of refuge, rather like a monastery. But suddenly some screeching rooks flying overhead conjured up images in her mind of soldiers in mail armor with colorful banners flying in the wind, crying out in the heat of battle, the clash of sword upon sword. No fortress was ever built which did not challenge others to possess and conquer it.

She started on her way back to the farm. At the crest of an incline, she sat and sketched the château with its backdrop of woods and winding river in the valley below. Well satisfied with her efforts, she returned to the farm.

Back in the guest house she found a note inviting her go the stables to ride a horse which had been selected for her, provided she did not return too late. Philippe, the head groom, would be expecting her.

She changed quickly into her riding clothes and walked out to the stables.

By asking several of the men working in the area, she soon found Philippe and introduced herself. He was a strong, burly man with a dark stubble beginning to show on his chin. He told her to follow him and led her to a box containing a most regal white Arabian. Madeleine drew in her breath in awe. She was a good rider, but she had never ridden anything so magnificent.

"Are you sure that this is the horse that I am to ride?" she queried Philippe.

"Monsieur le Comte was most specific. This is one of his favorites. He comes from a very distinguished blood line and has a gentle disposition."

She spent nearly an hour in the paddock. At first, she felt intimidated by his size and power, but he had a gentle mouth and responded to her every move. It was an exhilarating experience that she would always remember. As she was trotting to the gate, she saw Marc watching her. She dismounted and led her mount through the gate and towards the stables. He fell into step with her. The horse nickered at the sight of Marc and got a friendly pat on his neck.

"You looked very compatible together."

"How can I ever thank you for such generosity? That was marvelous. I shall never forget it."

"Well, perhaps we can go for a ride tomorrow morning together. But I would like to return to Paris after lunch."

Supper that night was a unique experience for her. There were ten men she did not know. They had weathered hands and faces and very muscular physiques. They bantered between themselves, as men do only from long acquaintance. They were deferential to de la Croix although they were not above gently teasing him. Madeleine they carefully ignored, except for the most basic table courtesies. The conversation was general and she could not glean any information about them. Luis Brazzini was not one of the group. He and his family had their own house on the property.

Madeleine excused herself after dinner and retired to her room. She tried again to reach Sir Francis but all the lines were busy.

So much fresh air had made her sleepy. She climbed into the big bed and turned out the light. She slept without waking.

The next day dawned crisp and sunny and they spent the whole morning together. It began with a tour of his stables. His horses were magnificent and Madeleine was able to comment knowledgeably on both their condition and their bloodlines. They talked animatedly throughout their inspection. It was an hour of shared pleasure. Finally, he closed the door to the last stall. They were both silent. He turned to her and asked, "How would you like to ride my other white Arabian?"

"You are not serious?"

"I have never been more serious."

He called one of the stable hands and the white Arabian was saddled. He was led into the paddock where she mounted him. They circled a few times. It was a spirited stallion but she rode him well and Marc recognized her as a fearless and experienced rider.

"Shall we go?" He looked distinguished and very much at ease as he joined her seated on his favorite chestnut mare.

They had ridden for about two hours. It was a beautiful and warm autumnal morning. They set out at a trot. Later when they reached the open fields they gave the horses their heads and galloped. It was heady and exciting with the wind in her face and the strong and beautiful animal beneath her. They reined in their horses eventually and slowed to a walk. Her face glowed and he could see her jubilation. He turned his horse so that he sat facing her. He lifted his riding crop and gently traced the outline of her face. He let his crop run down her neck and across her shoulder and back again where he let it sit under her chin. She could scarcely breath. A deep longing enveloped her. The intensity of his appraisal of her seemed to be overshadowed by a great sadness. The moment seemed to pass as quickly as it had arisen. He tapped her on her hand and without a word, turned his horse in the direction of the stables.

Finally, their departure could no longer be delayed. It was time to leave. They left the horse farm behind and were back on the road to Paris. They hardly spoke. Madeleine was musing on the morning she had spent. It had been a special interlude. She would always remember the thrill of riding two such magnificent animals; the exhilaration of being with a man such as Marc de la

Croix. He was an enigma in so many ways. She knew little about him. But she felt instinctively that he was a man of great depth and substance.

Somehow she was not ready to return to England. But she had little reason to remain much longer in Paris. She felt guilty that she had not reached Sir Francis. Marc broke into her thoughts, "You seem pensive."

"Yes. I have not been able to speak with Sir Francis since telling him about the man who I discovered in my room at the Fleuri. I promised that I would let him know as soon as I had seen you."

"What man in your room?"

She told him.

He was silent for a long time and she wondered if he was thinking of something entirely different, but he came back to the subject as though there had been no interval.

"Did you get a good look at his face?"

"I did see him, but his appearance was distorted by the neon lighting from the adjacent hotel. I have no idea what his coloring was. He looked a bit like one of those street mimers with white faces. It has been one of those strange holidays. I feel as though I have been two steps ahead of some shadowy figure that has been following me everywhere. I think that if I had stayed at the Malesherbes, I would have felt that I was part of a real life spy story."

"What has the Malesherbes got to do with you?"

She recounted the whole story in more detail than she intended and also told him about the newspaper article which mentioned the death of a guest. She regretted the allusion to a spy story. It was a bit of a Freudian slip. It really was too far fetched. She did not believe it herself. But she was uncomfortable about the various coincidences. Was she being used?

They had left the countryside behind and were now traveling in more and more built up areas. They would soon be on the outskirts of Paris.

"Does Sir Francis know everything that you have told me?"

"Everything except the newspaper article."

"When you get back to the Fleuri, you must do your utmost to reach him. Do not leave the hotel until you do."

"Is it so important?"

"Important enough that he might prefer you to return to England rather than attend the horse show which begins on Wednesday this week. Brazzini and some of the assistant grooms will be coming up tomorrow with the horses. I shall be very busy with arrangements for it, so I would not have much time to keep an eye on you."

A shiver went through her. "You think I am in some danger?"

"I think there have been too many coincidences. But I am a suspicious man. The war did that to me."

"But now that I have given you the envelope, surely there would be no need to pursue me?"

He did not respond.

She forced herself to change the subject.

"And to think that I came all this way to try and persuade you to bring your team to play polo in Dorset."

They were stopped at a traffic light and he turned and looked at her. "Considering all the circumstances, I think we owe Sir Francis a chance to beat us at his favorite sport. Tell him that we will be happy to visit him in Dorset, provided he promises to play us here in France."

"You don"t mean it?" She smiled, delighted.

"I do."

With that they drove the rest of the way in silence.

She was back in her suite at the Fleuri. It was as she had left it, for Alphonse had not worked that week-end. There was one message for her. A rather cryptic one from her parents that asked her to contact her cousin Elisabeth. She could guess at its meaning and felt she might ignore it. Strange that the operator should have made a muddle over the name of "great-aunt" and "cousin." She tried unsuccessfully to reach Sir Francis, but his housekeeper said he was away for the week-end and expected back by midday on Monday. She was frustrated and upset.

She was sitting there wondering what to do next, when the telephone rang. She picked it up. It was Marc.

"There was a message from Sir Francis for me upon my return here. I will come and see you after dinner tonight." With that he rang off and she was left wondering what he meant.

She enjoyed a pleasant dinner in the charming, candle-lit dining room of the Fleuri. The staff were attentive and friendly. She had the impression that they all knew that she had been somewhere for the week-end with the Comte de la Croix.

Dinner over, she went and sat in the small anteroom where coffee was served after meals for those who wished. There were magazines to read and she picked up one and started to browse through it. She spent the best part of an hour reading and sipping her coffee in the company of other guests. She looked at her watch and was surprised to find it was nearly ten o'clock. If Marc came as he had promised, she realized he would probably not want to sit and chat in front of strangers, so she returned to her room.

The telephone rang a little after ten.

"Are you still awake?" he asked.

"Yes."

"Then may I come up?"

He arrived looking preoccupied.

"I do apologize for being so late. There has been much to do. You have not been able to reach Sir Francis, I presume, because he left me a message. He was unable to reach you."

She nodded and waited.

"He wants you to leave Paris as soon as possible, but you are not to return to England just yet."

"But why?"

"He did not elaborate. I think he was careful in case his message should be intercepted. We have been working on something together and suspect that someone has infiltrated our organization. You have to understand that there are many loose ends after such a bitter conflict as the war we have so recently fought. The cold war continues."

"But where can I go?"

"Could you return to Liechtenstein? You have a relative there."

"It is a coincidence that you suggest that because I have just had a message from my parents telling me to get in touch with my cousin Elisabeth, except she is my great-aunt in Liechtenstein. I have not telephoned her yet."

"How was the message phrased exactly?"

She told him.

"It is possible that it is a message that was sent in collaboration with Sir Francis. The error was deliberate. Just to throw off anyone who read it. In small hotels like this everyone knows everyone else's business. You probably have more cousins than you have great-aunts."

She nodded. "Is all this cloak and dagger stuff because of the envelope?"

"It is possible that it has nothing to do with the envelope."

She felt suddenly very nauseous. Would it never end? She sat down suddenly and put her head in her hands.

"Has something else happened since you left England that might lead you to believe it could be something else?"

"Yes, but I thought it was over."

He did not ask her to explain, but looked at her with compassion and had a great urge to hold her in his arms, but this was not the time or the place and probably never could be.

"Why was your great-aunt trying to reach you? I am sorry if that appears inquisitive, but it is important that I know."

"It was nothing very important to anyone else. She wanted very much for me to join her in Monte Carlo and attend the Bal d'Hiver. I know no one to invite as my partner, but she said that did not matter. She would arrange everything."

He sighed with relief, but she was unaware of his concern.

"I think it is the perfect solution to our present problem," he said smiling broadly. "I could not be more pleased."

She looked up at him and took heart when she saw his face, He seemed suddenly to have relaxed. Perhaps, after all, things were not as dark as they seemed and she was fantasizing too much about the past.

"I have already thought of a plan to help you leave Paris. This invitation from your great-aunt makes it easier. My parents live in Provence where they also raise horses. I try and visit them as often as possible. It is where I grew up. I love it even more than my farm."

She looked at him in surprise. "It must be an exceedingly beautiful place, for I can hardly imagine a lovelier place than your farm."

He smiled and nodded.

"When is the Bal d'Hiver?"

"At the end of next week."

"Good. I was planning to send two of my older horses down to Provence to my father. I cannot go myself, but I was going to send Luis Brazzini's assistant. You could travel with him, and of course the horses, if you would not mind?"

She looked at him in surprise. "It is all rather sudden. I do not know what to say."

"I think that you start by accepting your great-aunt's invitation. But please do not use the telephone in your room as the whole staff of the Fleuri will know your plans. I believe there is a public telephone at the end of street. Use that. But come straight back to the hotel. We will not announce your departure. Instead I will pick you up tomorrow around six-thirty. Everyone will think you are dining with me. Can you rearrange your luggage so that you take only what you want in Monte Carlo? The rest I will arrange to send to England by train."

"How will I leave the hotel with my suitcases if I am only going to dinner with you?"

He thought a moment. "I could take them with me now, if it would not take you too long to pack. The man at the reception desk tonight is someone who does not know me, which is an advantage. Hopefully, I can leave without meeting any of the other staff I know. I can always come up with an explanation if necessary." He grinned boyishly and she knew that he was perfectly at ease in such a situation. Even though he had never mentioned it, she guessed that he had probably been in the Résistance during the War. It suited his personality perfectly and explained his present involvement with Sir Francis.

"I am going to move my car. I had to leave it rather a long way off. I will be back soon."

She was glad to be alone to do her packing. It would be less distracting. She would have felt very self-conscious doing it in his presence. It was a monumental task to accomplish in such a short time. But it made the decision making easier. It turned out to be easier than she anticipated because her gowns had been packed neatly with all their accessories. She could take the suitcases for Monte Carlo with her and leave the rest to be sent back to England. In a way, it was a relief not to have to struggle with them any more. She just hoped they would reach her home safely.

He was back before she knew it. She was just putting the finishing touches to the last suitcase.

"How did you do?"

"I hope that I have not forgotten anything important, or packed two left shoes or something equally annoying." She smiled, feeling her old self again.

"You are an adventurous young lady. You will go far." He smiled and continued. "My plan, which I will confirm in more detail tomorrow is this. You will travel to Beauvois with Alain, who is an experienced groom. He is a man in his early sixties and I can vouch for his integrity. You will be safe with him. I will let my parents know of your arrival. You can then stay there a few days before making arrangements for your onward journey to Monte Carlo. While you are there you will meet my wife, Alicia. She is not well. She was captured by the Germans at the end of the War and tortured. She will never regain her health."

Madeleine gasped. It was a shock. But it explained his demeanor and his reserve. He had told her in a very matter-of-fact way, but she could hear the edge of bitterness in his voice and marveled at his composure.

"I think that is all for the moment. I will see you tomorrow evening. Perhaps you can leave some things scattered around as you normally would if you were still in residence. I will see that everything gets packed."

She nodded. She was at a loss for words. He picked up the suitcases and she held the door open for him. He walked out into the corridor and disappeared from view down the staircase.

After breakfast, she walked down the street to the public telephone kiosk. Happily it was functional. She hoped very much that, after all her arrangements, her aunt was still planning to include her in the invitation to the ball. What a mess if she had changed her mind. What if she could not reach her? She forced herself not to think of that. The telephone was functional and after some delay she got through to Schönhof. It took another long wait until her aunt came to the telephone.

"Madeleine, my dear, how lovely to hear your voice. Where are you?"

"I am still in Paris. Why did you ring me, dear Aunt Elisabeth? Was it about the Ball?"

"Yes, dear. I want you to join me and some friends at my table at the Sporting Club. It is always such an elegant evening. You will love it. And don't worry about a partner. I have half a dozen prospects."

"I would love to come."

They talked about the details of their respective itineraries. Madeleine promised to telephone her aunt as soon as she had a more definite time of arrival. Accommodation, which was at a premium in Monte Carlo, was not a problem. Her aunt had a suite of rooms at the Hotel de Paris.

Madeleine hung up the telephone much relieved and returned to her hotel.

The day seemed to creep by. She had a substantial lunch in case she did not get dinner. She spent only the time needed in her room to make all the arrangements necessary for her departure. Alphonse was close to completion with his wallpapering.

In the late afternoon, she returned to her room to find the telephone ringing and Alphonse stretching to put up the last piece of border in the sitting room.

"I am sorry, Mademoiselle, that I could not come down to answer the telephone. This is the last piece."

The telephone had stopped as she was about to pick it up. She nodded and said. "I quite understand. I am sure that whoever it was has left a message. Why, Alphonse, it does look so very attractive with that border added. Such a change and improvement from when I first arrived."

"Yes, indeed. You should have seen the old paper. So very dreary. This will last a few years." He grunted in satisfaction and climbed down his ladder.

"This hotel seems to have survived the war without damage. Were you in Paris during the Occupation?"

Alphonse grimaced and swore quietly. "Les sales boches." She had struck a nerve, for his loathing of the Germans, for he continued without encouragement. "Those were terrible times. The streets were empty. Everyone who was able fled. The German presence was everywhere. The swastiska hung from all the major buildings. They requisitioned homes and hotels. In some ways, it looked very beautiful with no people and few vehicles. But at heart, Paris was a dead city."

"That is hard to visualize with all the vitality there is now. How did people manage?"

"For those left behind," he went on to say, "the shortage of food became an obsession. The most precious food items were bread and potatoes, and then fats. People would steal and barter precious objects for these commodities. If you had money, you could buy from the marché-noir. In fact, there were even marché-noir restaurants, where the food was still good, although the prices were exorbitant. But for the most part, women made it a daily ritual to queue for food and became the slaves of the providers such as the butcher and the baker. Those queues became social events which could not soften the discomforts of cold, rain and disappointment if no provisions were delivered. Some family members queued in relays. There was the search for lost relatives. The curfew. The bombing. Houses were boarded up. There was no coal. Gas and electricity were interrupted.

There was no water. I spent most of the Occupation making special deliveries of water throughout the city. I got to know a lot of families. There were some very sad situations. Great hardship; much courage. People left their homes at night with a case of their possessions to stay with friends or neighbors, or to camp in the metro, underground in tunnels, or house or garden cellars. It was exhausting and disruptive."

"What a terribly depressing existence"

"Indeed it was. However, the Parisians had great spirit and found many ways to alleviate their dreary and arduous existence. They spent a lot of time going to the cinema, theater or cabarets, despite the inconvenience of the curfew, which created transport problems and despite the continuing air-raids. Programs were generally planned early to avoid the night raids. The Germans would also attend these performances, but tended to frequent their own cinemas. There was also horse racing at Longchamps."

Madeleine burst out laughing at this. "That sounds so incongruous, in a time of such deprivation."

"Yes, I know," he said smiling, "but it is true. People were desperate to distract themselves. Young people became very active in sports. Others devoured everything they could read, but books were difficult to obtain as the Germans tended to censure everything. But forgive me, I have taken up too much of your time and bored you with my meanderings. I have not spoken of those days before. I think that I needed to do that." He shook his head as though to free himself of the past.

"Indeed you have not bored me at all. It would be difficult to imagine all you have described, unless one had experienced it oneself.

He started to assemble his tools and buckets.

"I shall be moving my things to another room down the end of the corridor. Then you will have peace and quiet." He smiled at her.

"I shall miss seeing you," she said with sincerity.

"I shall be here a couple of more weeks. How much longer will you be staying here?" It was asked more from politeness than any inquisitiveness.

"Until the end of the week. Then I must return home to England." She hated lying to Alphonse whom she considered above such deceptions himself. But Marc had warned her that idle gossip spread fast in a small establishment. She watched him pick up his buckets, his florid, lined face a gentle landscape of benevolence.

"Then, until tomorrow," and with that he lumbered out of the room.

When she enquired at the reception desk about the call she had missed, no message had been left.

She resigned herself to waiting for Marc and hoped he would not be late. He was not.

They had met at the public telephone down the street from the Fleuri. She had dropped her key off at the reception desk, but the clerk hardly paid attention to her because he was busy with newly arrived guests. It would not have mattered anyway. She walked out of the lobby, her bag over her shoulder, along the flagstone entrance passage and out into the street.

They drove to the outskirts of Paris and finally stopped on a quiet side street where the horse van was parked She was introduced to Alain, a grey-haired, taciturn man in his early sixties, although Madeleine thought he could have been older. He was short and muscular. Her heart sank at the prospect of a long journey with Alain. Conversation would be limited.

Marc wished her a safe journey and an enjoyable stay in Monte Carlo. He asked her to give greetings to his parents. Madeleine was surprised that he did not mention his wife. He kissed her hand before handing her into the van.

"I look forward to our next meeting."

"I do too." She meant it. "Good luck at the show this week."

He nodded and smiled. "And thank you for everything."

They made their way slowly through the outskirts of the city and were eventually on the main road south.

It was a long, slow journey. Alain, as suspected, was not a conversationalist and Madeleine decided to follow his lead and only speak when spoken to for the most part. She had a good book and she enjoyed watching the passing scene. It seemed that Alain was not in a hurry. He had made this journey before on other occasions. He stopped at small auberges that were clean and simple establishments. He made it clear that he did not expect her to join him at table, at which she was greatly relieved. His charges got royal treatment and he fussed over them as if they were his own.

When they reached Avignon they turned off the main route and wended their way into the foothills of the Alps.

They turned finally between two massive and ornately decorated iron gates and through a long avenue of ancient beech trees. The avenue curved to the left and they arrived in a large, open space. Before them stood a mellow stone house of large and beautiful proportions. Its central facade was spanned on each side by symmetrical wings. A shallow staircase with an elegant balustrade led up to the entrance. To one side, she caught a glimpse of a walled garden.

Alain drove past the house and into the courtyard that housed the stables.

Men came running to greet Alain as he climbed out of his van. It was obvious he was well-known to them. Madeleine climbed down herself and stood there waiting. Alain turned in her direction finally and asked one of the grooms to conduct her to the house. She shook hands with Alain and thanked him and he responded with a rare smile.

It was the cocktail hour and they were gathered together in the library. Marc's parents had welcomed her with great courtesy, but she felt also with some reticence. She could understand this in view of the fact that their daughter-in-law lived with them and that they must feel protective of her. Perhaps they wondered about her relationship to Marc. She had arrived in the early afternoon, but as yet she had seen no sign of Marc's wife, Alicia.

"As soon as Alicia arrives, we will go into dinner." announced Marc's mother. "She should be here any moment."

No sooner had she spoken than the door opened and in stepped the loveliest woman Madeleine had ever seen. She had long blond hair, an oval shaped face with the most delicate of pale pink complexions. She had the slender, lithe physique of a ballet dancer. She seemed to float into the room. The door closed quietly behind her and Madeleine thought she caught the glimpse of a woman in a white uniform.

The Countess de la Croix rose to her feet and went to greet Alicia whom she kissed gently on both cheeks. She then took her by the hand and brought her to Madeleine.

"Alicia, this Mademoiselle Devaux, a friend who has come to stay with us for a few days. Mademoiselle, this is Alicia de la Croix."

Madeleine extended her hand to take that of Alicia. It felt cool, limp and lifeless to her touch. When she looked into the blue eyes in that beautiful face, she was shocked to find them quite unseeing. She was not blind, but she might just as well have been for they were sightless and vacant. Behind the facade of an elegant woman was an empty shell. Madeleine had rarely felt so stunned. The shock in her face must have shown for the Countess said gently, "She never speaks. We are not sure that she even hears us. We are always hopeful that one day she might be healed, but the doctors hold out no hope. We try to surround her with love."

The Countess led the way out of the library and into the elegant dining room.

Madeleine spent three days with Marc's parents. Marc's father had taken her to the stables and introduced her to the head groom. He had told her she could ride as often as she wished. He was a slender, elegant man whose complexion spoke of someone who spent a lot of time in the open air. But there seemed a great sadness about him and Madeleine supposed that he was reminded daily of his son's loss and the sadness of never being able to look forward to having another generation to assume the role of custodian of this unique and tranquil place. It was a quiet interlude spent riding and walking the incredibly beautiful property of Château de Beauvois. But she was impatient to reach Monte Carlo. She had spoken to her aunt who awaited her arrival as soon as she could make the necessary arrangements. It was Alain on his return journey to Paris who drove her to the station in Avignon.

— 25 —

It was not far from the station to the Hotel de Paris. She drank in the rich tropical landscape with its rows of palms and the elegant pastel colored buildings. It really was a very special place. She felt a thrill of expectancy.

Her aunt appeared like magic as she was checking in at the reception desk.

"There you are at last, dear child," her aunt trilled. She was obviously in high humor, for she wore a floating two piece pale silk dress and coat. It was late afternoon, so she had either been somewhere elegant or was going somewhere elegant.

"Aunt Elisabeth, how beautiful you look."

"Thank you, dear, thank you. I was at a luncheon and a fashion show and managed to see many of my friends. But more of that later. Welcome to Monte Carlo. I am so very delighted that you were able to come. How was your journey?"

Madeleine sighed. "I thought that I never would arrive. The journey was interminable. But I am very excited to be here."

The Kandahar Talisman

"Well, let us go upstairs and I will show you your room. I hope you don't mind sharing the suite I have. There was no possibility of finding you one all to yourself."

Sharing a suite with her aunt was decidedly not a hardship. There was a large communal sitting room decorated in pale turquoise and gold with floor to ceiling doors which led out to a balcony with a view of palm trees and the sea beyond. There were two bedrooms, each with very spacious bathrooms. This was a feature that Madeleine cherished after her sojourns in cold and drafty locations in German-occupied France.

Madeleine stood in the middle of the sitting room and drank in the splendor surrounding her. She did a small pirouette and sat down in one of the overstuffed armchairs. Her aunt came out of her bedroom with a pencil and pad in her hand.

"Now, I am going to make a list of all the activities that are taking place this week. I will tick the ones which I plan to attend. You can join me if you choose. Then we will discuss what you will wear to each occasion."

"I did not bring a very big wardrobe with me. I thought that I only had to plan for the Ball." Madeleine's heart sank at this unexpected social dilemma.

"Never mind, dear. What you do not have, we can always purchase." When she saw her niece about to protest, she raised her hand. "You are my guest while we are here and I do not want you to fuss or worry about anything. We are here to enjoy ourselves."

There were three days before the ball and they were filled with luncheons and teas and dinners with friends and acquaintances of her aunt's. A certain amount of time was spent shopping, since her aunt maintained that she did not have nearly enough clothes for the occasion. Walking back to the hotel one day through the old town, which was full of tiny alleys and picturesque buildings, they came upon one of the many luxury designer boutiques in the window of which was displayed a single, elegant sea green chiffon dress.

"You would look perfectly ravishing in that dress with your golden blond hair. Let us go in and try in on."

"But, dear Aunt Elisabeth, it is going to cost a king's ransom. It is perfectly beautiful, but I really do not need it."

Her comments seemed only to galvanize her aunt for she was through the door and beckoning her niece to follow.

It was a very exclusive place with thick carpet and opulent armchairs and sofa. The owner of the salon glided into the room and smiled reservedly in welcome. She wore a plain black dress with pearls, real pearls and too much make-up. Madeleine was hypnotized by the length of her dark red nails. Her dark hair was coiffed in a severe chignon. She made Madeleine feel uncomfortable. However, great-aunt Elisabeth was more than equal to her surroundings, having obviously spent a lot of her life in similar boutiques.

A seamstress was called and asked to remove the chiffon gown from its model. It was then carried into one of the spacious changing rooms where Madeleine tried it on. To her amazement, it fit her perfectly. She stepped out into the main salon and twirled in front of her aunt. She did not know why she should have behaved in such a theatrical way, considering the eyes of Madame Baudette were upon her, but the effect was to bring pleased smiles.

"It could not be more perfect, dear child. I just think the color is most becoming to your fresh English complexion. We will take it. Could you please have it delivered to my suite at the Hotel de Paris? Also, please charge it to my hotel bill."

Madeleine was impressed that all this was acceptable to Madame Baudette, who responded. "It will be a pleasure. May I show you anything else? We have a few exceptionally elegant gowns that are newly arrived."

"Since we are here, why not?"

Madame Baudette clapped her hands and a young woman appeared immediately. She must have been hovering behind a silk curtain that divided the front of the salon from the work room. Madame whispered some instructions and she disappeared again.

"May we offer you a glass of champagne?"

"It is a little early for that, but some coffee would be most acceptable."

There followed an enjoyable half-hour of viewing. It was a most glorious palette of colors and fabrics. The designs ranged the spectrum of traditional to contemporary. Madame Baudette had gauged her market well for all her creations were supremely wearable. She did not risk anything too avant-garde. She left that to the Paris market.

Madeleine sighed in contentment as the last gown was carried away. It had been a quite different experience from that of the Dior fashion show. She had been able to touch the fabrics and look closely at the workmanship. Her aunt had kept up a running commentary with the owner. One dress had stood apart from all the others. It was an off-white chiffon sheath which was sprinkled with tiny silver and glass beads. They twinkled like fireflies under the salon's soft lighting. Madeleine thought it was the most romantically beautiful gown she had ever seen.

The Countess rose to her feet and thanked Madame Baudette. The door was held open for them and they stepped out into the late afternoon sunshine.

The Countess entertained that night in the main dining room of the Hotel de Paris. There were twelve guests. Madeleine wore the pale sea-green chiffon. Her aunt wore the royal blue that was so becoming to her. It was a festive evening and a sumptuous dinner. The guests were a mostly mature group. An elderly French colonel and his wife, two sisters who were close friends of the Countess, a famous French painter and an equally famous Italian dress designer, a Lithuanian diplomat and his wife and a Swiss banker and his wife.

Madeleine felt she had nothing in common with any of them, but she was seated next to the Italian dress designer and found him to be a great storyteller. She only had to listen. The evening passed agreeably and there were many interchanges between tables for the room was filled with long-time habitués of the Hotel de Paris who came every season, long before the war.

The following day her aunt took Madeleine to a tea that was held in the nearby villa of a long-time friend. The salon was filled with elegant women of all ages. The hostess, the Principessa Bracciolini, was elegant in a flowing gown of peach-colored silk. Madeleine guessed her age to be in her mid-forties, but she had an ageless look to her. Madeleine was introduced to more people than she would ever remember. Her aunt was in her element. They were finally seated at a small table where they sipped their tea and sampled the many small sandwiches, gâteaux and petits fours displayed on silver platters.

Their group included three other elegant matrons, whose gowns were timeless classics with a pre-war quality to them. The conversation was centered around the Ball, and those who were attending and with whom. The chairman of the Ball, Countess de Beauchamps, was well-known to them all. Madeleine had the impression that she was a most influential woman who was not liked because of her domineering personality. However, they conceded that she alone could make a success out of such an undertaking and that they were not the least bit envious of all the attention she received as a result. It was also understood that they would not have refused, had they been invited to sit at her table, despite their negative feelings. Such was society. Anything for visibility and to be seen in the right circles. There were to be several guests of honor sprinkled amongst the crowd at selected tables. Countess de Beauchamps, it was rumored, had at least one such guest up her sleeve, but nobody knew who they might be. Gossip had it that there was a Russian prince, a Polish count, an Italian principessa, and on and on. It really did not matter. Soon all would be revealed. They debated how the Count de Beauchamps tolerated all the activities and antics of his wife. Gossip maintained that he had long ago sought consolation elsewhere and that there was a tacit understanding between the two of them not to infringe on each others territory, provided appearances were maintained. Most of society seemed to side with the Count, but he was rarely seen and only appeared on grand occasions. There was speculation as to whether he would appear at the Sporting Club on Saturday evening.

After dinner, the Countess was determined that Madeleine should experience yet another social side of Monte Carlo, namely the gaming rooms in the Sporting Club's Casino. This Belle Epoque gem was built in 1861, with its grand staircase and elegant gaming rooms, it was the attraction for all those in society who wished to be seen and wished to try their luck in the various salons. It was always a glittering scene with the chandeliers, frescoes and the glamorously and elegantly attired guests. The Countess, herself, never gambled, but she loved to watch those playing for high stakes and witness the drama engendered by those occasions. Besides which one saw so many of one's friends. It was always an animated evening.

Thus Madeleine found herself in a tightly packed room with people crowded around the roulette tables. Smoke hung heavy in the air. There was the low murmur of voices, the click of the roulette ball on the wheel, the chink of glasses. She stood watching, fascinated. The piles of chips rising in pyramids on certain numbers. The hush as the ball spun in its groove around the wheel, and then the slow click, click as it jumped from one slot to the next, until at last it fell and settled on a number. The momentary gasp when a high stake was won or lost.

Her aunt was back at her side.

"I have just seen an old friend. Would you mind if I left you, dear, while Georgette and I have a drink together?

"You can leave me for as long as you like, dear Aunt Elisabeth. I find this absolutely fascinating."

"Good. Then try your luck with this thousand francs and I will come back and find you later." With that she was gone.

Madeleine looked with astonishment at the money in her hand. The thrifty side of her was aghast at the thought of losing such a sum. She would prefer just watching. The thought of worrying about losing would spoil all the fun. She browsed the room and was soon able to pick out the tables where big contests were taking place. She was staggered at the sums which were changing hands or sitting in front of the various players. There were bejewelled dowagers, exotic Arabs, and smooth and elegant people rubbing shoulders together at each table.

She finally squeezed her way between a large gentleman and an even larger lady enveloped in a black and white taffeta gown. She had probably watched for nearly an hour when she realized that she had lost her fear of losing and wanted very much to try her luck. She left the table and went and changed her note into chips. She was soon back and found the large gentleman had left, his place having been taken by a very thin, grey-haired gentleman of some considerable age. She found there was plenty of room between him and the next player.

Madeleine was much too cautious to start out playing on the full numbers. Instead, her plan was to play the red and black, odds and evens, as a beginning.

"Rien ne va plus," intoned the croupier. Madeleine held her breath and watched the wheel intently.

The ball fell and she was astonished to find that she had won her first chips - red and even. Her heart raced with excitement. She caught the eye of a man across the table and she saw him smile at her. He was good-looking and dressed in a tuxedo. She turned her eyes once more to the table and went on playing. An hour had passed and she had accumulated a small pile of chips.

The man was still standing across the table. He rarely took his eyes off of her. She was not sure whether to feel flattered or offended. She was wearing a fitted black chiffon cocktail dress with a heart-shaped neck line. It was exceedingly flattering to her figure and her coloring. She wore a crescent shaped gold and sapphire brooch on her shoulder and pearls at her neck. She was unaware of the many admiring glances, except for those of the man across from her.

Her aunt was once more at her side.

"It seems I have possibly corrupted you, dear Madeleine. You seem to be having beginner's luck. I see that I must leave you and come back much later."

Madeleine lent over and kissed her. "Yes, much later."

When she looked back across the table the man had gone. She wondered briefly about him, but soon became absorbed in her game.

Two and a half hours had now elapsed and she had a very large pile of chips. She had not counted them, but she knew that soon she should walk away before she began losing.

Finally after six straight losses, she felt that her luck had turned and she got up from the table. Anyway she was stiff and thirsty. She walked over to the cashier's booth and cashed in her chips. She was disbelieving when he counted out ninety thousand francs. She picked up the enormous notes and stuffed them into her black suede evening purse. She must find her aunt. As she turned she saw the handsome man from across the table walking towards her.

"You have had a successful evening, Mademoiselle," he said in French that was obviously not his native tongue.

"Yes."

"Would you join me for a drink?"

"Thank you, but I promised to take my aunt home once I had finished playing. She is waiting for me impatiently, I know."

"That is too bad. Will you be at the ball tomorrow evening?"

"Yes, I will."

"Then perhaps we shall see each other there. I should introduce myself. My name is George Vladimirovich."

"Madeleine Devaux."

"With whom will you be sitting tomorrow evening?"

"Countess von Altenburg."

"Then with your permission I shall come looking for you."

She smiled and turned away.

She found her aunt sitting on a large and comfortable sofa with a small group of friends.

"Madeleine, at last. I thought that I should have to sit up all night. Did you have fun?"

"Yes, dear Aunt Elisabeth. It was so exciting. I apologize for keeping you up so late."

"No, I am happy that you had a good time. But I am ready to go now. We have to save our strength for tomorrow which might be an even longer evening." She turned to her friends and bade them all good night and with that, she took Madeleine's arm and they walked out of the Casino.

Madeleine slept late and got up and dressed in time for lunch.

Her aunt had already spent a full morning. Her stamina was amazing.

It was a beautiful day and Madeleine went for a long walk. Later she went down to the harbor and watched the boats. She had a hair appointment later in the afternoon. Her hair being naturally curly did not really need much attention, but for the Ball she wanted something sophisticated.

She had almost reached the hotel on her return, when she saw a familiar figure approaching her. It was George Vladimirovich. He stopped in front of her.

"What good fortune to see you again. Would you be free to have tea?"

"I have a hair appointment in less than an hour. That does not leave much time."

"I promise that you will not be late. There is a tea room not far from here.

They were settled comfortably at a table for two.

"So tell me all about yourself."

"There is not a lot to tell," responded Madeleine. But he persisted and asked her lots of questions so that before she realized it, he knew a lot about her.

"I think it is now your turn to tell me something of yourself."

"I think the less you know about me the better. Your aunt would not approve."

"That is not fair. So where were you born?"

"I was born in Georgia not far from Tbilisi."

She nodded. "So where were you during the war?"

"I ended up fighting the Germans. It was a terrible war."

"Yes, it was."

"I think you must be too young to know about it."

She smiled. "Unfortunately, not."

They talked of other things and then Madeleine looked at her watch and jumped to her feet. "Now, I must go or I shall miss my appointment."

"Please do not leave. We have only just begun to get to know each other."

"You promised that I should not be late."

"But I did not realize how much I would enjoy your company. Just stay a little longer."

"No, my appointment is too important."

He tried to persuade her, but she shook her head and hurried out of the door.

She was exasperated. She did not want to be late and she was annoyed that her companion was sufficiently self-absorbed to be indifferent to her agenda.

She reached the hairdresser's five minutes late and was saved from a scolding because Robert had been called to the phone. She knew that today of all days was not the day to keep him waiting.

She got back to her suite and found her aunt sitting drinking a Perrier with lemon, looking relaxed and lovely.

"Why, Madeleine, how elegant and sophisticated."

"Yes, I love it." She looked in the mirror. "It is slightly French Empire, don't you think?"

"The perfect hairstyle for that elegant gown of yours.

The ballroom was filled to capacity. The dance floor revolved in a rainbow of colors with gowns in all shapes and designs. The glitter of jewels, the soft candlelight and the romantic strains of the orchestra created an ambiance of old world elegance, which, of course, it mostly was. People were picking up their lives from where they had left off in the days before the war.

Madeleine had discovered, during the years since the end of the war, that enough money could overcome anything, be it a shortage of food or commodities. During the war, it could buy freedom, if one was lucky.

Madeleine seemed to have danced all night. True to her promise, her aunt had provided an unlimited number of elegant and eligible partners. Almost without exception they had been excellent dancers. They ranged from sophisticated to shy, from intellectuals to sportsmen. They were all she could wish for, dancing partners with impeccable manners and old world courtesies. But none had struck at her heart-strings. She wondered if she was being unfair. She had danced with George Vladimirovich and later her aunt had asked how she had come to meet him.

"My dear, he is very well-born, but his reputation is not of the best, if one is to believe the rumors. Do be careful."

"Do not worry, Aunt Elisabeth. He really is not my type. The only difficulty is that he does not seem easily deterred."

"His kind succeed where others fail." Her aunt shook her head. Then she changed the subject. "How I wish that Yvonne and Charles could be here with us tonight. They would have loved it. However, I am sure that they are having a wonderful honeymoon."

Madeleine nodded in agreement. It left her feeling momentarily dispirited. Would she spend the rest of her life alone?

It was past midnight and she excused herself from the table. It was time to take the shine off her face and repair her make-up, not that she wore much. She did not need to.

She threaded her way out of the ballroom and to the doors leading out into the vestibule. There was an animated group, blocking this exit, chatting and laughing. The Countess de Beauchamps was the center of attention, looking immensely glamorous in a black and white satin ball gown which was off the shoulder on one side and rose in a fan of fabric on the other. A dramatic creation that silhouetted her classic profile and suited her dark complexion. The group broke up and moved back in towards the ballroom. Madeleine edged her way around them.

"Do not stay at the tables too long, you have hardly danced all night," called Jeannine de Beauchamps over her shoulder to one of the party as he was moving towards the exit. He was looking back over his shoulder as Madeleine was about to step through the doorway. They collided gently and Madeleine would not have stopped, but for the grunt of pain which surprised her. Expecting to see an elderly gentleman, she turned to apologize and found herself looking into the face of her husband. She was transfixed. She could not believe her eyes. It seemed that her heart stopped and she could not breathe. The room began to turn slowly as she sank to her knees.

Erich stepped forward and quickly caught her around the waist and lifted her into his arms. A passing waiter rushed up to him.

"Is there a quiet, private place where I can take her?" he asked. The waiter pointed to the other side of the vestibule to a door leading into a small salon, where cocktails had been served earlier in the evening.

"Bring me a glass of water, a towel and a cognac," ordered Erich and limped slowly across the room.

But for the limp body in his arms, Erich was not sure if he too would not have been rooted to the ground by shock, but disbelief, anxiety and an overwhelming urgency forced him into action. This could not be happening to him. He was desperately afraid. Afraid that this was a mirage, that this beautiful woman in his arms was an illusion. One of life's incredible coincidences. A likeness so similar that only a mother or lover could tell the difference.

He entered the salon and saw a sofa at one end. He made his way towards it and gently lay his charge upon it. He got an extra pillow and placed it under her head. He looked for a chair and brought it and placed it beside the sofa.

He looked down into her face, very white, the blood drained out of it. She had hardly changed. Her face was perhaps a little fuller. Her complexion was unblemished, except for the slight thinning of an eyebrow where she had injured it in a childhood accident. Surely this was his Madeleine, not some duplicate copy to torment him. He sighed deeply and realized that his thigh was throbbing. It had been sensitive all evening. That was the worst of old injuries, they could never be relied upon to remain dormant. Bumping into her had not been anything but a minor event, but it had been like a needle thrust into a raw nerve. Momentary, but painful.

The waiter was back. Erich took the tray and sat with it on his knee. He wet the towel and lay it on her forehead. He handed the tray back to the waiter and thanked him and then placed the cognac on the floor.

Her eyelids fluttered and closed again. She stirred and then moaned gently as though seeking to delay the moment of consciousness.

Her eyes opened and stayed open. "Is it really you, Erich? Or have I died and gone to heaven?"

This remark, which caught him by surprise, broke some of the tension in him and he laughed spontaneously.

She looked in wonder at him. How incredibly handsome he was. She must be dreaming. His eyes were just as blue, accented by those long dark lashes, which she had always envied. His thick, black hair was combed away from the dark outline of his eyebrows. A strong and slightly sensual mouth, when he was relaxed. But now, his forehead was furrowed with concern.

"Yes, it is Erich. You are not dreaming. Would you like to sit up a little more? I have some cognac here. A sip might make you feel better and put a little color in your cheeks."

She struggled to sit up and he helped her. He handed her the brandy and she took several sips, choking a little. Color crept back into her cheeks.

"I was afraid you were dead."

"I thought you were dead," he responded with emphasis.

She dared to hope that this was not a dream. "Is Max still alive?" She did not know what prompted her to ask this, except that Erich and Max had been symbols of love and loyalty that were intrinsically intertwined with her relationship with both of them.

Erich's heart lightened and he smiled. No one but Madeleine would have asked after Max. She was no creation of his imagination. "Max lives. He is pretty old and stiff, but for his age he is healthy. He hates my absences."

She laughed. "I can dare to believe that you are no figment of my imagination?"

"No, I am flesh and blood. I cannot believe, however, that I am seeing you. What are you doing here?"

"I am a guest of a relative. What are you doing here?"

"I am also a guest."

She gave him a long look. "Of the Countess de Beauchamps?"

He nodded, his look completely neutral.

She suddenly noticed that he was holding the Kandahar medallion in the palm of his left hand. She stared at it in fascination. It was like reliving another moment of her life but, this time, one so unreal that she was afraid it might be a taunting mirage which would evaporate at any moment. He saw her eyes focused on the medallion and smiled. "This became entangled in your beautiful butterfly brooch, so I thought it best to remove it. Shall I slip it back over your head?"

"No, thank you." She took it from him and kissed it as she put it safely into her evening purse and snapped it shut. "It was a gift from my father. I do not remember if I ever told you that." He shrugged his shoulders as though dismissing the statement. Whatever the unknown associations attached to it, the medallion would always be her special talisman, now more than ever since being reunited with Erich.

"Do you feel well enough to get up? I would like to take you home."

She nodded and with his help, stood up. The color had returned to her face. She bent slightly to arrange her dress. He was overwhelmed by her loveliness. The crimson brocade with its train and billowing golden pink scarf was enormously flattering and gave her a regal appearance.

"I feel a little shaky."

"Would you like to sit a little longer?"

She shook her head.

They made their way slowly to the entrance of the Sporting Club. He seemed surprised when she told him where she was staying.

They arrived at the door of her aunt's suite and he unlocked it for her and guided her inside. He appraised the room in a quick glance but said nothing. She felt that he was disapproving, but she could not be certain.

"Will you be able to take care of yourself, if I leave you alone?"

She nodded. "My aunt should be back soon, except she is probably wondering what has become of me. I wonder what I should do?"

"I have to return to the ball. If you want to write a short message, I can have it delivered."

She nodded and quickly wrote a few words on the hotel notepaper and put it into an envelope and addressed it.

"Have you any free time tomorrow?" he asked. "We have to talk."

"I have no plans at all."

"Then meet me downstairs at three o'clock. In the meantime, I hope you will rest and feel restored tomorrow."

He kissed her hand and was gone.

— 26 —

She stood holding on to the back of an armchair. Her happiness was muted by his reticence. Why had he seemed so distant? He had not kissed or embraced her. Was she a terrible intrusion in his life? A great fear suddenly took hold of her. What if he had remarried? It would be almost worse than thinking that he was gone forever. She felt shaken at this unwanted thought. It had never occurred to her to ask him. She now realized that she dreaded their meeting tomorrow. She felt miserable. There were so many unanswered questions.

She went to her room and undressed. She would have liked to have had a bath but felt too tired and listless. She got into bed and lay looking at the ceiling. Eventually she slept. She awoke later and lay thinking. The remainder of the night she tossed and turned alternatively awake and asleep. She finally got up at midday, feeling tired and jaded.

Her aunt had left a note expressing the hope that she was feeling better and that she would see her at the cocktail hour. She sensed a slight coolness on the part of her aunt. She probably had offended her by disappearing from the party without the appropriate courtesies.

She made her way downstairs and sat herself on the central circular banquet. She was wearing periwinkle blue. The color was flattering to her and accented her eyes. She had made up her face carefully, for she wanted to give herself more color and try and eliminate the dark circles under her eyes. She was not sure she had succeeded at all. There was nothing she could do to counteract how tired she felt. She had rarely felt more nervous or anxious. She had forced some soup into herself at lunch, but she felt light-headed and nauseous now. She dreaded this encounter. She got up and paced, unable to sit still. He was fifteen minutes late. She wondered if she would feel any worse if he did not come. But the suspense was more than she could stand. She had just turned to walk once more towards the door, when she saw him enter the hotel. He had seen her almost immediately. She had stood still, uncertain of her legs.

He took her hand and kissed it and looked keenly into her face.

"You look a little tired. How do you feel?"

"I feel tired," she responded. She noticed that he, by contrast, looked fresh and rested. Her spirits sank lower. "Where can we go to be alone?" he asked. "I think this is a bit too public."

"I really do not know Monte Carlo that well. I have been here only three days."

He stood thoughtful for a moment.

"Come," He took her by the arm and led her out of the hotel. The doorman called a taxi and they got in.

"We will have tea at La Réserve in Beaulieu."

Madeleine tried to enjoy the lovely scenery as it flashed by them. But she was too preoccupied by his mood to be able to relax. They hardly spoke for the eleven kilometers. They arrived at last.

When they were settled finally at a small but comfortable table in a corner, he turned to her and asked, "You seem very preoccupied. What are you thinking about?"

She felt like weeping and remained unable to speak for a time.

"When I learnt that you had been arrested and imprisoned, I thought that my life had come to an end. I had never been unhappier."

He smiled sadly. "Yes, it seemed like the end of all my hopes."

"Once the war was over, I wrote to you. None of my letters were returned. I thought of writing to your parents, but decided against it."

"I never received one letter. Where did you send them?"

"So many letters, all to Waldesrauschen. Then finally, I asked the authorities to write to the prison where they thought you were incarcerated."

"I am not surprised if any written to the prison were not delivered to me. It was a pretty primitive place, where those who were suspected of plotting against the Führer were sent and treated with the minimum of human dignity."

Madeleine winced.

"I cannot understand why I did not get the ones you sent to Waldesrauschen. Once I was released, I wrote to you immediately. But finally my letters were returned stamped 'Unable to deliver.' 'Residence demolished.' Some with scribbled notations by hand to the effect that the residence was no longer occupied due to bomb damage. I also wrote to you at your parents' address, but received no reply." He could have said more but refrained from doing so. This was not the time to tell her that someone had intercepted his letters.

"Our first flat in London was demolished." She clenched her hands tightly together and finally, in a rush, asked, "Erich, did you remarry?"

He stared at her a long moment before answering. Her heart was in her mouth and she thought she might faint all over again.

"No," he replied. "No."

Whereupon she burst into tears and sobbed silently.

He took her hand and asked her gently why she was so sad.

When her sobs were spent, she told him that she had been so dreadfully afraid that he had remarried.

"But I loved you too much," he told her.

She smiled weakly. "Oh, Erich, I love you so much. Will we be able to pick up our life together again?"

He kissed her hand and smiled. This time, there was great warmth and his face was illuminated with love. "I am counting on it. It is going to take a little organization. I hope there are no obstacles." He looked at her quite seriously now.

"None. What do you mean?"

"What was that fedora doing in the sitting room of your suite?"

"Fedora?" She frowned.

"It looked like a man's fedora."

She laughed. "Yes, there probably was a fedora. My aunt wears one occasionally. She looks marvelously elegant in them. You have to meet her. She will approve of you."

He smiled. "I saw the hat and was immediately suspicious and jealous."

She took his hand and kissed it and held it to her cheek.

Their tea was served. They ate and drank without noticing, for they had become more and more absorbed in each other.

It was the beginning of a healing for them both. Madeleine already felt rejuvenated and it must have showed in her face and demeanor, for she was glowing.

Suddenly in a moment of silence, he said, "You look so beautiful."

They sat and reminisced about many things. They did not speak much of the years of separation. That was too painful. That could wait.

It was getting late and it was time to go. "We have much to decide and organize," he told her. "It is going to be a bit of a shock for the world that knows us. We must time it carefully."

"I can tell my aunt, I hope?"

"Of course, and I want to meet her. Tomorrow perhaps?"

They rode back to the Hotel de Paris hand in hand. He delivered her to the front door. "I am late. The Countess is giving a cocktail party. Forgive me for not coming in. I will ring you in the morning."

She longed for him to kiss her, but she knew he would never do so in public.

He kissed her hand, got back into the taxi and she walked through the hotel entrance.

Her aunt's suite was empty. A note was propped on a credenza. It informed Madeleine that her aunt expected her at dinner at eight-thirty promptly. It was not her usual loving greeting. It was obvious that Madeleine had offended her. She hoped that it was only a matter of explaining her extraordinary encounter. Anyway, she was far too happy to worry about it. She had plenty of time before dinner. She was tired from all the excitement, but most of all from a poor night's sleep. She would lie down and rest briefly.

She fell instantly sleep and awoke with a start. She had no idea what the time was for it was dark outside. She felt wonderfully refreshed. She turned on the light and discovered to her dismay that she only had fifteen minutes before being expected at dinner. It was not possible to prepare herself in time, but she would do her best.

She arrived in the dining-room ten minutes late. She was flushed from rushing, but also from the enormous excitement that filled her. She was still fearful that she would suddenly awaken and find that she was dreaming.

She was wearing a long purple silk gown that accented her youthful figure.

Her aunt smiled a rather frigid smile and waved her to the only empty seat, whereupon she introduced those already seated.

It was an evening that passed without leaving much impression on Madeleine. She conversed with both of her table companions. They were young and attractive, but she had no interest in them. She suspected that her aunt had made a special effort to produce them. In other circumstances she might have been grateful. She ate well, but had no memory later of what she had eaten. She was altogether too euphoric at the encounter with Erich. Too excited at the prospect of being one day reunited with him as his wife. She hoped fervently they would not have to wait too long for such a moment.

It was obvious to Madeleine's aunt that something special had happened to Madeleine. She looked radiantly happy, but completely preoccupied. She is in love or having an affair or both, she thought silently. In any event, she was more than a little annoyed at her niece's erratic and unreliable behavior. After all her efforts on her niece's behalf, she felt ill-used.

The dinner party came to an end and the guests started to leave. Her aunt claimed that she was tired and was going to retire. It was obvious that she did not wish to encourage conversation, but Madeleine touched her arm as she was about to turn away and said, "Dear Aunt Elisabeth, I have something very exciting to tell you. Do you have a moment now or shall I save it until tomorrow?"

"Tomorrow will be soon enough. I also have a few things to say." With that she turned and left Madeleine.

It was unlike her aunt to be so abrupt and Madeleine recognized it as a rebuke. She sighed. She was sorry if she had ruffled her aunt's feelings or offended her. She hoped it would be easily straightened out in the morning. In the meantime, she thought that she would return to the gaming tables. After her late afternoon nap, she felt fresh and energetic.

The gaming rooms in the Casino were as animated as ever with elegantly dressed men and women. Madeleine settled herself at a table and played for nearly two hours, until she felt stiff from sitting so long. She had not won much, but had ended the evening having been pleasantly entertained.

As she arose from her place at the table, she caught the eye of George Vladimirovich as he moved away from another table. She sighed. There was no way to escape him. He came up to her.

"What a delightful surprise. Will you join me for a drink? I will not take no for answer."

"How ungallant of you. Suppose I wished to retire because I was tired?"

"But you do not look the least tired. Come, I will not keep you up too late."

She shook her head. But he took her by her arm and led her towards the bar.

"What will you have?"

"A tonic with a twist."

He ordered himself a brandy.

"So what are you doing for the rest of the week?"

"I am returning to England."

"You cannot do that. Stay on and keep me company."

"I am sure that you have a dozen other most eligible ladies who can fill that role."

"I am interested only in you. I could show you the whole of the Riviera. We could have a very good time."

"Thank you, but no. I have to get home. I have some very important things to do."

"What could be more important than enjoying this beautiful place. England is cold and wet, especially at this time of year."

"Yes, it is, but I cannot wait to get there."

"There is someone else in your life?"

"As a matter of fact there is." She regretted saying that as soon as she had opened her mouth. She knew that his unquenchable curiosity would be aroused. "I have to go. It is late." She got up and half turned. She saw across the room the Countess de Beauchamps and her heart gave a skip. If she was here, could Erich be far behind? She must not let him see her with George. He would never understand.

George was holding her arm. "You cannot leave now. The night is far too young. Let us go and dance."

"I really want to return to my hotel and go to sleep. If you were a gentleman, you would not force me to stay here against my will."

"But you do not understand what a good time you would be missing."

She sighed. This was going to be more difficult than she feared.

"I do not wish to dance."

"So who is this special man in your life?"

"It is none of your business and you would not know him anyway."

She had to get away, but he still had her by the arm.

"Perhaps one more drink."

He smiled in triumph. He turned towards the bar and let go of her arm as he did so.

She turned quickly and ran out of the room, dodging between the crowded tables. She did not look back, but kept running all the way back to her hotel. It was not a very sophisticated thing to do, but she knew of no other way to disengage herself from him.

Her aunt's door was closed. She was relieved at that.

She took a long, relaxing bath and went to bed. She lay reliving the day, Erich's face vivid in her mind. It was hard to believe what strange fate had brought them back together. She was afraid to wake and find it all a dream.

The telephone awoke her the next morning. She picked it up.
"So will you elope with me, my darling.?"
Her heart leapt in happiness. "Oh, Erich, you know I will."
"I think we need to spend some quiet time together, but we need to plan it. You sound as though you are still in bed."
"I am. What time is it?"
"Ten o'clock. Could you be dressed in an hour if I were to come and fetch you?"
"Yes, of course. Perhaps, if my aunt has not left, you can meet her then. I think she is very upset with me. If she were to meet you she might be ready to forgive me for upsetting all her plans."
"Well, I want to meet her too. I will come and collect you at eleven o'clock."
She lay there thinking of Erich, longing for him. What if she had never come to Monte Carlo. Did it mean that she might never have known that he was still alive. She shuddered at the thought.
She washed her face and brushed her hair and put on her lace robe. She hoped that she might make a good impression with her aunt. Most of all she hoped that her aunt had not already left.
She went out into the sitting room. Her aunt's bedroom door was closed. She picked up the phone and ordered some coffee and croissant. She had just put down the telephone when her aunt came into the room.
"There you are. I have been wanting to speak to you ever since the night of the ball. Your behavior has been, to say the least, extraordinary."

"I know, dear Aunt Elisabeth, I am so sorry to have kept missing you. But the most extraordinary, the most wonderful thing has happened. It is like a miracle. I have found Erich. I have found my husband. I was so afraid that he was dead. If I had not come to Monte Carlo I might never have known that he was still alive."

Her aunt stood there speechless. Madeleine could see the disbelief in her face.

"Please sit down and let me tell you the whole story."

Her aunt sat down and Madeleine recounted all that had happened. When she had finished, her aunt smiled and said, "I could not be more happy for you. It truly is the most incredible story that I have ever heard. I am so relieved too. I was really beginning to have doubts about you. Your behavior was so out of character. I was afraid that you were having an affair with that terrible Vladimirovich character."

Madeleine laughed. "You know, if you had not asked me to this ball, I might never have known that Erich was still alive. Do you realize, dear Aunt Elisabeth, how well you have fulfilled your promise to find a suitable husband for me? You could not have made me happier." They embraced.

"Erich is coming to fetch me at eleven this morning. He wants very much to meet you. Will you still be here?"

"Well, dear, I had promised to meet a friend at eleven o'clock downstairs, but I suppose I could delay that a little."

"Please do, it would make me so happy."

While her aunt went to telephone her friend, the coffee arrived on an elegant tray with a rose in a vase.

Erich arrived promptly. He was looking especially handsome in a pale blue cashmere sweater and dark brown suede jacket.

Madeleine introduced him to her aunt.

"Aunt Elisabeth, may I introduce Baron Erich von Brandenburg. My husband. Erich, Countess von Altenburg." He kissed her hand.

"My dear Baron, I can hardly believe the story that my niece has just told me of your reunion. It sounds rather like a fairytale."

Erich smiled. "I think in many ways our meeting has been a fairytale, but one with many twists."

"What do you propose doing now? You have both been leading separate lives. It is going to require considerable thought and planning."

"Yes, it is. I was wondering if I might have your permission to take Madeleine away for a few days? We need some time together away from people who might know us."

"My dear Baron, you do not need my permission. I am so very happy for you both."

"As I have to be back in Berlin at the beginning of next week, we shall not be gone more than three or four days. Upon our return, would you kindly consent to dine with us, so that we may tell you our plans?"

"I should be more than delighted. I can think of nothing that would give me more pleasure."

Madeleine could see from her aunt's expression that she was quite captivated by Erich's gracious manner and natural charm.

"Then I will go and make all the arrangements. Perhaps you could pack a few things, Madeleine. I should not be long."

He took his leave of the Countess, smiled at Madeleine and went out.

"My dear Madeleine, what a delightful, cultured man. How very lucky you are. I could not have done better for you had I spent the rest of my life interviewing prospective husbands."

Madeleine smiled and hugged her aunt. "I was so afraid that I should wake up and find that I was dreaming."

"I understand, but I can assure you that you are not dreaming. Now what are you going to take with you?"

"I have no idea what to take. He did not say where we would be staying."

"You can be sure it will be a lovely place. I really do not think that you need much. Let me help you pick out a few things. Then I will have to leave you."

— 27 —

The next four days were a time of great enchantment for them both. Erich had reserved a suite in a small hotel on Cap Ferrat. Surrounded by lush tropical vegetation, it had a beautiful view of the sea through the pine trees. At night the lights along the coast twinkled and flickered.

They were shown to their room and their bags placed side by side on two luggage racks. The porter opened the window overlooking the bay and they stood together looking at the sailing boats gliding across the blue expanse of the sea before them. It was as if she were with him for the first time. She felt very shy and self-conscious. Erich finally turned towards her and tipped her chin up towards him. "You know, it has seemed like an eternity for this moment to come. This is the first time that we have been truly alone. I have wanted so much to kiss you ever since I first laid eyes on you. I have gone to bed at night thinking of you, wishing that you were beside me, wishing that I could hold you. Afraid that it was all a dream."

"That is just what I said to my aunt. We are so indebted to her. I cannot bear to think that we might never have found each other. I go cold thinking of it..."

He bent down and pulled her closer and kissed her with a hungry longing.

There was a knock at the door, but they ignored it. It came again a few moments later. Erich lifted his head and responded, "Yes?"

"Champagne, Monsieur le Baron."

Erich smiled at Madeleine. "I thought we might be willing to give up eating for an hour or two, but a really good bottle of champagne might help us bridge the present and the past."

He opened the door and a waiter with a trolley entered. The waiter laid a white linen cloth on the small table near the open window and placed champagne, caviar, melba toast and a bowl of fruit on it, as well as glasses, plates and an ice bucket.

As the door closed behind the waiter, Erich picked up the bottle of champagne and began to unwind the wire from around the cork. There was a loud pop and the champagne bubbled out of the bottle in a light golden froth. With the two glasses filled, Erich handed one to Madeleine.

"We should make a toast. What shall it be? To a long and happy life together."

"To our family and friends."

"To love and friendship."

"To us."

He refilled her glass and his own. He walked into the bedroom, put down his glass and threw himself on the bed. She followed him in and he lay there smiling lazily at her.

"It is very comfortable. I highly recommend it."

She took another sip of champagne and placed it on the bedside table.

"But I don't feel tired." She smiled provocatively.

He rolled over and, before she could react, he pulled her onto the bed beside him. He wrapped his arms around her and buried his face in her hair. He lay murmuring her name over and over again. Then one hand slowly slid up her back and took hold of her hair. He pulled her head back and kissed her neck and gently worked his way upwards until he reached her lips. She felt that she was drowning from the intensity of her emotions.

He was leaning on one elbow looking down at her. How much she loved looking at his face. His lips were curved in a smile.

"I am glad you don't feel tired. It would be such a pity if you were to go to sleep now. I have all sorts of plans for us. I think that I shall begin by undoing the buttons of your jacket. To save my strength, why don't you change into something different."

She got up from the bed and bent to kiss him lightly on the nose.

"I shall try not be long," she said with a provocative smile.

He threw a pillow at her.

She returned wrapped in a pale pink satin robe. He was standing at the window and was wearing his favorite color of dark blue silk robe. She went up to him and he turned and folded her in his arms. She lay her head on his shoulder as he stroked her back and ran his fingers up and down her spine. She lifted her head to look at him and he kissed her fiercely.

Scarcely removing his mouth from hers, he picked her up and carried her to the bed and laid her gently down. He stretched out beside her kissing her mouth, her neck and her breasts. He could feel her quiver. Her hand ran up and down his side like a feather and then extended across his back as he rolled towards her. She clung to him fiercely as his hand entwined itself in her hair again as he pressed her closely to him. They murmured endearments, which spilled out of them intermittently, only partially heard. It was as if they were living in the center of a great storm. The power and the force building and building, sweeping them away in a great tide of passion that spoke of years of sadness and longing, of despair and loneliness.

Their days were sunlit and carefree. They breakfasted in their suite on marvelous French coffee and fresh, soft croissants and brioches. It was a light and airy space, the rich scent of pines drifting in on a morning breeze. The sea in the distance twinkling and sparkling through the trees. There was a great sense of peace and serenity around them. If there were other guests in the hotel, they were not aware of them. There seemed no sounds from within. The only sounds that reached them were the songs of birds, the sighing of the pines and the braying of a donkey in the distance. They had a great sense of being quite alone.

They took long walks in the crisp sunlit air through the woods and to the beach and along the narrow promontory. They relived the frantic days before their wedding in Ulm and her eventual escape back to England. They felt again the pain of their abrupt and sudden separation as the balloon lifted from the earth, when they became once more two individuals seeking to survive in a cruel and devastating war. They talked of the years of their separation. The hope that when peace came they would be reunited. The frustration, the anxiety and then the disbelief when neither of them could trace the other. And as time passed, the disbelief turned to despair. Much was not spoken of and Madeleine was relieved that Erich did not seem interested to know all the details of her life during the war years. It was as though there was an unspoken agreement that some subjects should not touch this reunion, this special world which they had created for themselves.

At lunch time, they would find a small café on or near the beach. They did not wander far from the seclusion of their hotel. It was enough to be together. They did not want the intrusion of traffic and people. It was a time of healing from the pain of loss and separation. It was not possible to regain the years of separation lost, but the intensity of their relationship now brought them both exquisite pleasure. Such intense passion could not last, but would, with time, transform itself into a more comfortable and serene emotion. But for the present, they were living in a time of intense joy. The joy of their present togetherness almost overwhelmed them. The rediscovery of their physical attraction absorbed them totally. Only sleeping and eating intruded. And sleeping was only an extension of their loving. With desire once satiated, they would lie enfolded in one another's arms and often fall asleep. The knowledge that soon they would have to separate, for however long it would take to reorganize their lives, brought them both pain. The uncertainty of the weeks ahead stimulated a possessive quality in both of them.

They were lying in the darkened room. The sun had set and only a pink glow remained in the sky to warm the ceiling of their bedroom. They were discussing the weeks to come. Erich had to return to his office in Berlin. He warned her that he would not be able to retire immediately from the Navy. It might mean some brief separations. But now that they had rediscovered each other, the need to work to fill his days was no longer a necessity. He would not wait to be pensioned off. His parents' estate was in great need of a custodian. His father had died just after the War, but his mother was still living and not able to cope with the many demands made on her by such an extensive property. His own home needed him too. He would have his hands full. It would be wonderful to have Madeleine's help in many matters.

As for Madeleine, it would be less complicated to extricate herself from the life she had been leading. It would be hard to leave her parents, but the distances between them could easily be bridged. Besides which, she wanted them to meet and know Erich. She had always felt that they did not really believe that he existed. She had not even had a photograph of him to show them.

It was their last evening on Cap Ferrat. They dined in the little dining room of the hotel. The distant lights across the bay twinkled like fireflies. The dining room was not filled and the low murmur of voices rose and fell like the sound of the sea beyond the window. They ate and drank well and felt satisfied and contented. His hand covered hers as it rested on the table. He looked at her searchingly. How beautiful she was. Such blue eyes and soft enticing lips. The most amazing creamy pink skin and curly hair. She had not lost that air of innocence which had so captivated him when they first met. She was like a promise of spring. He had often wondered at her startling appearance on his train. It was an incident that was so beyond belief that, in the days after the war when he believed her dead, he had wondered if he had not hallucinated the whole incident. There were those who, if told of her existence, would have suggested that she was a spy. It was hard to believe the explanation she had given. It was too simple. His friends, who had met her, never spoke of the possibility that she might be suspect. He was grateful to them for that. It was beyond logic that anyone so incredibly attractive would be used for such a purpose. She could never be inconspicuous, however hard she might try. Besides which, she did not act the part. She was much too ingenuous. He had to admit that he did not care. But he also had to admit that he would never actively try and discover more about her wartime activities.

They lay together that last night listening to the ever present gentle murmur of the pine trees and the sea. They were loathe to relinquish to sleep their last few hours together. But after a languorous interlude of murmured endearments they both fell into an undisturbed and tranquil sleep.

They were dressed and ready to leave. It had been a magical interlude and both were reluctant to turn their backs and walk out of the hotel that had somehow drawn an invisible curtain about them and sheltered them from the world to which they now had to return.

"Before we leave and before we separate to go our separate ways, I want you to have this." He produced a small box and handed it to her.

She looked at him in surprise. She took it from him and gasped in astonishment, for inside was a pear-shaped diamond ring surrounded by brilliant baguettes. It was a magnificently designed piece of jewelry. She had never seen anything like it.

"Erich, it is unbelievably beautiful. Wherever did you find it? I love it. I am almost speechless."

"It is to remind you of me during the time we are away from each other. From your husband who loves you, very, very much."

She flung her arms around his neck and kissed him.

"Let me put it on your finger." He took it from her and placed it on her wedding finger. It was only slightly loose, an almost perfect fit. She stretched out her hand and rotated it this way and that so that the diamonds caught the morning light and flashed and sparkled.

"Dearest, darling Erich, I shall treasure it always, as I do you." She laughed with joy and hugged him again.

He smiled, well pleased with himself and with her reaction.

The ride back to Monte Carlo was as spectacular as ever, but they hardly had eyes for it.

It was like returning to an old friend when they crossed the threshold of the Hotel de Paris. But whereas they had been invisible in their anonymity in Cap Ferrat, this was far from the case in Monte Carlo. They had hardly passed through the door of the hotel than a voice cried out in greeting,

"Erich, my dear, where have you been. I have not seen you for days?"

It was Principessa Bracciolini, magnificent in silver grey crepe trousers and matching hip-length suit jacket, with a marvelously bright colored silk Hermès scarf floating around her shoulders.

Madeleine did not break her stride, but continued walking to the rear of the lobby. She and Erich had discussed just such an incident and had decided that it was far too soon for explanations. It was better, for the time being, that no one knew the truth of their relationship.

"I have been away for a few days," was his reply. "How elegant you are looking."

"Thank you. How kind of you to say so. I thought you were together," she waved her hand towards the departing Madeleine. "Would you be free to join me and some friends for dinner tonight?"

"How kind, but I already have other plans and tomorrow I leave to return to Berlin."

"We shall miss you. But I shall be in Berlin in the Spring. I hope that I may see you there."

"It would be a pleasure."

She smiled archly as he kissed her hand. "Then I shall write and let you know when I plan to come."

In the meantime, Madeleine had reached her aunt's suite and found her aunt on the telephone. She deposited her suitcase in her room and returned to the elegant sitting room and sat down.

Her aunt's conversation concluded, she turned to her niece who embraced her and then immediately burst into tears.

"Oh, my dear child, don't tell me that you had an unhappy time."

"No, no," sniffed Madeleine, "It was the happiest time in my whole life. It is just that I love him so much and I cannot bear to see him return to Berlin without me."

"There, there, dear, the time will pass soon enough," said her aunt much relieved.

Still sobbing, Madeleine stretched out her hand to display her ring to her aunt.

"What a magnificent piece. If I did not already know it, this is proof indeed of how much he loves you." Her aunt smiled with pleasure. "I have seen nothing like it in all my long years, and I have seen some wonderful jewelry in my time. How very fortunate you are, Madeleine dear. A man of taste, too. But you must stop crying, you will make your face ugly."

Madeleine nodded and went back to her room to repair the damage.

For the sake of privacy, they dined in the Countess' suite that evening, the three of them together.

They spoke of their plans, some still unformulated. They had not yet decided when and how to inform their friends about their reunion. Madeleine's aunt said she did not know how she was going to contain her urge to tell all her friends about them both, but she promised not to break the news until they told her she could do so.

"I am planning to meet some friends at the Casino, so I shall leave you two alone. I want you to know, my dear Erich, that I could not be more pleased to know that my niece has such good fortune in having you as a husband. I wish you both many, many years of health and happiness together. I hope that we shall see each other again one day soon."

"Countess, we should be honored if you would be one of our first guests, once we have settled in our home together."

"I should be delighted. But do not wait too long. I am getting too old to travel much any more."

At this they both laughed. No one could ever imagine great-aunt Elisabeth as ever being too old to do anything.

She left them then. Madeleine sat with her head on Erich's shoulder and they talked intermittently. It was a poignant time.

"Come back to my room for a short time." he said to her. "I do have to get up and leave early in the morning."

As she lay in his arms, a great nostalgia enveloping them, he turned his head towards her and said. "We are only as far away from each other as the time for a letter to arrive, so you are not to be sad. We shall be back together again in a few weeks."

"I want to believe that. But I am left with the awful memory of all those years when we were separated. I marvel at the incredible chance that brought us together. I am overwhelmed by the thought of what might not have been. It is unbearable."

He held her tightly and kissed her. "Now it is only a bad dream. But there are still some things that I would like to know. I still find it strange that I never received any of your letters. The Germans on the whole are very efficient. I shall look into it on my return."

They bade each other a lingering farewell. It was painful for both of them. Erich left Madeleine in her aunt's suite. She went to bed, but it was a long while before she slept, her pillow wet with tears.

Another day and Madeleine, herself, would be on her way home. With Erich no longer in Monte Carlo, she would be glad to leave that beautiful Mediterranean playground behind. There were too many memories. Wonderful memories, but painful to her now that she was alone.

Her aunt was sympathetic, but much more practical and suggested that Madeleine should lift her spirits by keeping herself busy making some concrete plans for when she returned to England. They sat down and made some lists together.

"Erich spoke of giving a big party once we have settled down. We want you to come to it, dear aunt Elisabeth. You will be the guest of honor, being the person responsible for our meeting again."

Her aunt smiled.

Madeleine brightened suddenly. "I would need a very special gown for such an occasion. I have just had an idea. You know all that money that I won on my first night at the Casino. I think that I will buy one here. Do you remember that wonderfully romantic silver and white gown at Madame Baudette's? I think that I would love to buy that if it is not too expensive and has not been sold."

"What an inspired idea. Off you go."

So it came to be.

Madeleine and her aunt parted with great affection. She could never repay her aunt for her generosity during her stay in Monte Carlo. For the life-changing meeting with Erich, that was a miracle beyond thanks.

— 28 —

Her parents welcomed her home with affection. It was a wet and dismal afternoon and they sat in front of the fire and had tea together. There was so much to tell them that she hardly knew where to begin. She decided to recount it in sequence, as hard as it was to contain her excitement. But in the end that was not to be, for in the middle of her narrative, her mother had noticed the ring which she had tried discreetly to hide.

She saw the disbelief in her parents' faces, the uncertainty and what she recognized as the beginning of a sense of loss. Their beloved daughter would leave them. But in general they seemed to be pleased for her. After all the years of yearning and sadness, they had to be happy for her that she had found her life's partner.

For the time being, life would take on its normal routine. There were too many decisions yet to be made before any definite plans could be completed.

Madeleine's first impulse after she had been home a few days was to visit Madame Fez. She wanted to share with her some of the highlights of the social events that had taken place while she was in Liechtenstein and Monte Carlo. Madame Fez welcomed her like a long-lost daughter. She wore a scarlet satin hat that hugged her head, with a black dress with red reveres. Her house was in its usual state of chaos, with fabric and half-made outfits spilling everywhere. It was morning and they drank coffee together. Madame Fez was not prepared to accept the shortened version of Madeleine's account. She needed to know every detail. Had the dresses survived the journey? Almost in perfect shape thanks to Madame's professional help. This was received with a satisfied smile. What comments did she receive? At the end of nearly two hours, Madeleine had relived the whole trip which was of interest to Madame Fez from beginning to end. She suddenly remembered that she had not mentioned the Dior fashion show which she had attended in Paris. Madame Fez's face lit up in delight. It was something she had never done herself, but was every dress designer's dream. How truly fortunate Mademoiselle was to have had such an experience.

Madeleine longed to tell Madame about Erich, but it was too soon. However, she told her that she wanted to make some new additions to her wardrobe and would return soon, when she had selected some fabrics.

Before leaving, she presented Madame with a prettily wrapped gift. It was a small Limoges dish which could be used for many purposes. When Madame Fez undid the wrappings and saw the beautiful dish she burst into tears. Madeleine was embarrassed to have precipitated such a flood of emotion. She realized then that Madame Fez was probably a very lonely lady and that such a gift represented a rare occurrence in her life. Madame kissed Madeleine on both cheeks and told her that she would always be able to fit her in to her schedule, given a little notice. It was with a sense of nostalgia that Madeleine left the little cottage. She would miss this association once she moved to Germany.

It hit her with a jolt that she was soon to leave England behind to live in a country against which they had so recently been at war. It left Madeleine in some trepidation as to the reception of a British woman in Germany.

It was a great relief to find that her luggage had arrived safely from Paris. She gave silent thanks to de la Croix for his efficiency and thoughtfulness. She could not decide whether to unpack everything or just leave the trunks and suitcase and forward them in due course to Germany. In fairness to the beautiful ball gowns she decided she had to unpack and hang them up. She owed that much to Madame Fez.

Sir Francis Winterbottom was someone else that Madeleine had to see. She telephoned him to make an appointment, but he was not at home.

Unpacking one day, she found the sketches which she had made while at Marc de la Croix's horse farm. She was surprised how much they captured the mood of that lovely place. She spent the next few days working on them with her watercolors. It was a very satisfying experience and helped to distract her from the limbo she was living in. She had not heard from Erich, but he had told her that he would probably not be in touch with her for at least a week.

She managed at last to speak to Sir Francis and they arranged to have lunch at the Club. She arrived at the appointed hour. He was his usual jovial self. However, she now knew that there was a totally different side to him, a side that most of the world never saw.

They were sipping their coffee. Sir Francis pulled at his greying moustache and cleared his throat as a prelude to business.

"Your stay in Paris proved to be a little more adventurous than any of us expected. I want you to recount your whole stay there leaving out no details."

He did not interrupt until she had finished.

"What is so disturbing to me is the fact that you might have stayed at the Hotel Malesherbes as a result of someone's cancellation of de la Croix's reservation for you at the Prince de Galles. It means that it was known that you were traveling on my behalf, but who the devil could have found that out? We now think that de la Croix's telephone was tapped. It left me thinking that there was a leak at this end, but that is rather unlikely due to the special arrangements and precautions I am careful to make. Sadly, we can never let our guard down. There are always infiltrators busily engaged in their devious tasks. Who besides your parents knew that you were going to Europe?"

"Mary, the cook. Madame Fez, my dressmaker. Guy Hamilton. Also some of my friends in London."

Sir Francis was silent for a moment.

"This is an awful long shot, but would you mind if we tested the telephone in your London flat?"

"Of course not. In fact, I would welcome it. Although I do hope that this game of cat and mouse is now over. I seem to have been followed by shadowy figures for a very long time."

He did not hasten to reassure her and she felt suddenly depressed. It really was not fair to involve her in their war games.

They should choose someone who enjoyed and thrived on that kind of thing.

He sensed that she was irritated and tried to make amends.

"My dear, we have accomplished so much thanks to you. We have just a few more pieces of the puzzle to put in place and then we can close the file. I want you to forget everything and put all your adventures behind you." He smiled benevolently.

She brighten a little. "You know, I forgot to tell you that de la Croix said that they would be happy to arrange a polo match here in Dorset, provided that you would reciprocate with a match against their team in Paris."

Madeleine thought she had handed him the world trophy. His smile was beatific. "My dear, how brilliant of you. How can I ever thank you?"

"You said that you would fill me in on the Peter Weiss story. Would this be a good time?"

"Well, I do have an appointment after our lunch together." He paused, unprepared for the question and reluctant to give her too many details. "Just briefly. He is British. Was educated at Cambridge, where he was active in left-wing political groups. He began life working as the editor for a left-wing socialist magazine in London. Unfortunately, there are a number of such people around. He was trained as a paratrooper, a rather useful credential in the circumstances. He was obviously an opportunist. It seems he did not mind who he worked for - British, Germans or Russians - whoever was prepared to pay him the most. We think he mostly worked alone. He was basically a very efficient assassin. He had done work as an informant. We are a little bit concerned that he might have tried to infiltrate one of our networks." Sir

Francis did not attempt to qualify how he had come by all this information. He felt that Madeleine now accepted his involvement in intelligence gathering.

"Would it not be a little difficult to infiltrate a network? "

"Yes and no. But if he had managed to do that, it would be difficult for him to betray any of the operatives without a long association. We do not think he had time for that." Sir Francis paused, twiddling his coffee spoon between his fingers. He hoped desperately that Weiss had not infiltrated their network years ago before hostilities began in earnest. He put down his spoon and continued. "Fortunately, the director of a network uses various names and identities, so it is very difficult to uncover such a vital person. A director is not even known to the leaders of his group. Only he knows all the members involved. It would be through the network director that we would have to attempt to trace our infiltrator. Only some erratic behavior by an operative is likely to give us a lead. Weiss would be too professional to give himself away easily. Also, none of the members understand the real purpose of all the small bits and pieces of information they are instructed to collect or the small actions they are asked to perform. So if Weiss' plan was to try to leap-frog the Channel, backtracking the conduit from France to England, he would have to be exceptionally lucky to discover even one member of the network. But you can imagine the value of such information to the opposite side."

She sighed. "I hate to think that he might have been successful."

"My dear, thanks to you, I do not think he succeeded." He did not add that the Paris file had yet to be closed.

"I am so annoyed that he should be British."

"Yes, it is hard to accept that a fellow countryman should be such a nasty character. Please do not worry yourself about all this. With Weiss in custody, you are now perfectly safe. Well, I have to be going, my dear."

"Thank you for the delicious lunch."

Sir Francis got to his feet, picked up his briefcase and smiled at her. "I will be in touch with you when I have any more news about our polo match."

She nodded and watched him leave.

He hoped that he would never have to confess to her how often her path had crossed with some of their operatives and those of the opposition. There had been risks for her, but she had been lucky and for that he was infinitely grateful. He realized that in many ways one could become too focused on the success of an operation to take into account the dangers to bit players, who were generally totally unaware of their involvement. Their innocence was their greatest protection.

Christmas would soon be upon them. Her mother was very involved with the Christmas Fair at the Women's Institute and was counting on Madeleine for assistance in her many and various tasks. It helped keep Madeleine from pining for Erich.

He finally telephoned her one evening. Madeleine could not get over how lightly Erich treated such an extravagance, especially when connections were often quite bad. They talked at length. He told her that as much as he had hoped to be together with her for Christmas, that he planned to go to Hohenfels to be with his mother. He had not yet told her about Madeleine and their wartime marriage. He hoped his mother would forgive him. He planned to take some leave after the holiday. Perhaps Madeleine would travel to Germany then so that they could be together again and make the final plans for their new life together. She was content at last to have a focus and a date for their reunion.

Madeleine had just returned from a trip to London. It was tea-time and her mother was bustling about in the kitchen.

"Where is Mary?" her daughter asked her.

"She was at home. She rang after you left for London to say that she was feeling very unwell. I have rung her several times, but get no reply. Then about an hour ago, her cousin telephoned to say that Mary had suffered a slight heart attack and was in hospital. It means that I shall have to try and go and see her tomorrow, but it is the day we are setting up the Fair and I could not be more busy."

"Can I go instead of you?"

"I think that this first time it should be me. If you could substitute for me in some general areas at the Institute, that would be an enormous help."

The Christmas Fair was one of the more important events of Whickam's social calendar. It meant that nearly every woman in the village was involved in one way or another. Madeleine was known by nearly everyone present and it was not hard for her to act as her mother's substitute, even if she did not have her experience or have at her fingertips all the plans that were involved.

The morning passed quickly. They were sitting eating their sandwiches, when Claudia Devaux returned from her visit with Mary. There was a chorus of enquiries about Mary who was as famous for her baking as she was for her long-term association with the Devaux family.

"She did not look well to me," was Claudia's response. "But then I suspect she has never been quite truthful about her age. I think it is possible that she is nearly ten years older than she has admitted. In which case, she has been working far too long and should have retired years ago."

"But Mary's life centered around you and the life in the village. She could never have sat at home alone, not being needed," said the grocer's wife with a wise smile.

"I agree with that, but I now feel terribly guilty that this has befallen her."

"Do not fret. This is what she wanted for herself. To be needed and useful to the end of her days." This from the postmistress.

"Yes, but she could have been needed and useful and worked half-days. I feel perfectly dreadful."

The rest of the afternoon was consumed in an hive of activity. It was late by the time both Claudia and Madeleine returned home.

"I feel too exhausted to lift another finger. What are we going to do about dinner?" said Claudia as she sat collapsed in an armchair. "We are going to be in a mess at this very busy time without our dear Mary."

"I will get us a soup and a sandwich, if that is enough for you."

"Darling, bless you. It will be perfect."

The next few days were hectic and the Fair took all their time and energy. Madeleine enjoyed herself. She got to know better many of the villagers. More importantly it took her mind off of Erich.

Claudia had several offers of help at the house as a result of Mary's illness. It was difficult not to offend so many kind-hearted people. She knew that she could not substitute Mary. All that was needed was someone who could just keep the house in shape. The cooking could take second place, as much a deprivation as that would be. In the end she compromised. She took on a woman who would clean the house and do the laundry and come in three days a week. She found another woman who would come in five afternoons to prepare the dinner. It could never make up for having Mary, but it would work well enough.

The fair was over and soon it would be Christmas. Madeleine decided that she should go and see Mary and take her Christmas present with her.

She found her lying with her eyes closed, looking pale and very frail. She drew up a chair and gently took Mary's limp hand in hers. Her eyes fluttered open and then closed again. She opened them a few moments later and focused on Madeleine's face. To Madeleine's great dismay she saw tears trickle slowly down Mary's lined cheeks.

"Please don't cry. You are going to get well again. But you need all your strength and crying is not good for you."

Mary shook her head slowly from side to side, the tears still coursing down her cheeks.

Madeleine got up and found a small hand towel hanging by the wash-basin. She brought it back to the bed and dabbed it gently on Mary's face.

"I am being punished for something terrible I did," Mary whispered at last in a voice filled with anguish. "I can never be forgiven."

"Mary, Mary, how can that be possible? You are such a good, kind person. You have never spoken an unkind word in your whole life."

"I did a terrible thing to you, I know."

"To me?" Madeleine was astonished.

She nodded. The tears came faster and she was unable to speak again for several minutes.

At last she said, "A letter came from Germany, shortly after the war, addressed to you, care of your parents. It was from him." There was another flood of tears and Madeleine waited until they had subsided, before asking in a whisper.

"Go on."

"I wrote "Deceased" on the envelope and "Return to Sender." When another came, I wrote a short note to say you had died. That I was writing on behalf of your parents since they did not wish to write themselves."

Madeleine was so shocked, it took her breath away. "Oh, Mary. Why did you do that?"

"Because I hated the Germans. They killed my sister. They made a misery of so many lives. I could not have you marry one of them. It just would not have been right. You deserved better."

Madeleine was silent, unable to find an answer. She thought of all the years of anxiety, fear and sadness. Of the chance encounter that had brought her and Erich together again. There was a moment of anger that coursed through her. But it was almost immediately replaced by a great compassion and sadness. However misplaced, she realized how great Mary's love and devotion for her was. It was obvious that Mary was weighed down by guilt. Now here she was struck down by this heart-attack that left her old and helpless and very much alone. How could she be angry now that she and Erich had found each other? Could she convince Mary that it was possible for her to forgive her?

"But you do know that I did marry him? That I loved him very much. That I knew that he loved me? I could never have escaped from Germany without his help. He risked a great deal. But what you do not know yet, because only my parents know, is that I found him during this trip to Europe. It was a chance encounter. I should have found him eventually, but it probably saved months of enquiries. We shall be able to be together and start our lives again. So what you did was wrong, very wrong, but it did not change my life. It was just an interruption."

The tears started to run down Mary's cheeks again and she gripped Madeleine's hand fiercely.

"I feel better that you have found each other. I really do. I could not go on living with the guilt of possibly ruining your life."

"I was terribly lonely and afraid all those years, but in some ways it would have been too soon for us to begin our lives in either country after such a dreadful war with so many painful memories. It still will not be easy, I am sure. But there has been time for healing. The Germans suffered terribly too."

Madeleine got up and went and soaked the towel in warm water and brought it back and wiped Mary's face and laid it on her eyes.

She sat holding her hand wondering what she could say. Her own emotions were still in confusion.

She removed the towel and wiped her face again.

"Listen, Mary. Erich, my husband, is a wonderful man. He is a naval officer, a family tradition. He was not one of those dreadful Nazis. He comes from an old, aristocratic family. He truly is a gentleman. I know he is German, but then so are the royal family's ancestors German. I understand how you feel about him. I am sure my parents, in particular my mother, feel very much as you do about my marriage. They wish that I had fallen in love and married someone British. But I haven't and they seem to have resigned themselves to the situation. Hopefully, when they meet Erich they will understand better and one day come to accept him."

Mary had closed her eyes, but gently nodded her head.

"I think that I should leave you to rest. You are quite worn out. Before I go, I want you to know that I do not plan to tell my mother about this. I think we should keep it between ourselves, unless you feel very strongly to the contrary."

Mary shook her head and said nothing. She was obviously exhausted.

"I have brought your Christmas present. When you feel stronger you can look at it. We miss you very much, Mary. So you must do your best to get well."

She bent and kissed her and Mary grasped her arm and squeezed it.

"Thank you," she whispered.

Christmas came in a flurry of cards and invitations. The days were filled with activity. Her mother was very involved organizing gifts for needy children and food for those confined to their homes. Inevitably Madeleine was drawn into the action and the days sped by.

She missed Erich especially at this time of the year, when most family and friends were together. She longed to be with him, but understood that she had to be patient. She would see him after Christmas. They had spoken. He was still in Berlin, but about to leave for Bavaria and his family's estate at Hohenfels.

The cocktail parties were a strain. People wanted to know all about her recent trip to France and the wedding in Liechtenstein. She found it hard to talk about much of it. It had become a precious memory that she did not wish to share. However, she could speak of the promised polo match, the horse farm she had visited and the horses she had ridden.

Christmas Day was spent with the Vicar and his wife and family. Madeleine would have preferred to remain at home, but this was a gesture of gratitude to her mother for all the work she had done towards the Christmas Fair. It had left Claudia tired and, without Mary, with many extra burdens. It was a delicious Christmas luncheon and a pleasant afternoon. But they took their leave in due course and made their way home.

A fire was still burning in the hearth and they settled down to have a cup of tea and exchange their gifts. Madeleine had purchased her parents sweaters during her stay in Switzerland. They were thick and warm and attractive. She had also selected cosmetics for her mother and pipe tobacco for her father. They, in turn, gave her books, records and personal items and a check, which had originally been intended for her riding club membership. It could be put to other uses now. It was a relaxed and intimate time and they were able to relive many of their previous family gatherings. It would perhaps never be quite the same again.

Claudia went to visit Mary on Christmas Eve. Mary had a little more color in her cheeks and was more tranquil than on her first visit. She told her daughter this. Madeleine made no comment. She hoped that Mary was feeling less anguished.

She had not heard from Sir Francis as expected and wondered what devious cloak and dagger games he was up to now.

She realized that he certainly led a double life, but that few people would ever have suspected this.

There was to be a New Year's Eve dance at the Club and it was customary for most of the members to attend. She felt sure that she would see Sir Francis that evening and perhaps that was the reason he had not telephoned. There was certainly no urgency anyway.

Once Christmas was over the time seemed to pass very slowly. Erich had written again to say that he was not able to take leave as soon as he had hoped. He had considered having Madeleine come and stay in Berlin with him, but he feared she would be terribly lonely, as he would either be working late or away part of the time. When she answered his letter, she did not try to change his mind, because she was not sure she wanted to be alone in a strange city, as much as she longed to be with him. If it were their own home, as opposed to his home, she might have felt differently, for then she would have the responsibility of running it.

The New Year's Eve dance at the Club was a pleasant interlude as she knew so many people. Sir Francis was not present, which she found rather surprising.

She felt restless and decided to give herself something to do for a week and go up to London. She could see some of her friends. Before leaving, she tried to reach Sir Francis, but he was out. She decided not to leave a message that she would be in London.

The flat seemed unchanged and untouched. She wondered if Sir Francis' team had been in to test the telephone. Perhaps that was not necessary. She was not very well informed about electronic surveillance.

She went and opened a few windows. She looked in the refrigerator and found it empty but for a few odd bottles. She would have to go and shop for food.

The remainder of the day and evening was spent organizing the flat and planning for the week ahead. She managed to speak to a number of her friends. She would be kept quite busy during her week in London.

Madeleine had spent the day browsing in most of her favorite shops, including Dickens and Jones, Libertys and Harrods. London would remain badly scarred for years to come, but the pace and renewal of life was like a rebirth after such an extended period of oppression. She had lunch with an old school friend at Fortnum's. They had not seen each other in several years and had much to catch up on.

She returned to the flat in the late afternoon feeling weary.

She dropped her packages on a chair and went into the spacious kitchen and put on a kettle of water. She got out a cup and saucer. When the water was boiling, she made herself a pot of tea. She walked into the living room with her tray of tea and some digestive biscuits which she placed on a table. Kicking off her shoes, she collapsed on the sofa with a sigh of relief. She wiggled her toes and sipped her tea in contentment.

She loved her parent's flat. They had owned another, more spacious home in London, but it had been badly damaged at the beginning of the war and sadly they were forced to have it demolished. Their present flat was not large, but nevertheless had a spacious high-ceilinged living room with pale lemon-colored walls that always looked sunny even on the dullest of days. Three sets of book shelves with cupboards beneath added color and character to the room. The kitchen was spacious enough to serve as a dining room. Whereas the living room overlooked the gardens on the square, the kitchen had only an angled view of a neighboring terraced garden, with a blank, white brick wall blocking out most of the sky. A long corridor divided the main living area from two small bedrooms and bathrooms in the rear. It was a very convenient and comfortable floor plan. She resolved to spend the remainder of the afternoon reading when she finished her tea. She had purchased a ticket to a concert that evening and had several hours in which to relax and make her supper. She was comfortably reclining on the sofa with a book when the telephone rang. She picked it up. It was her mother.

"There you are. I thought that I might catch you at this hour. Have you had a good day?"

Madeleine gave her mother a brief account of her day.

"I am ringing because we had a telephone call from Sir Francis earlier this afternoon wanting to speak to you. He seemed upset to have missed you. He said he could not ring you right away, which seemed strange, but asked me to tell you to wait in for his call."

"Well, he better ring me soon, because I have a ticket for a concert this evening."

"I am sure he will, dear. Anyway, that is the message. I hope you have a lovely week. Ring us when you know which day you are coming home." After a few more words, her mother rang off.

Madeleine was puzzled by Sir Francis' cryptic message. It really did not make much sense, but she did have a feeling that whatever he had to say to her was important.

She had a simple supper of scrambled eggs and sausage and a slice of apple pie. She washed up the two plates and then changed into something a little more dressy. There had not been time to find a friend to accompany her, so she had purchased only one ticket. It was an organ concert in a local church. The money raised would go towards repairs and renovations. So many churches had survived the bombing but, due to age and neglect, and the ravages of the war, were in dire need of repairs.

It was time to leave and despite Sir Francis' message, she decided not to wait to hear from him. It surely could not be that urgent, otherwise he would have given her mother a more informative message. Besides, she was once more leading a private life and the club and horses were her only connections to him now. She put on her coat and took her umbrella. She closed and locked the front door behind her and went out through the front entrance of the building.

She had not been gone more than a few minutes when her telephone rang. It was Sir Francis. When he got no reply, he immediately started contacting the various members of his team. There was no time to waste. Peter Weiss had escaped the previous day while he was being transferred from one prison location to another. The men guarding him had totally underestimated their man. He had feigned an apathetic, slovenly attitude. It made him look slow and uncombative. Sir Francis was later to berate the prison warden who had failed to inform the guards of the identity and notoriety of their prisoner and his infamous reputation as a very deadly and lethal antagonist. When the transfer was being made, Peter Weiss had swiftly floored his two guards. Then he had tackled the two guards in the front of the van and driven off at breakneck speed, quickly distancing himself from the second van, which had to lose time turning around to take up the pursuit. The van driven by Peter Weiss was later found abandoned at a tube station. He could be anywhere in London. However, Sir Francis was not going to take any chances with Madeleine. He must make provisions to protect her, although he did not believe that she was a target anymore.

The concert was a pleasing and relaxing experience. The first half of the program featured a young woman pianist who performed a selection of Bach which included an Italian concerto in F Major, a Gavotte and an excerpt from one of the Brandenburg concertos. Madeleine hoped that the inclusion of that particular piece was a good omen. The organ recital followed. The rich, deep tones of the old organ filled the church and Madeleine felt uplifted and renewed by the purity of its enveloping sound.

She returned home feeling content but weary. She was glad to be home safely. She had no sooner got in her front door than the phone rang. She picked it up, but there was no one on the other end. She wondered if it was Erich with a bad connection, as was so often the case. It did not ring again and she was soon in bed and asleep.

She awoke the next morning feeling still fatigued and somewhat light-headed. She hoped that she was not catching a cold.

She ate a light breakfast and was dressed when the front door bell buzzed. She went to the intercom and answered. A voice announced that it was a delivery of flowers. She pushed the buzzer to open the front door and waited. At last there was a knock on the door. She looked through the spy-hole, but could see nothing but flowers. Her heart sang. Flowers from her beloved Erich. How romantic.

She opened the door and was stunned when the man holding the flowers stepped across the threshold and slammed the door behind him. It was Peter Weiss.

— 29 —

Erich returned to West Berlin as a man whose future was changed so radically that he could hardly believe that he was not fantasizing. His apartment, on the outskirts of the city, seemed strange and unfamiliar, as though its spirit had also gone through a metamorphosis. He felt infinitely restless. His joy at finding Madeleine was something he had not been able to put into words. If he had expressed himself it was in his unabashed love-making, in his total absorption in their mutual physical pleasure.

The years of their separation had been stark, loveless and overwhelmingly fraught with danger. He had been immensely relieved that his injury, which had so nearly cost him his life, had not resulted in his being pensioned off. The fact that he had been still able to walk, think and give orders had been sufficient. Germany needed men, but more importantly it needed leaders and Erich had been recognized for his leadership qualities. After his convalescence, he had been assigned briefly to serve in submarines and had distinguished himself by his daring and brilliant strategies. But to his immense frustration he had not seen as much active service as he would have wished, for his leg had rebelled against the strains and stresses he had imposed on it. He had been withdrawn from active duty. Instead he had been kept busy shuttling to and fro between meetings and assignments. Time had passed very quickly, for the most part. But the ever present threat from the skies above had never let him forget his frailty or that of the German nation. They had been hard pressed on all fronts. Uniformed personnel had outnumbered civilians, from the humble women's auxiliaries to the military police, as well as the ever present Gestapo and all branches of the wehrmacht, the armed forces. They had been times of enormous tension, for whether one was a civilian or a member of the wehrmacht, there was a sense that, as a result of a mistaken word or gesture, arrest could be swift and terrifying. Unluckily for Erich, he had been caught in a meeting of military professionals who were suspected of planning a plot against Hitler. He had been arrested, interrogated and sent to a prison in East Germany. Once there, all communication with the outside world had ceased.

Once the war was over, it had taken Erich years to be reinstated. Although the process had been incompetent and unbearably slow, the sacrifices Erich had made for the Fatherland had not been forgotten. His reputation as a superior naval officer was a matter of record.

His task, now that the war was over, was to help redesign Germany to meet post-war needs, which inevitably would mean considerable reorganization after so much chaos. He had little patience for the resulting complaints and disgruntlement of those affected.

Berlin had been badly damaged during the reign of terror inflicted on it by both the British and the Americans. However, there was a great resurgence of energy and industry as the rubble was cleared, unsafe buildings demolished and new buildings constructed. The more elegant social life still took place in the country residences. However, the Berliners were not slow to pick up the threads of a social life that had been almost, but not totally, stilled by the time the war ended.

Erich was always in demand as one of the more eligible bachelors on the social circuit. His greatest problem had been to keep the more ardent and determined hostesses from battling over his person and intruding on the little privacy he was able to glean for himself. His life had not been totally celibate, but he had never come close to losing his heart.

Thus, now that his destiny and life with Madeleine was once more assured, his greatest challenge was to fend off all the unwanted attention from the society matrons and other voracious females.

He considered it too soon to introduce Madeleine until she could be present in person. He thought a very special party would be the occasion to introduce her to his circle of friends and acquaintances. He recoiled at the thought of having to stem the endless questions that would arise at such an unlikely match. He anticipated criticism, but felt confident that Madeleine's extraordinary beauty and charm might quell some disapproval, even if it aroused envy in others.

He felt very frustrated that she could not join him in Berlin, but felt that she would be lonely during the many absences that he anticipated in the next few months. She needed a better entry into society. He wondered if his mother could provide that for her. He had not yet told his mother of his precipitous marriage during the war. There never had been a good opportunity to do so. He was planning to spend Christmas with her at Hohenfels. It was only as the time approached for his visit with her that he realized the difficulty of his task.

His mother had longed for him to marry, even before he was of marrying age, to fulfill her overriding desire to have a grandchild or, more particularly, a grandson. It was a large estate and she knew that her husband's everlasting wish had been the assurance of a continued line of inheritance. But the doctors had warned her that there was a great probability that her son was infertile as a result of a severe case of mumps in his early twenties, so she no longer dwelt on the hope of grandchildren. Instead she hoped that he would find his life's partner and return home to Hohenfels to manage the estate. Since losing her husband at the end of the war, she had worried considerably about the future. There was her brother's son, but she did not welcome the idea of his managing or inheriting the estate in place of Erich. However, it must remain in the family, that she knew and would accede to the nephew's inheritance if necessary.

Thus Christmas had come and with it Erich's journey to Hohenfels.

He was out all day driving around the estate with the gamekeeper and the manager. Partridges and pheasants were raised at Hohenfels for sport and for commercial use. It was a complex and interesting process and very finely tuned. The eggs were incubated. When the young birds reached a certain maturity they were released into a protected area from which later they were allowed to roam free. It was a big estate of several thousand acres, a mixture of forest and open terrain. A small herd of cows was kept, which helped make the estate self-supporting. There was much to see and discuss. The management of the forested areas, the maintenance of the peripheral boundaries, the gates and the barns. It all involved considerable expenditures.

Erich had enjoyed his day in the fresh air and arrived to take tea with his mother with a glow in his cheeks and a large appetite. He knew that his mother adored him. But he also knew that she could be unforgiving and inflexible in certain circumstances. He realized that he was not well prepared to present Madeleine in the best light. He was offering his mother a daughter-in-law who was not only foreign, but a national of a country so recently at war with Germany. His good mood was beginning to slip away from him. He sipped his tea and ate voraciously. He talked of his day's activities and his thoughts on various aspects of the estate's affairs.

"You have other things on your mind than Hohenfels," she commented. "I know it is not your work in Berlin as you have never chosen to discuss that with me. It must be an affair of the heart."

How was it that mothers had that uncanny ability to read the minds of their children? Erich gritted his teeth and did his best to look nonchalant. Here he was an adult, accustomed to leading men into battle, to making life-threatening decisions, and yet he felt like an infant about to be reprimanded by his elegant and beloved mother. The subject had to be addressed, but how best to present it? Would it make any difference?

"You are in love." It was a statement and not a question.

"Yes, mother. Very much in love. In fact I fell in love several years ago, at the beginning of the war."

"Uncertain times can breed impetuous decisions."

His heart sank. She seemed to be one step ahead of him.

"We were separated. We both thought the other was dead. When I was in Monte Carlo in December for the Bal d'Hiver we literally bumped into each other. It was a great shock. Madeleine fainted."

"And you revived her."

He could not tell if she was being sarcastic or laughing at him.

He sat morosely stirring his tea. The thought of his mother's disapproval weighed heavily upon him. She might eventually forgive him, but she might never accept Madeleine. He had always known that he had taken a great risk, but his love for Madeleine had always overridden all else. It had been easy to avoid this moment of confession. But no longer.

"In many ways, Madeleine was instrumental in saving my life at the time that I was injured during the devastating explosion in the station in Stuttgart. She helped me through my convalescence. We got to know each other very well. When I was healed and we could arrange it, we were married."

He watched his mother's face for some sign of emotion. She showed none. It was as though she had already known.

"I am sorry that I have deprived you of the pleasure and excitement of a wedding."

"I must say that I have always suspected that something very momentous had happened to you. You always had that faraway look in your eye. It made me very sad, for I suspected that you had experienced some personal loss. I cannot say that I am not a little disappointed that you took so long to confide in me. I do love you and do want to support you in all that you do. For the most part, you have always shown good judgement. I have to assume that Madeleine is a very special young lady?"

Erich swallowed. "She is."

"I feel there is more." His mother's hands were folded in her lap, like some mother superior interviewing her novices.

"She is British."

His mother drew in her breath and looked at him in astonishment. She clasped her hands together as if in supplication. "You must have taken leave of your senses."

"I think I did." Erich tried not to smile. He really did not want to antagonize his mother. "But she is the most beautiful and exciting woman I have ever met." It came out with a rush. It rather surprised him.

"Well," said the Baroness, "I am grateful that you are convinced that you have done the right thing. There is perhaps hope after all."

He waited for her to go on, but she was silent.

"This has been rather a shock. I think that I will go for a walk before taking a rest and changing for dinner. You know that we will be sixteen for dinner tomorrow night."

"Yes, you did mention it."

She rose and walked out of the room, slim and elegant in her silver grey dress which matched her beautiful hair. Erich sighed with relief. He was glad that he had at last confided in his mother. He had not been happy keeping this secret to himself. He was grateful that there had been no angry outburst. That might still come later.

Christmas at Hohenfels hardly lasted a week before he had to return to Berlin. They entertained family and friends on several occasions. It was festive and beautiful in the luxurious reception rooms of the old schloss. Although it had been closed and shuttered during several of the war years, it had escaped the destruction that had befallen many of the old country estates. It had been more a matter of an enormous cleaning and restoration job. The replacement of pictures and tapestries, carpets and precious furniture, which had been hidden in safe places.

It was a residence where one moved from one beautiful salon to another, a place where walls and ceilings and doors were covered with either carvings or murals. There were molded ceilings and inlaid parquet floors with varying designs. An extensive collection of arms and armor from the Middle Ages adorned some walls. Other walls were covered with graceful antlers. A three-storied Baroque schloss, with a beautiful terraced 18th century garden. A schloss of mellow and muted stone sitting on a rock above a deep ravine on one side and a small lake, once the moat, on the other. A natural stone bridge spanned the lake where once had been a drawbridge over the moat. It had been a very secure retreat in earlier times.

Erich and his mother hardly spoke of his marriage. It was mutually agreed that it was not timely to announce it yet. Erich knew that he had to allow his mother to become reconciled to the idea of a daughter-in-law and a married son. He was prepared to await her lead.

Although Erich was kept very busy with administrative duties after his return from Hohenfels, he knew that he would be able to find time in the immediate future for a visit to Waldesrauschen in Riquewihr. There was much to organize at his hunting lodge in the forest, for it was there that he wanted to bring Madeleine on her return to Germany. It had special meaning to them both. Also at Waldesrauschen was the beloved Max in care of Gretchen who had replaced Maria after the latter's death some six months earlier.

At last Erich managed to find a five day interval in which to make the trip to Mitteldorf. He was met at the station there by the beaming and still rotund Schultz in the trusty Daimler. Schultz and his wife, Gretchen, had lost their home during the war and Erich found, to his great satisfaction that Schultz and his wife were happy to move to Waldesrauschen and take on any of the tasks needed to run the estate. The aged Otto had moved to be cared for by a slightly younger sister.

"Schultz, how very good to see you again," exclaimed Erich with enthusiasm and a smile. "I do hope that both you and your wife have settled down comfortably at Waldesrauschen?"

"Indeed we have, sir. We both love the country. We are very happy to be here and hope that we can give you all the assistance needed to keep the property in good condition."

"Schultz, I am grateful that you are here. I know that Waldesrauschen is in good hands."

Gretchen, a portly woman in her middle years, was waiting at the front door as the Daimler drew to a halt in front of the lodge. She was rosy-cheeked and smiling; such a contrast thought Erich to the severely stern Maria. But Maria, for all her faults, had been a meticulous housekeeper. Erich had never wanted for anything. Her cooking had been plain, but good. Only Maria's lack of patience and sympathy for Max had resulted in some discord. It was something that Erich had been forced to accept.

Gretchen bobbed a curtsey as Erich greeted her. He strode into the familiar entrance hall and took a deep breath. It smelled of recently waxed furniture and had, too, the mouth-watering smell of baking bread. Gretchen had been hard at work since receiving von Brandenburg's telephone call informing her of his planned visit.

He turned to Gretchen and asked, "Where is Max?"

But before she could answer, a bark of greeting announced that Max, now a little harder of hearing, had heard his master's voice. He came trotting out of the kitchen and pranced with joy around Erich. Erich fondled his ears and patted his shoulder and the two of them made their way together into the library. It was good to be back in familiar surroundings. It had been months since he was last here.

"Gretchen, come. We have things to plan. But first, bring me some tea, if you would be so kind."

In due course, she returned with a tea tray and a mouth-watering selection of pastries which she set out on the table next to Erich's chair. She also placed on the table a pile of letters tied together with a piece of string. "I found these in the back of the dresser in the kitchen. I think that Maria must have put them there and then forgotten them. She was really ill for a considerable time, I understand, before she would admit it." She smiled, bobbed a curtsey and left.

Erich sat mesmerized, looking at Madeleine's handwriting. So many letters, which he had longed to receive and which would have saved him from so much anguish. Letters which Maria had carefully put away for when she might see him? Or had this been her way of revenging herself upon a beautiful girl of whom she did not approve? Maria was gone. He would never know. Perhaps it was better that way.

Later he sat, while Gretchen scribbled rapidly the list of instructions that he had mentally formed in his head during the journey from Berlin.

He wanted the whole placed spring-cleaned. What furniture she had polished she was not to do over. She was not to wash the curtains, unless needed; instead she should take them outside to air. The rugs she was to beat until they were dustless. Windows to be washed and copper to be polished. Linens and beds to be aired.

Gretchen was smiling broadly as she wrote, not the least inconvenienced at the prospect of so much work. She had missed her husband during the war and life had been lonely. She welcomed the prospect of bringing the house back to life, as much as she welcomed the arrival of the Kapitän's wife. They would be a complete family.

She had left him then to prepare dinner.

Thank God, thought Erich, for the cheerful Gretchen. He could never have presented Maria with such a formidable list without meeting her frowning countenance. It would have seemed a criticism of her housekeeping.

He sat and contemplated the faithful Max whose head rested on his knee. The thought of Madeleine made him ache for her presence. How much longer they would have to wait before being together, he did not know. But he hoped it would not be long. He picked up the pile of letters and settled down to reading them.

— 30 —

Madeleine was stunned. She could not believe that Peter Weiss was standing there in front of her. She had thought of him as out of her life forever, behind bars, never to threaten her or society ever again.

"At last," he said. "I have spent far too much time trying to find you. Time is a particularly precious commodity for me at the moment. I thought perhaps I would be out of luck. But this is the final reckoning. You have messed up my life for the last time. You are going to help me escape. You are going to provide the means for me to do this."

She gasped.

He smiled, his eyes cold and menacing. "You have crossed my path once too often for it to be coincidence. I don't know what your connection is with the copy of the coin I had in Berne, but obviously it had special significance to you. You have to be the person I took it from in Ulm, when that other stupid bitch messed up that operation and got me shot. I don't even care. That is in the past. Only the present matters."

She could hardly breath, she was so afraid, but she knew that to let him see her fear would give him even more power than he already had. She had to think very fast, to stall him to gain time, but to what purpose? He could kill her any time he wanted. She remained important to him as long as he felt she was useful.

"You must have fooled a lot of people for a long time doing whatever you were doing. So you were working for the English, but also for the Germans too, I have a feeling."

She had touched his pride.

"Yes, I did hoodwink the whole bloody bunch. The British were too stupid to ever work it out. The Germans got lucky because they caught the stupid whore who was working with me. It did not take long for them to get the information they needed. I was the number one agent for the Russians in my particular field of activities. They paid well. I liked their philosophy. They had never had anyone as good as me. Most of their operatives were uneducated fools. Peasants."

"So you were passing the Russians military information and names and all the usual stuff." She tried to make it sound commonplace in an effort to prod him into being boastful.

"Some of those things, of course, but much of it was a little more specialized."

Like killing people, she thought. Aloud, "I suppose you would have preferred to work alone, but then you have to get instructions from someone. It always weakens the chain of command to have other operatives."

She had touched a nerve. "I did not need instructions. I knew what had to be done. When you have to work with half-wits it puts the whole operation in jeopardy."

"True, but then you had to let them know progress, otherwise how could they pay you whenever you managed to complete an assignment? Waiting for the payment part must have been rather worrisome."

"I always completed an assignment. I never failed. They always paid me, but I need a substantial sum of money immediately to make my final plans. You are going to provide it. You have a bank account, I presume?"

So that was it. So how was she to play this?

"Well, I do not have much in it."

His face contorted into a snarl. "You better find enough money or I will make your last moments a living hell."

She felt ice-cold and nauseous. "Shooting me is not the solution."

"I very rarely shoot people. There are quieter and more efficient ways."

She felt such a threat a hundred times more menacing.

"My bank is around the corner."

She saw him visibly relax. She had decided that if there was any hope of her survival, she had to get out of the flat and into the street. Some years ago, she had told David Johnson, the building's caretaker, that as a result of her wartime activities, there could be times when she might be in some physical danger. As a result, she hoped that she could call on him to help her out, if asked or if he suspected she was in danger. She had given him two telephone numbers to ring in such a circumstance. She prayed that she would see him if they left the flat.

Peter Weiss stepped towards her and twisted her arm, so sharply that she cried out in pain. "Now don't try to be clever. You will only get hurt."

"Only a coward would enjoy threatening a woman. You have me confused with someone else." Now she was angry.

He twisted her arm harder and she cried out again, louder.

He released her, pushing her roughly so she fell.

"How far away is the bank?"

"Around the corner on Brompton Road."

"Get up. We will go right now."

At that moment the telephone rang.

"We are not going to answer it."

"But I am expecting a call. If there is no answer, my mother will ring the caretaker to ask him to see if I am here."

His eyes were expressionless, which made him even more threatening.

"We are leaving immediately."

The telephone finally stopped ringing.

"I have to get my bag."

He gripped her arm in a vise.

"Do not attempt to get away from me. I can kill you in an instant."

She walked into her bedroom and looked around desperately. She could not escape out the window because she had to unlock the padlock which held together the protective retractable metal grillwork. The key was in the living room. She picked up her bag from the dressing table. There was nothing she could do. She was startled to see him standing by her bedroom door. Her spirits sank lower. There was no way she could outwit him.

She opened her front door and they stepped out into the hall. There was no one out there and her heart sank. She had prayed that David would be polishing the brass door knobs, which he did every morning.

They went out the front door and down the steps into the street. She looked in both directions and her heart leapt. She saw David down the street. Perhaps she could get his attention. He was standing talking to someone. Probably one of the other residents on the square. She turned in his direction and Peter Weiss held her arm firmly.

They were drawing closer to the two talking men. Her heart was racing. She felt dizzy again. What if she fainted? Would he still kill her? They were drawing level and David turned and saw her.

"Morning, Miss Devaux. It is good to see you again. It has been a while."

"Good morning, John. Yes, yes, it has. I was so glad to hear that your daughter had her baby safely."

They moved on. Weiss' grip was hurting her. She had done her best. She hoped that David would recognize something was wrong. He did not have a daughter. She felt weak. She was terribly afraid. She did have a bank account here, but only a small amount was in it. She did not know what she was going to do. It looked as though he would not loosen his grip. She was in despair. To think she would never see Erich again, after the miracle of their finding each other. It stirred a great anger in her, but she felt weak and dizzy and thought her chances of tackling her adversary with any success were nil. They reached the end of the street and turned the corner. Cars lined the street on either side all the way to Brompton Road. It was only another two hundred yards and they would be turning onto it.

"How much money do you need?" she asked in desperation.

"Five thousand," he responded curtly. "If I don't get it, I will use you as a hostage until I do."

As they crossed the road, she staggered, but he hauled her savagely upright.

Suddenly, there was a loud popping sound, like a cork coming out of an enormous bottle of champagne and Peter Weiss let go of her arm and sank to the pavement. She looked down at him in amazement. He was grimacing in pain and blood was staining the upper part of his thigh. He had been shot. She turned and saw the man who had been talking with David running towards her. He looked down at Peter Weiss and grunted in satisfaction.

"You all right, Miss? I was afraid for a moment that I might have shot a friend of yours. But then I saw how he was holding you when you nearly fell. Not very friendly, was he? Nasty piece of work. We were wondering if he would turn up. We are sorry that he got to you before we got to him. That was quick thinking tipping David off like that. It took him a few minutes to work out what you were saying."

"It was all I could think of."

"You look a little pale, Miss. I can't leave this one alone. Can you make it back to your flat without me?"

Before she could reply, David came pounding down the street towards them.

"The young lady is not feeling too well. Could you see her safely back to her place for me?"

"Of course I can. Now let me take your arm. We will just walk back slowly. I'll get my wife to make you a cup of tea. You will feel better in no time."

She was back in her flat once more. It was good to be sitting down. She still felt shaky and dizzy. She was annoyed that she should be demonstrating all the frailties so often attributed to her sex. She thought she was made of sterner stuff.

David had left and his wife was now fussing over her. She had tea and biscuits on a table beside her. There were pillows behind her back. Her feet were up on a stool. She felt pampered and cosseted. Finally she managed to persuade Sue that she was going to be fine and that she wanted to lie down and have a nap. Only then did Sue consent to leave her with the promise that she would drop back to see her later.

Madeleine slept deeply and awoke feeling better. She still felt tired, but the dizziness had gone. Sue returned bearing a dinner of shepherd's pie and apple tart. Madeleine was not feeling very hungry, but thanked Sue for her kindness and assured her that she would eat every scrap a little later.

She settled down with a book and had been reading for over an hour when the telephone rang. It made her jump. She was surprised that she should still feel edgy, but she was having a hard time shaking off the knowledge that Peter Weiss had actually been standing in this room. It had been such a violation of what she felt was her safe haven.

She got to her feet and reluctantly picked up the telephone. It was Sir Francis.

"My dear Madeleine. What a relief to hear your voice. I tried to reach you last night, but you were not in."

"I went to a concert."

"I had hoped to warn you that Weiss had escaped." There was slight reproach in Sir Francis' voice. "We really never expected that he would seek you out. There was no reason to suppose that he would be out for vengeance."

"Vengeance was only a secondary emotion. He thought I could provide money for his escape. Luckily it did not come to that."

"Well, it is a great relief to know that you are safe. Are you feeling better? Rawlings was afraid that you were suffering from shock."

"I am getting over a slight case of flu. It was a shock, but I am feeling better now." If she sounded unfriendly, it served him right. How dare they play games with her life. She could not believe the risks they took with other people's safety.

As if reading her thoughts, Sir Francis said, "We are truly indebted to you for all that you have done, for your invaluable contribution to the war against espionage. It has not gone unnoticed."

"My greatest wish is that I shall be allowed to live the rest of my life in peace from all your cloak and dagger operations." She tried to sound severe, but she was tired, and she really did not dislike Sir Francis, just his professional involvements.

He sensed this for he said, "Can I hope that you will forgive me in due course?"

She laughed. "Yes, it may take a few days, but I am sure that by the time I have returned to Whickham, all will be forgiven. At least, nearly all. I had no idea that so much was at stake." She could not count the number of times she had been nearly scared to death as a result of her association with Sir Francis and his colleagues.

"Thank you, my dear. We just could not tell you what we were trying to accomplish. It was for your protection. I know that you took enormous risks, both knowingly and in ignorance of the true facts. I would be deeply saddened if it had ruptured our friendship. You have my heartfelt admiration and most grateful thanks. Well, I must go. Give my best to your parents." Then he was gone.

The remainder of the week passed in agreeable social activities. Madeleine enjoyed herself, although she could not quite shake the feeling of oppression caused by the sudden eruption into her life of such a menacing personality as Peter Weiss. There had been no mention in the papers of the event. Too secret she supposed. She could not help wondering what the neighborhood grapevine had made of the event. David had been discreet and asked no questions. She was grateful for that.

Erich telephoned her the day before she was to return to Whickham. They had a long and languorous conversation. He told her of his plan to take her to Waldesrauschen. She was delighted. She had loved the place, despite the severely protective and critical Maria. Then there was Max. She really looked forward to seeing Max. Erich told her that he wanted her to redecorate the lodge and bring it back to life. He felt it was looking tired and faded. This comment made her laugh and she responded, saying that she would enjoy such a project. He did not mention his confession to his mother, but only said that his visit to Hohenfels had been pleasant. She was afraid to ask more.

She was glad to be home again, back in her own bedroom and near to her parents. She lay in bed and watched the sunlight create shadows on her ceiling as the curtains fluttered in a slight breeze. She tossed restlessly. She still felt unwell. A continued feeling of nausea which seemed to persist on and off. She generally did not catch colds and the flu as often as other people. She must really be run down. It was so annoying. Perhaps she needed a tonic. Although food was still rationed, there really was plenty of most things, so she should not be suffering from malnutrition.

Throughout the war, they had been short of so many essentials. During the intervals that Madeleine had lived with her parents, the three of them had survived on three-quarters of a pound of meat a week each, one egg each, hardly any sugar or butter. However, living in the country, as they did, there were times when neighbors would share their produce when there was a surplus. They never saw a banana during the whole war and very rarely oranges, and then only if they queued up for hours. She had only once been truly afraid that they might end up starving and that was when the shops ran out of potatoes and there were only mangle worzels. Horrible, inedible things normally fed to pigs.

She sighed. It was time to seek advice.

It was tea-time and her mother brought in the tray of cups and saucers. Madeleine placed the cakes and biscuits on the table. They had only to wait for the kettle to boil and the tea to be made.

Madeleine was alone in the sitting room. She was almost in a trance. She could scarcely believe what happened earlier that afternoon. She had seen Dr. Evans, the family doctor whom they had known since Madeleine was born. She described all her symptoms, expressed disgust that she should have this lingering flu and asked if she could have a tonic or some prescription so that she could start feeling better. He was a very solemn man, who spoke little and was not given to smiling often, but his reputation was lauded far and wide, as a wise and dedicated healer. He asked her several questions in his very quiet, dry voice. He listened to her heart and lungs and felt her pulse. Finally, when his examination was completed, he coughed, as though uncertain how to proceed. Finally, he asked her if she had some special young man in her life. Puzzled, Madeleine wondered how she should respond. Finally, she saw no reason to be secretive with this obviously very discreet man. Without going into too many details, she confessed that she was deeply in love with a man whom she had married some years ago. They had been separated during the war years, but had recently been reunited. She was astonished at the doctor's reaction to this information for he burst out into tinkling laughter.

"That is splendid news. I am so happy for you. It gives me great pleasure then to tell you that you are expecting a baby."

She looked at him in amazement. "That cannot be possible," she responded. "My husband told me that he had a bad case of mumps when he was in his early twenties and had been told that he probably could never father a child."

The old doctor, who had always reminded Madeleine of a Chinese mandarin because of his yellowed paper-thin skin and aesthetic appearance, responded with a smile and said in his soft, dry voice, "I assure you that I am not mistaken. As for your husband, he may or may not have been misdiagnosed as sterile, but nature has been known to produce a few miracles of her own."

She returned home in a dream. She could hardly believe that the source of her many queasy moments could be the symptom of such a monumental event. It was totally unbelievable. Erich had assured her that he could never father a child. She had been bitterly disappointed, but considering the desperate circumstances in which they had found themselves she had been accepting of the situation. Now, she was electrified with excitement. She loved Erich with all her being and to find that she now carried within her the child that would personify their love was the most thrilling discovery. As impatient as she was to be reunited with him, she knew she could wait patiently and calmly in the knowledge that a part of him would always be with her.

She now had to decide whether to tell her parents or wait until she had told Erich. Why were there always so many decisions? Anyway, it was very early in her pregnancy and she secretly believed that the doctor could be mistaken. She decided that as eager as she was to share this knowledge, she really did want to relish it a little longer in private. So she held her peace. But her mother noticed her distraction and wondered at its source.

The days passed slowly. She was not very interested in village activities. In fact, her erratic moments of queasiness made it rather awkward for her to disguise her condition. She spent a lot of time working through her wardrobe, trying to eliminate items she felt she would never use. She longed to hear from Erich. He wrote to her regularly once a week.

Madeleine knew that she would have to confide in her parents soon. It was a small community and it would be easy for her parents to run into Dr. Evans. He would have no reason to keep the secret from them, even though she knew he would be the model of discretion with everyone else. It was just a matter of finding the right time.

It finally came one wet afternoon when they were again together having tea. Her mother commented on her lack of interest in the cakes for tea. She also thought her a little pale.

"Dr Evans says that I am pregnant, but I really do not think that is possible." She explained why. "But I do feel nauseous quite frequently and I find it upsets me just to look at food some days."

"Well, that is a classic symptom, darling. Well, this is very exciting news should it be true. But like your marriage, we will have to wait before announcing it. I must say that I shall feel relieved when we can talk openly about you and Erich. It is very hard not to let something slip in conversation."

Madeleine nodded.

She was surprised that her parents seemed so accepting and happy about her possible pregnancy. She thought they would be more negative about her child than she suspected they were about her marriage. What she did not realize was that they had reached an age when they were ready for grandchildren. They were beginning, as they aged, to need another focus. That Madeleine might possibly be expecting a baby was a great joy to them, even though they had never met the father and even though, in their hearts, they disapproved of his origins. It did not mean that they were not prepared to like the man.

— 31 —

The weeks dragged by and Erich was becoming increasingly more frustrated with the continuing calls his career made upon him. Finally, he saw that he might at last extricate himself from his work and take a few weeks away. He managed to telephone Madeleine and told her this and was gladdened to hear the happiness in her voice. She sounded very tired, which he found rather surprising since she said she was leading a very quiet life. He decided that this inactivity was probably very unhealthy for a person as normally active as Madeleine. They discussed dates and the possibility of meeting first in West Berlin and then traveling together to Riquewihr. Madeleine was going to research the possible travel choices available and they would then finalize their plans the next time he was able to ring. At least his official ranking gave him some advantages where communications were involved.

But it was only a few days later that he received a letter from his mother inviting him to visit her and asking him to bring Madeleine with him so that they might meet. This reaction surprised him. He had hoped his mother would in due course invite them both, but he had not expected such a spontaneous invitation.

Then to complicate his life he had received an invitation to a Mardi Gras Ball from his faithful friend, Anton, from Langenhof. A handwritten note urged him to come and bring the lovely Madeleine. Erich sat pondering this invitation. It would be a great opportunity to introduce Madeleine to a large cross-section of friends. He felt it might be the least stressful way of having Madeleine meet a lot of people at a ball of the dimensions that Anton was apt to plan. Conversations at such an affair would be haphazard and fractured and she might be spared the scrutiny of a more intimate social event. There was much to commend it. He sighed in frustration. He desperately wanted to be alone with his lovely wife. Waldesrauschen was the perfect retreat and he hated to have to postpone their arrival there. They would have to decide in which sequence to plan this itinerary, provided that Madeleine would consent to any of it.

Erich was surprised when he next telephoned that Madeleine was enthusiastic and prepared to participate in all the proposed social events and did not seem intimidated at the prospect. He was flattered that she wanted to meet his mother and slightly irritated that she did not want to be alone just with him. He smiled ruefully at himself. He was being difficult to please, he had to admit.

The days passed slowly, but at last the day of her departure arrived. Her parents accompanied her to the train. They bade her a most affectionate farewell and made her promise to keep them informed of her every movement. They cautioned her not to get overtired and to let them know how she was feeling on a weekly basis. Madeleine had to smile at their solicitous attitude. She was wearing the Kandahar medallion under her suit jacket. It had mixed associations, but she would always consider it her good luck charm, not just because it was a gift from her father, but because she had worn it the night she had been reunited with her beloved Erich.

The journey to München was long, but uneventful. She felt her heart beat faster as she stepped off the train. It now seemed a very long time since she had last seen Erich. She felt shy and self-conscious.

He was there waiting for her, looking sophisticated and vibrant in a knee length suede coat with fur collar. The blue sweater that showed at the neckline enhanced the vivid blue of his eyes. His face lit up when he saw her and her heart skipped a beat. He kissed her hand. He stared at her keenly and said, somewhat surprised, "You look thinner. I would have thought that your sedentary life in Whickham would have produced the opposite result. However, it becomes you. You look almost luminous." The intensity of his look took her breath away.

With her luggage collected, they walked out to the street and found the chauffeur-driven Mercedes awaiting them. They sat in silence at the beginning of the three-hour journey. Erich could not seem to take his eyes off of her. She was infinitely desirable. Slowly, they began to pick up the threads of their lives.

The city had been left behind and they were now in the countryside driving eastwards towards Passau. It was a relief to be together again. They had not realized what a strain these last few months had been, living apart. They stopped for a simple lunch in a country inn, after which Madeleine fell asleep with her head on Erich's shoulder.

At last they were approaching Hohenfels and Madeleine sat turned looking out of the window. They had passed through the entrance and were following a winding road through woods and open parkland. Erich told her how they raised pheasant and partridge there. She was delighted by the unspoilt beauty of the estate although a little awed by its dimensions. But she was surprised to find Hohenfels itself to be very lovely and not pretentious, despite the size of the surrounding property. The mellowness of its stonework and the pleasing lines of its facade made it an historic house that was welcoming. She found that, for the moment, she was not nervous, but she knew that might change in an instant. Much would depend on the welcome that she would receive from Erich's mother.

They were shown their rooms which had lovely views overlooking the lake on one side with a backdrop of woodland on the other. When they had unpacked, they walked back along the corridor of their west wing until they came to the main body of the Schloss. Here they turned at right angles and walked another corridor filled with portraits until they came to the main staircase, which descended to a central hall. Madeleine was dazzled by the richness of the carvings that adorned the doorways they passed, as well as the intricate and varied moldings that covered all the ceilings. Once in the central hall they walked through several salons until they came to the library.

"If you will wait here, I will go and find mother."

She stood looking out the window. A narrow garden lay between the Schloss and the lake and Madeleine imagined it filled with a profusion of color when summer came. For now there were masses of red, yellow and pink tulips swaying in the light breeze. A backdrop of low boxwood hedges embraced the central area of the lake. A pair of elegant swans floated calmly away from a flock of ducks foraging busily at one end. It was a very dramatic, but peaceful scene. The outer fringes of the garden enfolded this central area with semi-circular beds already cultivated and prepared. Only a few green tips of summer flowering perennials showed; the promise of what would later burst forth in magnificent splendor.

She was unaware of how long she had been standing looking out on this tranquil scene, when she felt Erich at her side once more.

"My mother is waiting to have tea with us in one of the small sitting rooms. Come, let us go and join her."

Madeleine was surprised that Erich had made no attempt to prepare her for this momentous encounter. But she was not to know that Erich was much more nervous than she could ever guess at the impending meeting of the two most influential women in his life. He had no idea of his mother's attitude towards this unknown daughter-in-law. He expected her to be courteous, but he wondered if she would be aloof and distant. He hoped desperately that she would not.

Madeleine, for her part, now felt fluttering uncertainty and anxiety begin to overtake her. She felt a little nauseous and was gripped by fear that she would embarrass herself and Erich by becoming ill. She tried to take deep, slow breaths. She hoped that she had selected her outfit well. She had on a deep lavender woollen suit, but she wondered if she should not have worn a dress. Too late now. Anyway, Erich had not given her the time to change. He said that she had chosen a most becoming color for her arrival at Hohenfels. He kissed her with warmth and tenderness.

They reached the small and charming salon which also overlooked the water, as did half the rooms in the Schloss.

Erich's mother was dressed in her favorite color of silver grey. It became her so well and flattered the soft petal pink of her complexion.

"Mother, I have the great honor to introduce to you my wife, Madeleine. Madeleine, my mother."

Erich's mother surveyed the young woman standing before her and was immediately captivated by her loveliness. There was a purity of spirit about her which enhanced the natural freshness of her appearance.

There was a moment of silence, which was broken by the older woman.

"I now understand why my son risked so much when he chose to marry you. You are a very beautiful woman. Welcome to Hohenfels."

"Thank you, Baroness. You are very kind."

"Please sit down and let us have tea."

The conversation was general and focused on Madeleine's journey, the early spring and what was planned for Erich and Madeleine's visit.

Tea was a pleasant interlude. Erich's mother turned to her son and said, "Gregor has been asking for you. He is very impatient to discuss the coming season. He implored me to send you to see him as soon as you returned today. He has some new ideas for the pheasants. Why don't you go and find him now. Then Madeleine and I can have some time alone."

Erich's eyebrows arched in surprise as he stared at his mother. He could never predict the moods of women, least of all his mother. He hoped that his mother would continue in the benevolent mood that she had shown throughout their tea together. He looked protectively at Madeleine. She seemed more relaxed than when she first sat down and less pale.

He got to his feet and smiled at his mother. "I sense that you are trying to get rid of me."

"Darling, of course not. But Gregor really has been bothering me daily and you still have not spent much time with him since your arrival. So off you go. Madeleine and I have so much to discover in each other."

Madeleine's heart fluttered slightly. But she was feeling a little better and hoped that she could put on a good face.

"Now tell me a little about yourself."

With kindly encouragement, Madeleine found it easy to talk about herself; from early childhood to her school years. The Baroness did not ask for details of her meeting with her son and Madeleine presumed that Erich had told her. But she was sure that he had given her only the briefest of details. It was something that she had not thought to ask him. As she relaxed, there grew between them a companionable relationship.

"You are looking a little pale. Are you feeling quite well?" the older woman enquired.

Madeleine hesitated. She was uncertain whether she would be betraying Erich if she confided in his mother and decided that she would not.

"No, I have not been feeling well for quite a few weeks. I am expecting a baby."

The older woman gasped. "Are you sure?'

"I was disbelieving when the doctor first told me, especially as Erich had said that he probably could never father a child. However, I am now quite certain that I am."

"My dear, I never expected to live to hear such joyful news. I am afraid to believe it. What an incredible surprise. I could not be more happy for you, or for myself. I have longed for grandchildren in vain. I wanted so much that this property would remain in our immediate family. I have to assume that Erich does not yet know?"

"No, I wanted to wait and tell him when I saw him. Why do you ask that?"

"The news will upset him. He will not believe you. You have to be prepared for that."

"I know you are right. I was afraid that might be his reaction. He is the father. There has been no other man."

The Baroness reached out and took Madeleine's hand. "My dear child, I have absolutely no doubt of that. I can see by your face how much you love my son. However, you must understand that he has lived too long with the belief that he would never produce heirs. Until he observes your expanding waistline, you must be prepared for his scepticism."

Madeleine sighed. It was such a wonderful piece of news. It was sad that she should now be hesitant at sharing it with her beloved husband.

Erich's mother smiled and said, "You must count on me for support, if needed." She got to her feet. "Come let me show you some of my favorite rooms in this lovely old place."

Thus they set off on an extensive tour of the Schloss with the Baroness giving a long and detailed lesson in history and architecture. Her knowledge was impressive. She glowed with the love she felt for this beautiful and historic place.

They returned at last to the library where they found Erich sprawled on a sofa reading. He got to his feet as soon as he saw them. "Where have you been all this time?"

"Showing Madeleine Hohenfels. If she is to come here often, as I hope she will, it is important that she know her way around."

Erich was stunned. He could not believe that his mother had accepted and welcomed Madeleine into her life so easily and unquestioningly. He was delighted, but mystified. He had thought his mother would be slower to accept Madeleine, if at all.

Their stay at Hohenfels far exceeded Madeleine's expectations. The fact that her mother-in-law had accepted her so unconditionally was both a surprise and an immense relief to her. They spent a lot of time each day in each other's company. The Baroness von Brandenburg was protective of her new daughter-in-law and saw to it that she both exercised and rested regularly. She tried to provide meals that were appealing to her fragile digestion and was gratified to see some color creep back into her cheeks.

Two dinner parties were held in honor of the newlyweds, both gracious and elegant affairs. Later the Baroness complimented Madeleine on her excellent German. For she herself had been complimented on the graceful elegance of her new daughter-in-law.

Their stay came to an end all too soon, as far as the Baroness was concerned. She was loath to see them leave.

But Erich was eager to return to Waldesrauschen and the ball at Langenhof would bring him there that much sooner. They made their farewells and the Baroness embraced Madeleine and told her that she should return soon, especially if Erich should be called away on duty.

— 32 —

It was a different experience returning to Langenhof. They were given the same apartment, hung with priceless tapestries that held the canopied bed of rich blue satin. She stood at one of the windows and looked out over the immense park and lake. She remembered the dark night she had lifted off in Anton's balloon and floated over those same woods in the distance to freedom and safety in Switzerland. How long ago that seemed. It had been such a wrenching moment to leave Erich with no guarantee that she would ever see him again. It had been a time of great uncertainty, but a time when their love had been as exquisite in its intensity as it had been painful in its fragility. She subconsciously shook off the dark fears and memories that swept over her and turned away. She walked over to her luggage and began to unpack.

Anton welcomed them as if they were long lost family. He gave Erich a bear-like hug. He kissed Madeleine's hand with a flourish and commented on how much more captivating she looked than he remembered, that he had thought of her often over the years. She shook her head at him in fake disapproval. He was an incorrigible flirt, but it was hard to take offence. Erich seemed not to mind in the least.

They dined together that evening and reminisced about their last meeting. Later in the conversation, Anton wanted to know details of Madeleine's journey to Switzerland and by stages to England. The conversation was light-hearted throughout and no details were asked about more personal war time experiences.

They wanted to know more details of the ball planned for the following evening. Anton told them that 350 guests had been invited, that some would come costumed, but that others would not. They would dine at ten o'clock. There was to be a firework display at midnight. Erich wanted to know how many of his friends might be present and was gratified that he would know a very large number of the guests. People were traveling from all corners of Europe to attend. A large number of guests would stay overnight at Langenhof. This was apparent to them on arrival, for there was a great hustle and bustle inside the Schloss. It was a light-hearted evening of shared memories and gentle humor.

The evening of the ball dawned bright and clear with a gentle, warm breeze. This was the occasion that Madeleine was looking forward to wearing the lovely soft, off-white sparkling gown that she had purchased in Monte Carlo. Erich had not seen it and she hoped desperately that he would like it. As yet, they had not been together long enough for her to know his taste and all his likes and dislikes. It made her nervous. Her mother-in-law had asked her what she planned to wear and had seemed approving of her selection. But mother and son were quite different people.

It was time to get dressed for the ball. Madeleine had arranged her hair and made up her face and was now ready to put on her gown. She slipped it over her head and stood in front of the long mirror in the ancient armoire and did it up. It made her look even more slender than she remembered. She realized that she had lost weight in the first two months of her pregnancy. She appraised herself in the mirror and was surprised at her slenderness. She was about to turn away when she saw Erich's face in the reflection over her shoulder. She turned and saw the look of incredulity on his face.

"I thought that I could never see you looking more radiant than when you arrived in München, but I was mistaken. You look positively regal in that spectacular gown. Where did you find it? It becomes you in a way that I could never imagine." He took her by both hands and held her at a distance. "If this is the night that you are to meet all of my friends and acquaintances, you could not have chosen a more elegant gown to enhance all your natural attributes." He drew her gently towards him and kissed her lightly. He stared intensely into her face and then released her. His nearness always triggered a tremor in her. There was a virility and sensuality to him that never failed to stir her.

The ballroom was filled with a throng of brightly gowned and costumed guests. The walls were lined with large topiary trees and tall candelabra with cascading vines and sweet-smelling roses, peonies, lilies and other beautiful flowers. It was a magical spectacle. Liveried servants were everywhere passing glasses of wine and hors d'oeuvres. Anton was at the head of the staircase that lead down into the ballroom. His eyes opened in wide admiration at the sight of Madeleine.

"Tonight, my dear Madeleine, you will outshine all present. You promise to reserve a dance with me?'

She smiled. "If Erich gives his permission." She slanted a look at him and found him frowning at Anton in mock disapproval.

"As our gracious and most generous host, how can I refuse him? However, you should know that I really do not trust you an inch!"

"I promise that I will be nothing if not correct. But if there had been any way that I could have stolen the lovely Madeleine from you in a previous lifetime, I assure you that I would have done so." Erich smiled and nodded. He knew that Anton in jest was speaking his feelings. He did not resent it, but took it as the ultimate compliment.

They had arrived late to the ball for, at the last minute, Madeleine had a brief dizzy spell. Erich assumed that it was nerves. Madeleine knew better. But it passed and she hoped that she could survive the rest of the evening in better style. She wished that their arrival could have been less conspicuous, but it was not to be. The trumpeters, dressed in medieval costumes, raised their banner-decorated instruments and a crescendo of magnificent sound filled the air. The guests below still bubbled with conversation and laughter, but slowly they raised their heads to the sound and as slowly fell silent. For as Erich and Madeleine began their descent to the ballroom, they were announced as Baron and Baroness Erich von Brandenburg. A gasp of admiration and awe floated up to them as those below drank in the sight of Madeleine in her softly shimmering gown and diamond coronet making a regal entrance with Erich beside her. He, in turn, looked equally imposing and distinguished. They had almost reached the ballroom when a burst of voices drowned all else as those next to each other turned and speculated upon the handsome couple they had just seen. Erich and Madeleine were immediately surrounded by Erich's friends and acquaintances. They did their best to field the questions and congratulations, but it took them a good hour to extricate themselves, by which time Madeleine was feeling limp with exhaustion. Fortunately, dinner was announced and they could take their places at the festive tables in one of the great salons. Surprisingly, Madeleine was revived by the dinner. It was a six course meal, and although she was horrified at the quantity of food set in front of her, she found that by eating a little from each course she seemed to gain strength.

It was a magnificent spectacle with the glow of candlelight from each table as well as the sconces on the walls and then, above them, the soft glow from the enormous crystal chandeliers. Flowers were everywhere.

After dinner there was dancing in the ballroom. Many of the guests were wearing period costumes, both medieval and 17th and 18th century which lent a most theatrical and opulent mood to the evening.

Suddenly, Erich got up from the table and turned to Madeleine and said, "Baroness, may I have the pleasure of this dance?" She looked at him in wide-eyed amazement.

"We have never danced together."

"True." His smile was provocative. "The thought of it has made this exhausting social environment bearable."

She blushed. His ability to stir her emotions seemed limitless.

"I am not sure…" She broke off as she saw his expression. He had stiffened slightly.

"Are you suggesting that you do not want to dance with your new husband or that you suspect that in some way I may be inexperienced or awkward as a dancing partner? You have not failed to let me know how much you love to dance. In fact, it seems that you spent your whole stay in Liechtenstein and Monte Carlo dancing with endless partners provided by your devoted great-aunt! I have not been without quite a variety of dancing partners over the years."

She stood up abruptly. He really had challenged her and made her slightly jealous, stupid as that was, she knew. It was obvious that she had offended his male vanity.

"I was going to say, before you jumped to erroneous conclusions, that I could not tolerate another conversation with any more curious individuals."

"My exact sentiments," he smiled at her gently, mollified by her answer. "We will ignore all those around us and shut out the world." He took her hand and led her out onto the dance floor.

He slipped his arm around her and stood looking down at her. He could hardly resist the urge to kiss her. His desire to hold her, naked, in his embrace almost overwhelmed him. It was a slow waltz and eventually they took their first steps and were as one. It was such a new experience for them both. He held her slightly at a distance, but soon held her closer and they danced as if alone. At one point his grip tightened about her slender, seductive waist and he murmured in her ear, "You feel and smell wonderful. I wish that we were already at Waldesrauschen. I want you all to myself."

She smiled and nibbled on his ear. They danced on oblivious to those around them, to whom they were the center of attention as one of the most glamourous and romantic couples at the ball.

The orchestra finally stopped playing, to take a brief rest. Everyone stayed on the dance floor and chatted. Madeleine and Erich were soon surrounded by a number of couples who came to congratulate them and bombard them with questions. The magic interlude which they had enjoyed was broken.

The music began again and before Erich and Madeleine could move back to their table, Anton came and touched Erich on the shoulder.

"You promised to let me dance with her. It will soon be time for the fireworks, so it may be my last chance of the evening."

Erich smiled at him and shook his finger without saying anything, but implying that he would have his eye on him.

"You should know that I am terribly envious of your handsome husband." He smiled at her and she gazed back at him softly, but said nothing. She knew that this was an enormously attractive man who was used to seducing any woman who attracted him.

They danced in silence for a time. He danced well and she enjoyed the brief interlude with him.

"Before we come to the end of this moment together, I want to thank you, Anton, from the bottom of my heart for the truly generous gift of freedom that you extended to me during our last visit here. Without you, I do not know what might have become of me. I know you did it for Erich, but it was an exceptional act of unconditional friendship to do it for a stranger, and a foreign one at that."

He smiled at her, gazing at her intently. "How could I not help someone so special? You could say that I did it out of selfishness. You see, I have my reward tonight. I am dancing with you, something that I could scarcely have anticipated at that moment in time." He kissed her on her forehead. Then, he added as an afterthought, "You know there is something different about you tonight, but I cannot put my finger on it."

She blushed for she was afraid that he was close to guessing her secret. Then he led her to where Erich was standing talking with a group of friends. Anton bowed to Madeleine and handed her to Erich, nodded to his friend and moved away.

They watched the fireworks in awe, until Madeleine said that she was feeling cold. Erich did not complain at leaving the spectacle before the grand finale. His only desire half the evening had been to have Madeleine to himself. He had more than fulfilled his wish at having Madeleine formally presented to his friends. It had been a vivacious and enormously successful occasion. But he could see that Madeleine was very tired. It was time to leave the revelries.

Once back in their apartment, he helped her undress. She handed him the glittering diamond coronet that his mother had asked him to give to Madeleine as a surprise gift for the occasion. Such an unexpected gesture of acceptance and generosity had brought tears to her eyes. He expressed astonishment at Madeleine's instant and unexpected friendship with his mother. He was delighted, but mystified at the unexpected humors and moods of women in general, and of his mother in particular.

They had fallen asleep in each others arms.

They got up late and breakfasted in their room. Finally, they joined the other guests in one of the smaller salons where a light, late lunch was served. They went walking as a group. It was refreshing to be in the woods. The clear, pure air had helped to revive their jaded senses.

They were not to spend time alone with Anton until the following morning when they were preparing to depart. He insisted that he fly them to Waldesrauschen in his old, small twin-engine plane of which he was extremely proud. Rather like Erich's Daimler, Anton had seen to it that his plane had been well cared for throughout the war. It was only when peace was declared that he had been able to fly it again and only then, when fuel was obtainable. They had not planned on this generous offer, but Anton would not hear of their refusing him. While Erich was seeing that their luggage was safely stowed, Anton was making a last minute check with his mechanic.

Erich sat in the co-pilot's seat with Madeleine behind them both. Their take-off was somewhat bumpy on the man-made runway, but they were soon airborne. It was not a long flight but it was a windy day and they had a fairly bumpy ride. Madeleine, who had looked forward to this speedy means of reaching Waldesrauschen, was soon regretting the experience. The motion was making her dizzy and she closed her eyes in the hope that it would calm her stomach. After an extended period of turbulence, Erich had looked over his shoulder at her and saw her closed eyes and her paleness. He told Anton that she looked unwell. Anton nodded, but said nothing.

They made a good landing in a field not far from the lodge. Erich jumped out of the small plane and strode off to wave to Schultz in the Daimler that he could see parked on the far side of the field. Anton helped Madeleine to the ground.

"You look awful," was his only comment.

"I feel awful. But it will pass." She could see that he was about to say something more, but she put her finger to his lips and he looked at her with a gleam of recognition. He knows, she thought.

Erich was back and Anton embraced Madeleine and whispered in her ear, "He is such a lucky devil."

Erich and Anton embraced. They thanked him for his wonderful hospitality and the memorable party.

"It is nothing. But one day, when you are tired of being alone, you must invite me over." With that he climbed into his plane and taxied off. They watched as the plane rose skywards and Anton waggled its wings in farewell.

"Such a good friend," was Erich's only comment.

They were standing in the high-ceilinged entrance of Waldesrauschen surrounded by Madeleine's luggage. She looked about her and remembered with nostalgia those dark, uncertain days when she was first there. Those had been very dangerous times, but she looked back on them as holding the first important steps in their relationship. There had been many challenges, but they had been tested by them and survived. She drank in the fresh smell of waxed furniture. She noticed how much brighter and more welcoming the house seemed since she had last seen it. Obviously the lodge was in the care of an eager housekeeper who wanted to please. Gretchen had met them at the door. Madeleine had liked her immediately. She was everything that Maria had not been. Cheerful and welcoming, young and energetic. She had to admit that it had been difficult to live under the same roof with Maria, but Maria's allegiance had been to Erich and his family and not to some suspect foreign relative. It was understandable.

Erich disappeared with some of her luggage. In that, he was a typical naval officer. He liked to have everything stowed away in an orderly fashion. He was back again, smiling at her. She could sense his great pleasure at being home. She knew how much he had wanted to have her all to himself.

He turned to Gretchen. "Is Max in the library as I asked."

She nodded smiling. "Yes, asleep as usual beside your chair."

"Madeleine, let us go and see Max. I know that you cannot wait a moment longer." He was right. She had wanted to see Max nearly as much as she had wanted to see Waldesrauschen again.

They went through the door of the library and saw the great dog stretched out on the rug asleep. His deafness was apparent, but he must have sensed their presence from the current of air that came in from the front door, because he raised his head and looked up. When he saw Erich, he scrambled stiffly to his feet and came joyfully across the room to him. Madeleine remained standing in the doorway, not wanting to compete for his attention. But he must have sensed her presence for he turned towards her and stopped in his tracks. Then with a bark of sheer joy, he hurried towards her, reaching up to lick her face. She laughed happily and bent down and hugged him. It was a moment of great poignancy. Erich was smiling with pleasure. "I think it is safe to assume that from now on, he will not let you out of his sight for a moment." She smiled and nodded, as Max continued to prance around them both, as much as his aged limbs permitted.

The remainder of the day was spent organizing Madeleine's possessions. Her luggage was spread out in various rooms in the lodge. Erich had decided that his room was not large enough for them both and had arranged in his absence to have two rooms made into one. The result was an attractive bedroom and sitting room. He was eager to show Madeleine the changes he had made. She was amazed at the spaciousness which had been created by removing the adjoining bedroom wall. It had always been a large, airy room because of its high, beamed ceiling and enormous window with its intricate pattern of lead panes which gave onto the garden. But it had been a long, narrow room, with very little color other than the dark oak furniture and the dark brown and red oriental on the floor. With the sitting room addition and the lighter-colored sofa and chairs, it seemed less masculine and austere. An additional armoire had been placed in the sitting-room for Madeleine's use.

"I know that these are not your colors, but I want you to redecorate Waldesrauschen in due course and give it more life. The colors seem very drab to me now."

She smiled. "That would be fun and would give me something to do."

They spent several days settling into their surroundings. It was wonderful to be alone at last. They lingered over breakfast and talked of what they would do each day. At night, they curled up on a sofa in front of a log fire with Max at their feet.

Their nights were moments of lingering tenderness for Erich was concerned by Madeleine's seeming fragility and moments of fatigue. His passion was ever present, but he was fearful of her delicacy and of breaking a spell so infinitely precious. It was almost as if they were together for the first time. They were totally absorbed, yet again, in discovering each other anew. There had been several beginnings and each one had been unique and special. This time, however, they were finally home and liberated from the challenges and difficulties that had pursued them for so long and this was as intoxicating as almost any other emotion.

Madeleine was impatient to tell Erich of her pregnancy, but at the same time hesitant to spoil the special relationship they were now enjoying. She could not decide whether to make an occasion of it or wait for an appropriate moment.

In the end, it came about spontaneously.

She was sitting at breakfast one morning, feeling more nauseous than usual, but knew it would probably pass soon enough. Erich had noticed her pallor and expressed his concern.

"You have not seemed well recently. Perhaps you should see a doctor," he said.

She nodded, not feeling like talking, but knowing now that she could tell him everything once this spell passed.

Later that morning, they were out walking with Max. Madeleine turned to Erich, smiling.

"You are quite right, I do need to see a doctor." She saw the anxiety reflected in his eyes. "But I know exactly the reason for my symptoms. I hope it will make you very happy when I tell you that we are expecting a baby."

He stood stock still, an expression of surprise and confusion on his face.

"Please do not tease me so cruelly. You know that is not possible."

"That is what I said to my doctor in England. But he said that small miracles happen all the time. This is one of them."

He was silent for a moment. "My darling, you should perhaps get another opinion. I do not want you having a terrible disappointment. Your symptoms could have another cause."

"Erich, Erich. I am as certain as I have ever been about anything. Besides, your mother had no doubts whatsoever. She, like my own mother, said that my symptoms were classic of an expectant mother."

"My mother. Your mother. How is it that I am the last to be told?" He was frowning.

"I wanted to be absolutely sure before I told you. Because I was afraid that you would not believe me. Oh, darling, I am so very happy and excited."

She saw a glint in his eye that told her that he was prepared to believe what she was telling him. But she knew too that his mother was right when she said that until he saw her expanding waistline, he would be afraid to hope for the miracle that he believed could never happen.

It was a few weeks before the baby was due and they were sitting in the garden on a lovely, warm evening.

"You know, my beloved, we have to choose godparents for the baby. What would you think of asking Anton to be the godfather?"

"I think that is a wonderful idea. Actually, he would be terribly offended if you did not ask him, considering he has known about it for so long."

"What do you mean by that? I have never mentioned that you were expecting a baby."

"Well, nothing was said in so many words, but I knew he guessed that I was not just being airsick that day in his plane. He had that knowing look."

"What do you mean by that? He has never been a father. He knows nothing about such things," Erich said with slight indignation.

"I think that dear Anton is much more a man of the world than you are, dearest Erich."

"Well, I grant you that he might be more worldly than I, but he does not have the most beautiful expectant mother as a wife," and he gently pulled Madeleine to him and kissed her with great tenderness.

About the Author

J.D. Smithyes was born and educated in England. Her professional career first took her to Basle, Switzerland where she worked for The Bank for International Settlements. Thereafter, she accepted a position in the private office of the Secretary General of The Council of Europe in Strasbourg, France. Her experience and knowledge of languages resulted in her being elected to the Institute of Linguists in London. She later worked for the Belgian diplomatic corps in New York. During this period, she met her husband-to-be. They were married in England and have two children. She and her husband reside in the United States, in Michigan.